Slingshot

MERCEDES HELNWEIN

WEDNESDAY BOOKS

NEW YORK

First published in the United States by Wednesday Books, an imprint of St. Martin's Publishing Group

SLINGSHOT. Copyright © 2021 by Mercedes Helnwein. All rights reserved. Printed in the United States of America. For information, address St. Martin's Publishing Group, 120 Broadway, New York, NY 10271.

www.wednesdaybooks.com

The poem on page 244 is an excerpt from "Used" written by Tiffany Steffens. Used by permission of the author.

Library of Congress Cataloging-in-Publication Data

Names: Helnwein, Mercedes, 1979– author.
Title: Slingshot / Mercedes Helnwein.
Identifiers: LCCN 2020048627 | ISBN 9781250253002 (hardcover) |
   ISBN 9781250253019 (ebook)
Subjects: CYAC: Boarding schools—Fiction. | Schools—Fiction. |
   Dating (Social customs)—Fiction. | Family problems—Fiction.
Classification: LCC PZ7.H375955 Sli 2021 | DDC [Fic]—dc23
LC record available at https://lccn.loc.gov/2020048627

Our books may be purchased in bulk for promotional, educational, or business use. Please contact your local bookseller or the Macmillan Corporate and Premium Sales Department at 1-800-221-7945, extension 5442, or by email at MacmillanSpecialMarkets@macmillan.com.

First Edition: 2021

10   9   8   7   6   5   4   3   2   1

TO ALL THE JERKS AND SOUL MATES OF MY YOUTH

IT WAS THE LAST DAY BEFORE THE CHRISTMAS holidays, and I sat in a bathroom stall at school dressed as a witch. The long, black fabric of my dress was trailing out under the stall door because of its ridiculous volume. I was crying. My knees were pulled up to my face and my arms wrapped around my legs, head burrowed in the black folds. My whole body felt tight, every muscle strained to the point where I was certain that a gentle tap could snap me in half. My face was hot and glazed with snot and tears, and I had to shove some of the fabric of the dress into my mouth so that my choking sobs wouldn't reverberate through the entire bathroom.

I had never cried like this before. This was the way ladies in Lifetime movies cried, clinging to some guy's leg as he was trying to walk out the door. I was the opposite of that. I had been one of those tough-as-nails, little shithead kids that didn't cry—not when I got hurt, not when I was yelled at, not when I was picked on. And even when I did cry, it had always been short and to the point, secretly performed without witnesses and no evidence left behind of any kind whatsoever. I had always considered myself to be pretty unbreakable, and I was. Or at least I *had* been up until that point in the bathroom.

Just like that, my childhood armor was obliterated, and all it took was my soul mate ramming a butter knife into my heart.

His name was Carl Sorrentino. Mr. Sorrentino—my biology teacher. It was true that he was about twenty years older than I was, and I could see how that could be a thing for some people. Small-minded people. There were hurdles to overcome, sure, but what are hurdles when one is faced with destiny? This was destiny. It wasn't just that I thought we were soul mates—I *knew* we were. I just *knew*. My reasoning was that when you know things on that level, they don't need to make any practical sense, because love is a bigger truth than logistics, and basically anyone who wanted to have a problem with that could go suck it. Love is *love*. It's all that matters. How does age even play into it? It doesn't.

I knew that Mr. Sorrentino felt the connection too. I knew I wasn't delusional, because despite the fact that we didn't exactly address our feelings openly (which would have been technically totally illegal), there were actual things I was basing my inevitable conclusions on. Real things that Mr. Sorrentino did and said. Signs.

For example, the smiley faces he drew on my tests, next to phrases like "You got it, Gracie!" or "The Grace-monster strikes again!" And he would draw little eyes into numbers on the tests—for example, when he wrote 99 percent on a test, he'd make the circles of the nines into eyes. Sure, it was corny as fuck, but that wasn't the point. The point was that it was adorable.

Then there was the way in which our eyes met when he told one of his biology jokes that no one got except me. I'd smile knowingly at him across the classroom, and he'd smile back and the whole world would pass between us in these moments.

Or at lunchtime he would sometimes let me hang out with him in the classroom, and I'd ask him detailed questions about whatever the hell we were studying at that moment. I honestly never cared much about what we were studying, but my grades were excellent because of the amount of energy I put into my biology work. He was so patient. He looked at me while I talked. He'd sit there and wait for me as I worked out my questions, trying to be witty and deep and challenging. And then he'd nod and say, "You know, that's a damn good question, Gracie. You're taking this to the next level. Here, let me show you something." And he'd draw diagrams for me on the chalkboard. He would draw detailed cross sections of animal and plant cells, or the entire respiratory system, or DNA strands—complex diagrams with arrows and descriptions— all just for me.

Plus, he high-fived me a *lot,* which would have been nauseating had anyone other than Mr. Sorrentino been doing it, but with him it kind of worked, and really, it was the only kind of touching we were probably allowed to do, so I got why he did it.

There were lots of other things. And yeah, I wasn't an idiot—I knew they were all small things that could have easily been dismissed as nothing, but the whole point was to look at the bigger picture. All you had to do was connect the dots. And the bigger picture was crystal clear: Mr. Sorrentino and I had a powerful, earth-shattering connection. The kind that defies all rules and traditions. The kind that reinvents the game. The kind of connection that is too strong to follow in the well-worn paths of any prototypes.

But whatever. It turned out I was delusional after all.

It was the last performance of the school's production of

Macbeth, in which I played one of the three witches. I hated drama, but I had auditioned for the part after Mr. Sorrentino had called me a witch for getting 100 percent on a pop quiz. I figured maybe it turned him on to think of me that way and that it couldn't hurt to play out the fantasy—black gown, hat, and all.

As I got off the stage from my second scene, Mr. Sorrentino came up to me and pulled me over to where a brunette lady stood.

"Gracie, I'd like you to meet Judy, my fiancée. She's going to be doing some substitute teaching here starting in the new year."

Judy had voluminous hair and smiled so broadly that it looked like she had about four thousand teeth. She had freckles and thick eyebrows, and she was wearing this Dillard's-looking Christmassy dress with little Christmas-tree-ornament earrings. Her lips were pulled tight across her face due to the smile, and the soft pink goo of her lip gloss glistened in the light. I shook her outstretched hand. Her fingernails were painted the same soft pink as her lips, perfectly manicured.

"So nice to meet you finally!" she said. "I've heard so much about you. Top student in your biology class, huh? Not bad at all!"

I stared at her blankly. She continued talking for a while about all the great things Mr. Sorrentino had told her about me. She seemed truly thrilled about my grades. I just stared. When you first get injured, you sometimes don't even feel it because of the shock. The pain is there, but it's still anesthetized by the suddenness of the circumstances.

Judy continued smiling. "Oh, and Carl tells me you're interested in studying biochemistry after school."

"Uh-huh," I said.

"How amazing is that?" she said, her wall of teeth gleaming.

I turned to Mr. Sorrentino. "Mr. Sorrentino, can I talk to you for a second?"

He looked at Judy quizzically. She smiled.

"Sure, Gracie."

I led the way into the nurse's office, which was the closest empty room available down the hallway.

"What's up?" Mr. Sorrentino asked, smiling. "Hey, you did great out there, by the way. Shakespeare isn't easy. Not everyone can memorize that kind of language."

"You never told me you had a fiancée," I said.

His smile didn't exactly fall off his face, but it froze in a way that made him look displaced. "Well . . ." He halted, looked at his elbow for a second, and then continued, "Judy wasn't my fiancée until yesterday, but quite frankly, that's my private life, Gracie. I don't see how—"

"She didn't exist before yesterday? She just appeared out of thin air? I didn't know that was possible—scientifically speaking."

He looked at me, bewildered. Eyes almost unfocused with noncomprehension.

"Hey, what's going on?" he asked after a beat.

I turned my back to him and wiped away a tear that had started to flood my right eye. "Are you for real with this lady, Mr. Sorrentino?" I asked. "Is this actually a real thing?"

"*Excuse me?*"

With the tear out of my eye, I whirled back around to him. "Are you serious about marrying her? She's a fucking joke. I mean, do you even see what she looks like?"

"Whoa!" he said, backing up a step. "That's way out of line, Grace!"

"Sorry, it's the truth."

"*Hey, that's enough!*"

I jumped a little. He had never said anything to me in that

tone of voice before. It was an alien sensation being at odds with him. I could feel my face getting hot, and although it was jarring, about a quarter of me was definitely turned on by it.

"You mind telling me what's going on here?" he asked.

"Are you in love with her?"

For what seemed like a very long moment, he just stood there doing nothing. An *oh shit* expression began to materialize on his face. It was here that he seemed to realize the gravity of the situation. Or at least *some* of the gravity. He probably thought I had a crush on him. I doubt he realized that he was my soul mate.

He took a deep breath. "Sit down for a second, Gracie."

I didn't sit down.

"Okay, listen. Life can get confusing. I know that. It gets confusing for all of us, believe me, but when we're young, things can seem even stranger. I want you to know that you're a very intelligent, gifted young woman. And what I see in you is someone who's going to go far. You're an exceptional person, Grace. I really mean that. And I hope you know how much respect I have for you. You're going to make one hell of a biologist someday."

My dinner began to crawl up my throat. The absolute last thing in the world I wanted was to have his respect for me as one hell of a fucking *biologist*.

"You might be drooling over her *now*," I said, "but you're delusional if you think there's anything to back this little charade of yours up."

His mouth fell open. He had no words for a moment.

"Oh, wait, you're right," I added, rolling my eyes at his reaction. "I'm sure what you and Judy have is *true love*."

Mr. Sorrentino crossed his arms with a grim finality in his face. "I'm sorry, this conversation is over, Grace."

I was drawing the courage to act blasé almost solely from

my full witch's regalia. "Whatever. Congratulations, Mr. Sorrentino, on finding a real *gem*."

I turned and walked out, the long folds of my polyester dress trailing out behind me dramatically. I walked down the hallway with all the attitude I could muster, clinging hard to the remnants of my bulletproof façade, but even the remnants were synthetic at that point. I had already been destroyed.

Noreen came running down the hallway dressed as a tree. "Holy *shit!*" she called. "We were so fucking good! Nobody forgot the words! It was crazy!"

She was one of the "rapping trees." She and a bunch of other trees did a rap at the end of the second act. A way to dust the cobwebs off the play, I suppose. I was always against it personally, but I wasn't a big enough drama nerd to care.

I ignored Noreen and turned into the delicious emptiness of the girls' bathroom. I went straight to the last stall, slammed the door shut, and fell apart without further ado.

I WENT HOME FOR THE CHRISTMAS HOLIDAYS FEEL—
ing like a carcass. My soul, as far as I was concerned, had been
digested by fate and spewed back into my body, where it re-
sided with no will or purpose left to itself. Or in any case, that
is how I had recorded my feelings on the matter in my journal.

"Hi, bug," my mom said when I walked up to her at the
bus station.

I was the only student who attended my school and traveled
home on a bus. If you could send your child to the almost-but-
not-quite-prestigious preparatory boarding school that I went
to, you could pay for economy plane tickets. Just not in my
case. I was from a different income bracket—more of a mobile-
home-community-type income bracket that doesn't tradition-
ally jibe with private school tuition fees. Honestly, it never
entirely stopped being bizarre that I went to a private school
for high school, but my father paid for board and tuition and
wouldn't budge on the matter. He said a solid education was

all I needed to be all right in life, but I think really it was all *he* needed to be all right—with the fact that he had made me accidentally, and there was nothing much he could do about it at this point. He had to do *something* to not be a scumbag, and sticking me with a bloated education was his solution. He was never fully a scumbag, though—more of a dickface, maybe— but he meant well. Anyway, that's a whole story in a nutshell. More later.

"Hi, Mom." I had stopped in front of her and just stood there for a moment, arms hanging limply at my side.

"Come here," she said, pulling me into her embrace. "How was school?"

"Normal."

"Oh, good. I hate that you're gone so much," she murmured into my hair. "I hate it so much without you."

I grabbed onto her hard. There were many things wrong with my mother—real things, not melodramatic teenage imaginings, but she was the only person I could hold on to without shame or even a good reason. She'd never ask questions.

"I decided that we should get doughnuts right now on the way home!" she said, giving me a kiss. "What do you say? Should we do it?"

The thought of eating a doughnut made the nausea well up in me all over again, but I smiled all the same and said, "Yeah!" Exclamation point and all.

I spent the holidays coming to terms with this new crippled existence that was evidently my destiny. I read a lot, as I always did. I couldn't help my obsession with books. Try as I might to be cooler than that, I just wasn't. I also wrote journals and poems and novels, so that didn't help. I had just finished *A Clockwork Orange,* and having thoroughly enjoyed that mindfuck, I moved on to Stephen King's *It.* I figured it was safer to stay with deranged subject matter. It seemed to settle my stomach.

At night, I read and listened to music and cried. During the day, I spent a lot of time with my mother, which was harder than it had ever been before. I liked laying my head in her lap while we watched TV with her hands playing in my hair, but talking to her took the kind of energy and patience that was painful for me to scrape together under the circumstances.

My mother was a special kind of person. She was young—thirty-four. And she was beautiful. Not in a trailer park kind of way. She was beautiful in a totally unprocessed, gift-of-nature kind of way. She had the same coloring as I did—dark hair, pale skin, blue eyes—but on her it somehow worked. She didn't look pasty or "contrasty" the way that I did. She looked otherworldly and mesmerizing. People stared at her when she walked by. And on top of the looks (or despite the looks), my mother was also an insanely nice person. Gentle, loving, kind. She wanted everything to be good for every living creature on the planet at all times, and she was genuine in her good-will and peace-on-earth vibes. She meant it. She was nice to everyone, even plants, even furniture and inanimate objects. Everyone got the benefit of the doubt.

But the problem was that she was also an insane person. For real. I guess the easiest way to describe her condition would be with the word *delusional*. She was ruthless in the way she ignored reality, like little kids are when they pretend to be astronauts or cowboys or princesses, building worlds around themselves. My mother had built a world around herself in the same way. She disregarded the actuality of things as much as possible, and when it wasn't possible—when reality got too loud and began to exert too much pressure against the fairy-tale world she lived in—that's when she shattered. And then you fumbled with the pieces to put her together again. The way to do it was always more or less the same: you had to reassure her that what was real wasn't real at all and that her mythical, nutball world was the truth.

I didn't blame her most of the time. She wanted to be happy, and life wasn't set up like that for her, so she cheated the system and decided to short-circuit everything via fantasy. She wasn't stupid, and it worked. I understood the logic, and I supported it the best I could. Sometimes it was better the delusional way. My mother could be a lot of fun—painting the world a smorgasbord of ridiculously pastel-colored, unicorn-flavored hues of glittering bullshit. Sometimes, after a bad day of school, that was exactly what I needed. On the downside, however, you could absolutely forget about discussing anything real that was on your mind, ever, because reality = booby traps = nuclear holocaust of emotions. The short circuit could only handle so much before it blew a fuse.

That Christmas was hard. I had never been in love before. I'd never had my heart broken before. Keeping that kind of shit creek out of view wasn't easy.

"You don't mind that your dad couldn't be here for this Christmas, do you?" my mother said, patting my knee as we were watching TV together. "You know he really wanted to, but work got in the way. His company is merging in January, and there's just too much he needs to prepare."

"Yeah, I don't care."

"Honey, don't say you don't care. *He* cares he can't be here, so you should care too."

"No, I just meant I understand. I know he has to work."

She smiled. "Isn't that a cute necklace he sent you?"

"Yeah, it's nice."

Here's the story.

The reason why my father wasn't with us for Christmas was because he was a married man with a wife and three daughters in California who didn't know that my mother and I existed. All this stuff about a merger in January was made up. My mother and I were a secret offshoot of his otherwise ordinary life. I didn't blame him for having been helpless against my nineteen-year-old mother on a Floridian business trip all those years ago. Naturally, he had to fall in love with her. She was beautiful in a way that was unusual and bottomless. It's no mystery at all that he could never get her out of his head no matter how convenient that would have been. Their affair had never ceased and grew like a fungus in a damp basement. I was a side product, and here we all were. There was real love between my parents, I can't deny that. Maybe there was more real love there than with his actual family, and maybe that's why it "worked." Whatever the reasons for my parents' longevity as lovers, my mother and I were his alternate universe, coexisting with his dominant universe, side by side. We knew of "them," but they didn't know of us. The only rule was never talk about it.

I had my mother's last name: Welles. My father sent a little bit of money monthly via a complex system that included his best friend and business partner. He paid for me to go to boarding school via the same system of funds, and he visited us a couple of times a year under the guise of business trips. We all stuck to the rules, and as I said, it worked.

It had never been any other way, and so it was never anything other than the norm. When my dad came to stay for some days or a week or two, I was always pleased to see him. He brought presents, and we went out to eat every night. When he left, I was all right too. At least I think I was all right. Sometimes I would inspect my emotional constitution after one of his visits, sitting on my bed and wondering if I had been damaged somehow. I could never be 100 percent certain. It depended a lot on what music I had playing during these inspections, but mainly I felt I was all right until I got jealous of something like the girl across the street being yelled at by her dad to stay away from some loser boyfriend. That kind of stuff sometimes got me. I could probably have sex with every questionable variety of boy all day long and nobody would stop me.

The thing I was absolutely certain I didn't understand about this scenario was why my mother had fallen in love with my *dad*. That is the part that made no sense at all. He looked so incredibly ordinary to me. There was nothing exciting about him, except that one never quite knew when he would appear and disappear. He was sixteen years older than she was, with a moderate belly, and he was pretty bald. I just couldn't figure it out. Sure, he had money. He was an entertainment lawyer, and he lived in Beverly Hills (or at least that's where his firm was), but this didn't make him any more interesting in my mind, and he certainly didn't shower us in money. He couldn't—it would have been too dangerous.

My mother could have had any man she wanted. She could have left Florida with the lead singer of any band stopping through on a tour. She could have met a brilliant scientist or been the muse to a writer who would use her as inspiration for his Pulitzer Prize–winning novel. She was that special. At the very least, she could have married a ridiculously wealthy man, or even just a normal man who actually loved her enough to stay.

She could have put a spell on anyone, but instead, it was my dad who had put a spell on *her*.

I looked over at my mom and wondered if I would end up like her. Trapped forever in some kind of love purgatory. *Probably,* I thought. I was probably fucked.

MIDHURST SCHOOL WAS FOUNDED IN 1973. IT WAS A
preparatory boarding school somewhere on the lower spectrum
of private boarding schools. It wanted to be prestigious, but it
was too accessible, too short of funds, and also, it was in the
swamps of Florida.

It lay nestled in the midsection of the appendix of the USA,
as we liked to call it—closer to the Atlantic side than the Gulf
of Mexico but not near enough to either side to be close to a
beach. The countryside surrounding the school was thick, flat,
and green, with Spanish moss hanging off all the trees, lizards
darting across the sidewalks, snakes in the bushes, and that
thick, stocky grass that feels fake to the touch.

I've always liked the Floridian vegetation, actually, even
back when I was a little kid. There was something forgotten and prehistoric about it. It was fertile and romantic.
Everything dripping and hanging. And I loved the danger—
the fact that you had to watch out around lakes because of

alligators, the hurricane and tropical storm warnings, and the rattlesnakes that were sometimes found in the bushes around the school. But beyond the natural vegetation, the location of the school had little to offer. The closest town was a little down the road from the school. It was small, uneventful, and lacking in most things.

The school itself consisted of a large whitewashed Spanish-style building that used to be a hospital back in the '30s. That was the main building. It housed the offices, most of the classrooms, the assembly hall, and the dining room. It was a bit rundown, like most of the school was, but it was imposing in its quiet simplicity. The other buildings spread out behind it. The dormitories, the gym, the extra classrooms that didn't fit into the main building, the art rooms—those were a mixture of '70s and '80s buildings, added over the decades.

The majority of the kids at Midhurst came from upper-middle-class backgrounds. Their parents weren't *rich*-rich, but they had enough money to want to imitate the patterns of the class above them. There were a few legitimately wealthy kids. I imagine their parents had tried to get them into better schools, but without the right grades or connections to those schools, they had failed and moved down a notch in their ambitions.

Midhurst School had no waiting list. There were no rigorous entrance exams. You could get in even if your grades were not above average. If you could pay the tuition, your child was in. As a result, there was a wide variety of kids. A bunch of smart kids who'd end up making it into impressive colleges. Lazy kids who had no ambition whatsoever and coasted through like they would have done at any third-rate public school. The kids whose parents didn't want them at home. There were a lot of kids from other locations in Florida or neighboring states, a few local kids, and even a small group of international kids—Germans, predominantly, for some reason.

We had a stupid school slogan (*Holding the Key to a Brighter Tomorrow*) just like all the other schools did. And a logo that had a medieval-looking tower in the middle with two palm trees on either side of it and a goblet above it. It made little sense, except for the palm trees. Midhurst believed itself to be "steeped in tradition" and made all kinds of attempts to appear elevated in its institutional ranking—a springboard to the Ivy League. The tower in the crest was no doubt an attempt to wrangle some tradition out of nowhere. Lord knows what the goblet was about.

The school website featured laughing kids, the sun shining through their hair as they sat on lawns with their homework. Shots of kids playing tennis and horseback riding. Kids in front of computers, presumably learning to code. Kids hanging out in sun-filled dorm rooms, playing guitar or board games. One kid playing a saxophone. Seniors throwing their mortarboards up in the air. Teachers hanging out together, looking like they've bonded over great adventures and had come out the other end with a lot of hilarious in-jokes.

In reality, Midhurst was the kind of school that had gum stuck to the bottoms of the desks, outdated furniture, teachers who drove shitty cars, and weird musty smells in random parts of the corridors. We had school uniforms, but even those were half-assed. They were just the blue T-shirts with the school logo printed large on the front, and then dark pants or pleated skirts. It borderline looked like a PE uniform or something you'd wear at summer camp.

And then there were the school rules. In this respect, Midhurst kept up quite well with all the other boarding schools. The curfews, dress codes, rules about hair, makeup, socks, shoes. The zero-tolerance rules on smoking, drinking, and drugs. No congregating in dorm rooms past 9:00 p.m. Absolutely no boys in the girls' dormitory or vice versa. No cell phones allowed in the dining hall or during class. Definitely no use of the lavatories during class without a bathroom pass. No food in the laundry room, classrooms, or hallways. No gum. No leaving the school grounds without a pass. No sports equipment in the main building. No music after 9:00 p.m. No music louder than a "pleasant midrange" at any point in time. No card playing or balls in the dormitories or hallways. No borrowing money from other students. No running in the hallways. And so on. Boarding schools are good at thinking up ways in which to claustrophobize your life. That being said, 75 percent of these rules were being broken on a regular basis, and everyone knew it to some degree, including the staff.

It was all right. Once you got the hang of it, it was all right.

School started up again a week into January. I arrived the night before and found my roommate already in our room, unpacked and listening to *Mamma Mia!* (yeah, the musical) on her speakers.

I threw my bag on the floor. "Oh no. No fucking way."

"Hi, Grace. Nice to see you too," she said, giving me the finger.

"Not this shit. Turn it off!"

"It's my room, too."

"Yeah, but my ears!"

She sat at the edge of her bed, watching me unpack my suitcase. I was putting my clothes away and lining up my composition books next to my bedside table. There were about fifteen novels I had started in those composition books. I started a novel about almost everything, but it was hard for me to get beyond the first chapter on any one of them. The only other item of real significance I had brought was my slingshot. I stared at it for a second before dropping it into the sock drawer. I had been a six-year-old when I'd first gotten it, and I had used it every day for years. In a way, it was the most substantial proof of my childhood—the object that defined those years of my life more fully than anything else. I wondered why exactly I'd brought it, but I figured it had something to do with wanting proof of a time when I didn't cry myself to sleep next to toilets and when nothing could intimidate me. I liked to be reminded that I'd had a backbone once.

"So, what's wrong?" she asked, her eyes still sucking in every movement of mine.

"Besides the fact that your music is raping my eardrums as we speak?"

"Seriously. You look bad. Like, unhealthy," she said. "Your face looks puffy and fat in weird places."

"Thanks."

"I'm not trying to be mean. Just pointing out the truth."

"I really appreciate it."

Georgina Lowry and I got along well enough despite our many disagreements. We weren't friends, but we weren't involved in each other's lives enough to be enemies either. In fact, I'd go so far as to say there was a softly pulsing loyalty hidden somewhere among the many layers of outward irritation. Like a tiny vein embedded deep in a mass of excess fat. We would have rather died than acknowledge this verbally, of course, but still, we knew it was there—the inevitable bond of being holed up together in the same tiny space.

She had dark blond hair, a broad face, and superlight eyes. That crystal-blue color that can come off as beautiful but also extremely unnerving. She was athletic in build, stocky and dense looking, but full of muscles, not fat. I'd often find her doing weird leg lifts and crunches on the floor between our beds. She knew all the tricks of how to breathe—inhaling and exhaling at the right moments and pushing the air out in aggressive, little, professional bursts. I had to constantly step around her while she was doing something on the floor with her legs pointed up and her abdomen bouncing left and right in little twists. Her big thing was the volleyball team, which sometimes seemed to serve as her religion.

Also, she was rich. Our room was crammed full of her things: clothes, shoes, and sports equipment, decorative pillows, hair flatteners and curlers, framed artwork featuring inspirational quotes, a dehumidifier, a mini fridge, family photos, little boxes for jewelry and hair bands, and so on. I had a few articles of clothing, a few books, and a laptop, which was issued to every student at the beginning of the year. In a way, it was really *her* room more than it was mine, and although she was never malicious about it, she did get a kick out of my being *underprivileged,* as she liked to call it. That word in itself was fun to her—exotic. She found it fascinating that I couldn't just buy things or that a decent amount of my clothes was from St. Vincent's or Goodwill. When she'd see me debating whether to use a few quarters for the snack machine, she could never resist making a joke about it. Every time. She would be playful in the way she said it, always in good fun, but she didn't have any tact. Sometimes, it got to me. Georgina was a real elephant in the department of wit and social graces.

But still, despite our fights or arguments, I couldn't ever take it out on her. There was something desperately uncool about her that forever kept me bound to her in loyalty—the kind that you can only have for a roommate, a stupid sibling, or a countryman in a foreign place. The hot-pink athletic headband that she wore every day, her impossible taste in music, and her way of wearing clothes. She was the kind of girl who everyone in school knew was hopeless. Boys didn't give her the time of day, and girls dismissed her as a nonentity. Even the volleyball team wasn't a huge fan of her. She wasn't directly an outcast or someone who was bullied or picked on—she was too rich for that, and wealth did mean something at school—but she was uncool in the plainest sense of the word. Painfully so.

"What did you get for Christmas?" Georgina asked after I had taken a shower and was getting into bed.

"Books, mainly."

She waited for me to ask her the same question, and when I didn't, she said, "I got clothes and these cowboy boots that I've wanted for a superlong time. Oh, and also—the best part is my parents are taking me on a trip to Paris for spring break."

I looked over at her, too exhausted to be interested in anything she was saying.

"Freaking Paris!" she squealed.

"Yeah."

"God, you're no fun at all sometimes," she said, turning the lights off and moving around on her bed aggressively.

I didn't reply. I thought about the next day and how unreal it seemed. I'd have to see Mr. Sorrentino. I couldn't imagine a reality in which Mr. Sorrentino and I could ever share the same space and time again. I had thought of him so much over the holidays that he was no longer a normal person. He had grown into a creature of mythical proportions. He was no longer mortal. No longer a charismatic, friendly, flesh-and-blood human being who could laugh with me over mitochondria jokes and draw winky faces on my tests. He was a terrifying deity that held my entire life in its hand. I didn't belong to myself anymore. I belonged to him now.

I turned on the light again to write this thought down into my journal, but Georgina made a stink about it, and I turned the light back off.

BIOLOGY WAS THE FIRST PERIOD AFTER LUNCH. I
stood outside Mr. Sorrentino's classroom terrified, pressing
myself against the opposite wall of the hallway and staring at
the door. My slingshot was wedged into the waistband of my
skirt for emotional support. It had seemed like a great idea that
morning, pulling it out of my drawer and jamming it into my
skirt, but as I stood there, I realized it was no support whatsoever. I don't know how long I waited outside Mr. Sorrentino's
door. Kids were streaming in with their usual noise. Their
flushed faces laughing and joking. Eyes wide open, mid-joke,
or just looking bored out of their minds, moving in the sluggish,
dazed stagger befitting a Monday morning.

Then the bell rang for the last time, and I was still standing
there, holding my books, immobilized against the school hallway. I heard Mr. Sorrentino's voice begin to call roll, and I
turned away.

I didn't know where exactly I was going, but it didn't matter anyway. I slipped out the back entrance of the building,

past the tennis courts, and I didn't stop until I had reached the very back end of the school's property. There was nothing much back there except a wall running the length of the place and a couple of utility and equipment sheds. I dropped down by a tree and closed my eyes, enjoying the feel of the warm tears spilling down my cheeks. There's something to be said about crying when you're sad. As much as I wanted to punch myself in the face for being such a spineless pissant, I simultaneously couldn't help wallowing in the glory of the absolute blackness of the emotions. So, I just let the moment be. And then I groaned and pulled the slingshot out from my skirt because it was digging pretty hard into my back. I threw it on the grass next to me and pulled out my notebook, opening it to a fresh page, where I wrote *Midnight in My Heart* at the top and underneath it: *Chapter 1*. I took a breath and thought for a moment, and then before I could get any further, I was interrupted by the sound of yelling and footsteps crashing through the grass.

I wiped all traces of tears frantically off my face, closed my notebook, and turned just in time to see a group of boys come running across the field toward my general direction. Three older boys chasing a fourth kid who looked to be a little younger. I thought I recognized some of the older boys—they were all seniors—but the other one must have been new to school because I had never seen him before. He began to slow down when it was obvious that he was at a dead end. The wall was stretching out before him in both directions—no way out. He came to a stop and turned to face the other three, breathing heavily. They began to circle around him. I definitely recognized them. The larger one was Derek McCormick—he was a senior and the guy who got all the girls because of his looks and general asshole credentials. The other two were Neal

Gessner and Kevin Lutz. They were a well-known trio that stuck together like a chemical compound.

When it became apparent to them that they had their victim cornered, they began to take their time about it, savoring the lopsided quality of this fight. There was an introductory shove, and the new kid stumbled back a step before catching his balance again. Derek, the obvious leader of the trio, stepped forward with a wholesome grin that spread across his face as if he were in a commercial, throwing a Frisbee or something. I mean, he looked like such a piece of shit, it was kind of fascinating. Out of nowhere, the new kid cut Derek's monologue short by landing a surprisingly solid punch in Derek's jaw, catching everyone off guard, me included. After reeling back a few steps, Derek straightened up and punched him back—in the stomach, and then the other two jumped in, practically frothing at the mouth. He went down. I grabbed a few pieces of gravel off the ground almost without thinking at all. The little group didn't notice me. They were closed in around the boy on the ground, taking turns kicking. When I was close enough, I placed a decent-size piece of gravel into the pouch of my slingshot and pulled it back, twisting it as I did so, for a soft shot. It would allow the rock to fly straight. I aimed it at Derek's face. His left ear, to be precise. He was standing back just then, taking a moment to catch his breath. The piece of gravel hit him hard where it was intended to, and he jumped, letting out a loud yelp.

Derek's head swiveled around wildly, and then, catching sight of me, he stared dumbstruck with his hand on his ear. I don't think he knew what had happened. His mouth hung slightly open in confusion, and he kept his face perfectly still, which is exactly what you want when you're aiming at something. Which I did.

"What the *fuck*!" he cried out when the second piece of gravel cut his cheek.

I had been somewhat sure that I could still aim, but when I hit him exactly where I had intended to for the second time in a row, I was thrilled. It must have been at least a year since I'd last shot at anything. Back in the day, I had gotten to the point where I could hit anything in my sleep, but that had been in my junior high school days at home. Standing there, I could feel my breathing speed up. I felt a sense of accomplishment, and I remembered how much I had liked the taste of adrenaline when I made a perfect shot.

Nobody knew what to do next. All four of them were staring at me now, and I was staring at them. I wasn't a boy, and they weren't girls, so all the usual ways out weren't exactly available to us. They wanted to move, but where to and for what? To be honest, I didn't really know what to do either. I had outgrown my schoolyard altercations.

"Hey, what the fuck!" Derek called again, massaging his ear and glaring at me like an injured rhinoceros—spooked and indignant, as though the laws of the African bush had been tipped sideways.

"Did she just hit you?" Neal asked with a constipated look of noncomprehension. "Is that a slingshot?"

Then the new kid, who had picked himself up off the ground meanwhile, took this opportunity to kick Derek hard in the back of his knees. Derek collapsed almost automatically to the floor. His pals stood there confused for a moment before taking off after the new kid, who was coming straight at me. He grabbed my hand as he passed by without stopping and yanked me almost completely off my feet with the force of his momentum.

"*Move it!*" he yelled back at me, not letting go of my hand.

We ran. I don't know if we were followed or not. I didn't

turn around. I kept my eyes on the boy pulling me across the field. He had his free arm wrapped around his body, holding his side, and his footing was arrhythmical and stumbling, but he ran. Once we had picked up speed, I was able to pull my hand out of his grasp. It was easier to run that way, and besides, I didn't want to hold his hand, which was sweaty and tight around my fingers and a random person's body part. We continued running until we crashed through the back doors to the main building, where Mrs. Gillespie, one of the English teachers, seemed to have materialized out of absolutely nowhere with a bunch of papers clamped under her arm and a coffee cup in hand. Her bulky little form was suddenly right in front of us—loud floral blouse, matching blazer and skirt combo, fresh beauty-parlor hairdo sitting on her head like a fluffy bird's nest. For a terrible moment, it seemed that we would take her down, but I managed to skid to a halt a few feet in front of her, and the boy I was following dived out to the side in the last second, just barely grazing her shoulder as he went crashing to the floor. Mrs. Gillespie jumped back with a scream and let the cup of coffee go flying into the air. The cup exploded against the wall. It rained coffee. The boy was lying on the floor, and I stood frozen a few feet behind him, still holding my slingshot. I turned to see if the others had followed us this far, but there was no sign of them.

5

"I'M WADE, BY THE WAY," HE SAID.

I gave him my name reluctantly and then made a point of focusing elsewhere in the room. We were sitting in the main office, waiting for Mr. Wahlberg, the headmaster, to see us.

I had never gotten into very serious trouble at school, but I did have a consistent if innocuous relationship with Mr. Wahlberg due mainly to Algebra II and PE, in which I made little to no effort of any kind. I found both of these subjects completely irrelevant to my existence and had no objections to being sent to the office about it. In fact, I preferred it to either PE or algebra class, and with time, I had become pretty familiar with the place. The potted plants, the bad oil paintings of Mr. and Mrs. McCleary, who had started the school in 1973, the announcement board, the staff photo, the light gray carpeting, and the stain on the ceiling by the door to the hallway. In a way, I liked the office. It was comforting in its predictability. Plus, it was full of adults, and sometimes I needed to get out of the raging hormonal bloodbath that was the majority of life at school. Grown-ups were so much more lethargic. It could be very relaxing.

This time was different, though. Waiting to be called into Mr. Wahlberg's office, I felt the cold sweat start to build at the back of my neck and my stomach become detached and queasy. There was no doubt that we were in a fairly sizable amount of shit, but that wasn't what was making me nervous. It was the social implications of what I had gotten myself into: this person sitting inches away from me, bouncing his leg up and down, trying to talk to me as though we were now on the same side of something. I had never asked for this. All I had wanted was to shoot Derek in the face for being such an A-1 piece of shit. It was supposed to be a distraction from Mr. Sorrentino—something to make me feel better—but it had backfired on me. Somehow, I had been packaged off onto the same team with this sweating, breathing stranger who was a boy and whose elbow had bumped into my arm twice already because he couldn't sit still. It was nauseating.

"Hey!" Wade tapped me on the shoulder, oblivious to my attempts at blowing him off by not-so-subtle means of body language.

I gave him a nervous glance.

"Hey, that was insane—that thing with the slingshot," he said. He kept his voice low so that Mrs. Martinez wouldn't be able to hear from where she sat at her desk, but his words were full of breathless excitement. "How come you know how to shoot with one of those things?"

I turned away, focusing on the staff photograph—top left-hand corner, to be exact—where Mr. Sorrentino stood smiling back at me with his devil-may-care hair flopping into his face.

"I practiced a lot when I was younger," I said.

"Why?"

"I don't know."

"I didn't think slingshots actually *worked*—you know, that you can actually hit things with them accurately."

"That's what they're made for."

"I just always thought they were toys."

"They're not toys."

"Yeah, I believe you," he said with a laugh.

The way he laughed caught me off guard. There was an unapologetic warmth in his manner. Boys didn't laugh like that—at least not the cool ones, who usually had a derisive, overconfident, joker-asshole vibe going at all times. I couldn't tell if Wade was the cool kind or not, even when I stole a furtive glance. He sat with a defined slump to his shoulders. His fingernails were dirty and bitten low. No particular haircut, just hair grown out slightly too long, probably out of carelessness. Undone shoelace. Bruise under his eye, courtesy of Derek. Baby fat still in his face.

"Thanks, by the way," he said. "For helping me out."

His eyes were fixed on me with that same magnetic innocence that had been in his laugh. It really seemed that he gave no fucks about me being a dick.

"Yeah. I wasn't doing it to help, though," I said.

"Then why'd you do it?"

I concentrated back on Mr. Sorrentino's smile. "It's just Derek. His stupid face, I guess."

"I can live with that," he said with another laugh.

I angled my body slightly away from him, trying to make it clear that just because fate had thrown Mrs. Gillespie into our path did not make us a duo of any sort.

The wait was taking forever. Wade sat next to me, fidgeting as the minutes drained away. He made one or two more attempts at conversation, and I shoved them back into his face. Eventually, he got up to help Mrs. Martinez find her glasses, which she had misplaced. Mrs. Martinez was the keeper of Mr. Wahlberg's office—a large lady (height more than width), probably in her late forties with a penchant for cozy wear (e.g., oversize sweaters, often with cats on them, and slip-on shoes that looked like something one would wear at home on the couch). She was all right as far as school personnel was concerned. Anyway, she and Wade sorted through the mess on her desk for about five minutes, and the whole time, they talked about these two crazy cats that Mrs. Martinez said she had who liked to carry off her glasses and hide them in weird places at home. Wade laughed at her story and told her about some dog he once had as a kid. It was bizarre. I didn't get his angle.

"Look," Wade said, holding up the glasses.

"Well, I'll be!" Mrs. Martinez exclaimed, delighted. "Where were they?"

"Under all this stuff," he said, pointing to a messy pile of papers. "Don't you ever clean your desk?"

"Oh, I'm terrible, aren't I?" she said as he handed them to her. "Those are the old timetables for the Christmas charity fundraiser. What are those still doing there? Pass them to me will you, hon?"

He grabbed the stack of papers and passed them over to her.

"Those were supposed to be in the recycling bin."

"You want me to drop them off there?" he asked.

She stopped her bustling around and took her time to look him over. Her small eyes narrowed in concentration, as though trying to make sense of an undiscovered form of life. "You're a real sweetheart, you know that?" she said. "Your parents sure did something right."

Wade let out a small snort of amusement.

"I mean it," she said. "You're a gentleman."

His amusement turned quickly into discomfort. "It's not a

big deal," he said, scratching his arm. "I can drop them off if you want."

"Thanks, hon, but Tara will get to it in a minute, and I think Mr. Wahlberg is almost ready for you."

He walked back and fell into the seat next to me. I quickly looked away again, and we continued to wait silently.

Mr. Wahlberg was a wiry man. Tall, thin, probably in his fifties, and not much appetite for life left in him. He wore pale yellow shirts and combed his hair straight back from his receding hairline. On that day, he wore a tie that had musical notes all over it, which struck me as bizarre since I couldn't imagine him listening to music. He seemed too miserable— certainly too miserable for a tie with musical notes on it.

"This qualifies as a weapon," Mr. Wahlberg said, holding up the slingshot.

He let the significance of his statement sink in.

"I wouldn't call it a *weapon,* per se," I said eventually, staring hard at my knee.

Mr. Wahlberg sighed. "I'd really appreciate it if we could skip the song and dance this time, Miss Welles. The rules and regulations are very clear about objects that could be used as weapons."

"Right. Totally. I just think that's super vague, though," I said. "Because per that rule, anything could be used as a weapon. I could technically use a *sock* to strangle someone. I mean, who decides if a slingshot or a sock is a weapon anyway?"

"*I* do," he said.

"Right, but that's what I'm saying—it's arbitrary. Like, there's no need for any real logic, per se. It's just what you decide. But anyway, that's all I'm saying."

When I was nervous, I tended to say *per se* a lot. It was easy to throw in pretty much anywhere in a sentence.

Mr. Wahlberg closed his eyes and began massaging his eyeballs, which is something he did when it was necessary to prove to people that he didn't have it easy in his line of work. Wade and I sat watching the eyeball massage. After a moment, Mr. Wahlberg dropped his hands on the desk and pulled himself together.

"We're not here to discuss why I have risen to the exalted position of school principal, where clearly my powers know no limits and my whims are the law. Let's keep it simple: the two of you were caught running through the hallways during lessons this morning, very nearly taking Mrs. Gillespie's head off in the process, and you were carrying a slingshot. And that, Miss Welles, puts you in very hot water."

"It's my slingshot," Wade said, raising his hand.

Mr. Wahlberg focused on Wade with a blank expression, and for a second, I thought he was going to go into another eyeball massage, but he didn't.

"My dad gave it to me when I was a kid," Wade started to explain. "It doesn't even really work—like, the elastic is totally worn out—and anyway, it's just a toy. I just keep it around, you know, to remind me of home. I didn't know it was such a big deal. Sorry."

Mr. Wahlberg took Wade in for a long moment. His eyebrows drew together. "How are you settling in?" he asked Wade.

"Really well, to be honest."

Mr. Wahlberg's expression remained unaltered. His eyes drooped down a little on the outer edges, and his mouth was an almost perfectly horizontal line of non-emotion.

"I know you had a difficult time at your last school," he said.

Wade didn't reply but seemed undaunted. Polite, wide-eyed, attentive.

"Your parents were hoping this would be a fresh start for

you," Mr. Wahlberg went on. "This is, what—your fourth school in two years, I believe?"

"Yeah . . ." He squinted up at the ceiling for a moment as though counting the number of schools in his head. "Yeah, four."

"Two of those were expulsions."

Wade nodded with a shamefaced grimace that looked pretty bogus to me. Mr. Wahlberg regarded him carefully for a moment.

"I like to believe that this is the kind of place that can give you all the resources you need to turn over a new leaf," he said eventually. "I'll tell you, we've had plenty of success with kids being able to find themselves here. I've seen it happen. I'm not interested in who you were at your previous schools. What I'm interested in is who you intend to be here at Midhurst."

"Right. Well, that's what I'm interested in too actually."

"Is that so?" Mr. Wahlberg didn't seem to buy it.

"Yeah. No joke," Wade said. "I know it sounds like I'm full of sh—or, like, I can come off insincere and stuff sometimes, but I'm not. I'm actually being sincere right now about turning over a new leaf and all."

God, he was either so good or so bad at talking his way out of a scrape that I couldn't figure out which it was. I didn't think Mr. Wahlberg knew either. He folded his arms over his chest and proceeded with some caution.

"Well, listen, I'm going to give you the same chances I give anyone else. Clean slate. No judgment. I'm not going to sit here, expecting you to fail just because that would be the easy way out for us all. I'm afraid I'm going to expect you to succeed like I would expect any of my straight-A students to succeed. That is my promise to you: a fair chance. But what you make of that chance is up to you. And I'm not going to lie—it worries

SLINGSHOT   33

me that the semester has just started and here we are. It's a bad start, Mr. Scholfield."

No one said anything for a moment. Wade had lost a small trace of his absolute cool. He remained attentive, but his right leg had started bouncing again.

"I would hate to have to call your parents and tell them that we have a problem."

Pausing after saying something like that was a particularly low move, I thought.

Mr. Wahlberg continued, "Let me ask you this: Do you want to be here?"

Wade nodded.

"Are you sure about that? Because if you're not, I'm not interested in wasting anyone's time."

"Yeah, I know," Wade said. He was rubbing the arm of his chair. "I get that. It would be stupid if anyone wasted their time on me, but I like this place. I really do. I'm serious about not wanting to screw it up."

Mr. Wahlberg leaned back in his chair with a thoughtful frown, no doubt still trying to determine whether that had been penitence in Wade's voice or just really high-end derision. For a moment, we just sat there, listening to the ticking of Mr. Wahlberg's wristwatch, waiting for the verdict. The phone rang out in the main office, and Mrs. Martinez's pleasant voice answered. And then Mr. Wahlberg opened one of his desk drawers and pulled out a piece of paper, which he placed in front of Wade.

"These are the school rules and regulations. I'd like you to copy them out thirty times over the weekend and see me on Monday. You think you can do that?"

A wide smile broke out across Wade's face. "Yeah, absolutely."

"If you're serious about wanting to stay here, Mr. Scholfield, I am perfectly willing to be convinced of it."

Wade was full of relief as we walked out of the office, and I, in contrast, was in a real stink of a mood because Mr. Wahlberg had also assigned us a week of cleaning the dining hall after dinner, which ranked only second to cleaning the toilets.

"Yikes!" Wade said, wiping his brow in an exaggerated manner as we walked back into the hallway. By the way he acted, one would have thought it was all a big joke to him, but his hand was trembling a little when he made the motion of wiping his brow.

"You didn't have to pretend the slingshot was yours," I said, sounding heartless in a way that I couldn't control.

"Can't help it if I'm that kind of guy," he said.

I didn't even crack a smile. "Well, it was pointless, because I don't care if I'm expelled or not. All those empty threats wouldn't have bothered me personally."

He looked intrigued. "Wait, you think he was bluffing?"

"Of course he was. He needs your tuition fee. You think Mr. Wahlberg gives an actual shit about you 'turning over a new leaf'?"

"Well, maybe. I don't know the guy."

"He doesn't. He just likes to hear himself talk."

I didn't know if Mr. Wahlberg just liked to hear himself talk or not, but I said it because I couldn't think of anything else to say, and besides, I didn't want to have to thank Wade for taking the fall. It was chivalrous in a way that I was ill equipped to handle.

"Hey, hold on a second," he called out when I turned to walk in the opposite direction he was heading.

I stopped reluctantly. "What?"

"I can't tell if you hate me or if that's just your personality," he said. "Not your personality, but your—you know—the way you act when you're uncomfortable. My best friend at my last school had a way of losing his nerve in front of people, and some of the stuff he said made him seem like a jerk. I figured that was maybe the same thing with you too. Or *do* you hate me? It's all right if you do, but I don't want to jump to conclusions—in case you *don't* actually hate me, I mean."

I hesitated, and not fully certain of what he was even asking, I said, "It's my personality."

He smiled, seemingly with relief. "Okay, awesome."

My face began to feel hot again. His effortless insight made me sick. It only added to my humiliation, being dissected like this and having my unattractive traits thrown into my face.

I didn't bother answering him. I turned and walked away.

And Derek McCormick. I could no longer remember why exactly I had shot Derek. Maybe I was a psychopath.

6

I DREAMED THAT I HAD WEIRD SEX WITH MR. SOR—
rentino in a tiny car that night. A lot of the dream had to do
with the mechanics of getting into the car, but once that had
been accomplished, there was some very definite offbeat sexual activity. I was a virgin, so almost all sexual activity in my
head was offbeat and unrealistic, but ever since Mr. Sorrentino
had entered my life, the dreams had gotten somewhat intense
and totally out of control. My pristine lack of experience ne-
cessitated this rampant overdrive of my imagination, which
just wasn't a good thing. I had a *lot* of unorthodox sex with
Mr. S. almost every night, and honestly, when the dreams were
not sexual in nature, they were worse. We'd be trying to fit a
giant-size saltshaker into a suitcase all night or something.

Anyway, the weekend came. I gave myself bangs on Saturday afternoon when Georgina was out at some volleyball meeting or practice and I had the room to myself. The bangs were
crooked, but I was afraid to straighten them out because of

how short they already were. I wanted to avoid having one-inch bangs, so I put the scissors back in Georgina's desk drawer. Rain was streaming down the window. It was one of those unexpected subtropical rain showers where the sky breaks loose, and the light turns weird and you can feel the electricity in the air around you.

I read some more of *It* before putting it down and staring at the ceiling, not able to concentrate. I hated every angle of my life just then.

After a while, I got up and wrote Stephen King an email. Initially, the email had been about how much I liked *It*, but it quickly turned into a detailed account of the Mr. Sorrentino situation.

"It's hard as hell to hate him, and yet I do. And I love him even more than I hate him. And maybe I hate him more than I love him. I don't know anymore. I really thought we were soul mates. That's a thing, right? Being soul mates with someone? I was so sure that Mr. S. was my soul mate. It's not like he told me so, or even did anything specific, but I figured you don't need proof like that. Don't you just know when someone is your soul mate? And anyway, he's marrying that lady—Judy. What a joke . . ."

I peeled myself off the bed, and, saving the email into my drafts folder, I decided I might as well go downstairs and fill up my water bottle in the common room. There really wasn't anything better to do.

The common room was attached to the entrance hall of the dormitory building, easily accessible by both the girls' and boys' wing. It had some snack machines, a microwave, a TV, a pool table, and a collection of old couches. There was also a filtered tap where you could fill up your water bottles. It was crowded with kids due to the rain. I stopped at the doorway and decided not to get the water after all. Too many people. It was loud and jumbled in the room, full of motion and animalistic energy born out of pubescent ennui. I mean, it's not like I was actually older than these kids, but that didn't stop me from considering them juvenile and moronic in their pursuit of amusement. My newfound heartbreak made me world-weary in a way that I believed far removed me from this ocean of toddlers around me who clearly had no clue how painful life actually was. It never even crossed my mind that any of these kids might have had their hearts pulverized too. I mean—not for real. Not like I had. It wasn't possible.

Anyway, I backed out of the room quickly and began to make my way over to the girls' side of the building again. I was thinking about Mr. Sorrentino—the way his stomach was a little soft. It wasn't a paunch exactly but just a slight soft-ness, something that set him apart from boys as a man. The small wrinkles around his eyes when he smiled too. The warm, patient, attentive way in which he talked and listened to me. I didn't think I'd ever be capable of liking a boy—what would a boy ever be able to do for me? They lacked all the things that made the male species attractive to me. Having a boyfriend in my own age bracket seemed like it would be on par with taking care of a two-year-old who constantly wanted to stick his fingers in an electrical outlet—or maybe like babysitting an iguana at best. Boys were crass and loud, full of the need to perform in front of their friends at all times. They made infantile jokes about girls, they had terrible haircuts and the attention span of gnats. Being repellent was somehow their way of existing. Even the senior boys were a joke. And yeah, there were the quiet, introverted ones too—but half the time I forgot that they even existed, and when I did remember, my instinct was to feel bad for them, not to be turned on.

The thing about Mr. Sorrentino was that he made me feel good about who I was. In a world where I dangled at the end of the food chain almost constantly, he made me feel like someone with a legitimate future. Judy didn't need him the same way that I did—she was *born* with a legitimate future. It wasn't fair. She didn't even seem mentally equipped to really appreciate how special Mr. Sorrentino was. She would have been just as happy with some random insurance agent guy or accountant or used car salesman—I was convinced of that.

I was really starting to feel sorry for myself right around then, and maybe I would have made a whole afternoon out of it if I hadn't walked into someone's shoulder. I fell back a step, startled, and there was that guy Neal Gessner, one of Derek's friends. He was the one going through the experimental soul patch phase of his life, and plus he had one of those terrible haircuts I was talking about. Kevin, the other sidekick, was there too—and of course Derek, coming up behind them with a Band-Aid across his cheek where I had hit him with the piece of gravel. It almost made me laugh, except the situation wasn't hilarious enough.

"Hey, if it ain't the little cunt with the slingshot!" Neal announced happily.

Neal and Kevin were slowly backing me into the wall.

"Excuse me. Do you *mind*?" I said, sounding as unimpressed as I could while I tried to push the soul patch guy aside to no avail.

"Hey, what's the rush?" he asked. "We just want to communicate about what happened the other day. You traumatized this guy over here—see that guy? You made him feel pretty bad. Don't you think we need to communicate about that for a second at least?"

He was pointing at Derek, who was shaking his head like his friends were a couple of adorable idiots.

"I think you need to try to communicate with your brain cells before you hurt yourself," I said.

Kevin started laughing. Neal smiled a little.

"That's pretty funny," he said. "But you know what? Here's the thing—if you fuck with us, we fuck with you. We have to. That's just the natural order of the world. Nothing I can do about it."

"It's called karma," Kevin said, jovially.

Neal ignored him. "And your little fucknut boyfriend—will you tell him we said hello? We miss that little turd. Tell him we'll catch up soon, okay?"

I felt a cold splatter of liquid hit my face a moment later. It streamed into my eyes, down my back, into my bra, and some of it into my mouth—the sickly sweet taste of stale Gatorade. Neal was holding the bottle upside down over my head. When it was empty, he let it drop. It bounced off my head and hit the floor.

"Watch your back, baby," he said with a wide, friendly smile.

"Or what?" I asked, wiping Gatorade off my face with my sleeve. "You have some 7 Up you're going to pour on my head next?"

He shifted restlessly, all the energy in his face and hands needing something to do, but beyond pouring liquid over my head, there wasn't much he could do.

"Just watch your back, bitch," he repeated.

"Whatever, dickweed. Good luck with that soul patch."

He gave my shoulder a hard shove, and I fell back into the wall behind me.

"All right, all right," Derek said, pulling him back. "Let's go before this gets any weirder. Maybe we can find you a pre-schooler to pick a fight with next."

He pushed his friends back in the direction of the common room, accompanied by Kevin's high-pitched laughter. Derek looked back at me over his shoulder with an expression I couldn't decipher.

I leaned back against the wall for a second and took a deep

breath. It wasn't that I hadn't been scared but rather that all the guts and social skills I was lacking in most departments usually came together pretty solidly during moments like these. I couldn't talk to a boy who was trying to be nice to me or join a bunch of girls who invited me to be their friend, but I was fine with almost any kind of asswipe. There was comfort in the adrenaline. Or perhaps it was just the sense of having nothing to lose. When people were trying to be nice, there was everything to lose; when they were already assholes to begin with, there was nothing you could say to ruin it. Less pressure. Far more freedom.

I pushed my sticky, dripping hair out of my face and started back to my room, my heart thumping heavy and loud in my chest.

Upstairs, I passed the room with the music spilling out of its open door. It was Angela and Chandra's room. I saw a bunch of the girls from my grade lounging around in there, on the floor and on the beds, talking and laughing, singing along to the lyrics, their legs carelessly propped and dangling over various pieces of furniture. They made being alive look so easy. They had their idols, and their lyrics to sing along to, and their adorable emotions to feel. Their Instagram accounts to curate, and the boys that they effortlessly cultivated. They all knew how to flirt—that was another thing. They were cute and cool, and somehow they just knew how not to be lumbering assholes. They had the makeup, and the parents to rebel against, and their table at lunch, and their bedrooms at home, which I imagined to be full of pillows, stuffed animals, candles, and posters of hot guys.

"Hi," one of them called, seeing me look in at them.

I couldn't help feeling the crushing loneliness of my existence just then. My hair and face sticky with Gatorade and no one to confide in—seriously, no one. Except maybe Stephen

King, but I doubted he would ever read my letter even if I did find a place to email it to. I gave a quick nod to the girls in the room and moved on.

"Do you think eyelid skin is the same kind of skin as penis skin?" Georgina asked me that night.

I could always depend on my roommate to make my day a little weirder.

"No," I said. "I think it's different skin."

We had already turned out the lights, and it was that part of the night when philosophical thoughts tended to strike.

"It's weird how similar they seem, huh?"

"Yeah," I said.

I was disturbed to think Georgina would even know what penis skin looked like. *I* certainly had no idea. Although, from then on, I always imagined it to be made of the same material as eyelid skin.

"Good night," she said, and I could hear the rustling of her blankets as she settled herself in bed.

"Good night."

7

MONDAY, DINNERTIME. LASAGNA NIGHT. THE cheese oozed bright orange from the block of pasta and meat on my plate and pooled around it like a lake. The grease visibly floating in the cheese. The sick thing about it was that it tasted pretty good. I dipped my fork into the cheese lake and pulled it out, a thin string connecting fork with plate.

The dining hall was one of my least favorite places in the known universe. It defined you almost more than anything else at school—where you sat, how you walked, how you wore your school clothes (or worse: your real clothes on the weekend), what kind of food you picked out to eat, what people you talked to. Every movement you made was fair game in the dining hall. And whereas at a normal school you could get around the lunchroom, at boarding school, that was not an option. Even if you skipped breakfast or cut lunch short, you couldn't stop eating entirely. To stay alive, you had to deal with the dining hall. You had to walk in there every day and face the noise and the chaos, armed only with a tray of food.

And of course, if you were a girl, you couldn't eat any of the stuff you actually wanted to eat—like, forget about loading your plate with lasagna or pizza or anything deep-fried. You had to get the salad option if you weren't a pig. Always. Occasionally, you could get away with the baked potato as a side (without the butter)—but generally speaking, if you were trying to be taken seriously as a girl by the girls that mattered, you had to do your eating on the sly.

I always ate the wrong meal. Because fuck it. I'd be damned if I ate salad all day with my life already sucking as much as it did.

"Hey!"

I looked up from my lasagna. It was Wade Scholfield. He was holding his tray, standing on the other side of my table.

"I had a dream about you last night," he went on. "You were about three hundred pounds and you were getting onto a Greyhound bus. You might have been Australian too. That part I can't really remember, but I think you said something with an Australian accent." He shrugged quickly when I didn't reply. "I don't know what that means. Probably nothing. But . . . just thought I'd mention it."

I had no idea what to say, so instead, I nodded and flicked a piece of imaginary dirt off the table.

"Anyway, how was your weekend?" he asked.

"Um . . . shit, I guess."

He smiled a little. "What a coincidence—so was mine. Twenty-seven school rules, times thirty, is eight hundred and ten. I copied out eight hundred and ten rules. And some of those are about a paragraph long."

"Oh. Right."

I looked back at the table, hoping he would evaporate. He didn't.

"So, are you ready to clean this place after dinner?" he asked.

"I guess."

He stood there a moment longer. "Can I sit down?" he asked.

My stomach turned. I straightened up in my seat, suddenly terrified. "Oh shit. I don't know. I usually sit by myself," I said.

"So . . . yea or nay?"

He is actually going to make me say it, I thought. Why would he do that? He continued to stand there with his tray and the bright innocence in his stupid eyes, waiting for me to be a cunt.

"Nay," I said, instantly feeling weird about having used the word *nay.* "I'd rather you just sit somewhere else. Or if you want to sit here, I can leave too. I'm pretty much done."

"No, don't do that. It's okay. I'll sit somewhere else. I'll see you later anyway."

"Yeah."

"Okay, see you in a bit," he said. He scanned the room for a second and then walked off.

It's his own fault for not taking a hint, I told myself. I had made it perfectly clear that we were not going to be a team. I was certain I had been repellent enough to make that apparent. If he couldn't take a hint, then he'd have to deal with the consequences. I wasn't about to feel terrible about any of it. Only, I did. I watched him amble hesitantly into the ocean of tables, and I felt like turning myself off. I just needed to stop being me for any of this to be palatable. Unfortunately, that wasn't possible. I grabbed my tray and made my way to the trash.

"Do you know how bad that combo of gluten and dairy is?" a girl asked, suddenly standing next to me with her tray.

She was looking at the remnants of my food dripping into the trash can.

"Uh-huh," I said.

"Those are literally the two most inflammatory foods that exist."

"Okay, thanks for the info."

What a jackass, I thought, although I knew she was probably right.

An hour later, the dining hall had cleared out, and it was just Wade and me standing in a wasteland of splattered food, questionable liquids, and the general smell of a deep-fried sock. We could hear the kitchen staff clattering around in the kitchen, listening to terrible music. They had set us up with the cleaning supplies. Wade was holding a bucket in one hand and an assortment of rags and a bottle of industrial all-purpose cleaner in his other arm. I was holding the mop.

"I'll mop if you want," Wade said. "You can do the tables."

Mopping was generally considered to be the raw end of the stick.

"It's fine. I can mop," I said.

"I know you can, but I'm saying I'll switch."

"I can do it."

"Just give me the mop, will you?" he said, holding out his hand.

"Fine."

I gave him the mop and took his supplies in return. Clearly, *I* should have been the one to mop. I really could have used that speck of redemption, but he wouldn't let me have it. He took the mop and then pushed the large bucket with the wheels off to fill it with water. I thought he might say something else, or linger, or make a joke. Or anything. But he said nothing more. Perhaps he was pissed off. I certainly hoped so.

"No half-assing it, all right, folks?" I heard one of the

kitchen ladies call to us. She was holding open the door to the kitchen and leaning out. "None of that smearing the food all over the table with the sponge. I'm not signing anything off unless the place is clean. And you'd better believe it."

"Roger that," Wade called back.

I walked slowly over to the farthest corner of the room and sprayed a grease-covered table with the industrial cleaner. The chemicals landed in droplets, and I watched them eat into the grease. Then I pushed a wet sponge over the surface. All I seemed to accomplish with this was smearing the grease across the table just like the kitchen lady had predicted. There were jellylike lumps all over. I tried to remember who had sat there earlier.

Wade Scholfield and I didn't talk the entire time. I went over all the tables, methodically covering each one in chemicals and then scrubbing off the grease and food. I never looked up to see what he was doing. When we were done, we put away the cleaning supplies and went our separate ways.

"HEY, WAIT UP!"

I turned around and almost lost my footing as I found Beth Whelan strolling toward me.

It must have been Thursday by that time, because every Thursday for PE, Mrs. Randall dropped us off a few miles down the St. Angela's trail for a cross-country run. Even when it rained, she dropped us off. On average, it took about an hour to get back. The idea was that you jogged all the way back to school, where Mrs. Randall would be waiting with her stopwatch and note down your time and ranking. Some girls really cared about their cross-country ranking, and they'd warm up and stretch and time themselves with their own special sports watches and then argue with Mrs. Randall about timing. Some of them had crazy-looking professional running shoes, and they braided their hair tight to their heads to make them more aerodynamic or something. I usually just hung back as long as I could, and then I'd amble leisurely behind the rest, savoring the solitude. I loved it when I could get somewhere devoid of people. Sometimes I would imagine that there had been an alien invasion that wiped out 80 percent of the population, and I was one of the few people still roaming the earth. I imagined there was no one up ahead, no one behind. No one back at school. Nothing.

Beth Whelan's sudden appearance behind me tore me out of my daydream with a violent jolt.

She was a senior. I'll describe the obvious things about her because, in a way, describing her accurately is nearly impossible. Strawberry-blond hair, long and creamy, almost peach colored, always parted on the right side of her head and tumbling down over her left shoulder. Her hair always smelled freshly shampooed but looked messy and neglected. Freckles. Hazel eyes. Curves. Lipstick lips, perfectly outlined. No eye makeup, just the lips. And the velvet choker that she wore religiously, like a talisman rather than a fashion statement. Even during cross-country runs.

She wasn't pretty—she was stunningly beautiful in a way that almost had nothing to do with her simple features. It was something about the way she moved and talked—a cross between teenage sloppiness and the kind of adult sophistication of shady film noir ladies. A combination of precision and laziness—every movement measured, filled with the burning confidence and unwholesomeness that oozed out of her every pore. She was able to cultivate an air of dangerous beauty but then treat it like an unimportant side effect of who she actually was. A trick that always blew my mind. It was like she couldn't be bothered about her own perfections or the lust she inspired so effortlessly in the male population. She tossed it aside carelessly, whereas all the other top-of-the-food-chain girls at school spun their entire existence around that kind of thing. It mattered desperately to them—their desirability quotient. It hardly mattered to Beth at all, which made her untouchable. Add to that the fact that she smoked cigarettes and read books that said *Kafka, Camus,* and *Isaac Bashevis Singer* on the spines, and there wasn't even a point in trying to be in her stratosphere of cool no matter how great you thought you were.

I stared at her, shell-shocked. The fact that Beth Whelan was suddenly here, walking up to me, was incomputable. Like a glitch in the universe.

"Hey there," she said.

"Hi . . ."

"God, I hate these cross-country death marches!" she said, closing the distance between us and producing a cigarette and a lighter from some dimension within her T-shirt. "Isn't torture technically illegal?"

"I think so," I said stupidly.

She glanced at me with a small smile as though she just now noticed me. "What's your name again?" she asked. Her voice was low and husky and melodic.

"Gracie. Welles."

"That's it! Gracie. You're a freshman, right?"

There was no way in hell she had ever heard my name before. "Sophomore."

"Oh, right. Right."

She lit her cigarette. Her hair was up in a high ponytail, but she had left one long strand of it hanging down into her face. "Thanks for walking with me," she said. "Usually, I don't do the Thursday cross-country, but I missed the Tuesday one, so here I am. I don't really know this crowd."

This crowd being the freshman and sophomore girls.

"Yeah," I said.

She looked over at me curiously after a long stretch of silence, exhaling a cloud of blue, translucent smoke into the air between us. "So, I was thinking," she said, "and please tell me if this is totally bananas—but I was thinking we could have a conversation on our way back to school. You know, a mutual exchange of words—where we both say things. Not just me. What do you think?"

"Okay," I said, face burning.

More silence. Her eyes were still on me as we walked, and she said nothing, creating a vacuum.

It worked. I went through this wobbly throat-clearing intro and then, rubbing my eyebrow, I said, "Sorry. I'm just . . . I guess, going through a bunch of shit currently, so that's why maybe I'm a bit out of it."

"Well, there ya go," she said. "Let's talk about that. What kind of shit?"

I found myself looking around, as though searching for an exit. "Nothing really. Just stupid and complicated shit."

"What, some boy pulverized your heart?" she asked, sounding underwhelmed by the possibility of this being the case. "And now that your heart is disintegrated, you don't know how you're supposed to pump blood through your body, and so you're dying a slow and painful death?"

"What?" The terror must have been thick on my face.

Beth rolled her eyes with a small smile and handed me a cigarette. I took it even though I didn't smoke. She flipped the spark wheel of her lighter, holding the flame out to me, and I held my cigarette toward her, not totally sure how this was done.

"Put it in your mouth and suck on it," she instructed with a little amused snort. "You know—take a deep breath."

I did, and she lit it as I inhaled. When the smoke hit my lungs, I went through the obligatory coughing fit. Then the dizziness. I stopped walking and planted my feet more firmly on the ground for balance, pulling my shoulders up and hunching over a little.

Beth was watching me from where she stood a few feet up ahead. "Just take another drag," she said. "The dizziness will go away."

I took another drag, inhaling deeply, concentrating on the smoke as it disappeared into me, filtering through my body down into the farthest reaches of the bronchioles or alveoli or whatever those things were called. I tried to picture the diagram of a lung that Mr. Sorrentino had drawn them for me before the Christmas holidays. He had sacrificed his lunchtime, and we had sat in his classroom together alone with the rain pounding against the windows and the smell of his vegetable soup and the soft tone of his voice. The dizziness came again, but it was not as bad as the first time. I watched the smoke drift out of my mouth. It was strange, but the bleeding pain that was supposed to be there accompanying the memory wasn't fully there. I mean, it was there—but covered in this weird layer of quiet.

"I just somehow assumed you smoked," Beth said as we continued walking. "You kinda look like smoking might be the least of your bad habits. I don't mean that in a bad way."

"Thanks."

"So, who is it?" Beth asked.

"Who is what?"

"Who's the boy?"

I said nothing for a second.

"We *have* to talk about it," she said matter-of-factly. "We're going to be stuck out here at least another hour at the rate we're going."

The last thing I wanted was for Beth Whelan to find out the nauseating details of the Mr. Sorrentino situation. She inhabited the dizzying heights of the glittering and untrustworthy. I had read *Carrie* like any normal person, and I knew exactly what *not* to do: you don't trust the beautiful people.

You lock up. Especially when the beautiful people are nice to you, you lock up. But then again—fuck, I wanted to talk about Mr. Sorrentino so much that it hurt. I had to get it out of me. I looked over at her, and I could feel all my secrets welling up inside of me, wanting to be sucked out.

"It's not a boy—per se," I began tentatively.

She waited for a moment, and I stalled.

"So, who or what is it?" she demanded impatiently.

"It's a man," I said. "I mean, like, an actual grown-up man."

Beth's face brightened up. "How old—like fifty?"

I shook my head. "No! Oh my god."

"Older? Please tell me he's older than fifty!"

I laughed a little, even though I was still somehow terrified of everything that was happening underneath the comforting layers of the nicotine calm.

"He's just, like, a normal grown-up age," I said. "Like, maybe twenty-nine? Or I don't know—thirty-five?"

"Damn, I really would have preferred if he were your best friend's grandpa or something. That would have been on another level," she said, putting her arm around me. "But whatever, it's okay. At least it's not someone your own age. There's something so dumb about teenage kids falling in love with each other."

I happened to agree with her on that one. "Yeah, totally."

"Do I know him?" she asked, letting out more smoke from her mouth.

I thought about lying for a second and telling her it was our neighbor Norman Dressler (who didn't exist), but instead, I just said, "Mr. Sorrentino." I figured I was too far in already, and besides, it was nice talking to her.

I expected her to ridicule me in some sophisticated cool-girl manner, but instead, she nodded, still smiling broadly, and said, "Right on. He's not my type personally—his ankles are kind of delicate looking, and his hair is insanely perfect, but I can see Mr. Sorrentino capable of crushing your soul. It's not a bad choice."

"His ankles are delicate?" I asked.

"Yeah, a bit. Also, his teeth are really small."

I wasn't sure about the ankles or the teeth, but Mr. Sorrentino's hair definitely *was* insanely perfect, and that was the whole point!

"Okay, so what are you doing about it?" she asked.

"Nothing."

"How very proactive of you."

"Well, he's engaged. He's marrying this lady—Judy." I made a puking gesture after Judy's name. "And she looks way worse than she sounds. Just like some lady who sells underwear at Dillard's or something. I mean, it's depressing."

Beth laughed. It felt so good to be able to talk about it that I forgot how much I didn't like talking to people. Plus, everything I said seemed to entertain her. She looked at me with interest and maybe even understanding. Nobody had been this interested in the minutiae of my bullshit existence ever. Certainly, nobody on her level. I felt encouraged.

"Anyway," I said with a sigh after I had recounted all kinds of unnecessary details about Mr. Sorrentino and my supposed "connection" with him. "I think this is where the story ends."

"Did you know that stories don't actually have endings?" she said, pointing her finger at me.

I stared at the finger in my face. Some kind of pale glimmer of hope came with that finger. "What do you mean?"

"Stories don't end," she said. "Even the last word of the last sentence of a book is not an ending. That story continues whether the author writes about it or not. More so even in life—there's the illusion of things ending, but really nothing ends. Life is one long sausage of things happening."

She put the cigarette to her lips and pulled at it, her eyes falling shut for a second in this beautifully poetic way. "My point being," she continued, exhaling, "men are super horny, and if you wanted the story with Mr. S. to continue, it would be the easiest thing in the world because all the advantages lie in your court." She laughed when she saw my expression. "I'm saying the male body is definitely on your side, Gracie. Boys jerk off about thirty times a day. Mr. Sorrentino obviously a little less because he's a grown man, but you get the idea."

"Yeah, I guess."

Beth gave me a little shove with her shoulder to emphasize her point. "*Mr. Sorrentino is a man. He has a wiener. You can do whatever you want with him!*"

I giggled, powerless against the word *wiener*.

"It's not a joke," Beth said.

I swallowed the rest of the giggle. "No, I know. I just . . . I don't think I can directly apply that—like, to my life right now. Per se."

"I'm not saying you have to break up his engagement. My point is just sit down in the front row in your next biology class and open up your legs so he can see your underwear a bit. Or don't even wear underwear if you want. Give yourself some dignity back and throw the poor guy a bone while you're at it."

I was officially out of my depth at this point. My face had turned hot, and I didn't know where to look. I concentrated on my cigarette.

"Am I embarrassing you?" Beth asked cheerfully.

"No," I said. "I'm just . . . I didn't think it was going to be anything like this when I finally fell in love. I thought it was going to be pretty simple. Like I'd love someone and they'd love me. I thought that's the way it worked."

Beth patted me on the back. "I know."

We walked in silence for a while.

By the time we got back to school, we were drenched. It had started to rain heavily out of absolutely nowhere, but the downpour didn't last long, and the sun was out again as we walked up the school driveway. It had felt somehow exhilarating and cleansing, like a baptism. A baptism of whatever religion Beth was the high priestess of. Mrs. Randall was no longer waiting for us at the finish line with her stopwatch. She no doubt marked us down at last place and called it a day. It was almost dinnertime. I couldn't quite believe I was walking down the school driveway, talking with Beth Whelan.

Someone called Beth's name, and we turned to find Derek trotting up to us.

"Lookin' good," he said, taking her in for a moment.

Beth gave a look of such utter un-reaction that it seemed to suck some of his essence out of him. Derek drove his hand through his hair, as was his custom. He glanced at me, and I became extremely uncomfortable in my wet clothes clinging to my skin, revealing my ratty bra underneath. He still had the Band-Aid on his cheek.

"Connie wanted to know if you're coming tonight," Derek said to Beth.

Beth seemed not at all concerned about all her curves being so loudly on display. She could move and talk as if Derek were just an afterthought to humanity—but at the same time, she moved with all her feminine powers subtly in gear. "Did she?"

Derek said, "Yeah. So, are you?"

"What's with the Band-Aid?" Beth asked, ignoring his question.

His eyes flicked over to me briefly. "Nothing. So, are you? Coming tonight?"

"Where?"

"Hillsboro's room."

She made a face.

Derek's hand went through his hair again. "Come on, if Connie doesn't come, none of the other German girls are coming, and Connie doesn't want to come if you and Dawn don't show up, and we need the German girls."

"Yeah, I'm not coming," Beth said.

"Why not?"

"I don't know. Maybe I'll wash my hair tonight or do a puzzle or something."

"Come on!"

"Believe it or not, getting Mark laid by a German girl isn't my top priority right now."

"It's not about that! We're just . . ."

But there was no point in finishing the sentence, because Beth had already begun to walk off. It had happened so fast that for a moment I was standing there alone with Derek in the see-through T-shirt clinging to my skin. We exchanged a look, and then his eyes went down to my chest in an inevitable sort of way. I ran off after Beth.

"GRACIE—BUG?"

My mom's voice came through the phone sounding bright and childishly excited, the way her voice always sounded when she finally got me to answer one of her calls. My phone calls home were invariably long overdue by the time they finally happened. I felt bad about it, but there was no other way. I had to build up the stamina and prepare the mindset to deal with a call home. It wasn't that I didn't love my mother. I did. And sometimes I even missed her quite a lot, but that didn't make any conversation with her less of a minefield. The explosives were always there, just below the surface, and the objective was to step around them. I had to be a certain person when I talked to her. I had to reorient myself to the fantasy terms of her existence. Not that it was brain surgery at this point in my life, but it took focus, and if I slipped, I wouldn't be there to help her back to normal.

"Hi, Mom."

"Oh, bug, I'm so glad you called! I tried to call you on the weekend, but you weren't around."

"Oh yeah. Sorry. I was . . . well, I told you I joined the volleyball team, right?"

"Did you?"

"Yeah, I'm pretty sure we talked about it last time. Anyway, we have practice a lot, so it's hard for me to get to my phone. I'm kind of their best player at the moment. It's one of those things that takes over your life at school."

"How fun!"

I sighed. Two seconds in and the conversation had already turned bogus. "Yeah, it is. It's pretty fun," I said.

"Did you bring that sports bra we bought you?"

"Yep."

"Aren't those amazing? I use them for yoga. Did I tell you about the yoga class I'm taking?"

There was no chance in hell that she was doing yoga. We were both full of it. Our conversations were beyond pointless sometimes.

"Yeah, you did, but hey, Mom—when you were in high school, did you ever, like, have a soul mate? Or, you know, were you ever in love with someone and just knew there was a connection, and there didn't even have to be any concrete evidence?"

She giggled. "Oh, you have no idea how good looking the boys were back then. Your dad—the first time I saw him—he was already a man, of course, but oh my god, he was just beyond anything I'd ever seen. He had this long hair. Ha ha! I showed you pictures, didn't I? He was already so much of a man compared to those guys that ran around at school getting high and cheating on their math tests. Your dad was already past all that. He owned his own company. It was real magic—the first time we saw each other. Just like in a movie. Love at first sight."

Oh shit, I thought. I had been bored to death of these dad stories ever since I was about ten years old, but hearing them now chilled me to the bone. It hit me hard that I was the exact same person as my mother. Mr. Sorrentino was basically my dad!

"Well, I gotta go, Mom!" I almost yelled into the phone. "There's a fire drill. Bye!"

I skipped biology, because how could I possibly ever look at Mr. Sorrentino again when he was some kind of psychological substitute for my dad? I shuddered at the thought. I told the nurse that I had food poisoning, and she let me go to my room, where I lay in bed for a while before grabbing Georgina's fancy headphones and taking them into the closet to listen to *Siamese Dream*. My phone was from the Neolithic era, and I'd lost the earbuds that came with it, so the only way I could ever listen to music now was through the speaker of my phone, and to do that to the Smashing Pumpkins would have been sacrilegious, especially when you needed them to save your life, which they could do for sure, just not on shitty iPhone speakers.

It had been about a year and a half earlier when I'd first came across the "Bullet with Butterfly Wings" video on You-Tube, and ever since then, the Smashing Pumpkins had been the only truly infallible thing in my life. I kept them a secret. Never listened to their music out loud anywhere. I don't know exactly why; I think it had something to do with the fact that I liked them too much. People would have opinions, and I didn't need that. This band wasn't a group activity for me—they were just mine.

I sat in the closet with my eyes closed and my head propped back against a bunch of Georgina's clothes, and when I got to "Rocket," I was already fully dislodged from planet Earth. SP had a way of making me feel like being me was all right. I don't know—like, that planet they put you on was definitely *not* Florida. I would always gain a kind of freedom listening to them that was impossible to attain in the real world.

> *Consume my love, devour my hate*
> *Only powers my escape*
> *The moon is out the stars invite*
> *I think I'll leave tonight*

I could reach a trancelike state where I had no memories of me or my life left. It was just a pure obliteration of everything. The laws of existence were out the window. Gravity, time, space—nothing held up when the music was loud enough.

Then the music stopped abruptly. I opened my eyes just as Georgina attempted to pull the headphones off my head.

"Oh my god! Do you know how expensive those were?"

"Five billion dollars?" I asked, handing them over to her.

"Ha ha!" she said, snatching them away. "You could at least ask me before you use my stuff!"

"Not if you're not here, I can't."

"Then don't touch my stuff when I'm not here! That's the whole freakin' point!"

I rolled my eyes and got out of the closet. She was probably going to blast *Mamma Mia!* now or *Dear Evan Hansen*. She loved blasting musicals whenever we were in a fight because it was a legitimately effective way of getting back at me. Musicals were exactly what it took to cripple me. It hurt my ears and my dignity to be in contact with them in any way, shape, or form. Pop music was bad enough, but the idea that a whole group of people would suddenly jump and start singing and dancing together—it was nauseating.

"You really need to learn to respect other people's property," Georgina was saying as she scrolled through her playlists looking for the right ammunition to plug into her speakers. "Just 'cause it's lying around doesn't mean it's there for the taking. Do you know what would happen if we all did that? There's a reason people make laws."

"Oh my god, relax, I borrowed your headphones! I think the economy is going to survive."

"It's not even just about this one time. You always do this! I'm sorry, but just because you don't have your own things doesn't make it okay to grab whatever someone else has."

"Fuck you."

She turned on the speakers. I slammed the door behind me.

She had managed to suck me back to the three dimensional confines of reality. Fully. The cherry on top of everything was the dining room. I had lost track of how many days we had been cleaning it and how many more days we had to go, but it was beginning to really get to me. It seemed never-ending and gross and socially unbearable because of Wade and how consistently mean I was being to him despite not even wanting to be mean. It was like I was trapped in this nightmare of food smells, and slowly crawling minutes, and my own stupidity, and other people's saliva. And plus, I was my mom, in love with my dad. So, it really couldn't get any worse.

After about five minutes of pushing a sponge over yet another grease-covered table, I stopped. I sat down and stared at a small piece of chicken stuck to the table's surface with the help of a translucent green sauce that had the effect of superglue. I pushed the sponge away and laid my head down on the table in defeat.

I stayed like that for a while.

"What're you doing?" Wade asked when he had worked his

way over to my side of the room with the mop and I still hadn't moved.

I didn't answer for a while, but then I sat up. "Nothing," I said.

"You sure?"

It wasn't just a single piece of chicken but rather a scattered line of little lumps—an archipelago stretching across the table. It was nothing out of the ordinary. I had been scraping little food islands off tables for about a week now, but somehow this island was throwing my life into my face.

"This chicken is superglued to the table with some asshole's saliva, and somehow it's my job to get it off," I told Wade. I wasn't even whining. Just stating depressing facts. "I mean, why *me*? Why is this my life? Why isn't it Constanze's life? Or Chandra Carr's?"

After a short silence, he said, "Wow, who knew you were such a baby."

I looked up at him. He was smiling a little. Not a lot. Just enough to show that he was bored by my crisis.

"I'm not depressed about the actual *chicken*," I said, black annoyance pervading my insides. "I'm depressed about what it represents—*life*. You do get that, right?"

"Yeah, I get it. Symbolism."

It annoyed me how he didn't buy my misery.

"I'm not being melodramatic," I said.

"Oh yeah?"

"I'm *not*, okay? My life happens to be the worst joke in the known universe."

"What about the *un*known universe?"

I glared at him.

He was still looking amused. It was driving me nuts.

"Okay, fine," he said. "What makes *your* shitty life so special?"

"Lots of things make my life special, okay? More than you could ever imagine."

"Like what?" There was a challenge in his voice.

"Like, none of your business."

"Yeah, that's what I thought."

My MO would have been to tell him to go fuck himself, but instead, I found myself too outraged to be indifferent. I turned to him, fueled with indignation. "My dad has a whole family in California—in Beverly Hills—and I live with my mom in a trailer park outside of St. Petersburg, and the other family—the 'real' one—they don't even know that we exist. We know *they* exist, but they don't know we exist. We have to keep it a secret, because god forbid their boat gets rocked. The real family's life has to stay perfect, that's the thing. But we're the side family—the one that wasn't ever meant to exist anyway, morally speaking. The ones in Beverly Hills are actually the victims, if you can believe it."

The moment I stopped talking, I was horrified. I was struck dumb by my own words. I didn't even care about my father as far as I knew. I wasn't traumatized as far as I knew. Not right then anyway. And I certainly did not care enough about Wade to tell him something that I had never told anybody else except this one kid Ralphie when I was six, because I thought it was a cool story. The whole outburst was insane. I felt so white trash I could hardly take it.

Wade screwed up his lips for a second, and then he sighed. "Sorry," he said.

I wanted to sink into the ground. It was so much worse now that Wade's eyes turned all clean and compassionate.

He added, "But if that's the kind of guy that your dad is, then maybe it's better that he's not around, you know? It could be that you're just lucky."

"It's not really a trailer park," I said flatly, focusing back on the chicken archipelago. "They're more like mobile homes. I didn't mean 'trailer park'—not the way that you're imagining it, at least."

He nodded.

"And anyway, I don't even care about any of that," I went on. "I don't know why I said that. That's not even what's bothering me."

I must have looked miserable as hell judging by the empathy in Wade's eyes.

"I gotta go use the bathroom," I said, getting up so fast that my chair clattered to the floor behind me.

"I can finish off here if you want," he offered.

All my time at school, I had strived to hide my trailer-park circumstances in whatever way possible. Now I had somehow managed to *brag* about them.

"I'm supposed to do half."

"I'll finish here," he said. "Seriously. Don't worry about it."

I didn't know what to say. I wanted to get the hell out of there, but I also didn't want to be indebted to this dumb boy any more than I already was. He was looking at me, and I couldn't handle it. So, I got up. Maybe the next day I would be able to be a better person and say something nice like *thank you* to him. But right then, I could barely manage to breathe. I walked out without saying anything and spent the rest of the evening arguing about pointless things with Georgina while the *Technicolor Dreamcoat* soundtrack was playing.

FUCK IT, I THOUGHT.

I put my tray down opposite Wade's at breakfast the next day, and it landed on the table a little more violently than I had intended it to. The juice spilled out of my cup, and the silverware rattled. He looked up, startled out of his daze. He had been on another planet, listening to music on his phone with his head propped on his hand and his eyes fixed on the edge of his plate. His food was mainly untouched.

Slowly, Wade pulled the headphones off his head without saying anything.

"Hey," I began. I almost stopped myself right there and walked away because I didn't know what else to attach to that word. It seemed like the worst word in the universe now that I had uttered it. And there it hung.

The silence stretched as long as it would go, and Wade began to look lost.

"I was thinking of sitting down here." I forced the words

out of my throat. "But I'm . . . I guess I'm just warning you that I'm not making any promises that it'll be easy to be sitting with me. It's not that I'm planning on making it hard, but I'm just not good at . . . manners. I guess. Even when I want to be good at them."

He pushed out the chair opposite himself with his foot and said, "I know."

I stared at it for a while before I sat. "I poured a ginger ale over Mr. Sorrentino's desk," I said. Something had to be said, and that's all that came to mind.

"You did?" he asked. "Why?"

"Doesn't matter."

"It would be a way cooler story if you said why."

"Who said I was trying to tell a cool story? It's just a thing that happened. *Jesus*."

Although I didn't want him to participate in the problem, I really *did* want him to be aware of it—sit inside of it with me. I wanted him to say something, but I didn't really want to hear it. Maybe I just wanted to talk now that I had started. I didn't exactly know what I wanted. I just had too much energy to be alone at that moment.

"I also broke all his pencils in half. You know how he only uses those vintage pencils?"

He nodded.

"I broke all of those."

"He's probably going to have to special order those from somewhere," Wade said.

"What a pretentious prick."

Wade looked puzzled. "Really? He doesn't seem like a pretentious prick to me."

"You don't know much about him, then."

"Yeah, but he seems cool."

I could feel a slight outrage tingling in the very tips of my fingers. It was irritating that he would disagree with me so effortlessly, especially after making such a big deal about trying to be my buddy. I had given him what he wanted, hadn't I? I had actually walked all the way over to his table and sat down with him. Here I was. It had almost killed me to do so. For a moment, I thought I was going to grab my tray and walk away. I had already curled my fingers around the tray, in fact, but something held me back. My eyes caught on the bruise under his eye, which was green now—fading, but there, and suddenly I was desperate to know what his deal was. How could he sit there and look like he was okay? I mean, there was no way his life was that great. I didn't get it.

I forgot for a moment that I was the center of the universe, and my fingers uncurled from the tray.

"What does Derek have against you anyway?" I asked him.

"Nothing. We're just nemesises," he said. "Or nemesi. What's the plural for that?"

"You didn't answer my question."

Wade stuck his fork into a pile of food on his plate, leaving it there like a statement. "Fine," he said with a confession in his eyes. "Not that this makes him any less of a douchebag, but technically *I* started that whole thing with Derek. Technically."

"What do you mean?"

"I mean, technically, I started a fight with him on my first day here. I started it, and then they got back at me on that day when you were there."

I glanced at him, confused. I had been pulling my bread roll apart and pressing its soft interior flat into the plate, but I took a break here.

"I hit him first," he clarified.

"Why?"

"He's a dick."

"So?"

"You don't think that's a good reason?"

"For hitting someone? Not at all. If I went around punching everyone in the face just because I think they're dicks—I mean, I'd be a lunatic. Who *isn't* a dick? I'd literally have to punch everyone in the face all the time."

"Your dick versus non-dick ratio perception is way off."

"It's not."

"Hold on a second," he said. "You're the one who shot Derek with a slingshot just because you didn't 'like his face'—those were your words. I don't know if you're even in a position to chew me out about this."

"That was different!"

"How?"

"Excuse me, I was saving your ass, remember?"

"Weird. I was under the impression that you were specifically *not* doing it to help me."

"Yeah, I *wasn't*," I protested. "You're not getting it—I didn't do it for you. I would have done it for anyone. You just happened to be there as, like, a total side element to the big picture."

"I was a '*side element*'?" He started laughing. "Oh fuck, that's the most depressing thing I've ever been called in my life."

"Well, it's true. It had nothing to do with you, per se."

"Yeah, I get it."

Wade Scholfield was not booby-trapped. I thought maybe I liked that about him. He was easy and accommodating to all my hitches and drawbacks. He was sweet. I didn't understand why I was trying so hard to be an asshole.

We ate in silence for a few seconds, during which Michael Holt squeezed by our table with his tray of food. Michael "Pizzaface" Holt was a senior. He had some kind of acne condition that ravaged his face, turning it into an inflamed mess of craters and angry mountainous terrains. It was terrible. But it didn't even matter, because the phenomenon of Michael Holt went beyond just the acne. He filled that spot that needs to be filled at every high school for it to be legally certified—that sacred spot of the ultimate loser—the leper. Michael Holt fit the bill better than anyone could have hoped for. Medical-grade acne aside, it was the way he wore his clothes—tucking his T-shirt into his pants and wearing that stupid cowboy-looking belt every day. It was his hair, his ears, his shuffling walk, the boniness of his shoulders, and besides that, it was everything else as well. It made him the ideal communal dumping ground. Everyone used him. Freshmen, chess nerds, Christian kids, cheerleaders, hipsters—it didn't matter. Michael Holt was fair game. In a twisted way, it was almost like he was the school mascot. A fixture to the school that made it possible for everyone to feel a little more comfortable about themselves. Kids would back away from him when he walked by, pressing themselves dramatically against the walls of the hallway, holding their breaths. No one sat with him. No one talked to him—unless they were calling him names.

Wade's eyes followed Michael Holt for a moment. "Derek was making fun of that guy," he said, nodding in his direction. "The guy with the acne. That's how I got into a fight with him."

"What?"

"Derek and those other two jerkwads he hangs out with had that guy with the acne cornered. He was about to start crying, and he was holding this weird cardboard science experiment that he was about to drop. I honestly didn't need to see that."

"Jesus. You mean *that's* why you started a fight with Derek?"

He nodded.

"They wouldn't have actually *hurt* Michael Holt. You know that, right?" I said, irritated. "*Everyone* is kind of mean to Michael. It's just a game—they all make fun of him, but it's not like anybody actually ever *hurts* him."

"Oh, *fuck*. I wish I'd known."

The sarcasm wasn't acidic—it was playful, but he made his point all the same. I felt stranded.

"He was almost crying," Wade said when I wasn't coming up with a comeback. "It was depressing. You would have done something too."

I wouldn't have, though. It sucked that I knew that.

I took a bite of my roll just to be doing something with my mouth other than talking for a second. I wasn't a fan of how weighty we were getting, especially since it was perhaps evident that Wade was a better person than anyone else at school.

"I think there's a good chance that you're the *real* Derek in this Derek scenario," I said, just to be a dipshit about it. "Like, I thought Derek was the asshole, but maybe it's you."

He shrugged like it might be a very real possibility. "But still," he said, "I think on an official Derek Scale, Derek would out-Derek me."

That was true. Derek was the ultimate of all Dereks, but I wasn't about to admit it.

"Or who knows—maybe not," Wade continued, since I wasn't saying anything. "There's always the chance that everything is actually the complete opposite of what we think it is—parallel universes existing simultaneously and all. I could totally be on the wrong side of things. Maybe secretly that guy Michael is a real piece of shit, and Derek lies in bed at night and cries himself to sleep, humiliated and traumatized by life. And we have no clue because at school Michael pretends to be this downtrodden guy, and Derek is too embarrassed, so he pretends to be a dick, and that's all we ever see here."

What a dork. I smiled for the first time since I had sat down.

"I've thought of that before," I admitted after a second. "I mean, that whole opposite-reality thing."

"I wouldn't mind it," he said. "The world would probably

make way more sense if I were 180 degrees wrong about everything."

It unnerved me a little that I understood what he meant, but I really did. "Yeah," I said. "I guess it would be an easy way to explain the majority of stuff that happens. My roommate, for example—the only way anything about her would make sense is if I'm wrong about everything—like you said." I turned this over in my head for a second and then laughed. "Holy shit. What if she *is* right? She always says musicals are like the 'perfect protein' of music. I mean, what if that's true?!"

"Yeah, exactly," he said. "Don't just assume that you're in the correct universe."

It was around here the conversation began to lose its weight. I stopped driving my sentences like a funeral procession and instead just said things as they came to my mind. Easy and thoughtlessly. We talked for a while longer about the ultimate reality of existence and what the proof was that anything was actually real. Then we moved on to time travel and eventually wormholes. He demonstrated how wormholes work by folding a napkin in two and then pushing a straw through it. Somewhere along the way, I forgot about everything: The fact that he was that guy I was stuck cleaning the dining room with. The fact that he was fidgety and restless, constantly threatening to start conversations or fall into action. The fact that he was intrusive with his friendliness. Most of all the fact that we had opposite body parts. I just forgot about it all.

Most kids had layers upon layers of social mechanisms for dealing with life at school. Especially at boarding school, which was a twenty-four-hour, seven-days-a-week deal. Nobody was as tough or cool or hilarious or even as malicious as their bloated school personas would have you believe. That included me. It was just about survival in the end. You could cry at home in your bedroom with your mom downstairs in the kitchen making a casserole, but you had better not let your guard down at school. I'm not saying all the kids managed this, but they at least all tried. They tried to be things, and they tried not to be other things. They worked hard, and therefore you noticed when someone didn't work that hard. I didn't know Wade well enough to pass accurate judgment on how cool or uncool he was, but at least it was evident that he lacked the telltale signs of putting any hard work into himself as a commodity to be bought by others. Maybe because he was too lazy. Or maybe because he was too dumb? I had no idea.

"What were you listening to anyway?" I asked him.

He pushed his phone over to me. The screen was cracked, but not badly enough to obscure the image in his music library. It said *Wipers—Is This Real?* I couldn't tell anything by the artwork. It looked like some kind of crazy modern art.

"What's that?" I asked.

He handed me the headphones.

I hesitated a moment. I hated being forced to listen to music that other people liked. They always waited so expectantly for you to be blown away.

"Don't worry, you don't have to *like* it," he said, reading my mind. "You're more than welcome to hate anything I listen to."

"I can't be fake nice about it," I warned.

"Noted."

"Really, though. I'm not good at finding anything nice to say if it's crap. I'll end up saying something super mean, and I'll be so nervous I won't be able to *not* say it."

"Yeah, I heard you the first time. I think I'm immune to your shit attitude at this point anyway."

I put on the headphones and started the song he had paused from the beginning. "Return of the Rat." The music was loud and fast and relentless in its attack on my eardrums, and it was about something dumb like rats returning from somewhere, but it didn't matter, because that beat pretty much ate me up right away. There was something about the song, and unlike the *Siamese Dream* vibe, which was poetic in its nuclear sadness and vast and took you light-years out of this world, this music somehow left you right in the middle of reality, but it gave you the means to stand a fighting chance against it, if that makes sense. It somehow evened the playing field. In that sense, it was a religious experience, and also simultaneously orgasmic in that inexplicable way in which music can affect parts of your body that might in fact be your soul, and not your body at all.

Wade leaned across the table and turned the volume all the way up for me. Then he sat back, waiting for my reaction. It annoyed me that he sat there, making me a science experiment, so I decided to do the same to him. Maybe it was the first time I ever even looked at him. For some reason just then, it didn't seem to matter whether I should or shouldn't stare. No care for potential signals being sent. The music blasting through my ears was a good soundtrack for his face—as though it made some sense of him. After a moment, he broke down and looked away, blushing a little. I felt triumphant about having made him uncomfortable.

"So?" he asked when I slid the phone back to him.

"I really hate it," I said. "A *lot*."

He laughed. "I have more music you might really hate," he said. "If you want, I can make you a playlist."

"Really?"

"Yeah."

"Okay. If you want."

"FOOD POISONING, HUH?" MR. SORRENTINO SAID.
"You missed three classes in a row—must have been pretty bad."

I stared intensely at the corner of my biology book. "Yup."

Mr. Sorrentino had asked me to stay behind after class. I stayed seated at my desk until the room had cleared out. He walked over slowly and then perched himself on the desk next to me, crossing his arms in a no-nonsense gesture. There was an exaggerated calm in his voice.

"That's no fun," he said.

"Nope." I looked away from him, across to the other side of the room.

Mr. Sorrentino sighed. "Grace, this isn't you. These grades, this attitude. Half your assignments are being turned in late, and the other half haven't been turned in at all. You've missed more than six classes altogether this semester. What's going on?"

I concentrated on the biology book some more, peeling back the plastic covering from the corner. "I don't know," I said. "Science doesn't really float my boat that much."

"Science doesn't 'float your boat.'" Mr. Sorrentino repeated my words with mock curiosity. "It seemed to float your boat just fine not too long ago. What happened?"

"Well," I said, "to be honest, it never really floated my boat to begin with. Not for real."

"You could have fooled me—getting straight As all year."

I shrugged. I wasn't going to get into it. But then I realized I *was* actually going to get into it, and there wasn't much I could do about it.

"Maybe I'm just not into the bullshit of 'education' anymore," I said, making air quotes around the word *education*. "I mean, when is knowing the difference between animal and plant cells ever going to bail me out of anything? Basically never. None of us in this class are going to be scientists, so that makes it all a charade. This class exists only so that they can tell our parents we're learning biology, and so that you can get paid and the school can have a Science Award. It's a ploy to keep everyone busy without any real purpose. I'm sorry, but that's what it is."

He sat there, arms still crossed. A tightness had settled into his entire body, but he remained more or less motionless. "That's incredibly disrespectful," he said evenly. "To me, to everyone who teaches here, to the students showing up every day to learn."

It was beginning to get on my nerves—that measured calm in his voice and the distinct lack of a proper reaction. "Why are you taking this personally?" I said. "It's just the truth of the matter."

"Nothing about what you're saying is the truth of any matter, and you know that well enough."

I rolled my eyes, this time without turning away. "Jesus *Christ*. Fine. Are we done with this yet? I'm going to be late for my next lesson." I had started getting up and scraping my book into my arms.

"Sit down."

I hesitated.

"I said, sit down!"

Finally, he was losing it. A little.

I let myself fall back into the chair, dropping the book on the table with a loud bang.

"I *care* about teaching. Did that ever occur to you?" Mr. Sorrentino said, getting up from where he sat and walking around to the front of my desk. He put his hands on the desk and leaned in to make sure the point stuck. Man deodorant all in my face. *How easy life would be if he were even* slightly *less hot,* I thought. "I've built my life around teaching science, and I have had students who went on to study medicine, chemical engineering, genetics, physics. Believe it or not, teaching biology is not just something to keep me busy because I have nothing better to do. And when I encourage you to compete for the Science Award or I call you back to discuss your grades having dropped from As to Ds, it's because I am fully invested in each and every one of my students' success, progress, and future. I will do whatever it takes, but I do not have a lot of patience for insults. If you come in here and disrespect what I teach or waste my time or any other student's time, we *will* have a problem."

"Can't I *not* be into science?" I asked, raising my own voice to match his. "Is there a law somewhere that when you go to school you have to be, like, super *thrilled* about it?"

Now he stood back. He began to look deep and a little sad, as though he were seeing through all the layers of my obnoxiousness and finding the tragedy beneath it. I thought I hated this version of him more—the understanding, patient version of him that reduced me to a child.

"You know, I really thought we were on the same side here," he said.

"What does that even mean, Mr. Sorrentino? Same side of *what*? The equator? You always say these things that can mean like ten different things, and it leaves everything hanging in the air with no way to really understand what you mean for real."

I could feel the anguish of the situation bubble up in me. Everything he had ever said and done I had interpreted in the wrong way.

"Grace, if you want to have an actual conversation about what's going on, I'm willing to listen, you know that—but you have to meet me halfway. You have to be willing to communicate."

"Never mind. It's not like you'd get it."

He studied me for a moment and then said evenly, "You broke all my pencils, didn't you? And the ginger ale on my desk—that was you, am I right?"

I had wanted him to find out all along, and now that he confronted me with it, I could feel my blood run cold with the thrill of something happening.

"Why would I do that?" I asked.

"You tell *me*."

"You don't have any proof."

"That's true."

A beat in which we were stuck in no-man's-land.

And then a loud: *"Hey, Gracie What the fu—!"*

We both turned, uprooted from the moment. Wade had bounded in the doorway.

"Oh shit—sorry!" he said quickly. "I didn't know—"

"It's all right, Wade," Mr. Sorrentino said, getting up. "We're done here."

He got up and walked to the front of the class to his filing cabinet, dismissing me. I got up too, grabbed my book, and joined Wade.

"What the hell was that all about?" he asked when we were out in the hallway.

"Nothing."

What Mr. Sorrentino had said echoed through my mind. *We're done here.* Did it mean we were done talking? Or we were done. Done as in *over?* Had he just thrown me in the trash for good?

"You okay?" Wade asked, giving me a shove.

It had been a playful shove, but it was accidentally strong enough to make me trip over my own feet. I caught my balance at the last moment and managed not to fall. I shoved him back much harder, and he went crashing into the wall, even if it was half-theatrical. I needed to be upset about Mr. Sorrentino, but it was useless to try to do it just then, because you couldn't hang out with Wade in a half-assed kind of capacity.

I hadn't had a real friend since middle school. I wasn't blaming anyone for this, because it had been my own decision all the way. Things had just grown stupid in junior high school with boys and girls becoming suddenly separated into male and female categories by their hormones and body parts—it wasn't just that boys treated girls differently and vice versa; girls started treating each other differently too. There was the sense of competition and comparison and falling short and humiliation. Mean girls were mean on a whole new level. And then high school—that was undoubtedly the worst as far as a social nightmare went.

The fact that I went to a goddamn boarding school and was totally out of my depth financially speaking didn't help either. Maybe at my local public high school I would have made some friends. I might have naturally congealed together with the people of my ilk. But in this setting, where all the kids came from a different dimension, there was no one of my ilk. Any field trip became a potential nightmare, because there were always snacks and sodas to buy and restaurants to eat in. Everyone seemed to be swimming in pocket money. All the money I brought with me to school was used for the necessities—toiletries, mainly—shampoo, tampons, deodorant, razors. If I wasn't hard-core about how I spent my money, I'd run out of something essential like toothpaste before the end of the term. I had learned this the hard way. My first term as a freshman, I'd had to borrow shampoo from Georgina for the whole last month before the Christmas holidays. It hadn't been fun. She made a big deal out of it, and in the end, I just stopped washing my hair.

If I actually ever made friends, I figured it would be too much stress. The amount of energy I would have to use to try to seem normal was exhausting just to think about. I would have to put on a show about how I was one of them, with the same-shaped problems and the same fantasies and dreams and opportunities. Of course, eventually, someone would find out all about the fact that a candy bar had to be planned into my budget with military precision, and it would all go to shit from there.

So how could I explain Wade to myself? I couldn't. Not really. Our friendship just made sense in one of those stupid ways that I couldn't do anything about. Of course, my natural instinct had been to back the hell off, but I didn't. For a while, I tried to keep him at arm's length, but then I'd find myself writing him a note in class about Mrs. Gillespie's under-boob sweat marks, or tripping him up in the hallway, or sitting down with him in the dining room. It was too incredibly easy not to back away. His reactions to me—to everything I said and did—were addictive. I found myself needing to be reacted to.

Maybe it finally dawned on me that loneliness was no fun. It could have been that ridiculously simple. I hadn't exactly thought of myself as lonely, but I guess it has a way of eating you up so quietly that you don't even notice. Maybe that was all there was too it—I had been lonely as fuck.

"YOU KNOW WHAT I HATE?" GEORGINA ASKED.

I looked over at her as she was reading a magazine on her bed and eating Cheetos. She wore a powder-blue bathrobe with frills around the sleeves and neck, and her hair hung damp down her shoulders from her shower. It was raining outside. A Saturday morning in early February with deep gray skies. All hell would break loose later on weather-wise. The air had that deadish, thick quality. The kind of stagnant calm that is pregnant with tornadoes and lightning storms.

"Gracie, you know what I hate?" she repeated, more urgently.

"What?"

"Having to pee. Especially right when you're about to fall asleep—or worse, when you're already sleeping, because if you don't get up and pee, you'll spend the rest of the night dreaming about finding a bathroom, but all the bathrooms you find in your dreams are always totally useless. Like, you open a door and the bathroom is only a foot wide, or the toilet is really high up, or only a few inches big, or the only toilet you can find is in a huge room and there are a hundred people in it."

I looked over at her from where I lay on my bed with my book. For a moment, I thought I was going to reply to her, but then I realized there was no point. I had no idea what she was talking about, so I returned to my book.

"*Right?*" she said.

I looked up again. "Yeah, I guess it can be annoying to pee. I've never really thought about it."

"Well, think about it right now for a second!"

"Okay, I did. Can I continue reading now?"

"Isn't it weird, though, how liquid is running through our bodies *at all times*? It's like a game we can't win."

I threw the book on the floor and lay back on the bed in defeat. "You're right, it's preposterous that we have to pee."

"You know, you have a way of sounding aggressive when you say things," she said, continuing to flip through her magazine. "It makes you seem like a bitch, which you are a bit, but not as much as people probably think."

It was going to be a long weekend. It always was when Georgina didn't go home to visit her parents.

"You should really try to be nicer," she suggested.

"Maybe I don't want to be nice."

"I mean, I don't care personally—it's pretty hard to offend me. But for your own sake. Unless you want to work at McDonald's someday, but even then, you'd have to at least *pretend* to be nice to people."

"Good point."

"I'm not kidding."

"Jesus Christ, Georgie! I know I'm a jerk. What do you want me to do about it?"

"You could *not* be one."

"I don't work at McDonald's *yet*. Until you're buying a Big Mac from me, I don't see why I have to make an effort."

"Whatever." And then I heard the Cheetos bag rustle and the crunching and mechanical flipping of the magazine pages continue.

The short knock on the door most likely saved my life. I didn't particularly care who it was. Being alone with Georgina, although always a candid experience, was at the same time exhausting and possibly fatal—I really hadn't ruled it out. Wade pushed open the door without invitation. Georgina yelped and pulled her bathrobe tighter around her torso as though there were anything indecent about the thick nightgown that enveloped her entire body underneath the bathrobe.

"You're not even allowed in here!" she yelled.

"Sorry, I'm not looking," he said. He walked over to my bed, grabbed my hand, and yanked me off the bed.

"Excuse me!" I said, pulling my hand free.

He grabbed it again impatiently. "Come on, don't you get sick sitting inside all day?"

Georgina got up. "Where are you going?"

"Nowhere," Wade said, pulling me to the door. Then he stopped. "Hey, you wanna come?"

Georgina seemed dumbstruck. She was still clutching her nightgown, confused and probably flattered without realizing it yet. "What? No!"

"You sure?"

"Yes—can you please leave?"

"Okay, see ya later," he called to her, pushing me out the door.

We ran down the hallway. The rush of the moment made me giddy, and all the girls in their rooms with the doors open saw us run by and perhaps thought I had a life of some sort, which maybe I did. It was nice being less pathetic than usual.

"Hurry up!" he called.

We ran down the stairs, out the back door, through the courtyard that tied the dormitories and school buildings together. We circled around the side of the main building and ran down the road to the entrance gate. There was a cab waiting there, and after pushing me into the back, Wade jumped in next to me and slammed the door shut. The car started driving, and we were catching our breath loudly.

"Where are we going?" I asked him.

"We're getting the fuck out of here! I have something in the vicinity of forty bucks for us to blow," he said, pulling out a ball of crumpled bills from his pocket.

"Did you get a pass?"

"A what?"

"A pass. You know—permission to leave the premises?"

"No, why?"

I fell back into the seat, laughing. "Wade, you know this is a glorified prison, right? You basically need a pass to wipe your ass. Didn't you copy out the rules like thirty times?"

"Yeah, I wasn't *reading* them. I was *copying* them." He threw the ball of cash at me. "No one is going to notice we're gone. And so what if they do?"

His idea of the future was pretty uncomplicated.

We went to a movie in town about a bunch of people who get murdered on a cruise ship. By the time we got out, it was almost dark, and there was a real storm going strong. Lightning, thunder, and pouring rain. We stopped by a strip-mall church of some kind and watched someone being saved. The place looked more like an insurance office than anything else, and maybe it really was an insurance office during the week. Plastic chairs neatly lined up. A table with coffee and pink-and-green cookies. A lady crying at the front as the preacher held her hand and said things about her soul. It was soothing, and we were captivated. Once the lady was done being saved, the preacher began talking about a picnic they were planning for next weekend, and we left. The drama had run out.

It was almost not raining at all at that point, but the air was still charged with electricity, and every once in a while, the whole sky would light up. We got some french fries and a Coke at Checkers and sat down on the curb of the insurance-office-strip-mall church. I pulled a cigarette out that Beth had given me and asked Wade if he wanted to share it with me, but he said no, and I was secretly glad I had it to myself. I had brought the lighter too, and he watched as I lit my cigarette.

For a while, we talked about whether or not the moon landing really happened. There was apparently a lot of controversy about it. Wade was telling me about a documentary he'd seen about it, and then I became distracted by his fingers as he lifted the Coke to his mouth. One of them had a Band-Aid wrapped around it, and the forefinger of his right hand was bleeding around the cuticle. The skin seemed to have been ripped off from around the nail.

"What the fuck, Wade," I said, taking his hand in mine to take a closer look.

"Yeah, I know," he said, pulling his hand away self-consciously. "It drives my mom nuts."

"You do that with your teeth?" I asked.

He nodded.

"*Why?*"

"It's just a habit."

I stared at him, horrified. "That's fucking psycho. Doesn't it hurt?"

"Not really."

I took hold of his hand again and pulled it over to show him the raw flesh exposed around the nail of his right forefinger.

"Wade, you're ripping skin off your body with your teeth! How is that not painful?"

"I don't know. It's just not," he said, looking from his hand to me. I could tell that he had lost some of his focus, and it suddenly occurred to both of us that I was holding his hand—warm and a little sticky from spilled Coke.

I dropped it. "Well, it's gross."

"So is smoking cigarettes," he said, giving my cigarette a light flick with his finger.

"Okay, but that's *normal*. That's a civilized thing to do. What you're doing is basically cannibalism."

"Smoking cigarettes is probably worse for you than this," he said.

"Are you really going to continue trying to defend eating your own fingers?"

"Nope, 'cause guess what? I don't have to explain myself to you!"

He got up suddenly.

"You wanna *walk* back?" he asked, smiling.

"How long is that going to take us?"

"I don't know."

"Okay."

"But if we're not going to get a cab, let's get rid of this first," he said, holding up the last of the money and nodding at the Piggly Wiggly that was at the end of the strip mall. It took about an hour, but someone did eventually buy us beer. It was a pissed-off-looking old guy who did it for three dollars but kept on telling us that he had cancer and didn't have time for this kind of shit. He got us a six-pack of Icehouse and kept two beers for "tip." We also had to listen to a few stories about his second ex-wife and how she'd robbed him blind during their divorce. He advised Wade to make me sign a prenuptial agreement before we got married, and Wade told him that was a no-brainer. Eventually, the old guy let us go, and we made our way back to the road.

"Fuck you and your prenuptial agreement!" I told Wade, giving him a shove.

"Sorry, Frank has a point. I need to know you're in it for *me*, not my money."

"Yeah, well, I'm not. Clearly, I'm in it for the money. Otherwise, I would have hitched my wagon to someone who's at least *somewhat* easy on the eyes."

"Ouch!"

I didn't know if this cheesy dialogue could be categorized as flirting, and for a second, my stomach dropped with panic. Had I accidentally sent a signal or opened a door of some sort? I glanced over at Wade, but he was preoccupied with opening his beer, seemingly totally unconcerned by our jokes about being married. I felt my stomach settle again in relief and followed his example by taking a sip of my own beer.

We walked back to school slowly, drinking and talking about stuff like how some trees smell like cum, to which I heartily agreed without having any knowledge of what cum smells like. It wasn't the first time I had had alcohol, but it was the first time I'd had it alone with a boy at nighttime, at the side of a road. The beer tasted like shit—noxious and bitter, coating my entire mouth in a layer of stale aftertaste—but it didn't matter; it was the most fun I had had in a long time, and the warm mood it created was soft and sloppy and hilarious. It wasn't all just the alcohol, though. I remember looking over at Wade and smiling like an idiot because he was such a great person to know. *Great person*—choice of words courtesy of beer. But regardless, I felt a sudden overpowering well of gratitude for him, and although I knew in my normal frame of mind I would have wanted to barf at the cheeseball quality of such emotions, I felt good about them just then. The way I was feeling seemed honest. Wade *was* a great person. There was nothing I could do about it. He really was.

When we got to the entrance gate about an hour or so later, we figured we weren't ready to get back to our dormitories, and we lay down on the grass behind the large stone sign that read *Midhurst School, est. 1973*. Wade asked if he could put his head on my stomach, and I said yes. Besides the fact that heads are much heavier than you'd ever expect, I remember feeling oddly powerful, lying there with the uncomfortable weight pressing into my diaphragm and the electric, Southern night-time breeze stirring in my bangs. I had never experienced that kind of intimacy with a boy. It didn't even seem to matter that he wasn't my soul mate, because this was something entirely different. It wasn't so much that I felt any feelings of love but rather that I was affecting someone else—putting a dent into someone's emotions. And that was a potent kind of thing to feel for the first time ever.

"Where the hell were you?" Georgina asked, sitting up in the dark as soon as I stepped into the room.

For a moment, I didn't move. "Town," I said.

"It's an hour and a half past lights-out."

"I know." I closed the door behind me.

"Did you even have a pass?"

"Yeah, totally." I sat down on my bed and pulled off my shoes.

"No, you didn't," she said.

"We did."

"I'm not an idiot. I know you didn't."

I got undressed and felt around the floor for a T-shirt I could wear to sleep. "Look, just rat on us if you *have* to," I said. "I can't stop you anyway."

She didn't answer, but she continued to sit up in her bed, watching me. I pulled on some T-shirt I found and got into bed. Georgina lay back down, and the silence of the room enveloped us.

"Did you guys make love?" she asked.

"Make *love*?"

"Did you?"

"No!"

"Did you make out?"

"No."

"Yeah, right."

"Just because he's a boy and I'm a girl doesn't mean the whole world has to, like, revolve around our reproductive organs."

"I feel like if a boy treated me that way, the world *would* kind of revolve around our reproductive organs."

I laughed a little.

"I'm serious," she said.

"Well, whatever. That's not what it is with us."

We both turned in our beds and drifted back into silence.

"Are you going to tell—about the pass?" I asked after a while.

"No," she said quietly. "I'm not a *jerk*."

"Thanks, Georgie."

"You know, you don't give me enough credit sometimes."

"I'm sorry," I said.

It was so much easier for me to be nice in the dark. I could just say things the way I meant them. And anyway, at that moment, I felt hopeful. I felt that I might actually have the breathing space to become a better person.

CONSTANZE KOCH WAS ONE OF THE GERMAN GIRLS—
the one dating Derek. She was a junior. Tall with naturally
platinum-blond hair cut shoulder length and almost white
eyelashes and eyebrows. Her skin, in contrast, was a perfectly
light golden hue. I had often seen her sunbathe on the weekends with the other German girls. They worked on their tans
methodically. Obsessively. Religiously, really. They had lotions
that they smeared on themselves, and they timed how long
each body part was exposed to the sun before they turned.

I watched Constanze meander across the back field with
two of the other older German girls. The other two girls were
not as tall or blond as she was, but they all shared the natural
undone beauty of a girl who rolls out of bed and walks out
the door without any concerns. A girl whose beauty regime
consists of nothing other than washing her face with water.
Erika had long brown curls tumbling down her shoulders, a
strand of which she twisted around her finger absentmindedly
as she walked. Kirsten had her T-shirt tied into a knot under

her breasts so that her golden stomach showed. None of them wore makeup or had their eyebrows shaped, their hair dyed, and still, they were beautiful. They had flaws, but so what? They had managed to understand that one's strongest asset at that age is youth, and they knew how to flaunt it in a way that was almost genius.

I was a little mesmerized, watching them. They weren't exactly otherworldly fascinating or original the way that Beth Whelan was, but they could definitely be in a music video, walking like that with the sunshine erupting all around them. *Well, maybe they're not cool enough for a music video, I thought, but definitely a tampon commercial.*

"How's the heartbreak going?"

I looked up from where I was spying on the German girls. Beth Whelan was suddenly standing there, smiling down at me, her eyes obscured by sunglasses, chewing on a Twizzler. Her hair was a crazy-beautiful color in the sun—like glowing, peach iced tea. It was messy and uncombed, tumbling down over her left shoulder.

I slammed the composition book shut that I had lying on my lap. I had been in the middle of writing a poem, and all my poems at the time had titles like "Drowning in the Aftermath of Eternity."

"Oh yeah," I said, totally unprepared for this conversation. "Normal, I guess."

"Normal?" She sat down next to me. "What kind of an adjective is that for a heartbreak?"

I found myself staring at a Twizzler that was suddenly looming in front of my face. She was holding it out to me. I took it, and she pulled out a new one from the packet she had pinned under her arm and bit into it.

"Thanks," I said. "Well, I just mean, I thought about what

you said—about trying to turn Mr. Sorrentino on and stuff, but I know he's never going to be into me because, for whatever weird reason, he's totally obsessed with the lady he's going to marry. Judy. So, I don't know. I'm just being an unhinged bitch to him, meanwhile, which kind of helps. It's like a way to feel good about feeling bad, I guess."

There was a high that came with making the Queen of the Underground laugh—a kind of bolstering of one's ego that couldn't be gotten anywhere else.

"That's a good line," she said. *"Being an unhinged bitch is a way to feel good about feeling bad.* Can I steal that for my yearbook quote?"

"Yeah, if you want," I said, embarrassed and pleased.

She laughed some more. "You're a weirdo. You know that, right?"

"I know I'm not normal, per se," I conceded with a nod. "It's pretty painfully obvious."

Beth ripped off another piece of Twizzler with her teeth, talking as she chewed. "There's nothing wrong with being normal, except potentially absolutely everything, you know?"

I nodded. It sounded cool, the weird way she had said that, all twisted around. The intoxicating fake-fruit smell of her shampoo wafted into my face as she pulled her hair around over to her other shoulder. She was wearing an old oversize T-shirt with a short skirt, her velvet choker and battered-up sneakers. It was perfect—the way that nothing about her attire was urgent or needy. And her lips were perfectly red and outlined, no smudges, no trace of having eaten any Twizzlers. I tried to take note of everything about her and store it somewhere safe where I might pull it out later and rabidly try to counterfeit it.

"You know what you should probably do?" she said, suddenly

lifting her sunglasses onto her head and fixing her eyes on me. "I think you should try to approach this Mr. S. thing again from a nonvirgin standpoint."

"What do you mean?"

"I mean, you should try to lose your virginity. Not to Mr. S., of course," she added quickly. "Someone totally different. Just don't do it with someone special, because that's the worst—having '*meaningful*' sex." She made a face to illustrate her feelings on the matter of meaningful sex. "Definitely don't do anything sexual that feels 'profound' or 'romantic.' Just pick a random guy and get it over with. It'll make you way less of a worm, which in turn will help you with the Mr. S. thing—and pretty much everything else too. Trust me. Bang someone."

I was a tad bummed out about the fact that my virginity was apparently tattooed to my forehead, and the idea of me "banging" someone was beyond ludicrous. All the same, I pretended it was something that was definitely worth considering.

"Really?" I asked. "Won't that make things worse? Like getting emotionally involved with another guy on top of Mr. Sorrentino?"

"Who said anything about *emotions*?"

I started picking at my nail polish. "Well," I said, "when you have sex—aren't there emotions that happen—like, in conjunction with the sex?"

She raised her eyebrows. "Is that what your guidance counselor says?"

I shrank a little at the stab. "No. It's . . . I mean, it's like the general consensus, right? That, like, passion has to be part of it for sex to work?"

"First of all, no. And secondly, passion isn't the same thing as being emotional anyway."

She wasn't talking down to me. I liked that. She was talking as though explaining something pretty self-evident and mundane to a fellow passenger on a bus.

"And technically, you don't even need passion to have great sex," she continued. "I know people like to make a big deal about it. Not to be crass or anything, but it's literally just a wiener going into a vagina. That's all sex is. And for it to be spectacular, all that needs to happen is for said wiener to hit the right spot in said vagina. And sure, it definitely helps if there is some decent foreplay and the guy isn't a moron or doesn't have, like, snot coming out of his nose when you're about to have an orgasm. Those are all good contributing factors, but listen, it's *not* a magical unicorn party. In fact, it's the opposite of that. The whole thing is so mechanical it's ridiculous. I can't believe people still have this obnoxious theory that it has to be special. I mean, why should a vagina be inextricably and automatically connected to an emotion?"

"I don't know," I said.

"One is a biological piece of tissue and the other an abstract mental phenomena. They have nothing in common."

I had never had a conversation where the word *vagina* was so effortlessly and philosophically tossed about. It felt exhilarating to be blasé about these things. "What about hormones?" I asked. "Don't they affect emotions?"

"Hormones my ass. I don't buy them."

"I mean, they *do* exist, though."

"So do aliens. It's all a matter of what you believe."

"Yeah, I guess."

"It's up to you, though," she said carelessly when we had finished off all the Twizzlers. "Don't lose your virginity if you don't want to. You should never believe anyone's advice anyway. Although that being said, the advice about not doing it with someone special is pretty solid advice. That one you should live by. Don't have 'special' sex, okay?"

"Okay."

"Get it from someone you're not going to care about afterward. It's all about freedom, and if you have some kind of sickening, romantic, candlelit event, then what's the point? You're just going to end up in a new Mr. Sorrentino situation."

"Yeah, that makes sense."

Someone called her name at this point, and we both turned to find her friend Megan Peffer and a couple of other seniors waving her over from across the field.

Beth got up and tossed a pack of cigarettes onto my lap that she had pulled out of her pocket. It was almost entirely full.

"Keep 'em," she said.

"Shit," I said. "Thanks."

"Later, masturbator," she said as she walked away.

MR. SORRENTINO GOT A NEW HAIRCUT THAT MADE
his ears more prominent—I couldn't decide if this was good
or not. Georgina became cocaptain of the girls' volleyball
team. Our new book in English was *A Separate Peace*. The
drama club had started rehearsals on their play: *Hard Times* by
Charles Dickens—but taking place in 2050. Beth did a pencil
portrait of me holding a fake fish for her art project. And a
kid was expelled for writing *My dick is awesome* inside every
new school pamphlet that had been freshly delivered from the
printers. A few of them had even been sent out like that.

This was March. A new kind of norm had settled in. A
norm in which I felt more freedom than I'd had in a long time.
I wasn't an idiot. I knew it was because of Wade that I felt this
way, and it scared me a little that he had that kind of power.
He was changing me. For example, I found myself listening
to Georgina's long-winded volleyball gossip one evening and
even contributed a sentence here and there, making it a civilized conversation. And when Mrs. Gillespie picked on me

in front of the whole class to point out how my bra strap was hanging down my arm, I had found myself cracking up about it rather than dying of humiliation as I should have. It was almost as though my nerves had ceased to be frayed. Somehow, almost imperceptibly, they had become fortified with some kind of vitamin-rich layer of nutrition, and before I knew it, I woke up one day feeling less of an asshole and generally more okay about the fact that the world was technically unbearable.

Maybe I'm even happy, I thought. I wasn't ruling it out. I remember standing in the shower wondering about it. I couldn't be 100 percent sure about what happiness even was. I had always been so sure about how miserable I felt that it was weird having to admit that I might actually be feeling kind of great.

Nothing happened between Wade and me, despite our growing intimacy. This was good. I was consciously thankful that Wade hadn't looked at me weird, the way boys looked at girls sometimes, turning them into dolls. It wasn't that it necessarily felt bad to be admired physically—just complicated. Maybe weird. It hadn't happened enough for me to know much about it, but I remembered how Derek's eyes had gone straight to my chest area after that cross-country run with Beth when my T-shirt was wet and see-through. Wade had never done that, which was good because being a doll wasn't something I knew how to be. Being a very human, very unsophisticated idiot, however, was totally up my alley, and Wade seemed to be all right with that, which is where the freedom lay. I loved that about him—the utter lack of judgment. The freedom to have all the flaws you needed to exist.

I mean, a couple of times I did wonder what it would be like if Wade looked at me in "that way." It gave me the chills, and I wasn't sure whether they were the good or the bad kind of chills. I never allowed myself to get lost in that kind of speculation for long, though. I swatted those thoughts out of my head as soon as they took shape, because they scared the shit out of me more than they felt good. Wade was Wade. He had to stay Wade. No matter what happened, he had to stay exactly who he was.

It was the tail end of March, and we sat in study hall together, working on our joint history paper. Study hall was a large room open to anyone wanting to work on their homework or study for an exam or whatever. The room was often occupied by study groups and raucous mathletes, or the debate team, or any of the other social entities and clubs that the school was teeming with. If you needed silence to study, the library was the place to go. Wade and I had a free period and decided to work on our paper, which was supposed to be about the Black Death. We had our laptops, notebooks, and some library books on the subject spread across the table, but all actual work had taken a back seat to finding the perfect title for the paper, which we had narrowed down to two options:

The Black Death: A Bacteria Terrorizes Humanity
The Black Death: Revenge of a Microorganism

We were toying with the idea of writing the whole report in the first person from the bacteria's viewpoint and getting super excited about how genius that idea was when Judy—Mr. Sorrentino's fiancée—appeared out of nowhere to throw a hand grenade into everything that had been so perfect.

"Hi there, Gracie!" she said, stopping by our table with a stack of composition books under her arm.

"Oh shit," I said. "Hi."

I felt disoriented by her appearance with the teeth and the hair and all. I still didn't fully believe Mr. Sorrentino was into her. It was impossible.

Judy's smile had wavered for a fraction of a second after my reaction to her, but then without warning, there was a full-blown grin on her face as she turned her teeth from me to Wade. "Who's *this* young man?"

She was too much for me.

"That's Wade," I said, gesturing toward him in the most unresponsive way I could.

"So nice to meet you, Wade. I'm Judy, Mr. Sorrentino's fiancée. I'm doing some substitute work here this semester."

Wade smiled at her. "Cool. I mean, about being Mr. Sorrentino's fiancée. The substituting probably sucks."

"You know what? It *is* pretty cool being Mr. Sorrentino's fiancée. I can't lie. But teaching is pretty cool too."

I wanted to groan, but Wade just took it in painlessly and with seeming interest. "Come on, it can't be *that* great to deal with a roomful of us," he said.

Judy, clearly enchanted by his wide-eyed interest in her cornball life, became even more animated. "Oh, I really enjoy it! The challenges can be so invigorating, you know. It's what I've always planned on doing—teaching. Between getting to do what I love most and having Mr. Sorrentino at my side, I'm a pretty happy camper."

"You beat the odds," Wade said.

She smiled, and then, not moving on, she asked, "So, are you two an item?" And the smile on her face becoming mischievous as though we were all in on some big, wacky secret.

A panic broke out in my entire body, and I opened my mouth to say I don't know *what*, when Wade said, "In her *dreams*, maybe."

Judy thought this was adorable, and she told us so.

"Well, we try," said Wade with a shrug.

She adjusted the composition books under her arm with a little laugh. "Look at you two," she said, putting her left hand on her heart. "You know, it's very evident how much respect you have for one another. It's lovely."

Even Wade was stumped at this point. He scratched his neck in lieu of a comeback, and I certainly was no use either.

"Well, I didn't mean to interrupt anything," Judy said, sensing that it was probably time to move on. "I just wanted to say a quick hello. Good to see you again, Gracie, and a pleasure to meet you, Wade."

She walked off with her stack of composition books, leaving us behind in a total vacuum.

I looked over at Wade, and we stared at each other for what seemed like an eternity.

"We don't have to talk about what just happened," he said at the end of that eternity.

I let out a breath of air in relief. "Oh my god. Good."

Then he flipped open the notepad for our history paper and added, "But just out of curiosity—you know that I'm kind of in love with you, right?"

I told him to go fuck himself.

Wade looked up from the notepad with a laugh. "I'm serious."

"Uh-huh," I said, pulling one of the books on the plague over to my side of the table and flipping through its chapters.

"Yeah, I swear."

I rolled my eyes. "Seriously, fuck you, Wade. Stop it."

"Come on, it's not obvious?"

The realization that he might not be joking trickled into me with cold terror. I froze. I was looking at the table, but I could feel his eyes on me. I don't know if he was waiting for a response or just making sure that the weight of what he had just said didn't leave a crater in me, which it definitely had.

"Don't say that stuff," I said after a beat. My stomach solidified into a heavy mass of what seemed to be emotional lead.

"Why? It's true."

"You actually can't know that."

"Yeah, I *can*, actually," he said in that maddeningly easy manner of his. "I was kind of in love with you right from the start. It would have been hard not to—you were aiming a slingshot at Derek's head. And then, when we were waiting outside Mr. Wahlberg's office and you looked over at me like I was this huge creep—I mean, my heart almost stopped completely."

It struck me how comfortable he was, saying something like that while everything inside of me was a bunch of pure chaos. He had detonated a bomb, and he didn't even know it. I looked across the room to where a group of kids were doing their homework. Girls and boys, intermingled, talking and laughing—more ammunition waiting to blow them all sky high.

"Seriously," I said. I couldn't look at him. "You can't say stuff like that."

"Why not?"

I couldn't believe that he might actually be so naive. "Do you really want to *ruin* everything?" I said, finally focusing on him. "You're practically the only person I can even stand having around."

"So, what's the problem?"

"*Love.* People ruin each other's lives by falling in love."

"Not always."

"Yeah, *always,* Wade. Always. It's the way it's set up—you can't even help being fucked in the process of being in love."

"Some people might say being fucked in the process of love is kind of the whole idea."

"Oh my god!"

"Sorry. It would have been weird if I didn't make that joke."

"Can you just be serious about this for a second?" I said, kicking him under the table.

He nodded and gave me his attention in that way that kids give their parents attention when they already know they're not going to give a fuck about the lecture.

"Okay, look." I took a breath. "I know it sounds easy, but it's not—being in love, I mean. It's complicated and rotten and gross and turns you into this nauseating dipshit you never thought you'd be. People in love—they pretend like they're normal, but inside they're all hollowed out and dead by the time they break up. Because nobody stays in love. And god, if they do, it's even worse."

Some kind of realization came to his eyes.

"I'm not talking from personal experience, okay?" I said quickly. "It's common knowledge. Have you ever read *Anna Karenina* or *The Great Gatsby*?"

"I read this study guide thing on *The Great Gatsby*," he said.

"Well, then, you get the gist of it."

He was finding all of this amusing more than anything else. "Are you really basing that theory off some books you read?" he asked.

"I also did this whole mathematical equation I can show you later that proves my point, which is: there's nothing about this idea of love that works out the way you want it to. It's completely booby-trapped from beginning to end. And anyway, it's not real. It's, like, a bullshit fantasy that everyone is brainwashed into. Probably to keep the planet populated."

"Wait, *what* mathematical equation?"

I waved off the question impatiently. "It doesn't matter. Just this equation—I figured it out with algebra."

"You're kidding, right?" he said with a laugh.

"Why would I be kidding right now?"

"I'm in that class with you, in case you forgot. I've seen your funky algebra skills in action."

"Shut up—listen, I'm serious!"

It was a little bit of a sore spot—the hilarious fact that I was the worst mathematician on the face of the planet, and for whatever unknown reason, Wade, who got no good grades anywhere else and was hopeless as a student, knew his way around numbers. He could get through an algebra class in his sleep. It was annoying.

"Even if my equation is totally bogus, it doesn't change the fact that being in love with people is a waste of time," I said, steering the conversation back to where it belonged. "That's the bottom line, okay? It's a creepy, bullshit waste of time. The way that you and I can be together, and talk, and sit together at lunch and dinner—all that wouldn't be possible. It would end in a bloodbath if we were in love. I'm telling you—everything would be bad. We shouldn't even be talking about it."

He seemed completely unimpressed by my vehemence. "Maybe you were just in love with the wrong person before?" he suggested.

"I told you I'm not talking from experience," I repeated, but it sounded like the lie that it was. All the Mr. Sorrentino emotions began to bloom up somewhere inside of me.

He shrugged. "Okay, well, then: Gatsby—that's where you're getting your theory from, right? Maybe *he* was in love with the wrong person. That girl in the book wasn't all that great, if you ask me, and so maybe that's why it sucked."

I thought about Daisy Buchanan and how disappointing and worthless she was. She was definitely the wrong person. It just didn't make a difference to Gatsby. That was the whole goddamn point Wade was missing by a million miles! It didn't make a difference to him that Daisy was worthless. And Mr. Sorrentino was my Daisy. Just like my dad was my mom's Daisy.

I was suddenly so embarrassingly sad about it all.

"But even if it's the wrong person," I said, not being able to keep it out of my voice, which made it even more embarrassing, "it doesn't mean it's not *real*. The wrong person can still be the real person that you're in love with. And that's all you need, to be fully screwed for eternity—to like someone hard enough. I'm telling you."

He put his arm around my shoulder and pulled me over so that my head ended up in his neck and I could smell his skin, which smelled nothing like a girl's skin. He just held me like that without saying anything else. It nearly killed me, because it was the cleanest form of affection I had ever felt from someone other than my mother. It wasn't a "move." It was just a gesture. It was one of those sudden ways in which he was beyond his years.

Incidentally, this was something I had fantasized Mr. Sorrentino would do. It was strange that it would come from Wade in the end.

After a long moment, he let go.

"It's not a big deal," Wade said with an effortless finality. "I just figured it was obvious how I felt about you and that saying it wouldn't make a difference. That's all. Forget it if you want."

An airborne calculator whizzed by our table accompanied by a loud squeal and then an eruption of nerd laughter.

"Don't you like the way things are?" I asked Wade, ignoring the nerds.

"Yeah."

"Me too. I really like the way things are right now."

"So, all right. Let's start this history report," he said, swatting me on the head with the notepad.

I pulled the pad of paper out of his hands and spread it open on the table in front of me. "Anyway," I said. "Beth says boys don't even know what love is because they're too confused what with their—you know—*wieners* dictating everything they do."

He covered his face with his hand, and for the moment, our

laughter mixed with the math-table laughter. *Thank God for the word* wiener, I thought.

"Is that true, though?" I asked after a while, when we had gotten back to work. "Like, does everything make you horny when you're a guy?"

"Well, not *everything*." He thought for a second. "Like, tap dancing doesn't really make me horny or—I don't know—berets? Or garage doors, or pretzels, or . . . well, *maybe* pretzels, actually—"

"What if it's a really hot girl doing the tap dancing?"

He nodded. "Right, exactly. You get how it works."

"Yeah. You're really only safe around garage doors and berets."

The truth of the matter was that I liked Wade too much to even consider being in love with him. Or maybe it went beyond just that. Maybe the truth was that I *needed* him. The way that he made me the center of his universe when he listened to me talk and let me live off his endless amounts of energy and imagination. On some days, I felt like I robbed him blind—took everything I could from him and went back to my room to wallow in it. I told myself that maybe it worked both ways. I probably made him feel good just the way that he made me feel good, but I didn't really understand what I was giving *him*. What I truly believed was that I had some dark magic powers that completely blinded and glued him to me. That's the only way it made any sense to me. And so what? I wasn't ever going to undo whatever spell I had accidentally cast.

WHEN THE EASTER BREAK CAME AROUND, I ASKED
my mother if I could stay at school for the holidays. I didn't
want to deal with that bus ride home, but also, I didn't want to
be stuck with her for a week and act with all the responsibility
that I had just learned to shed. My mother wasn't happy about
me not coming home. She complained about having planned
a big shopping spree to reinvent my whole wardrobe, and I explained how I really wanted to get ahead in my studies for the
next semester, especially since I was competing for the Science
Award. Again, we were both full of shit, but it didn't matter.
She agreed to let me stay, and I thanked her and went on to
explain how I was thinking of studying biochemistry at Northwestern. I didn't even know where Northwestern was, but I
presumed it was somewhere in the Northwest. I had heard a
girl talk about how she was dating a guy who went there.

Wade had a family reunion to go to.

"Are you kidding? Can't you get out of it?" I almost fully
yelled at him as we were walking to the dining hall for dinner.

There was no way a family reunion was more important than a week of freedom where we could do whatever the hell we wanted. "Tell them you're studying for some kind of national math-nerd competition or something."

He smiled but didn't bother with a reply.

"Why not?" I asked.

"There's no point. I don't carry that kind of weight with my parents. If I ask them for anything, they usually go the exact opposite way."

I couldn't believe he was being so defeatist. "So that's it? You're not even going to try?" I asked, giving him a shove.

"Look, I'd way rather stay here than be wedged into the middle of my whole extended family in Missouri for a week, but if I try to get out of this thing, it'll backfire on me. Trust me."

"But that's why you tell them you're getting extra tutoring or something. Lying to your parents isn't exactly brain surgery—you just tell them whatever floats their boat."

He laughed at this idea. "They don't believe anything I say, Gracie."

It was a no go. I could tell right away. Usually, it took no convincing at all to get him to go along with an idea, no matter how dumb. In fact, more often than not, *he* was the one supplying the dumbass ideas in the first place. This was different. There was none of that reckless disregard for eventualities in his response to my pleading. It wasn't even up for debate. The family reunion thing was iron clad for some reason.

"Ugh. Fine," I said, giving him another shove.

"Sorry. Really."

"Don't apologize when something isn't your fault," I said moodily. "You do that way too much."

He shoved me back this time. "You're a real goddamn joy to hang out with sometimes, you know that?"

I smiled, easing up on him. He was pretty good at giving me these adorable attitude adjustments. Nobody had ever been successful in that department before. Maybe Mr. Sorrentino—but not like this.

"Can you at least get them to buy you a new phone, *please*?" I asked.

Because that was the other thing. He had thrown his phone into the wash a few days earlier with his laundry. If he was gone for a week, it would mean complete radio silence.

"Yeah, I'll try," he said.

"Your parents have enough money, right? What's the problem?"

"I mean, they'll give me one, but it's going to be this whole thing first where they have to prove to me that money doesn't grow on trees and there are consequences to being irresponsible with my stuff—so just don't hold your breath, that's all. It might take a while."

I sighed. "God, why are your parents such *dicks*?"

He made a face like there were way too many worms in that can to open it up.

Whatever. It was just a week. I didn't care as much as I'd initially thought I cared, and by that evening, I was excited at the prospect of having a week to myself. As much as Wade had taken my life out of the dumps and made it palatable, I actually needed this radio silence when I really thought about it. I hadn't written an emotionally overloaded poem or started a new novel in far too long, and I had ideas piled up in my head, taking up way too much real estate. To have the luxury to be with myself began to feel necessary.

Only . . . when he stood with his backpack outside my door a few days later to say goodbye, it sucked a little more than I had anticipated. Out of nowhere, I felt this spasm of renegade panic in my gut.

"Okay," he said.

"Okay what?"

He shrugged. "See you in a week. I'll try to call from one of my cousins' phones."

"Sounds like a plan. Bye." I gave him a small wave.

Wade rolled his eyes and pulled me into a hug. After a longish moment, he said, "Please hug me back."

So I put my arms around him with a groan, just to let him know this was by no means *my* idea. Once my arms were around him, though, and my head squished onto his chest, I didn't let go. He didn't either. We held on, and just like that, the moment was charged in a way it hadn't been a few seconds ago.

"Get a room!" someone real original called as they walked by.

We both let go then, but Wade gave me a kiss on the cheek before he stepped back to pick up his skateboard.

"All right, see ya," he said, smiling, his face all lit up and bright.

I said, "Yup," and slammed the door shut, unceremoniously squelching the moment's momentum. Then I stared at the doorknob for a superlong while, wondering what—if anything—had just happened. Nothing, right? *Yeah, nothing for sure,* I thought, still staring at the doorknob. People hug. It's normal. Still, the week ahead now seemed like a relief—just in case something *had* happened.

I enjoyed the deafening quiet of the first day. The school was nearly empty except for the few kids who'd stayed behind either to study or work on projects, or because their parents weren't at home. A small crew of the staff remained too.

It was exhilarating at first—the emptiness and change of pace. I had never stayed behind at school for the holidays before, and it was a novelty that I was intending to wallow in. It was going to be great. I had the room completely to myself, and the first thing I did was plug my phone into Georgina's speakers and put on "Freedom" by Rage Against the Machine to clear the room of any invisible *Mamma Mia!* nanoparticles.

I liked older music, for the record. The late '8os and early '9os in particular, but earlier stuff too—like, for example, I had a huge soft spot for doo-wop, and I liked other '6os stuff like the Animals, the Who, the Sonics, and so on. More than a decade or genre, what mattered to me was whether the music delivered what it promised. Rage Against the Machine always delivered the promise. More so than you usually bargained for.

I turned the music all the way up and painted my nails. When it came time, I sang along: "*Freedooooooom! Yeaaaaah! Freedooooom! Yeaah, riiiiiiight! Freedooooom! Yeaaaaaahhh! Freedooooooommmmmmmm! Yeaaaaahhhhh, riiiiiiiiiiiiiiiiiiiiiiiiiiight!*"

I listened to RATM a bit longer and then found myself sitting on my bed with green nails and a weird side ponytail and nothing else to show for it. I was bored. I realized I was no longer as self-sufficient as I had been before I knew Beth or Wade. Especially Wade. Fuck, it was hard to know what to do without him.

I went to the common room and watched some TV until this Swiss kid I hardly knew sat down with me—like, right next to me, even though there were about a thousand seating options. I couldn't figure out if this was on purpose or accidental, and spent about fifteen minutes feeling weird, watching some reality show about people being naked in dangerous tropical locations before standing up nonchalantly and getting the hell out of there.

I took a walk and tried to write some poetry. Nothing was fully working out. I couldn't concentrate with the massive amounts of time I suddenly had on my hands. I went to the office with the intention of snooping around Mrs. Martinez's desk, but Miss Klein was sitting there, holding down the fort, so instead, I called my dad at his office. His secretary picked up the phone after two rings.

"Hall and Palmer. This is Larry Hall's office. How can I help you?"

"Good morning, I have Jean Dorf on the line for Mr. Hall," I said.

There was a pause. "I'm sorry, what is this regarding?"

"*Sorrentino v. Gillespie.*"

A longer pause. "What firm did you say you were calling from?"

"Dorf, Dorf, Dorf, and Dorf."

Hesitantly, she said, "One moment, please."

I waited, and after some phone-connecting noises, my dad's voice came over the line. "Hello?"

"Hi, Dad."

"Glorie?"

My heart dropped for a second.

Gloria was one of his other daughters. One of my three half sisters in California: Gloria, Helen, and Christine. I had seen a picture of them once when I was going through my dad's wallet while he was taking a shower. It was a photograph of the whole family, my dad included, probably taken at a professional studio, judging by the setup and the light gray backdrop.

I had studied it intently. Meryl, the mother, was blond—not naturally blond but *perfectly* blond. Her haircut was short—something like a boy haircut, but instead of making her look masculine, it made her look intriguing, cool, and unexpected. It was the kind of haircut you couldn't get in Florida. She looked older than my mother and not as beautiful but better taken care of. Healthier. More manicured. More adult. Everything about her looked perfect, and there was a sense of belonging—of the world being her private living room, a place she knew her way around like the back of her hand. I figured she probably understood contemporary art. She'd probably go crazy about a canvas with a sock nailed to it. She'd probably get it. It would touch her emotionally, deep down in her soul, and she'd say with mesmerized eyes, "This is the most beautiful thing I've ever seen. Larry, doesn't this turn your whole world upside down? We have to have this."

My mom's soul was touched when she was taken out to Ruby Tuesday for dinner. It made me pretty miserable to compare the two of them. It truly fucked with me.

The girls? They all looked older than I was—the youngest maybe by three or five years. I did my best to match their names to their faces. The older two girls looked friendly and happy. Laid-back in both attitude and style. Californian. Blond, like their mother, but naturally so, which meant their hair color actually came from my dad. But I was most interested in the younger one, Gloria, because she was the closest thing to my direct counterpart and the one my dad was always mixing me up with when he called my name. Life and adventure were practically spurting out of every pore in her face. There was a nose covered in freckles, bouncing curly hair, and the posture of someone who can't wait for the next moment of life to tackle them. I had tried to find traces of my own face in hers, but it was hard. I was nothing like that person in the picture. Not even remotely. Adventure and lust for life weren't necessarily things that spurted from my pores.

Anyway, I never went through my dad's wallet again after that. It wasn't worth it.

"It's *Grace*," I said to my dad.

"Gracie?" He sounded confused. "What's the matter?"

"Nothing. I mean, besides everything in the entire world. Nothing."

He chuckled, and it felt as comforting as it always did when he made that noise of amusement. "What's wrong, Gracie?" he asked again, although sounding more relaxed now. "I'm guessing there is some kind of emergency, since this is strictly an emergency line."

"Yeah, there is an emergency, actually," I said.

"Well?"

"I need to know what makes men tick. I figured you might know, being that you *are* a man and all."

No chuckle this time. "Listen to me, Grace—you do not need to worry about men. Men have no business in your life. Maybe in twenty years, but for now, you keep playing with your dolls, kid."

"Well, I *am* playing with my dolls, but I can't help it if men are falling at my feet. I mean, what am I supposed to do?"

"You walk over them. You step on them."

That made me giggle.

"I'm not kidding, Gracie," he said. "You're a beautiful young woman, and you're going to attract attention. Now, listen, I need to get back to work, but I want you to promise me you'll never believe anything a boy tries to sell you."

"But what if he's a nice boy? Like, the nicest person you ever met in your life?"

"There aren't any nice boys. They all just have one thing on their mind."

"Did *you* only have one thing on your mind when you were in school?"

"No, I was an exception. But everyone else was a pig. You can take my word for it. When a boy tells you things you want to hear, no matter how much you want to believe them, keep in mind that it's all just a load of baloney. They have one thing on their mind—one thing only. You can trust me on this one."

"You know far too much about pigs to not have been one yourself."

"I'm serious, Gracie. I want you to promise me to stay away from boys."

"Sure thing."

"Is that a promise?"

"Yeah."

Promising him things was easy—fun almost, since he really had no way of following up on anything. It was a true advantage to his kind of parenting.

"Are you doing all right at school?" he asked. "Do you need anything?"

I kind of needed a new hairbrush. A bra too, actually. Beth suggested I get one that had padding in it, and honestly, I figured it couldn't hurt to look like I had bigger boobs. But these were all things that took a back seat to what I really wanted.

"Actually, yeah, Dad. I need headphones for my phone. They don't have to be fancy or anything—I mean, they *can* be if you want—but mainly all I care about is that they work."

"Fancy headphones. Got it."

"You'll remember?"

"I have it written down right in front of me here."

"Okay, but don't forget."

"Of course not. You called the emergency line, so clearly this is an emergency."

"I know you think you're joking, but it *is* actually a life-or-death situation. Imagine if every time you wanted to listen to music you had to go to your nemesis and ask to borrow their speakers or headphones. That's my life basically. So yeah, I'd say this was an emergency, Dad."

"All right, kid," he said, and his voice took on that end-of-conversation tone. "I gotta go and explain to my secretary who

Dorf, Dorf, Dorf, and Dorf are. But we'll talk more about this, and meanwhile, just concentrate on your schoolwork. Forget about boys. Just work hard and you'll be fine. And don't call again, okay? Unless it's a real emergency. I mean, not this number—you can call the cell number that your mom uses if you need to get in touch."

"Yeah, yeah."

"All right, baby, have a good one."

"Bye, Dad."

I hung up in high spirits about the headphones I was going to get and was generally basking in the attention I had gotten from my dad. I liked that he had made such a fuss about me staying away from boys. I liked when he called me *baby* too, rather than just *kid*. And then I thought about the fact that Helen, Christine, and Gloria could call his office all the time, and they wouldn't have to make up a law firm to do it. I tried to figure out how fucked up that was. I wondered whether I hated those girls. I didn't think I did. A little maybe. They had everything that I didn't have. They had the year-round daddy who said things to them all the time about staying away from boys and how beautiful they were. And they probably had credit cards and bought whatever they wanted, and they went to schools that were not in Florida and never had to worry about buying toiletries. I imagined their bathrooms to be filled with bottles and tubes of beauty products that I wouldn't have known the use for. Bottles and bottles of different colors and shapes, lipsticks, expensive nail polish, perfumes, and whatever other amazing, frivolous crap people made for girls that I told myself I had no interest in because naturally I was far above that kind of stuff.

I figured I did hate them a bit. I couldn't be *totally* graceful about it, but on the other hand, I didn't feel as depressed about it as I maybe would have liked. The reason for this being that

I grew up in a different universe. My life was my home, and their life was like a TV show that I had never even watched, just heard about. And besides, if I lived their life in California, I would have never met Wade. And he was better than all their designer toiletries. I felt pretty good about having had that thought and left it at that.

Next, I tried curling my hair with Georgina's curling stick. I gave up halfway through and started a new novel.

"The night he was born, his mother died. It all happened under the crack of a lightning bolt. Boris would never not be alone again. He opened his eyes to a world that delighted in fucking him over every chance it got. His only friend from here on out would be a bone-deep loneliness . . ."

That's as far as I got. I shoved my composition book aside and went back to reading *It*.

BY DAY THREE, I WAS COMPLETELY AND UTTERLY
bored out of my wits. I spent a decent amount of time on YouTube
watching Stephen King interviews, where I learned all kinds
of stuff—like, for example: good horror is kind of like a peanut
butter cup, because you're supposed to have a combo of two
separate scary elements interacting, much like the chemistry
of the peanut butter and the chocolate. I noted this down in
my notebook and circled it a few times. Eventually, I googled
Stephen King's wife. The way he talked about her, I had to.
Which led to googling his kids. Which led to me closing the
laptop because they were all really cool and my dad, on the
other hand, was not Stephen King, and there was nothing I
could do about it.

I lounged around empty schoolrooms trying to read, trying
to work on the novel about Boris, and trying generally not to
suffocate on the nothingness that was crowding around me
thick and opaque. I called my mom. I almost called my dad's

office again. I went to Mr. Sorrentino's classroom and wrote him a letter that I folded up and put in the bottom of his desk drawer. I think I might have called him a *laughable Smurf* in it. I would take it out again before school started, but for the present, this illusion of unencumbered communication felt liberating.

It was hot outside, and the humidity was evil even though the sky was overcast and there was an occasional pale lightning off in the distance. I walked to the tennis courts and lay down in the middle of the last court, face to the sky, arms outstretched. It felt meaningful. *It's kind of sad that no one is here to witness it,* I thought. I had found an old Discman in the history room with a CD called *Masters of Baroque* in it. Mr. Ellerman would often listen to it while we were doing tests. I had taken it with me to the tennis court and was listening to it while looking up at the sky. Loud, crashing music filled my head, with trumpets, harpsichords, and instruments I didn't know the names of, climbing over each other in complex rhythms. It was mathematical in a strange way. Hypnotic. I closed my eyes, letting the music infiltrate my mind. It ate me up. There was one tune called Concerto for Two Harpsichords in C Minor that blew my mind. I skipped back to the beginning every time that piece came to an end and listened to it over again. There was something doomy and tragic in the fast-paced mechanical avalanche of music. It made the fact that I was lying there on the ground with my arms outstretched even more meaningful.

On the fourth time through the Concerto for Two Harpsichords, I opened my eyes and found myself looking up into Derek's face. He stood over me, staring down with a neutral expression, the harpsichord lending the scene an otherworldly complexity. It was so bizarre—visually and sonically speaking.

Sitting up, I pulled the headphones off my head.

"Hey," he said, hands in his pockets.

His face looked naked in a way that was hard to compute. That aggressive gleefulness that was so much a part of his features was not there. It somehow rearranged everything about him, making him look like a different person. Less maliciously constipated, I suppose.

"What're you listening to?" he asked.

Still slightly dazed, I said, *"Masters of Baroque."*

"Oh, right on. Bach, Handel, Scarlatti . . . good stuff."

I had no idea who the people were that he had named except for Bach, but I figured they were all *Masters of Baroque* guys. It annoyed me that he would know those names.

"I didn't know you liked baroque music," he said.

"It's not my CD. It's Mr. Ellerman's."

He nodded. "Oh, right. The one he listens to when he gives tests."

"Yeah."

He nodded some more, looking off across the tennis court in a thoughtful manner. "Good stuff. Good stuff."

And after a moment's silence with me still sitting and him still standing, I said, "Is this about the slingshot thing?"

He turned back to face me. "Hey, what was the deal with that?" he asked. "I don't even know you, and you almost take out my eye."

"But I didn't."

"So what? That's not the point."

"The point is that I *could* have taken your eye out, and I chose not to."

His expression soured a little. "I have a scar here. Right here. See? You can actually see it. That's there for good."

He pointed it out—a small indentation on his cheek, half the size of a neutron.

"Maybe if I had an electron microscope, I could see it."

I had meant to sound derisive, but everything just came out sounding limp and nondirectional. The humidity had sucked the attitude out of me.

"Seriously, why'd you shoot me?" Derek asked eventually. "I don't get it."

"I'm sure you can figure it out if you really tried."

"Is that guy your boyfriend or something?"

"*No.*"

"Then what do you care?"

I shook my head to indicate that he was hopeless. "God, this conversation is depressing." I made an attempt to get up, but he held out his hands in surrender.

"Okay, relax. Forget about the slingshot thing. Let's put it behind us, all right?"

I sat back, not knowing if I intended to stay or leave but curious and bored to death enough to linger.

"So, why'd you stay at school for spring break?" Derek asked.

"Because."

I wasn't exactly sure where to go from here. I didn't like Derek—that much I knew—but at the same time, everything was different when the school was empty like this. It was like the rules didn't apply, and his being a douchebag was somehow irrelevant. And honestly, he didn't have that hyena look, so I was willing to let myself be curious.

"You have the perfect amount of meat in your calves, by the way," he said, staring at my outstretched legs.

"What the hell is that supposed to mean?" I said.

I was trying to be offended because I was pretty certain I was being objectified, and all the older girls constantly talked about how they were sick of being objectified.

"It just means you have great legs," he said pleasantly. "You have a really beautiful shape to your legs. Some girls, even when they're stunning, have these legs that don't match how pretty they are—like, their ankles are too thick or their calves are too bulky or too skinny. When a girl is pretty and then her legs are awesome too, it's like a Christmas present. Just makes me happy. Can't help it."

He touched the calf of my outstretched leg lightly with his foot to point out what he was talking about. "See, that's what I mean right there," he said. "That perfect curve, and then how it goes in here and then ends in that ankle. It's really fucking awesome," he concluded.

He had done all of this with a nonchalant sincerity. I couldn't detect any sleazeball qualities in his tone of voice at all.

"Whatever," I said, pretending I wasn't immobilized by the situation.

Nobody had ever done anything like this to me—praised a part of my body like a work of art. It turned me into this *thing*. Like a monster, but the beautiful kind. It felt good. Despite what my facial expression might have been, I really wanted it to be true—what he said about my legs. Without ever having given much of a shit, I suddenly craved the kind of superiority that he said I had over other girls.

"To be honest, I've noticed your legs a lot," he said. "I'm kind of obsessed with them. At first, I was thinking you should wear your skirt shorter," he went on, encouraged by my silence, "but then I changed my mind about that because there's something really sexy about knowing what's under there but not getting to see it, except sometimes if I'm lucky. It's like your legs are a secret that nobody knows about."

I pulled my legs under my skirt. "Gross," I said. "My legs are not your special secret."

But I hadn't stood up and left. I was still sitting there, with my arms wrapped around my knees.

"Well, I was going to make a sandwich. You wanna come?" he asked, jerking his head toward the dormitory building.

"Make a *sandwich*?"

"Yeah."

"Like, literally?"

"Yeah. How else would I make a sandwich?"

"I don't know."

I figured maybe there was a sexual way to "make a sandwich" that I wasn't aware of.

"I'm hungry," he said, "and I brought sandwich supplies, which I'm going to assemble. You can come if you want. The cooking sucks ass here during the holidays."

He was right about that.

"Fine," I said, getting up from the ground.

It surprised me as much as it seemed to surprise him that I was on board with the sandwich.

"Cool," he said, giving me a wink.

Immediately, I wished I hadn't agreed to the sandwich. The wink was unbearably cheesy. It was like people high-fiving—you couldn't get away with that kind of thing unless you were Mr. Sorrentino, which Derek was not. *There is nothing cool about him*, I thought. *Nothing mysterious. Nothing beautifully tragic. Just nothing.*

However, being alone and bored was terrifying just then, and I jolted back into motion, following him. We walked silently to the common room, which had a small kitchen area. We made a couple of sandwiches and then ate them sitting at one of the tables. There was almost no dialogue during all of this until we had eaten about half our food.

"So what have you been doing here since the break started?" he said, holding his sandwich in front of his face, about to take another bite.

"Nothing."

There was some more silence as we ate.

"I might be going into town later if you want to come," he said. "We could see a movie or something."

"Eww," I said. I managed to add, "No, thanks."

He smiled. "You're an unpleasant person," he said with the thick-as-fuck, charming smile steady on his face.

"*You're* an unpleasant person."

"I'm not, actually. I get along with everyone."

"Except the kids you beat the crap out of."

"Hey, I thought we'd moved on from that."

Again I wanted to get up and leave, and again I didn't. The situation was somehow addictively bizarre. This was Derek McCormick. He was sitting here taking my crap and apparently enjoying it. He was applying his notorious sleazeball charm—on *me*. It was ridiculous. But I kind of wanted to see what would happen.

"I'm going to let you in on a little secret," he said, leaning over the table to secure our privacy, which was all just for show since there was no one else around anyway. He lowered his voice and whispered, "You're fucking hot as hell, Gracie."

I scooted back in my chair. It was a reflex. Like a flinch at an asteroid making straight for you.

"I'm serious," he said, enjoying my reaction. "You have this crazy little body that you don't even know you have, which makes it even better. In fact, I've got this whole theory that if you were a little less weird and mean and also, you know, dressed better and stuff, none of these girls would stand a chance against you. Connie—I mean, yeah her body is nice, but she knows it, and dealing with girls who know how hot they are can be a lot of work. She's boring too, if you want to know the truth. She likes to talk about how the bread in Germany is so much better than here, or how German gummy bears fucking rule the world."

Connie was Constanze Koch. The Amazonian German girl that was his girlfriend.

"First of all: gross. What the hell's your problem? And secondly, German gummy bears do rule the world," I said. As an afterthought, I added, "And you're lucky Connie even lets you near her."

He laughed. "Hey, Connie is great. I'm not saying she's not. All I'm trying to say is you're up there. Not even a competition."

"That's not funny."

"Hey, you'll figure it out for yourself in a year or two when everyone else figures it out too. Just thought I'd give you the heads-up."

"I'm gonna go puke now," I said, pushing my plate with the half-eaten sandwich at him. "Bye."

I got the hell out of there before he had a chance to say anything else, almost running down the same Swiss kid I had watched TV with the day before as he was making his way around the corner. I stayed in my room for the rest of the day, reading and getting up occasionally to study myself in Georgina's full-length mirror, holding the T-shirt up over my bra to get an accurate read on the status of my body.

The thing about Derek was that he was *Derek*. He wasn't some pimply faced virgin daring to have a crush—gingerly prodding the realms of female existence. Derek McCormick didn't have crushes. He had sex. Presumably a bunch of it— with all the beautiful, top-shelf girls at school. When he picked girls out, they responded, because it meant something when he did the picking out.

It was a system I had only ever observed from the outside. I had cringed a few times, witnessing it in action—the natural dismissal of a girl's existence as a person and the evil way in which the system invited the girls themselves to shift all their worth over to their physical assets. I couldn't ever decide what was worse—not being pretty enough to be eaten up by the system and therefore unceremoniously tossed aside like a defective toy (e.g., Georgina); or making the grade and being forever haunted by your most accidental virtues—DNA. Beth Whelan was really the only girl I'd ever met who remained somehow superior to the system, despite her beauty and curves.

I hadn't been involved in the game up until that point. I had been too much of a nonentity. Off the grid, off the radar. Invisible. I had no ambitions other than perhaps to one day grow up and be allowed the dignity that I imagined came automatically with adulthood. I didn't believe I had the wherewithal to be part of the game even if I had wanted to be part of it. And yet, here was Derek McCormick telling me I had a crazy little body. (Crazy in what way?)

The next day, he sat down with me at lunchtime. I had my composition book open and was working on my novel. The part where Boris gets adopted by a prostitute.

"So, you want to have another sandwich with me later?" Derek asked in a suggestive manner.

"Not really."

"Why not? You got something better to do?"

"Yeah."

"See, you're shitting on me," he said, a little of that gleeful hyena spark back in his eyes. "I love that about you! You're totally not in a position to shit on me, but you are. I mean, look at the way you're dressed."

"If you feel shat upon, it's accidental," I said flatly. "I'm actually writing a novel, if you have to know. It has nothing to do with you."

"Oh, man, that's even better!" he said. "You're blowing me off so you can write shit in your book! That's so awesome. Connie would never do that."

I closed the composition book. "Just . . . can you *not* be creepy like that, please?" I said. "I'm a totally different person from Connie. There's zero point in comparing us."

"Yeah, you *are* a totally different person. That's exactly it." He did this thing where his eyes burrowed into mine, as though delving into my soul—except my soul did not feel the delve at all, and so I knew it was one of his well-oiled asshole maneuvers. "You're totally different from Connie—from any of the girls here," he said.

But even if I didn't feel our souls connecting, it was creepy how good it made me feel to have him elevate me beyond the reaches of someone as perfect as Constanze—not just Constanze but girls in general. When he said I was different from everyone, he really meant I was different from all girls. With one sentence, he had lifted me out of a sea of "all girls" and made me unique, while the rest of them remained clumped together in a sad, collective cluster. It was hard not to take that bait. I became a little fidgety.

"Come on," he said, the smug charm thickening around him like a fog. "It's not *that* bad to have someone be into you, is it?"

I sighed in exasperation. There was a fine line of thrill and unease and pleasure and disgust that I was dealing with.

"Why the hell do you know those *Masters of Baroque* guys?" I asked. "It's bugging the fuck out of me."

He looked taken aback for a moment. And then I could see him processing the question and a new breed of mental activity take place in his head. The hyena spark in his eyes flickered out.

"I'm in the school orchestra," he said with a slight frown. "I play the trumpet."

"No, you don't." This was about the most bizarre thing I'd ever heard of in my entire life.

"Yeah, I do," he continued, looking at me like I was fucking with him, which must have been the exact same way I was looking at him. "My mom made me start taking lessons when I was about five. You seriously didn't know I was in the school orchestra?"

"Why the hell would I go see the school orchestra play?" I asked. "There's nothing mentally wrong with me."

"All right, all right," he said, holding up his hand. "We're not *that* bad. If you liked Mr. Ellerman's CD, you should come to the next performance because we're doing Bach."

"You're full of shit. You don't play the trumpet."

"I'm telling the truth."

It was unnerving having a civil conversation with Derek. Unnerving because when you decide anything about anyone and you have that set in stone, it's nearly impossible to have a new opinion about it. This was the guy who used girls like toilet paper and kicked kids who were already on the ground and drove his hands through his hair every third second. I hadn't seen the trumpet coming.

"I'm what they call a virtuoso," he was saying.

I laughed. "You're so incredibly full of it."

He wasn't, though. We went to the music room, and he got out a trumpet from this little case and started screwing it together and doing all this preparatory stuff to it. I played around with the marimba for a bit. When he was ready, I left the marimba alone and turned to watch him, making a big show about how bored I was by this.

"Okay, this is a part from the Brandenburg Concerto no. 2."

"Interesting choice of Brandenburg concerto," I said. "I would have gone with no. 16 myself."

"All right, just get ready to have your world rocked," he said.

"You can't 'rock' someone's world with a trumpet."

"If you shut up, I'll prove you wrong. And also, you should know that this is like one of the hardest trumpet solos to play."

I rolled my eyes.

He lifted the trumpet to his face, took a concentrated breath, and then began to play. The sound that filled the room was loud and clear and haunting, the melody moving under and over itself, creating complex patterns and musical shapes that infiltrated and hypnotized me the way that the music on Mr. Ellerman's CD had done. It went on for a while. I couldn't have said how long. I kind of got lost in it. When he was done, Derek stared expectantly at me, catching his breath, trumpet by his side.

"Pretty cool, huh?" he said.

"I guess."

It wasn't fair that Derek was a trumpet virtuoso. He wasn't the kind of person who should have complexities like that that I'd have to deal with.

"I still don't like you, though," I said. "Just for the record."

He sat down next to me. I felt like I had lost some battle. It was the trumpet playing. My whole headspace was off-kilter now.

"I think we should kiss," he said in a low voice next to me. It was more of a breath than a normal, verbal sentence.

I looked over at him and found his face unexpectedly close to mine.

"You're not my type," I said, scooting back a bit. "And can I also remind you that you're dating Constanze?"

He moved a strand of hair from my face. "It's not like I'm her boyfriend or anything. She knows that."

"You sit together to eat, and you walk around together," I said, moving the strand he had just tucked behind my ear back into my face.

"I can be friends with girls, can't I?"

"I fucking doubt it."

He didn't bother responding. His hands were now on my face, pulling it slowly close to his own face. I let it happen because when it came down to it, I was curious, in the plainest sense of the word. I had never kissed anyone before. I didn't *want* to kiss him, but I was interested in the circumstances. And so, just like that, my first kiss had materialized out of nowhere. It was the most mechanical thing that I had ever experienced. His mouth opened around mine and then his tongue was in my mouth, wet and warm. It moved around a bit and then retreated back into his own mouth and our faces detached.

Derek's eyes opened as he pulled back. There was a breathless, almost religious look on his face. I had seen plenty of kisses in films and had consequently deduced that kissing was something that would turn your soul inside out—something that would explode your reason, rearrange your cell structure and generally destroy your sanity in the greatest way possible.

"It's so anticlimactic," I said.

His expression fell a little. "Have you ever kissed someone before?" he asked.

"Yeah. Lots of times."

He clearly took this as a *no* and went on to give me instructions. "Okay, well, for starters, close your eyes when I move in. And then, when I draw back, kind of start closing your lips around mine—you wanna try to do that roughly the same time I start doing it. In other words, don't just leave your mouth hanging wide open at the end. Oh, and put your tongue in my mouth. But, like, with feeling, not just push it in lifelessly."

"Why don't you draw me a flow diagram while you're at it?"

"Come on, just do it the way I said. I know what I'm talking about."

"Screw you. I'm over this."

But whatever. The second kiss was better, and by the fifth one, we had worked it out. Our faces fit together, my tongue began to know what to do, and suddenly there was a rhythm, and it just flowed. His hand moved through my hair, and at least that felt good—like traces of a head massage. It was the first time that I stopped thinking for a second. Then Derek's hand moved down my back, and I pressed into him a little. That one small movement of mine made his whole body respond with a new level of urgency. A lot of mashing into me and his hands all over, trying to touch as much as they could. I wasn't particularly turned on by any of this. Derek, on the other hand, was fully invested. It was like he couldn't help it—eyes glazed over, possessed, seemingly robbed of his wits. Meanwhile, I was still on planet Earth, with my feet firmly planted on the ground, fascinated by my own untapped powers. Wondering, how did I have the ability to turn an almost grown man into something so desperate?

I was basically a god of some sort.

IT BLEW MY MIND THAT I HAD MADE OUT WITH A GUY.

Saliva of a male species had made it into my mouth by means of a tongue. It was pretty incredible—not the actual kiss, of course, just the fact that it had happened.

And things didn't stop there. Since the universe had clearly gone off the deep end and I suddenly had this sexual plotline to my life, I went with it. I was almost sixteen, after all, and some of girls in my grade were already having conversations about blow jobs they had given—a couple of them even discussed how the guys had come too fast and whatnot. I mean, they could have been making all that up, but I wouldn't have even known how to make that stuff up. My lack of experience had never bothered me before because, naturally: fuck everyone—I didn't need to be a sexual lemming. At one point, I had considered holding on to my virginity simply to spite the norm. However, "the norm" never realized that I was spiting it, so eventually I stopped caring either way. But now . . . I didn't know. Here was Derek, and we had four days left until everyone came back to school, and there was literally nothing else to do. So, we started messing around. In the empty music room, down the back stairs to the utility rooms, once even in the teacher's lounge when we found it empty with the lights turned off.

On the day before everyone returned to school, I thought about what Beth had said to me—the thing about how beneficial it would be for me to lose my virginity. How it would help me be "less of a worm." I thought about it a lot. I was really, *really* dying to be less of a worm. And plus, she had said not to lose my virginity in a special situation. I looked over at Derek, who was sitting next to me on the sofa in the common room, eyes on the TV. Derek was practically the most non-special way of popping my cherry imaginable. It was perfect. I was totally not into him in that way. This was exactly what Beth had been talking about.

And so it happened. I won't go into extreme detail, because no one needs that. I will, however, say that just as with the kissing—more so perhaps—the loss of my virginity was not half as neat as they had always made it out to be in movies. It was kind of like ramming down a door that had been locked from the other side, and the job required concentration and a lot of energy. On a scale of 1–10, the sensuality and romance of the situation was probably a -2. As I said, it was perfect. I couldn't have planned it better.

It happened a few hours past midnight. I was lying on my bed, almost fully dressed except for my underwear, which I had removed from under my skirt before I'd lain down because that seemed like an unavoidable necessity to what we were trying to achieve.

After some kissing and initial groping around and arguing about me taking all my clothes off (we settled on leaving my skirt on and pulling the T-shirt over my breasts but leaving the bra on), we got started. It took a surprisingly long time for Derek to "break through," and while he was thrusting around inside of me, I began to giggle, because—*what the hell were we even doing?* The whole thing suddenly seemed so abstract. How was the world revolving around this stupid activity? How did people get worked up about this and shoot each other out of jealousy and ruin each other's lives to feel better? For *this?* The whole planet was nuts as far as I was concerned.

Derek stopped thrusting, his trance interrupted. "What?"

"Nothing."

But I was still giggling.

"*What?*"

"*Nothing!*"

"Why are you laughing?" Derek said, pausing. Thankfully, over the previous few days, he had dropped the greasy charm that he had smeared on so thick initially. Underneath it, he was far more high-strung than he had let on.

"I'm sorry, but it's just so weird," I said. "You have to admit it's weird!"

"What is?"

"*This.* When you really look at what we're doing right now—I mean, what *is* this? And by the way, you have this look on your face that's really similar to when you're playing the trumpet. I swear to God, it's so weird—it's, like, the exact same expression!"

He propped himself up, and the religious/trumpet look wavered momentarily, replaced by a restless frown. "Okay, can you try to be normal about this, please?" he said.

"*You* try to be normal about this."

"I *am* being normal about it."

"Well, I'm sorry, your face isn't being normal about it at all."

"Just . . . just shut up at least, okay?"

"*You* shut up at least."

Anyway, it finally worked. I stopped being a weirdo about it, and Derek looked at my boobs for a second, the glazed look returned to his eyes, and we were back in business.

The next day, I woke up around noon and then remembered I wasn't a virgin anymore. The sunlight spilled over my face, and I smiled. It was going to be a whole new world. I showered, brushed my teeth, put on some lipstick Beth had given me, and smoked a cigarette out the window of my room. Then I braided my hair into two pigtails and went so far as to use some eyeliner. It was messy, since I never used eyeliner much, but it felt appropriate to try to make more of an effort now that I was no longer a worm.

I found Derek sitting in the dining hall for lunch. He looked up when I came in, and his face registered surprise at my abnormal appearance. I wondered whether I had to walk over there and sit with him now that he'd been inside of me; and after trying to convince myself that I did not have to sit with him, I ended up walking over there with my food all the same.

"Hey," he said with a small smile.

"Hey."

"You look pretty."

"Thanks." I sat down.

"So everything functioning—normal—down there?" he asked.

"Yeah—I *guess.*"

"Okay, good." He said, running his hand through his hair. "I've never done that before—you know, de-virgined someone."

"Wait, you've never slept with a virgin before?"

He shook his head. "Nope."

For reasons not totally known to me, this was unnerving—the fact that I had been the only virgin in his life. It had been better when I'd imagined he deflowered girls as a matter of routine. Now I couldn't help feeling that what had happened between us had been somehow weighted. I had been an innocent flower that he had introduced to the world, so to speak. Great. All I'd wanted was to mechanically lose my virginity, and now I felt like I had somehow deflowered *him*. He sat there, regarding me tenderly, like I might break if he breathed wrong.

"Look, normally, having sex is awesome," he went on, his voice respectfully lowered and apologetic. "I know it was weird yesterday, but trust me, sex is normally . . . It's just really unlike anything you can experience."

"Yeah, I can imagine," I said, starting in on my lunch, which was a small pile of toast with butter.

"I don't want you to think what happened yesterday is actually what it's like."

"Okay," I said, stuffing more toast into my mouth.

"Once you have an actual orgasm, you'll see what I'm talking about. Sometimes that just takes a little practice for girls."

"Yeah."

This was not Derek as I knew him. This wasn't even baroque-trumpet-playing Derek. I didn't exactly know what this was. I would go so far as to say he looked fragile in a large, meaty kind of way. Over the last few days, we had reached a level of comfort that allowed us to be partially naked in front of each other, yell at each other, grope and stick tongues into the other person's mouth, tear each other's lives apart, embarrass each other, be embarrassed without caring much, and lastly: copulate. But now it seemed that this calloused layer had evaporated and it was painful to talk about *anything*.

"So, school starts back up tomorrow," he said.

"Indeed."

"It's going to be kind of weird—all those people all over this place again. I think I'm going to miss this—how quiet everything is right now."

"I was getting kind of bored."

Hand through hair. "Well, we had fun, though."

"Yeah, but I'm sure it'll be a relief to have Constanze back, real woman that she is. I bet she doesn't call you a hamster while giving you a hand job. And she probably makes all the right noises during copulation."

I was trying to be light about the situation, but Derek looked pensive.

"She does," he said. "She always makes all the right noises."

After a moment, I said, "You're not going to tell her what happened, right? I wouldn't in a million years have done any of that stuff with you if you guys were fully together—you said you weren't a couple."

"Why would I tell her anything?"

"I'm just making sure."

I drove another toast into my mouth. I was not hungry anymore—if anything, I was repulsed by the thought of more toast, but I couldn't just sit there and not do anything with my hands.

"Hey, regarding the . . . *sex* . . ." I said through a mouthful of carbs.

His eyes flicked up, alert with hope.

I continued. "Obviously, it was nuts that that would have happened between us because—well, for obvious reasons— but it *did* happen, and whatever—it was nuts, but really it was also kind of a win-win situation for those particular circumstances."

"Yeah, totally. It was," he agreed, beginning to look unsure about where I was going with this.

"And now we're here."

"Yeah."

"On this plateau, so to speak."

"Right."

I hesitated for a moment because the way I was talking and using words was confusing even to myself. Who the hell says *copulation* every three seconds? Or *plateau*, for that matter?

Derek was paying close attention, waiting for the point.

"I guess what I'm trying to say is: you definitely don't have to worry about me being some kind of nutcase about this," I said. "I'm not, like, attached to you now emotionally or anything like that. Like, at all."

I had eaten all the toasts on my plate.

"Okay, cool," Derek said. "You wouldn't believe how some girls get when you sleep with them. This one girl left me a note every day for about a year and a half. Every fucking day, there'd be a note in my locker."

God, what a dickweed, I thought. And I was glad I could see him as such again. I kind of needed him to be a dickweed for things to make sense.

"Well, that sucks," I said, "for the girl probably more than for you, but fine—I can see how hard that must have been, opening your locker every day with the terrifying anticipation of yet another note."

"See, that's why I don't like you," he said with a small smile. "You're mean."

I got up and grabbed my tray. "Yup."

Beth had been spot-on about the "having sex in a non-special way" theory. It was clearly the best way to do it. If people only slept with people they didn't like, it would simplify everything. There'd never be any kind of mess afterward. No meaningful strings of romantic goo attaching you to whoever you slept with, keeping you nauseous and miserable and psychotic for weeks and months and years, until the feelings finally ran out.

Anyway, as I said, I felt pretty fantastic about having lost my virginity. I felt good about everything all day long—and that's saying a lot, because "good" feelings didn't usually have much stamina. I cleaned my room and washed my bedding, imagining how I would tell Beth about the sex with Derek. It had been perfect. All that stuff I had done with Derek—if I had done any of it with Wade instead, it would have been a disaster.

And then my merry little train of thoughts came to a crash. *Wade.*

I was in the laundry room pulling clean sheets out of the dryer, and I froze at the thought of him. I could feel my stomach crawl up my throat and the guilt drive into me like a bullet. I had no romantic obligations toward Wade, that was true, but I was presumably his best friend, and as such, I owed him the courtesy of not having sex with his nemesis, right? And then I remembered that hug before he'd left, which had been more loaded than anything I had done with Derek, and plus how he had told me that he was "kind of in love" with me, and I felt sick all over again. But I had never encouraged romantic feelings with Wade. How he felt wasn't my fault. But then again, I did also let him put his head on my stomach. *But so what?* Putting a head on a stomach didn't mean anything. Yeah, but that wasn't true, because I would never have let anyone else put their head on my stomach. Except Mr. Sorrentino, but that went without saying and would never happen anyway.

"Everything okay?" someone asked.

It was Anju Sahani. She was Indian, second generation, and all I really knew about her was that she was in my grade and had cool friends. She was wearing a yellow polyester '60s dress, cut off to make it very short, with ruffles around the collar. The whole vision of her was so displacing just then. Her black, glossy hair was parted in the middle and clipped to the sides of her face with the help of two plastic barrettes. Magenta lipstick, nose ring, and crazy, fake-looking, real eyelashes.

"Yeah," I said. "I'm just doing laundry."

"Same here. Did you just get back?" Anju began loading her stuff into one of the washers.

"No. I stayed here."

"Wow, you did? Why?" She continued loading laundry into the washer, acting natural, as though that's just what you did—striking up pleasant conversations with people that you usually didn't talk to.

"Oh. Just to catch up with schoolwork," I said.

"I've always wanted to stay here for a vacation week. Must be cool with everything being empty, right? Like living in a haunted hotel or something. Or was it just boring?" She glanced over her shoulder at me with friendly curiosity.

"No, it was fine."

"Cool. Yeah, I want to try it sometime—get, like, a whole group of friends to stay here with me. I bet nobody even makes sure any of the rules are being followed. God, I just fantasize about breaking all those dumbass rules. Like, I'd probably just run down all the hallways all the time and use the snack machine after 8:00 p.m. and use my phone in the dining hall."

She was bubbly as hell.

"You should hang out with us sometime," she said after she had closed the lid of the washing machine. "If you want."

She was friends with Angela and Chandra and Natalie—all the girls who lounged around together in their rooms, listening to music on the weekends, doing their homework together, and laughing and presumably braiding each other's hair.

"Yeah," I said. "Thanks. I should."

"We've tried to invite you to hang out before." Anju stared at me with a tentative smile. "You should come sit with us some-time at lunch or dinner," she added after a moment.

I nodded with no intent of ever doing so. "Yeah, that would be fun," I said.

Her smile suddenly widened. "Unless of course you're too busy hanging out with Wade Scholfield."

"Wade?"

"Yeah," she said, still smiling. "You're with him all the time."

"Oh." I shook my head. "No, we're just friends."

"You guys seem so close, though."

"Well, we are. We're probably best friends, I guess."

"I didn't know that was possible—being best friends with a guy."

"Why wouldn't it be possible?"

"Okay, maybe with one of those aviation-club guys or some-thing, but I mean, not with a guy like *that*."

I stared at her, confused. "A guy like what?"

"Wade." She added slowly and a little self-consciously, "He's hot. And kind of a dork at the same time, and that makes him even hotter."

"Wade is?"

"Yeah! Don't you think so?"

"I mean, I *guess*."

She laughed a little. "And that doesn't distract you?"

I finished pulling the sheets out of the dryer to make the moment a little less terrible. "I guess I see him differently," I told her. "He's just a person to me—like anyone, and his per-sonality is what matters. And he has a really good personality."

Anju seemed truly fascinated. Her dark eyes were wide and deep—I could see the thoughts climb across them. "You're like an advanced human being," she said.

I screwed up my face, not at all certain what to make of this ludicrous proposition.

"No, you *are*," she insisted more emphatically. "I can't even function around guys. It's like something inside of me clicks and all those parts of my brain that learned how to be a normal person who can talk and walk and pick up objects—it's like those parts of my brain are out of bounds when a boy talks to me. Like, for example—okay: Ryan Green once held the door open for me when I had my arms full of stuff, and I was just like 'Yup!'" She squeezed her eyes shut with a grimace.

"Why'd you say *yup*?" I asked, not understanding.

"Exactly!" she shrieked. "That's exactly my point! Why didn't I say *thank you*?"

I laughed a little, despite how uncomfortable everything was technically making me. "I'm no good around boys either," I admitted. "I can be really mean to them, though. I'm good at that, but that's about it. I'd probably have said, 'Fuck you,' if Ryan Green held the door open for me."

"That's not true," she said. "You're *friends* with a boy, and I've seen you guys together—you're so comfortable around each other. Not like other couples in school with all these lame little rules and games going on. You're just real. I mean, honestly, we're all kind of jealous of what you've got going on."

That freaked me out on a level I couldn't compute. Just the idea that all their eyes were on us. "Well, Wade is different, I guess," I said, feeling nervous again.

"Hell yeah." She tilted her head with a mischievous smile. "I get why you'd rather hang out with him all day than with us, but if you're ever bored, just say hi, okay?"

"Yeah," I said. "For sure."

I went back to my room feeling that everything had somehow gotten worse. It was bad enough that I had slept with Derek—that was a disaster that continued to crystallize with every passing moment into a more perfect pile of shit—but the way that Anju in her bright yellow 1960s dress talked about

Wade had left me unsettled. In a strange way, it made something inside of me come alive—the way her eyes had gone helpless for a moment when she'd said his name. It made him more necessary to me. It made him more mine. It made me detest Derek more. It made the whole world balance on something as precarious as the tip of a needle.

Georgina showed up after dinner and talked to me about volleyball, and this guy Chad that I didn't even know, and her goals for growing out her hair this semester. I began to feel better almost right off the bat. Being hijacked like this into the realm of Georgina's unfathomably strange existence was medicinal. I asked her all kinds of questions, and she brightened up, and we spent the rest of the night talking about the most mundane crap imaginable. It was nice. And as I sat watching Georgina talk, I realized that she was a human being with a whole complicated life attached to her. And then I thought, *Maybe everyone is a human being?* Anju Sahani and Derek and Wade. Probably even Beth Whelan. It was a humbling thought. We were all human beings, terribly intertwined in each other's lives. Everything I did potentially set off a chain reaction of events that could end up at someone else's doorstep.

"Are you listening?" Georgina asked.

"Totally listening," I said. "Chad knows swing dancing."

WADE WAS A DAY LATE GETTING BACK TO SCHOOL,
and the anxiety and loneliness of that first day of lessons—
the crowded hallways and the dining hall—without him hung
heavily over me. Sitting alone for meals with the school so full
and alive again was unbearable. I looked over to where Beth
sat with her friends. She smiled quietly, watching the others
as they screamed out conversations to each other and laughed.
Beth and I were probably friends, but there was no way I could
sit at that table with the top-of-the-food-chain senior girls. It
simply wasn't something that the fabric of reality would be
able to handle.

I looked over at the table where Anju and her friends were
sitting. She caught my eye and waved me over. I waved back,
but I didn't walk over to them. Instead, I got up, threw my food
in the trash, and left the dining hall.

I almost made it through all my classes, but when the last
lesson of the day came around, which was a computer science

class, I decided I'd skip it. I had two cigarettes left that Beth had given me, and I wandered out to the front gate with the vague notion that I would walk off the school's property and never come back. I lit the first cigarette and indulged in the romance of this fantasy. Abandoning all the unforeseen spectacles of life that had oozed unsolicited from the dark crevices seemed liberating. I had never asked to betray my best friend by means of sexual intercourse—that was far too sophisticated a way to fuck up for me. It had just happened. I sat down on the ground, ultimately far too lazy to run away and seek a blank slate. I examined a mosquito bite on my left leg without much interest and took my time with the smoke of the cigarette, pulling it as deep as it would go.

Maybe being a virgin had been better, after all, I thought. In a way, I felt like more of a worm at that moment than I ever had before.

I looked up at the sound of a car turning into the entrance driveway. Scrambling to my feet as the car slowed down, I dropped my cigarette quickly and stepped on it. It was one of those airport shuttle cars. It rolled to a stop, and I thought for sure some administrative person was coming back to school from their holiday and I'd have a lot of explaining to do. I began to frantically assemble a story in my head but stopped when the car door opened and it was Wade who got out of the back seat.

"Gracie?" he called over, shielding his eyes from the sun.

All I could see was half his face, and already I realized the magnitude of his absence and the magnitude of his presence—and the magnitude of Wade in general.

"What're you doing out here?" he called.

"Nothing."

I began walking toward him, downplaying my elation and my terror. "School started yesterday," I said.

"I know. I'm late."

His clothes looked like he had slept in them. He was wearing an old T-shirt with the Ghostbusters logo on the front, and there were pen marks all over his arm—what looked like childish doodles. He was also wearing a little girl's necklace—small turquoise plastic beads with a heart pendant.

"Come on," he said, "help me carry my stuff upstairs."

"You really need help carrying your stuff?"

"Yeah, what's your problem? Come on."

Blatantly disregarding my stiff reserve, he put his arm around me and gave me a squeeze. It was short and friendly in nature, but it was also honest, and I could feel my bones relax, as though I'd been holding myself up in an unnatural and painfully crooked way for the last week.

"So, what did you do while I was gone?" he asked once we were in the car.

I had to look away because all I saw was Derek, naked on top of me, thrusting with the religious look on his face. I blinked the memory out of my mind frantically.

"Nothing," I said.

"Yeah? That's a lot of time to be doing nothing."

"Maybe I did *less* than nothing—if that's mathematically possible."

"Actually, it is mathematically possible," he said, "but it's not possible in real life. You can't do 'minus nothing.'"

"Well, I really didn't do much," I said, looking out the window, watching the school's main building float into view. "I guess I read a bunch and listened to music."

I had officially lied to him. It made me sick.

I helped him bring in his stuff, which consisted of a plastic bag with socks in it, a backpack, and his skateboard.

"I hope these socks are clean," I said, holding the sock bag.

"They're new," he said, throwing open the door to his room. "My mom bought them yesterday."

I had never been in his room. It looked like a version of mine and Georgina's room, except it was not as cluttered and it smelled different. His roommate wasn't there, as the school day was not yet over, and the privacy was a little overwhelming. I placed the sock bag on the bed and crossed my arms, which is what I always did when it was hard to find a casual way to stand.

"Well, that's nice of your mom," I said fumblingly. "Buying you socks. It's pretty darn wholesome."

He glanced over from where he was emptying the contents of his backpack into a drawer. "You can sit down on the bed if you want," he said, stirring the clothes in the drawer with his hands to level them out—socks, underwear T-shirts, pants—all in the same stew of clothes.

I sat down carefully on the bed next to the bag of socks. "How was the reunion?" I asked, just to be talking about something far removed from Derek and his religious look. I wasn't sure whether I was nervous because I had never been to his room before and it felt so meaningful that I was sitting there on his bed, or whether it was because I hadn't seen him in a week, or because of what I had done while he was gone. Or because a girl like Anju might potentially be interested in him.

"Oh yeah," he said. "Terrific."

The edge in his voice gave me the chills a bit. "Why? What happened?"

He sat down on the floor with a dull, uncharacteristic lack of energy in his eyes. "Nothing much. Family shit."

"Oh."

"It's fine," he said before I could say anything else. "It wasn't anything out of the ordinary, to be honest. Maybe that's the worst of it. That everything is always so predictable. Even when you don't know exactly when it's coming, you can always count on it, you know? You can always count on taking it up the ass eventually."

He immediately rolled his eyes way up to the ceiling at his own words. "Sorry, I didn't plan on being such a whiny little bitch."

"No," I said, "don't be silly. It's nice seeing the whiny little bitch in you. You're kind of really good at it."

"Oh, thanks." He broke into an embarrassed smile. Somehow this was a massive relief. It had made me incredibly uncomfortable seeing his eyes go cold like that.

"Anyway," I added, "I guess at least you won't have to have another family reunion until like what—a year, right? Do you have those things often?"

"My relatives are actually all right for the most part. It's my parents I'm not a huge fan of."

It occurred to me that all the official facts I knew about him didn't add up to a whole lot. I knew he didn't have any siblings and that he lived in Georgia with his parents but didn't have the accent because he was twelve when they moved there. From Illinois or something. That was about it. I guess I hadn't exactly gone into detail about my own backstory either. Still, it was so strange imagining that Wade had a whole life—a home with a living room with curtains and décor on the shelves and wallpaper, and food smells coming from a kitchen, and rules about taking out the trash, and people that raised him. I had never thought about the background noise to his life before.

Eventually, I said, "Yeah, well, parents are the worst. Even when they're nice, they're basically hopeless dipshits. It's a law of the universe."

"Ha. Yeah."

"So, why aren't you a huge fan of your parents?" I asked.

He rubbed his eyes. "Because they suck." Then he laughed a little, genuinely seeing some kind of humor in his fate. "They suck big-time, Gracie. We all do—mushed-up together as a family. Me too. But they suck for sure."

"That's okay," I said when I was sure he wasn't going to expound on the matter. "My parents are certifiably insane. My mom, definitely. And my dad—he might be a lawyer, but I think just because he carries a briefcase around doesn't necessarily mean he's sound in the head."

I was so much less lonely just like that.

"It's fucked up, right?" I said, sitting up with new focus, "how you're born, and you never even had a choice about it? Two random people can just get together and *make* you. With no credentials or anything."

"Yeah."

"Like, if you want to drive a car, you have to take a test. Or if you want to be a cook, you need to take tests. I mean, listen—you need to learn stuff and take a test to paint someone's goddamn *nails*! But you want complete control over a living person? It's like, yeah, go ahead. Figure it out as you go along."

"Or don't. Nobody actually gives a shit."

"Right. Exactly my point!"

Wrong as it might have been, and as much as it creeped me out to see Wade gloomy, I felt a new unforeseen glow of intimacy thicken between us.

"You can sit on the bed if you want," I said. I realized he was sitting on the floor out of politeness to me. He must have picked up on the precarious way in which I sat perched at the edge of his bed, next to the sock bag, and decided I wouldn't feel comfortable if he were to sit down next to me.

I scooted over to the headboard. Wade got off the floor and lay down across the end of the bed, still giving me plenty of space.

"What's that all over your arms anyway?" I asked.

He held out one of his arms, covered in words and drawings. "Two of my cousins opened up a tattoo shop in their living room," he said.

"My Little Pony!" I said, taking his arm for a closer look. "Fuck yeah! I used to play with those."

"You did?"

"Yeah. For hours in the bathtub."

"I would have thought you played with decapitated Barbies or something."

"Shut up. I was adorable and sweet back then."

I followed the pen marks farther up his arm. Among the drawings of My Little Ponies and hearts and stars, there were some band names I'd never heard of drawn in wobbly, cartoonish-looking lettering. I twisted his arm a little farther.

"Hey!" he said. "You mind leaving my arm attached to my shoulder?"

"Stop being such a whiny little bitch." I followed the pen marks up his arm, and suddenly there was my own name, written in his cousin's cartoonish baby-lettering: *GRACIE* with an unsteady heart drawn around it. It had been way up his arm, hidden by the sleeve of his T-shirt, half discolored by one of those bruises he kept on getting from almost killing himself on his skateboard.

"You got my name tattooed on your arm," I said, looking at him, startled. "With a fucking heart around it."

He sighed. "Yeah, I know. I guess you'll have to deal with it."

I dropped his arm and started laughing. I don't know why I felt such a rush of relief just then. The room and everything in it seemed to expand back to its proper dimension, and there was space again. I lay down on my back next to Wade, and the two of us fell easily into our normal habits of conversation.

We listened to music and talked and lay on his bed. Our

conversation got lazy after a while, and we stared at the ceiling, saying things only occasionally. With the silence came new images of Derek and all the things we had done together. Finally, I looked over at Wade. His eyes were still fixed at the ceiling, but after a few moments of me staring, he turned his head and we were looking at each other. I couldn't take how blameless and tired he looked. It made what I had done so much more sinister in contrast. I was beginning to feel like a monster. He was everything that was the opposite of me. *I shouldn't be allowed to own him like this,* I thought.

I rolled over onto my side and lowered my face down to his. His eyes fell shut, and I kissed him. It wasn't a particularly long kiss. It wasn't a particularly deep kiss either. It was somehow just unthinkably simple. I rolled onto my back again, and for a while longer we continued looking at the ceiling as though nothing had happened. As though we hadn't just put our fingers into a crack to an alternate universe and pulled it wide open.

After a moment, I said, "I gotta go."

"Then get the hell out of here," he said.

I walked back to my room, spooked by my own stupidity.

Georgina wasn't around, and I decided I might as well try to figure things out on paper. Writing confusing things down in my journal sometimes helped to clarify them. It forced me to be explicit about blurry circumstances that would otherwise just come and go, perhaps never having fully been diluted and understood.

I kissed Wade because . . .

I paused here, my pen hovering over the open journal page, wondering why I had kissed Wade.

I kissed Wade because the circumstances demanded it.

But this, although true in a roundabout kind of way, was weak and useless in any practical sense. I crossed out the second half of the sentence and stared intently over at Georgina's side of the room, where my eyes focused on a framed picture she had on her bedside table of that guy Chad that she had told me all about, who I remembered her saying did an insane robot dance in drama class. It looked like she had probably ripped it out of the last yearbook. I stared hard at his features and felt that he looked a bit like a smug ferret. The kind of guy who knew he did a good robot dance and was going to shove it in people's faces whenever he could. He was probably only marginally aware of Georgina's existence, but that didn't matter, because Georgina had clearly claimed him. Maybe he was pretty cool, despite his smug look. *The robot dance actually speaks in his favor*, I thought.

I focused my attention back to what mattered.

I kissed Wade because I felt like a pile of shit.

This had the ring of truth to it, at least. What I had done with Derek was so unthinkable in Wade's presence—it felt like the only way out was to do something large enough to throw the past into its shadow. And who knows? Maybe I also did it to glue him down. To make sure Wade would never be able to leave, like a small animal that you pin down in a glass case for decorative purposes so that I could continue to suck the life out of him for as long as possible.

I put the journal away just as Georgina came back from her shower. I let her talk about volleyball for a while before we turned out the lights and fell silent. It can take a while for Georgina to shut up at night, but she fell silent quickly that particular night, and it probably had something to do with the unsuspecting, smug ferret whose picture sat on her bedside table.

The room was quiet far too quickly, and I began to trip up in the whole theory I had just worked out in my journal. It wasn't that I believed any of what I thought was not true. It was true. I loved Mr. Sorrentino, I regretted Derek, and I felt bad for Wade. Hence the kiss. The only problem was that the moment on the bed with Wade had maybe felt a little bit more like actual love than the biology teacher kind. So *was* I really still in love with Mr. Sorrentino? The quiet and dark of the room was suddenly too much.

"What do you think of Chad?" Georgina's voice came floating over through the dark.

I rolled over instantly to face her direction. "Oh, man, I think he's a really *real* kind of guy!" I was thrilled to bits that we were going to talk about Chad.

"That's true. He *is* real," she mused. "And I like his chin."

"Definitely a great chin," I said. "That's probably his best feature, actually. It's classy. Isn't that, like, a really manly quality? A good chin? Like something those guys have like Humphrey Bogart?"

I had never noticed a chin in my life, and I didn't even vaguely know what Humphrey Bogart looked like.

"What I also like is that he can take something seriously, you know?" Georgina was saying. "Like, he can be serious about stuff. Most of the boys in class act like they have to be idiots to be cool, but Chad just *is* cool. He literally can't help it. *Literally.*"

"Yep, exactly. And that's *so* rare. Don't take that for granted even for a second."

"I don't. Sabrina takes it for granted, though. I don't know why he likes her."

"What a bitch. Chad is too good for her."

I was still unclear as to who exactly Chad was, but I sure as hell didn't care. At that moment, I just wanted my life to consist of nothing other than Chad and Georgina and ideally Sabrina too. I wanted to know everything about Chad and his chin and the way that he took things seriously.

"Did you know he fly fishes?" she asked. "That's pretty cool, right?"

"Fuck yeah!"

We talked until Georgina eventually had to make me shut up because she was too tired to talk any more about Chad.

19

NOTHING WAS DIFFERENT THE DAY AFTER THE KISS
except that as we were walking to our last lesson, Wade yanked
me into a doorway and kissed me back. He didn't have the
religious look on his face the way that Derek had. There was
just a smile so faint that it was almost not there at all, like an
expression you might have while you sleep. He wedged me in
between the wall and door, leaned close over my face, and then
his eyes fell shut and so did mine. I would not have allowed
this to happen except that there was this perfect choreography
of the moment on his part. No hesitation, no faltering move,
no stumbling.

It was a much better kiss than the one I had given him the
day before, and instantly I had to wonder about who all the
other girls were that he had kissed to get this good. *There must
have been many girls,* I thought, unsure of how to feel about
that. But then it was suddenly too hard to concentrate on any
logical stream of thoughts because everything melted. It was
what I had expected a kiss to be all along. Even the bell in the

background added to the moment, supplying a soundtrack of urgency that made me dig my fingertips into Wade's arms. I could feel my stomach become light and unsteady as it began to register the weightlessness of the moment—like being flung through the air and my stomach trying to keep up. There was a taste of some kind of candy in his mouth, and when I opened my eyes slightly, I could see his closed eyes and the eyelashes on his cheeks.

We pulled apart, and Wade took a step back, pulling his shoulders up in a gesture that seemed to hint at the myriad of avenues to take into the future and his refusal to settle on any one of them. He was fighting a smile, but it broke out anyway when he looked to the floor. I crossed my arms tightly across my chest as some sort of feeling shot through my throat— the sinking feeling that ever since I'd known him, Wade had been *this* beautiful and I hadn't even noticed. And now that I did notice it, everything in my body began to hurt all at once. Full blast, like a fire alarm. It had snuck up on me because I had thought *good looking* meant a very specific thing—it meant that the guy looked like Derek—that asshole kind of smile, and the six-pack (no idea if Derek had a six-pack, but he seemed predictable enough to have one), the broad shoulders, and the stupid muscly neck. Or even like Mr. Sorrentino, who had the accidental dark and brooding looks of a dubious, romantic character from a Victorian novel. I had never imagined that it could mean Wade. The moment was oddly heartbreaking. I felt like I was losing Wade as I knew him. The safe version.

"What?" he said, studying me uncertainly. "What's happening?"

His eyes were so hauntingly beautiful. I wanted to vomit. "Nothing."

I had never felt bashful or scared around Derek. Everything had been so mechanical with him—romance was just fitting body parts into other body parts—nothing like this. This was . . . I didn't fully understand what it was.

"All right, come on, enough bullshit!" Wade said. He grabbed my hand, and somehow the day continued.

It seemed impossible that it would, but it did—without any deference to how absolutely changed everything would be from here on out. No visible cracks in the universe, no one acting any different—nothing.

I went to bed that night under the most mundane circumstances imaginable—with Georgina talking to me about this weird rash a girl on the volleyball team got under her armpit.

"The nurse thinks maybe it's like a fungal thing—like from too much humidity or something. It's weird because I've never even seen that before, and it's not like it's ever *not* humid, you know? Anyway, it's not super noticeable, but it sucks for Tracey because she can't use deodorant until the rash is gone, which could be a few weeks. Can you imagine not using deodorant for a few weeks? She's supposed to go on a date this weekend too."

"Huh," I said.

"Yeah."

After a thoughtful pause, Georgina added, "I'm so glad *I* wasn't the one who got it. Who do you think decides those things anyway? God?"

"I'm not sure God exists," I said.

"But what if he does exist—with all the important stuff he has to deal with every day, do you think he's also the one who decides who gets the fungal rashes?"

"Oh my god, you're insane, Georgie."

Georgina talked awhile longer before she finally ran out of steam, and just like every other night, she was the one who fell asleep first. I could hear her breathing even out as I lay staring at the ceiling. The ceiling was unchanged too. Everything refused to be altered.

But that was a lie. I was in love with Wade Scholfield. Therefore, due to the laws of physics and metaphysics and gravity and chaos math: everything had changed.

The next morning, when Wade sat down next to me for breakfast as he had done countless times before, I knew for certain that the simplicity of our bond had been obliterated. I knew this for a fact because of the strange way in which every part of my body became alive, demanding to be noticed. I could feel the inside of my fingers. My appetite dropped out of sight, and I began to cross and recross my legs with a manic urgency. Then I became suddenly worried that my eyes were not the right distance apart. I had heard a girl say her eyes were too close together the night before, and naturally I had written her off as psychotic—but what if *my* eyes were too close together? My heart tripped over itself in the pure terror of the possibility. While Wade talked, I tried to figure out whether I was breathing in double time or whether my breathing was at the normal speed at which I had always breathed. I thought I could feel the marrow in my bones as we walked to our first class, and then I almost tripped over my own feet because the rhythm of my steps threw me off. Wade caught my arm, and I thought for a moment everything inside of me would explode because he was touching me.

"What the hell?" he said with a laugh.

The more I tried to see Wade as I had before, the more the old version of him became extinct, and soon I couldn't remember him at all anymore—the way he was when I had met him. So I tried to fake it. I ignored his presence next to me and focused instead on the color of the walls or the haircut of the kid sitting in front of me. But like some backward mechanism of the universe, the intentional negative focus seemed to create a black hole of sorts that ate everything up, leaving nothing behind but Wade. By the end of the day, he was all there was.

His face, his body, his voice, his mannerisms. He was all I was capable of thinking about. Something as stupid as the shape of his lips or the thickness of his eyelids offered infinite depths to explore. I spent all of Algebra II trying to figure out the exact color of his hair, only to conclude that his hair was brown—something I had technically known to begin with. During computer science class, I thought about his arms— goddamn it, I loved how banged-up they were—and the blue of his veins in the crook of his arm. And other stuff. The strength in his fingers when he grabbed my arm to show me something. The way he always covered his face with his hand when he was embarrassed. His way of being on another planet sometimes, so much so that you had to shake him to get him to respond. The sharp canines. The laugh that exposed his soul to the elements.

Even the way he dressed. The striped T-shirts, and the neglectful quality of his clothes in general. Everything he wore was torn somewhere or had holes in it—somehow it was the perfect evidence of his method of existing.

God, it was everything. Everything about him.

I dissected him in my head as I walked down hallways and stood in line for food. I took him apart down to the cell structure of his being, down to the molecules, down to the atoms, and then I split the atoms.

I could only hope he was acting half as psychotic as I was.

I WAS LEANING AGAINST MR. SORRENTINO'S FORD
Taurus in the parking lot. It was Tuesday after school, and
most of the teachers who didn't live directly on campus had
already left. There were only a few cars parked in the lot. It
was hot, and I could feel my skin being eaten alive by the
sun. It didn't matter. I was going to do this. I was wearing
the stupid Busch Gardens baseball hat that I had gotten from
lost and found and was playing with a cigarette. I wasn't intending to smoke it, but my fingers were restless, and so I
flipped the cigarette over and over in my hand. Mr. Sorrentino slowed down when he saw me by his car. He stopped a
few feet away from me.

"I hope you remember that chapter on the respiratory system we did," he said, eyeing the cigarette with displeasure.

I stuffed the cigarette quickly into the pocket of my skirt.

"I'm still going to have to report that," he said. "You

can't be smoking on the premises. Or anywhere, for that matter."

"I wasn't even smoking!"

"Why don't you hand that over?"

"Are you serious?"

His hand remained outstretched.

"Oh my god. Fine!" I handed him the cigarette. "I didn't know you were such an elderly lady about the rules."

"Well, I am. And if you have something to say, I suggest you say it," Mr. Sorrentino said, glancing at his watch. "I have somewhere I need to be in less than ten minutes."

I thought about what *exactly* I wanted to say. He waited, looking impatient and shifting his weight around.

"I'm over you," I said unceremoniously. "I just wanted to let you know. I'm into someone else now, so you can relax."

For a moment, he was uncomfortably frozen. I couldn't remember right then whether either of us had ever openly acknowledged that I was in love with him.

"All right," he said carefully.

"And also, for what it's worth, I'm sorry for being such a fucking basket case, okay? Be—"

"Easy on the language," he said, interrupting me. "Your vocabulary is better than that."

"Wow. Can I apologize for a second? This is hard enough as it is."

He crossed his arms and waited for me to continue, pretending his fuse was running short. He was way too nice, though. His fuse was about forty miles long.

"Okay," I continued, picking up my train of thought. "So, I really shouldn't have said all that stuff about you just going through the motions about teaching. You're not that kind of teacher. You're like the only decent adult in this place. And biology isn't just a waste of time, I guess. At least for some people it's definitely not."

Mr. Sorrentino's face remained skeptical. "Does that mean you're going to focus back on your studies?" he asked.

"I doubt it," I said, honestly.

After a moment of studying me uncertainly, he said, "Well, I appreciate your apology, Grace, but I would still like for you to put some work back into biology."

"Yeah, I know you would."

He frowned. "I don't understand why you can't just make an effort. I've seen how brilliant you can be."

It still felt great to be praised by him like this. *Brilliant—who uses words like that?* I wondered. Especially to describe *me?*

"Thanks for always saying that kind of stuff," I told him. "It's pretty ludicrous—but thank you."

"Oh, you think I'm just trying to be *nice?* Why on earth would I try to be nice after the way you've been acting all semester? What I'm saying is the plain truth—you're a very intelligent, gifted student—I've seen it with my own eyes. I've read your essays, I've graded your tests. I'm not making this up."

I smiled. "You can't help being nice, Mr. Sorrentino. There's literally nothing you can do about it."

It seemed like he wasn't sure for a moment whether to be offended or flattered.

"Okay, look," I said. "I'm not saying I won't put any effort into my work, but I'm not going to go nuts about it either. It's just . . . I mean, biology—it's great subject matter, no doubt about it—but I'm not going to be a doctor or chemical engineer or anything. It's not your fault that I'm not. It's just who I am. I don't need to get straight As in biology to survive. I'm just being honest."

He got that passionate look in his face that he always got when he was fired up about something. "Grace, biology is the science of life," he said, flinging his right arm out to the side to emphasize the point. "*Life*. It's not just for people who want to become doctors. Biology is what's going on around us all the time. You don't think you need to know the fundamentals of the entire structure of everything around you?"

"I mean . . . not *really*."

He smiled reluctantly, like I'd won some kind of temporary battle, and began to fish for his keys in his pocket. "Well, you can try to ignore biology, but that's not going to change the fact that each cell in your body is a living kingdom."

Goddamn, he was adorable.

"True, Mr. Sorrentino. Very true."

"Knowledge is power, Grace."

And then, before he had a chance to continue spurting corny biology facts, I decided to steer the conversation into a more useful direction. "Hey, are you really in love with Judy?" I asked him. "I mean, like, *passionately*? Like, she's-all-you-can-think-about-all-the-time kind of love?"

He unlocked the door to his car and threw his briefcase into the passenger side. "I'll see you in class tomorrow," he said, ignoring my question and climbing into the car.

"Wait, this is a serious question!" I said, blocking the door so he couldn't pull it shut. "I just want to know what it's like when it's real—like a real feeling—being in love."

"Can I get to the door handle, please?" he said.

I backed off.

"Thanks," he said.

I wasn't going to get anything useful out of him. For a teacher who looked this hot and laid-back, he really had a stick up his ass about playing by the rules and not crossing any boundaries.

"Okay. Congratulations by the way on your engagement. Really. Judy seems nice. She talked to me a few times, and she always pats my arm or squeezes it, which is a nice gesture. Anyway, she seems cool."

"See you in class tomorrow, Miss Welles," he repeated, and then he slammed the door shut.

"Yeah. Bye."

I watched him pull out of the parking space and drive off.

APRIL WAS A GOOD MONTH. IT STARTED WITH ONE
of the ladies in the front office accidentally downloading a virus
that changed the backdrops of all the school computers to a
wallpaper of Nicolas Cage faces—a collage of them in all different sizes and expressions. And the great thing about it was
that since the computers were all interconnected, we too got
to enjoy the Nicolas Cage wallpaper on our laptops for a solid
week. Sadly, they called in a professional at that point, and the
backdrops went back to being of the school logo.

This was followed by the Freshwomen Unite protest where
the ninth-grade girls demanded that they be referred to as
fresh*women* rather than freshmen. The school was kind of
known for its protests ever since the legendary "BRAtest of
'96" ("*Ladies Show Support with Lack of Support*") when some
of the senior girls refused to wear bras for a week to make a
point about something or other, which naturally got lost in the
hubbub of the bralessness of the situation. Oh, and last but
not least, this guy Greg got into some trouble for pretending

his chicken nugget was a ray gun and aiming it at another student.

School could be entertaining, that was for sure, but almost nothing mattered much in the face of the unfathomable fact that I had a boyfriend.

I'd think about it sometimes without understanding any part of how it had come to be. Gracie + Wade. It had become a natural law in the way that all stable relationships at school become facts by which to orient oneself. At first, I found this public acceptance and sudden visibility intrusive. I didn't like how people made decisions about what Wade and I had, as though they knew any damned thing about us. I took offense to being thrown into the "high school couple" category with the likes of Porter + Brooke, Billy + Chandra, Jeremy + Nicole—all those shallow, hand-holding, lap-sitting, hand-job-bragging, prom-going duos that we had nothing in common with.

I noticed that girls occasionally gave Wade attention now that he was unavailable. I found it fascinating to watch how a girl like Eloise Smith, who had no genuine interest at all in Wade or the likes of him, tried to glue him to her all the same. She didn't want him. In fact, she was dating this guy Markus on the basketball team, but she wanted to make sure Wade was at least fantasizing about her, which was I guess her general expectation of all boys.

"Oh my god, Wade, can you do me the hugest favor ever and carry this for me?" she said, thrusting some stack of books into his hands. "Can they make books any heavier?"

Wade would say, "Sure." And Eloise cast a glance in my direction to make certain I was a witness to what was happening.

It was a spectacle I kind of enjoyed, actually. Especially since Wade obliged most favors asked of him, freak of nature that he was. He could hold books for girls and then walk away ridiculously oblivious to any of the traps that had been laid for him. He wasn't innocent or stupid; he was just wired weird. I felt a little bad for the girls who tried. Not that this was a regular occurrence by any means—Wade's social status was too ambiguous for that, but like Anju had pointed out and I had realized super late in the game: there were his looks, which I guess you could say really held up under scrutiny—so, yeah, some of the girls had to at least make an effort to get on his radar. Likewise, a few guys from our grade seemed to notice that I existed for the first time too. They didn't try anything. They were content to look me over, wondering if they were missing anything that should have been obvious. I tended to wear my clothes oversize, so it was hard for them to tell what was going on.

Anyway, none of it mattered. Nothing mattered. The novelty of our officialdom faded out soon enough, and after having been packaged off together, in the view of the school, we were more or less free to be in love at our own discretion. And we were. In love, I mean. Fully, utterly in love.

My grades going to shit was something I was only vaguely aware of in my very peripheral vision. It meant nothing to me, just like the whole world and all its consequences meant nothing to me. I didn't even care about the money issues or Georgina blasting *Cats*. Nothing hurt. It was weird. And if Wade had any cares, there was no evidence of it. He had always had an easy manner in the way he dealt with life, but now there was a true weightlessness to him. I could see the difference. In fact, that was probably the best thing about those days—seeing Wade happy like that. He was giddy. We were both giddy, I guess, but I got to see it in his face every day, and that became the proof—for pretty much everything.

"Oh dear *god*," Beth said.

She sat down next to me on the curb in the parking lot, where I was watching Wade and Calvin Meyer on their skateboards, getting obsessive about jumping over this bicycle rack thing. Calvin was a kid from our grade who had shoulder-length black hair and a band called Nonsexual Boner. He and Wade had hit it off one day when they were both stuck in Saturday detention and had become pretty good friends after that in an inevitable sort of way. The way that little kids become friends on the playground in about three seconds. I didn't mind their friendship. I appreciated it. It gave me a chance to play with a very safe kind of jealousy.

"What?" I asked Beth, a little embarrassed by the fact that I was caught red-handed, drooling over my boyfriend.

"You're so in love," she said. "It's disturbing."

I smiled and rubbed my face to try to hide some part of my predicament.

"I'm serious," she said. "The way you're sitting there with your head propped in your hand and your eyes all unfocused and dreamy, waiting like a good little girl for your boy to be done playing with his skateboard."

"Hey, I'm not waiting for him. I'm reading," I said, holding up *It*.

She smiled and ignored my protestation. "You know, it's a real pity that you've come to this. Especially after all that talking you did about how the two of you were just *friends* and how everyone else was living in the Stone Age if they couldn't handle that a boy and a girl might have a meaningful friendship. How clean and pure and fantastic and liberating it was to be pals like that. No strings attached—no mess. And yet, here we are," she said, "on a beautiful Sunday afternoon, and you're practically melting into a puddle of pink hormonal slush watching said boy ignore you."

I sighed, a little aggravated to have lost this battle but also incapable of being moody in my bliss. "He's not ignoring me, but yeah, I'm in love with Wade," I admitted, probably with my eyes all unfocused and dreamy like she had said. "He's all I think about every minute of the day. I probably don't even *have* a brain anymore. I'm probably 100 percent pure hormonal slush at this point."

"Nauseating."

"Yeah, but the thing is—it's *way* better this way. *Way* better. I'd choose hormonal slush over a brain any day."

Her eyes widened suddenly.

I looked at her warily. "What?"

"Have you guys *done it*?"

"Done what?" I could feel my blinking thrown a little out of rhythm.

Her mouth dropped open, and her eyes widened even farther. "You totally did!"

"What? No, we didn't!"

"Yeah, you did! You and that little shit had sexual intercourse!"

"Beth, I swear we didn't!"

She ignored me. "That would explain why you're a completely different person. Goddamn it, I knew something was up! I didn't really put it together until now—but yeah, of course—you're not a virgin anymore! *That's* what it is!"

"What are you talking about? I'm exactly the same!"

She shook her head. "No, you're not. Everything about you is different. Remember how I told you it'll make you less of a worm? Well, you're totally less of a worm! You have more confidence, and the way you move—everything. Good for you, Gracie! Fuckin' A!"

It was strange, I had wanted so badly to tell Beth that I was no longer a virgin, and now that she had figured it out on her own, I did everything I could to convince her of the opposite. Beth, however, didn't pay attention to any of it. She congratulated me and started asking questions, which I shot down, still insisting it didn't happen. I dreaded her figuring out it had anything to do with Derek. She was so good at taking one look at people and just *knowing* things.

"Ugh! I just wish you weren't in *love* with him," she said, looking grossed out by the notion. "Didn't I tell you to do it with someone non-special?"

"Yeah, well."

"Well, *what*? You did *exactly* the opposite! You should have done it with some random guy, preferably someone who kind of nauseates you. But now . . . I don't know, Gracie, you're kind of fucked now—pun not necessarily intended."

"I don't care. I wouldn't give up this feeling for anything," I said, closing my eyes to feel the feeling more perfectly. "I swear to God this is the reason any of us even exist—why the whole world even exists—so that we can feel this way."

"Gee-*eeez*," she said, throwing her head back dramatically. "That is totally and utterly the biggest untruth ever to see the light of day!"

"You can't know that."

"Yes, I can, because love is an *illusion*, G. It's a great marketing tool, but it's not an actual thing. It can't hold up to even the smallest amount of strain."

I shrugged off her comment with an abstracted smile.

"Art is the only real thing there is," Beth said.

"For *you*, maybe. I don't know anything about art."

"Not true. What about your band? You got their lyrics written on your shoes," she said, kicking my left Converse, where I had *Bored by the chore of saving face* written on the side of the sole. "Are you really going to tell me that Wade can save your life the way that music has?"

I had never thought to compare the Smashing Pumpkins to Wade, and it felt unfair and random that I should be asked to do so now. They weren't even the same category of "thing."

I moved my foot away and said, "Yeah. Wade already *has* saved my life."

She laughed, unconvinced. "Okay, fine. I am happy for you, Gracie. Kind of. *Maybe*. But there's an expiration date to this thing, you know that, right?"

I gave her a questioning look.

"Well, you know you're not going to end up marrying Wade and having his babies, right? Please tell me you know that, at least."

"I'm not interested in the future," I said. "It only gets in the way of now. And anyway, what if I do end up having babies with Wade? What if we get married and live happily ever after?"

She dissolved into laughter at this, her hair falling all over her face as she doubled over. "This is why I love you, Gracie," Beth said, wiping tears from her eyes and putting her arm around me. "You don't give a shit about the way the world actually works."

"I could say the same about you," I told her.

I was still not certain whether Beth and I were actual friends or whether I was some kind of protégé of hers—or maybe even just a toy. Somehow, it never seemed to matter what the exact foundation of our friendship was.

"Here comes your future husband," Beth said, nudging me.

We watched Wade walk toward us.

"Are you going to say something to embarrass me?" I asked Beth.

"I don't know. Maybe."

I had never seen Beth and Wade interact, and I watched not without some fascination at what the chemical reaction might be. In all the most obvious ways, they were polar opposites—godlike/human, clean/dirty, cold/warm, bad/good—and yet they were the only two people I knew that were somehow just who they *were*. No frills. No particular fucks given.

"Hey!" he called with that sunny disposition that always seemed so at odds with the hormonal quotient of our age group.

"You guys have met before, right?" I asked.

He sat down next to me.

"Not officially," Beth said, taking him in with a bored, half-assed smile, "but Gracie's told me all about you. For example, I know exactly what your eye color looks like in the shade and what it looks like in direct sunlight. Oh, and I also know a lot about the shape of your eyelids—the left one is a little thicker than the right. And your teeth, and the way you have a cowlick on the back of your head."

"Yeah, well, all those things are probably true," Wade said, with a small shrug, like there was nothing he could do about it.

"What about me?" Beth asked. "Did she tell you anything about me?"

He thought for a minute. "Um, yeah. She said you're really good at doing your lips—with the outline and everything."

"Wow. I can see I really left an impression on you," she said, giving my foot another kick.

"Well, I'm *sorry*," I said, "but it's not my fault you're good at lining your lips."

"Okay, hold on," Wade broke in. "I'm kidding. She also told me about your art and made me go look at all the drawings you have up in the art room."

Beth's eyes focused back on Wade. "Oh yeah? Did they blow your mind?" she asked.

"Yeah, you bet," he said. And then more seriously, "They definitely mess with your head, and once they're in there, it's hard to get them out. Not that I know what I'm talking about, but I'd say you're pretty good."

She regarded him for a second with a blatant, sober curiosity. "Huh. Gracie did say you were nice. She said if you saw a lawn mower accident and someone got mangled, you wouldn't secretly be excited that you had something to watch. I told her that most people probably wouldn't be excited to see something like that happen, but she insisted you were definitely different from the rest of the human race."

"Well, she has a pretty bleak opinion of the human race," Wade said, "but yeah, I wouldn't be into seeing someone mangled by a lawn mower. That's a valid point."

"All right," I said, cutting off the conversation before it could get any dumber than it already was. "That's great. Thanks, Beth. You can stop talking about the stupid shit I said now."

"Why? That's not even the tip of the stupid shit iceberg!"

I buried my head in my lap. I figured Beth was probably going to start talking about how I was planning our wedding next. She didn't go that far, however, and instead, I heard her cheerful and deceptively innocent laughter ring out over the background noises of a skateboard colliding with something solid and a curse.

Wade pulled me up and wrapped his arms around me in a way that must have been too adorable for Beth to handle, because she gave us a look of blatant repulsion.

"Well, I'm outta here," she said, getting up.

I dug myself out of his embrace.

"God, that was painful," I said when she was gone.

"Don't worry about it," he said, pulling me back. "You think I don't know the shape of *your* eyelids?"

"You know the shape of my eyelids?"

"Come on, Gracie. I know everything about your face—and believe it or not, I've noticed other parts of your body too. Parts that are *not* located in your face . . . if you know what I mean."

He flicked my arm lightly in the way that he had been doing ever since we were friends, and everything inside of me became that exact pink slush that Beth was talking about.

I put my head on his shoulder and said nothing. After a moment, we started to kiss. The background noises faded out, the world flickered away, and we found ourselves in a different dimension—the dimension of the make-out session, where time and space obey a foreign set of rules, and a minute is an eternity and vice versa. I can't say how long we were under, but we pulled apart when someone called Wade's name. Calvin was waving him over. Wade apologized and said he'd find me in a bit. He waited for me to shrug my approval before he gave me another kiss and got back on his skateboard. Walking back to my room, I felt light and a little unsteady in the pleasant unreality of reality. *Being alive is so easy,* I thought. *How had anything* ever *been hard?* I couldn't even remember. I glanced over my shoulder at Wade cracking up at something Cal was telling him. I pitied the rest of the world for having the bad luck of being neither Wade nor me.

THE THING IS, YOU CAN MAKE A BUBBLE AND SET up shop in it, creating a world where the laws of physics obey your own whimsical rules and the air smells exactly as you want it to and pleasantness abounds and the harsh light of reality cannot penetrate the confines of your fantastic little globular existence—but the fact remains that a bubble is meant for one purpose only. To burst.

I had forgotten about Derek. It seemed centuries ago that the sex happened, if it had happened at all. The deeper I got lost with Wade, the thicker the amnesia grew.

But here he was. I slammed the door to my room shut behind me after having left Wade and Calvin in the parking lot, and there was Derek, sprawled across my bed with one of Georgina's magazines on his lap.

I fell back against the door.

"Hey, what's up?" Derek said. "Didn't mean to scare you."

"What are you doing here?" I asked, unable to keep the panic out of my voice.

He threw the magazine aside. "This is your bed, right?" he said. "I wasn't totally sure, but I didn't think you'd have a picture of Werling on your nightstand. Does your roommate like that dumbass?"

I pressed myself harder against the door, scared to death that Wade would cut his hangout time short and come looking for me. "Derek, what the fuck are you doing here?"

"I just came to say hi."

"Okay, great. You said it. Can you go now?"

"What's the rush?"

"You can't be in here. Seriously."

"Why not?"

"Because," I said, "it's against the rules. You can't be in here. It's not allowed."

He got up from the bed. "Stop freaking out for a second, will you? Nothing's going to happen." He walked over to me, and as much as I wanted to move out of his way, I felt I had to guard the door. He took a second to notice that I was wearing a little kid's T-shirt, which was a change from my usual baggy attire.

"Excuse me!" I said, placing my hand across my chest.

"What? It's not like I haven't seen your tits before."

"Thanks for reminding me."

"Hey, what's wrong with that memory?"

"Seriously, can you get out of here? Constanze's room is like three doors down!"

"I told you, she's not my girlfriend."

"Yeah, okay," I said, rolling my eyes.

"You think she doesn't know that I fool around with other girls? And, hey, she's got a boyfriend in Germany, by the way. Did you know *that*? His name is Florian—I'm not making this up. She can't shut up about him."

I pushed him back, because he was suddenly very close to

my face. "That's super interesting, and obviously very relevant to my life, but can you get the hell out of here now? Please?"

"I thought we had a good time over spring break," he said, sounding offended.

I groaned. "Yeah, it was fine. But it's not like we actually *like* each other, so who cares?"

He took a minute to answer. "Yeah, well, I *do* like you, okay?" he said eventually, sounding annoyed about it.

"Oh god. No, you don't. Trust me. You don't."

Something about his whole body became less assertive—the way he stood, his jaw, his eyes. "I had a dream about you last night," he said.

I put my hands to my face, trying to keep from bursting out into tears out of sheer anxiety.

"No, listen, it's not what you think," he said, trying to pry my hands off my face and then giving up, settling instead on gently brushing my bangs off my forehead.

"Don't!" I snapped.

"Whoa! Relax." He moved his hands off. "Listen, this wasn't like a normal dream about girls. We didn't even bone or anything like that. It was just . . . you—naked, standing in the dining hall, but there were, like, trees and plants all around, and it was also kind of an airport at the same time—I don't know why—but anyway, no one was there—just you, looking at me, like you were talking to me but not with words. It's hard to describe, but it was real, Gracie. Like, realer than some actual real-life things that have happened to me."

"You've got to be fucking kidding me."

He was looking at me in this almost pleading kind of way. I could tell he probably was a little freaked out about the dream himself.

"You do realize I wasn't really *in* the dream, right?" I asked.

"You *were* in the dream."

"No, I wasn't! I was in my bed, sleeping. In my own dream—probably making a cake out of car parts or something. I was definitely not in *your* dream!"

"You know what I mean. Listen, it's freaking me out too, okay? You think I *want* to feel this?" he said. "I don't, okay? But it's a real thing. Something happened between us during spring break, and . . . look, I think we might have a situation here. That's all I'm saying."

"*No,*" I said pushing him back. "*We* do not have a situation. Leave me the fuck out of it!"

"Yeah, well, that's not the way it works," he said. "I like you. You're automatically part of the situation."

I closed my eyes tight in frustration. "Stop *saying* that! There's *no way* you like me, Derek! There's no way that's even a possibility!"

"How would you know?" He had drifted close to my face again and propped his hand against the door, right behind my head. "You can't tell me what I feel or don't feel, Gracie," he said.

I could hear laughter and footsteps coming up the hallway toward my room. "Shit! You gotta get out of here, Derek! I'm dead serious now!"

"Why? You expecting that little turdface boyfriend of yours?"

The footsteps and laughter passed my door.

"That's none of your goddamn business."

He stood back. "I guess not, but maybe it's *his* business that you and I . . . you know." He made the gesture of a penis entering a vagina with his fingers.

Without even thinking about it, my hands shot out, and my fingers were wrapped around Derek's neck, presumably to strangle him, which was a joke anyway because he was kind of a grown-up guy and my hands wouldn't have been up to the task. Still, he hadn't expected it, and his eyes widened in surprise. Then he laughed.

"You're going to strangle me?" he asked.

"I will destroy your life if you tell *anybody*!" I tightened my grip around his neck. "I mean it. If you tell anyone at all, I will kill you."

Derek's smile faded. He looked incredulous. "Are you in love with him?"

I stopped trying to strangle him. "I told you—none of this is any of your business."

He drove his hand through his hair again in a way that was automatic but also appeared oddly unpracticed this time, as though he were unused to being Derek but trying hard to fake it all the same. "You're in love with that fucknut?" he asked again in a voice that was all stripped down and wide open.

"Derek! Can't you just get the fuck out of here?"

"You're not answering my question."

"Please just leave me alone, okay?"

He stared at me a moment longer, and at last his eyes went to the floor. "Yeah. Sure," he said.

I opened the door carefully and stuck my head out. The coast was clear. But before I let him go, I fixed him with a glare. "Promise you're not going to talk about any of the stuff we did."

"No problem."

He made a motion to grab for the door handle, but I blocked it. "Not even your lame-ass friends. No bragging. Nothing."

"Jesus Christ. I said I wouldn't."

"Okay," I said. "Okay, thanks."

"It's not like I was going to hold a press conference about it."

"Okay, well, great. I appreciate it, okay?"

"Whatever."

I opened the door for him, making sure the coast was still

clear, and motioned him out. He made it down the hallway without anyone coming across his path. Then I closed the door again and sat down on the floor. My whole body was shaking. I took a bunch of deep breaths, telling myself over and over that it was all right. Derek wasn't going to tell anyone. He hadn't so far, and he had sounded sincere in his promise. He wasn't going to tell. Wade would never find out. Everything was all right. Everything was fine.

Two days later, I came across Derek in the hallway.

He was standing in the open doorway to the music room. His trumpet was under his arm. He just stood there and stared back at me, no movement or facial expression.

And his head was shaved.

I stopped dead in my tracks. This was *not* good. I didn't exactly know why it wasn't good, but I knew it was bad news.

"What the fuck happened to your hair?" I asked him, despite my decision never to talk to him again.

"I shaved my head."

"*Why?*"

His eyes looked like they had seen the end of the world and somehow survived it. Talk about melodrama. "I'm not going to fight who I am anymore," he said.

"What's *that* supposed to mean?"

He looked at me, a little bit of fire coming back into his eyes. "I'm not that guy that everyone thinks I am. I'm sick of being pigeonholed."

"What are you talking about? You think you're *this* guy?" I said, waving my hand at his head.

"Yeah. I do."

I took a step back in exasperation. "This can't be happening."

"What the hell do *you* care anyway?"

"Because your head is supposed to have hair on it so that

you can run your hands through it every three seconds, and now it doesn't, and it's fucking weird."

"Derek, you coming?" a voice called from inside the music room. "We want to practice the intro one more time. Morgan keeps on fucking up on the B-flat."

He turned and slammed the door in my face.

I was a big believer in omens, and this was not a good one.

AS MUCH AS I TRIED TO SCRAPE OFF THE GRIME, IT was too late. The reality of life all around us had already begun to push itself back into focus. For me, at least. Wade continued to be oblivious, and that was somehow the hard part. I found myself wishing that he knew. I wanted him to know everything and not to care. Well, I *did* want him to care—I wanted him to be adequately bummed out, but then to shrug it off and say it didn't matter because legally the sex with Derek was before we were formally together, and so it wasn't any of his business. *That* became my fantasy—that I would tell him I had sex with Derek and things would go on unaltered. I imagined Wade laughing and finding it adorable how terrified I had been to tell him.

I fantasized about him pulling me into his arms and saying, "Why would it matter what you did before we ever even kissed? I'm not a virgin either. I've had sex with other girls. Who cares?"

And the weight would be off my shoulders and the bubble would be mended and we would have babies one day.

I was sitting in English class with these thoughts crowding my mind. Wade looked over so clueless and sunny that it made me sick. He had told me some stupid story right before roll call, and I had listened and laughed and smiled, thinking about how I washed off the sticky aftermath of the hand job I had given Derek in the sink in the teacher's lounge kitchenette. I couldn't shake the hand-job thoughts no matter how hard I tried. I had seen Derek and his stupid shaved head right before class, which had triggered all the details I was fighting to forget. And here was Wade, wide-eyed and sweet, passing me love notes. I needed to get the hell out of there.

I raised my hand and asked to go to the bathroom.

"You couldn't go *before* class?" Mrs. Gillespie asked, looking at me with small, sour eyes.

"I didn't have to *go* before."

"Of course you didn't," she said. "Isn't that always the case?"

She held up the bathroom pass to me, which was a piece of laminated cardboard that read: *I am missing valuable portions of my education that I will never get back because I insist on planning my life around my bladder's schedule.* It had a string stapled to both ends of the sign. The idea was that you wear it around your neck and feel humiliated for having bodily functions to tend to—or I guess, if you're just cutting class. You could tell a lot about a teacher by their bathroom passes, and this said pretty much everything there was to say about Mrs. Gillespie. It didn't matter to me that day, though, the fact that Mrs. Gillespie was Satan—I had much bigger fish to fry.

In the bathroom, I pulled the cigarette that I had been saving all day from my skirt pocket and lit it with the lighter that was hidden under the sink. I didn't bother opening the little window or going into a stall to smoke. I sat down on the floor next to the last sink and let the knot in my stomach unravel. Slowly, I began to feel better about everything. The image of Derek and the hand job began to dissipate as I stared at the calming tangle of plumbing underneath the sinks. I knew I was going to be okay again in a minute or two. I just needed to smoke.

And then, the door opened and Judy, Mr. Sorrentino's fiancée, came walking in. I looked up at her from where I sat, cigarette in hand and the smoke curling around my face. I froze, and she did too for a moment. It was a pretty red-handed situation.

"Hi there," she said eventually.

"Hey," I said. I got up off the floor.

I turned on the faucet, but then stopped myself from holding the cigarette underneath the water. "Do you mind if I finish it?" I asked Judy, since I had nothing to lose at that point anyway.

I figured she would make me put out the cigarette and report me to the office, but instead, she said, "Go ahead," in her soft, friendly voice.

"Really?"

"Sure."

"Thanks," I said, a little stunned at my luck.

She began to wash her hands in the sink next to mine and glanced over as I took another drag. "What's that sign say?" she asked.

I had forgotten all about the bathroom pass around my neck. "Oh, it's just Mrs. Gillespie's cute idea of a bathroom pass," I said, holding it up so she could read it better.

Judy read it and made a face of disapproval. "That's a bathroom pass?" She was visibly put off by it.

"Yeah. She makes us wear it if we want to use the lavatory on her watch."

"That's terrible."

I began to smile. "It's fucked up, right?"

"Yes," she said. "As a matter of fact, it is. It's a little fucked up."

"Wow, don't let Mr. S. hear you use that kind of language. His little grandma heart would probably implode!"

She laughed. "It's not him. You know, there's a whole list of words we're not supposed to condone on school property. There's an actual list they give us."

"Really? I feel like I need a copy of that list."

"I think you're doing just fine without it."

Judy was wearing a T-shirt that had a bunch of crazy ruffles going down the front of it, and these pants that came with a sash-type-thing that tied into a bow around the waist. How could somebody who dressed like this be the first person on the faculty to realize that Mrs. Gillespie was a deranged psychopath? In all my time at Midhurst, nobody had ever seemed to have a problem with Mrs. Gillespie's tactics. They just let her run rampant.

"You know what? That bathroom pass is really rubbing me the wrong way. I think I'm going to bring this up to Mr. Wahlberg," Judy added with a resolution in her voice that eased the frown off her face.

"You *are*?"

"Yes. Why would you make children feel bad about having to use the bathroom?"

"Make sure you tell him it's Mrs. Gillespie's bathroom pass."

"I'll remember."

I thought maybe I got it now—why Mr. Sorrentino liked this lady. Her heart was in the right place. Plus, she had guts. It didn't matter that her purse had seashells stitched all over it. She wasn't a bad person. Not only because she disapproved of the bathroom pass. It was all the little ways in which she was always nice to me, and she *must* have known what a creep I had been to Mr. Sorrentino. He probably told her all about it—in a worried, responsible kind of way, of course.

"You know, smoking cigarettes makes you age faster," she said, putting her purse down on the sink and stirring around in it, searching for something. "They give you those fine lines around your lips when you get older."

"Yeah, I guess," I said, unconcerned by the mythical idea that I would ever be old enough for fine lines around my mouth. I watched her apply lipstick. Pale pink spread evenly over her lips. She had a pretty good upper lip shape, I thought—the kind that was made for lipstick.

"Hey, have you ever slept with someone who's an asshole?" I asked her. "Like Mr. Sorrentino's greatest nemesis?"

Judy stopped applying the lipstick and let out a short laugh of surprise. "Have I *what*?"

"Like, *accidentally*—not totally on purpose—accidentally slept with Mr. Sorrentino's nemesis."

"Mr. Sorrentino's *nemesis*?" She giggled.

"Yeah, like someone he really hates. I don't know—another teacher here who's just a total scumbag. Or like a twin brother who makes way more money and rubs it in his face all the time and drives some kind of obnoxious yellow sports car."

"Oh my gosh, you crack me up, Gracie! Carl is such a sweetie pie, he wouldn't be able to get himself a nemesis if you paid him. I'm sure you know that."

I nodded impatiently. "Okay, just pretend he *did* have a nemesis. And let's say you had sex with the nemesis. What would you do?"

She seemed a little put off by the question. "Well, why would I sleep with his nemesis in the first place?"

"Because obviously you're an idiot—for argument's sake."

She put the lipstick back into her makeup bag and zipped it up. Then she sighed and looked thoughtful for a second. "That's a bit of a toughie, but I really believe that a lasting relationship depends on honesty. Both Carl and I believe that. So, I'd probably have to tell him about it."

My stomach dropped. "Seriously?"

Judy looked at me with a patient smile. "We'd be living a lie as a couple if I never told him."

It was not what I had wanted to hear.

"But he'd leave you, right?" I asked. "Your whole life would be basically over forever."

"You know, sure, it's a possibility he would leave me after finding out I'd betrayed his trust like that. I would have to accept that as a consequence of my actions. But I wouldn't say my life would be over forever. That's a little bleak."

"But don't you love him?"

"Of course I do."

"So . . . I don't get it. Why would you ruin that?"

She put her hand on my arm in that touchy way of hers. "Listen, that's just me," she said. "And it's easy for me to do the right thing in a completely hypothetical situation like this. It would be a real toughie to work that one out in real life."

I said nothing.

My cigarette was at an end, and I held it under the faucet and turned the water on.

Judy packed up her stuff and pulled her weird purse over her shoulder. Then she halted for a moment and began tugging at her purse strap. "But if I *were* to sleep with Mr. Sorrentino's nemesis," she said, giving me a meaningful look, "I'd definitely use protection."

I nodded. "Yeah. Mr. S. would probably appreciate that."

She was trying hard to make the meaningful look hit home. I got it. Use a condom no matter what asshole you sleep with. I just wasn't going to let on that I got it.

"Well, I'll see you around, Gracie," Judy said with a final smile.

It struck me as unthinkable that one would sleep with the nemesis of one's boyfriend and then *tell* the boyfriend about it. The logic wasn't coming through to me on that one, and yet Judy seemed to think that this was the right thing to do, and Judy was exactly the kind of person who would know the right thing to do.

"I mean, what's the point of living if you're going to be a martyr about it?" I asked Beth that night. "Seriously, what's the point?"

We stood by the snack machine in the girls' dormitory. The light from inside cast a cold glow over her face as she leaned in to make a decision.

"You get what I mean, right?" I urged.

"Not even remotely."

"Well, I just mean, is there actually a point to doing 'the right thing'? Like, what *is* the right thing anyway? Wouldn't the right thing be to do whatever makes you happy?"

"Uh—*no.*"

"Really?" I bit my lip. I had bargained on Beth having looser morals than this. I hadn't told her any of the details, but I was trying to get advice from her all the same by making my dilemma as amorphous as possible.

She yawned and threw a Mars bar at me. "I'm thinking of bleaching my hair," she said.

This caught me completely off guard, not only because it was non sequitur as fuck but also because the beautiful peach color of her hair was part of what set her apart from an ocean of blondes and brunettes.

"Why?" I asked.

"It's time for a change."

I nodded in a trancelike stupor. Everything Beth said made sense on some level.

"Gracie," she said. "Whatever is on your mind—why don't you talk to Scholfield about it? He seems like the kind of guy who wrote long letters to the tooth fairy when he was a little boy and cried when Nemo got lost. I bet he's a really good listener."

I nodded again. "He is a good listener."

"So, take advantage of that. You might as well make him work for all the ass he's getting."

"Oh, Jesus."

"I'm serious. He'll probably love listening to you navigate the high seas of your indecisive moral dilemmas."

"Yeah, you're probably right. I'll talk to him."

"Okay. Good night, dummy," she said, walking off.

Needless to say, I did *not* talk to Wade about what was troubling me. I made an official decision that night that I would never come clean to Wade. Never in a billion years. I wasn't that kind of person. I was the other kind, and that was fine by me. I figured I deserved to be happy, and anyone who had a problem with that could go suck it. I dug myself into my sheets and fell asleep not much later with my conscience stored away high up on a shelf I couldn't easily reach.

24

THE MAKE—OUT SESSIONS WERE ALWAYS BEST when Wade knocked on my door late in the evening, sweaty and flushed after spending the afternoon with Calvin. They'd often leave school property to skate, and on those days, if nobody caught them coming back in, Wade would knock on my door around nine. If Georgina was in the room, we'd have to settle for a more PG-13 hangout, but she had a habit of taking forever in the bathroom at night with her evening showers and hair treatment routine. If that was the case, we wouldn't waste much time. And like I said, those make-out sessions were the best. Something about the adrenaline still alive in him from the physical exertion, and the guilt he always felt for making me wait had this way of making him vulnerable and starved for me. I could feel it in his fingertips when he was holding on to me. I imagined I felt the pulse in his fingers, which was probably impossible, but I liked the idea of it—feeling the blood racing. The fact that we were breaking a shitload of rules hanging out like this in the evening, past the curfew in my room, heightened the urgency of the already desperate need to be together. If the dormitory supervisor happened to stop by, we'd be fucked, which naturally made everything so much better.

"Hey, do you think Anju is pretty?" I asked him on one of these evenings, when we were lying on my bed, staring at the ceiling.

I don't know why I asked it. It was something I had occasionally fantasized about asking him. She was in a lot of our classes and hung out with the girls that liked to sit at the curb, watching the boys skate. I usually left when they showed up. Without them, I felt like I was just myself, exercising my natural rights to get turned on by my boyfriend, but when the other girls were there, it made me feel like a groupie. Plus, their clothes were better than mine.

"Yeah," Wade said in response to my question about Anju being pretty.

"You *think she's pretty*?" I said, sitting up.

He looked over, surprised by my reaction. "Yeah, you don't think so?"

"I *know* she's pretty," I said, giving him an exasperated look. "That wasn't the point of my question, you wiener!"

"Hey, don't use that kind of language with me, all right? That's uncalled for," he said, trying to pull me over to him.

I rolled my eyes with a laugh and pushed him back. "It's super called for, pal. I can't believe you think Anju is pretty!"

"Come on, girls are pretty. That's not *my* fault. And anyway, it doesn't change the fact that none of them do anything for me. Except, you know, *you*."

"Whatever. My dad said I should never trust anything a boy tries to sell me."

He laughed, and I pretended not to be appeased.

"You don't have to believe me," he said, "but I'm really screwed when it comes to you. Really, really screwed. Big-time."

I had no choice but to melt all over the place, and we made out some more until Georgina walked in and made her mood known by slamming the door shut behind her and throwing her gym bag down next to the dresser.

"Georgienator!" Wade called enthusiastically. You'd think he'd been waiting here all day for her to make an appearance.

"Hi, Wade," she said politely. "Do you guys mind not making out in here, please?" she said to me, less politely.

"We were just talking," I said.

"I saw you guys. I'm not blind. I'd prefer if you didn't do anything gross in here. It's my space too, and I don't always want to be the third wheel in my own room."

I rolled my eyes.

"Are you okay?" Wade asked her, breaking suddenly with his playful tone.

Georgina looked over from where she was kicking off her shoes. For a split second, she looked like she had been caught red-handed in an unseemly emotion. Then she said quickly, "I'm fine."

"You sure?"

"Yeah, I'm fine. I'm just . . . It's just not easy to deal with the volleyball stuff and then also the drama club stuff at the same time. I think I piled too much on my plate, that's all."

Wade was watching her. He was right—she looked off. She moved too fast. Kicked her shoes into the closet and shoved her feet into her slippers and pulled her hair up in a ponytail—all in a jerky, emotional, double-time speed.

"Yeah, sounds stressful," Wade said.

Georgina put on her weird frilly robe and tied it with a hard knot. "It is," she said.

Even I could tell that something was definitely up.

"Sure you're okay, though?" Wade asked again.

I just sat there, uncomfortable. I'd never seen Georgina up-set before. Not like this. My instinct was to get the hell out of there and not return until we could fight about music again, but Wade made no attempt to withdraw. The thicker the air grew, the more he pushed to get involved.

Georgina looked at him, suspicious, and then her eyebrows drew together, turning her face full of pain.

Wade walked over and sat down next to her. "What's up?" he asked. No concern that this was none of his business.

For a moment, she continued looking at him, half-spooked, half-grateful. It seemed like she was going to smile and say something normal, but she didn't. Instead, she turned away to face the wall, and then her shoulders began to quiver uncon-trollably as she lost it.

"I don't want to be here right now!" she said, through the sobs. Her body shook harder, and her words came out in spurts. "I need to be somewhere else. I can't be here. I just . . . can't . . . I need to—"

Wade put his hand on her shoulder.

I sat on my bed, digging my fingers into the mattress—terrified. Georgina cried for a while, her head on her lap, curled into as much as a ball as was possible from a sitting position. Wade kept his hand on her back and said nothing until she had stopped crying and her shoulders no longer shook. She straightened up eventually and wiped her face on her bathrobe before speaking.

"Chad is an asshole," was the first thing she said.

Her voice sounded thick and nasally from the congestion she had worked up with her crying.

"Who's Chad?" Wade asked.

"Chad Werling," Georgina said, still facing the wall. "You know. He's playing Mr. Gradgrind in the play."

"Who?"

"Thomas Gradgrind. In the play, you know? *Hard Times*—don't you know about the play? He's on all the posters."

"Oh, the drama guy with the ponytail?" Wade asked, making the connection.

Georgina nodded. "Yeah. He has amazing hair." She wiped her nose. "It's weird how he can be a total asshole and look like that—like, have perfect hair," she said.

"I think a lot of assholes have perfect hair, to be honest," Wade said. "It's probably something ridiculous—like 85 percent of them."

An unintended smile appeared on her face. It left as soon as it had shown itself, though, and her expression fell back deep into the abyss.

"He just seemed so different. He always did all these cool things," she said. "Like, he read one of his poems out loud at a drama meeting one time. It was about a tree that grows in the shadow of this really big other tree, and it's all about how the little tree doesn't get enough sunlight, but he continues to stretch his limbs toward the sun and never gives up. I don't remember it exactly, but it's a metaphor-type thing. It was so amazing to hear a guy have thoughts like that and be open about them. I thought I knew him—really understood who he was. I mean, shitty people don't write poems with metaphors, do they?"

"I wouldn't put it past them," Wade said.

"But he also fly fishes!" Georgina said. "He just seemed really different." She started crying again a little. "I'm such an idiot," she said through her tears. "I'm so, *so* incredibly stupid."

"Come on, no you're not," Wade said.

"I am!" she insisted, almost angrily. "I wrote him a letter. And if that wasn't stupid enough, I gave him the letter. I *gave* him a love letter! I mean, look at me! I know what I look like. I already knew that no guy would ever like me—especially a guy like *that*. I already knew it! So why did I give him the letter?"

She turned to face Wade with a rabid expression. Her face was red and raw from the way she had scrubbed her robe across it to wipe away the tears. There was a stain on her left sleeve from the Cheetos she always ate in bed.

"I read this thing online," she said, "where they said that guys like it when the girl makes the first move. That's what gave me the idea in the first place. But I wasn't actually going to *give* him the letter. I just carried it around pretending I was cool enough to make the first move. But then we watched *Dead Poets Society* in English yesterday, and . . . I just . . . It seemed like I should really stop thinking about things all the time and just seize the day already. So I gave him the letter, and he opened it right there in front of all his friends, and all the glitter I put in the envelope went all over the place, and then he read it out loud. He used this stupid voice when he read it, like he was in a soap opera, you know—like all dramatic, so what I wrote sounded even dumber than it already was."

I closed my eyes. I wondered how many stupid kids had tried to "seize the day" after watching that movie. I mean, even in the film it doesn't work out great for the guy seizing the day. There should really be a warning.

"Everyone thought it was hilarious," Georgina went on. "I was right there. I hadn't even left yet, and they were all laughing." She screwed up her lips and stared at the corner of her bed. "The worst were the girls who were like, 'Chad! She's right there. Don't be so mean!' while they're trying not to laugh, but really they were laughing more than anyone else. Brooke Foster was there—you know, she plays Sissy Jupe in the play."

The brunt of her emotions seemed to have passed, but

underneath the monotone of her voice was all the unquiet activity of despair.

"I just don't understand why I'm so stupid," she said. "That's what I don't get. I didn't think I was this big of a moron."

"You're not a moron," Wade said. "Writing someone a love letter and giving it to them—are you kidding? Do you know how hard that is?"

Her eyes flicked up at him, unconvinced. "Chad thought it was really pathetic."

"So that makes *him* a douchebag. Nothing about what you did was stupid."

Short silence.

"It doesn't matter. I can't ever see any of those people again," she said with finality. "I always knew that I was a loser, but now everyone else knows it too. I mean, they probably already knew it, but it's like this was the real proof. There's no use in pretending anymore."

"Oh, come on!" Wade said, giving her a little push. She had turned back to face the wall.

God, it was hard to watch her be like this.

"I'm a joke," she said to the wall. "I get grossed out every time I even think of myself. It's just the way it is."

More gently this time, Wade said, "Come on, don't say that."

She looked like she might start crying again. "Everyone thinks so."

"That's bullshit. *I* don't think you're a loser," Wade said. "Gracie doesn't."

Georgina glanced over at me. "Yeah, right. Gracie definitely thinks I'm a loser."

I squirmed a little. "I mean, mostly, I do, yeah," I said, "but now—I don't know. Wade is right; that was kind of impressive—writing a love letter and actually giving it to the person. Especially with glitter in it. I've never had the guts to do anything like that."

There was a short silence in which Georgina was presumably trying to figure out if she felt any better about the matter.

"And fuck Chad and his dumb poem about the tree, by the way," I added more emphatically. "I'm sorry, but that idea with the big and the small tree and the message and all that—it really sucked my mind's dick."

Georgina said nothing. She focused back on the corner of her bed, but her face no longer looked as terribly helpless as it had before. She was smiling a little.

"Yeah," Wade agreed solemnly. "It kind of sucked my mind's dick too, to be honest."

Reluctantly, Georgina's smile turned into a giggle.

We stayed up until about 2:00 a.m., Wade, Georgina, and I. When Wade left and we were alone in the dark, I heard the blankets rustle, and I knew it was Georgina Time.

"I used to think I'd hate to be you," she said after a moment. "I mean, not because there's anything wrong with you but just because of the obvious reasons. Like the fact that you don't have any money and stuff."

"Right." I rolled my eyes in the dark. It was good to have her back.

"But then you started having this boyfriend, and I got jealous. I've never had a first kiss yet. Boys don't look at me. Do you know what that feels like? To be this uninteresting, large person that nobody takes seriously?"

"Okay, Wade is nuts—that's why he likes me," I said. "And you're not 'large,' whatever that means. You just have muscles because you work out like a deranged maniac."

"Well, whatever. You're lucky, Gracie."

It was the strangest concept ever. I'd never been lucky. And I guess she was right. I had something to be envious of.

"Maybe," I said.

"You *are*. Wade is so cool and also, like, the nicest person I've ever met. I didn't know that boys could be like that. He even makes you less of a bitch. No offense."

"Yeah, that's true."

"Anyway, I'm still really jealous," Georgina said, "but if you guys ever wanted to 'do it'—have sex, I mean—I'd let you use the room."

"Oh. Thanks."

"But not on my bed or anything."

"Eww, what the fuck, Georgie! Why would we do it on your bed?"

"I don't know! I mean, you use my stereo and stuff when I'm not here."

"That's not even remotely the same thing!"

"I feel safer just saying it, okay?"

"God!"

"But I mean it. I'll give you the room if you want it."

"Okay, thanks. Jesus."

"You're welcome. Good night."

"Good night."

THE NEXT DAY AT LUNCH, WADE WAS HELPING ME
with some algebra homework that I had forgotten to do, when
his attention suddenly caught somewhere across the room. He
abandoned his train of thought mid-sentence, his finger resting on the open book, pointing out some dumbass formula
that I was never in a million years going to use in my life, his
attention hijacked.

"What?" I asked, scanning the room.

"Hold on a second," he said, getting up and leaving me
behind with the algebra book.

I called after him, but he didn't bother turning around. I
stood up and watched him as he crossed the room, his hands
clenched into fists—everything in him breaking with the easy
theme of his body's usual slacker language.

Then I saw Chad Werling with his tray of food, talking to
two friends from the drama club as they ambled toward their
table, and my heart sank. They didn't notice Wade until he
was right there. He pushed one of Chad's friends out of the

way, and without even the slightest hitch in the program, he slammed the tray out of Chad's hands. It went flying through the air. For the moment, everything seemed to go into slow motion. I watched the tray fly and the plate and cutlery and food dislodge itself from the gravity of the tray's surface. Everything was floating through the air. Chad stood there, dumbfounded, mouth hanging wide open, looking victimized and lost. His eyes followed the food moving through the air. Wade was saying something to him. Chad focused on Wade, and then he went flying backward into a table behind him, hands flailing in the air as Wade pushed him. Chad slammed hard into the center of the table. There was a lot of squealing as more food and soda spilled across the table into people's laps. Chad slid off the table onto the floor, and Wade stepped forward.

"You're a real piece of shit," Wade told him. "You should probably know that."

Chad looked terrified.

"What—I don't—" He stammered something, and Wade kicked him in the side. Chad, confused and blindsided as he was, let out a yelp and covered his face in case it was in danger. Someone pulled Wade back at this point, and Mr. Grant, who was on lunchtime duty, came running over.

"That's enough!" he called. "What the hell is going on here? What is all this mess?"

Eloise Smith stood among some of the onlookers. "It was Wade," she said, stepping forward, her finger feverishly pointed at Wade. "Chad didn't even do anything! He was just walking with his food. I was sitting right over here, so I saw everything. Wade just attacked him for no reason at all!"

She was finally getting her revenge for Wade's failure to drool over her. But then again, nothing she had said was an actual lie. It had happened just like that.

"All right, that's enough! Can somebody clean up this mess, please?"

Mr. Grant then ordered someone to help Chad up and grabbed Wade by the arm. "Let's go, buddy."

"Gracie!" I turned and saw Georgina rushing over to me. She grabbed my shoulders with both her hands, squeezing hard in excitement. "Oh my god! Did you see that?" She was out of breath. Mind blown. "Did Wade just do that for me?" she squealed breathlessly.

"I don't know," I said, dazed.

"I think he did! Holy crap! Can you believe that he just did that, Gracie?" Her mouth was hanging open in a huge frenzied grin, and there were tears building in her eyes. I'd never seen her this elated. Not even when the school printed her picture in the promotional brochure, holding a volleyball under her arm and standing by the front entrance. "Oh my god!" she was saying, trying to shake out the energy from her hands. "Nobody ever did anything like that for me. And oh my god—did you see Chad's face?"

I gave her a distracted look and then left to try to follow Mr. Grant and Wade.

"Your boyfriend is a psychopath, just so you know," Eloise said, giving me a shove as I was trying to get past her. Her eyes were wide with energy. She almost looked as happy as Georgina did.

I flipped her off without much interest.

"You know, the two of you really deserve each other!" Eloise called after me.

I had already passed her by and was pushing open the door to the hallway. I went to the office to try to find Wade, but they wouldn't let me hang out in there without a real reason. For the rest of the day, I was stuck wondering if Wade wasn't at all who I had imagined him to be. I remembered the story he had told me about how he had started the fight with Derek. At the time, I'd thought it was stupid, but beyond the utter stupidity of the matter, I hadn't thought much about it. It hadn't truly bothered me. I mean Derek was Derek—he basically *needed* to be punched in the face by someone. But this was different. Maybe it was different only because I had witnessed it first-hand. I had seen Wade be someone I didn't know. I had seen the way he'd slammed the tray out of Chad's hands. Pushed him into the table. Kicked him even though Chad was already on the ground, about to shit his pants. There had been something so callous about Wade's energy.

And the thing is, I had really loved the fact that Wade was not an asshole. It had been a turn-on—how he was sweet and caring and respectful of people in a way that I could never be. I wasn't perfect, I knew that, but somehow that didn't change the fact that Wade wasn't allowed to have any flaws.

I didn't see him at dinner, and so I sat down on the steps to the dormitories and waited, figuring it was the only way to intercept him without fail. He had never gotten a replacement for the phone he'd thrown in the wash before spring break, and tracking him down could be a real blast. I brought my book with me and read distractedly for about an hour or so with an uneasy stomach until finally I felt a tap on my head. When I looked up, there he was. Rubbing his arm and looking unfazed. Eyes full of life. As though the events of the dining room at lunchtime were just part of the normal humdrum smorgasbord that is life.

"What happened?" I asked.

"Nothing," he said, sitting down next to me.

"What do you mean, *nothing*?"

"International Space Station."

ISS = International Space Station = In-School Suspension. Both had about the same kind of isolating qualities.

"How long?"

"A week," he said with a shrug.

"That counts as a suspension, Wade!" I said, the anger flaring out around my words. "It goes on your record."

He seemed baffled and simultaneously entertained by my reaction.

"That's serious!" I said defensively. "It really affects your chances with colleges and stuff like that. It's on your record permanently."

I couldn't believe I was talking about colleges as though I had the capacity to give a rat's ass about that. Or permanent records. My emotional state was grabbing at anything.

"I hate to break it to you," he said with a laugh, "but my school records have been heavily besmirched since about middle school. Were you under the impression I was going to Harvard or something?"

Pissed that I was being turned into a parental figure without my consent, I scooted away from him. "You don't need to actively make things any worse!"

"I'm not trying to make things worse. I'm just doing my best not to make things *better*. It's not easy maintaining this perfect D-student/fuckup trajectory, you know—especially if you happen to be mathematically gifted."

"That's not funny," I said, getting up and holding my book to my chest awkwardly like I was trying to ward off evil with my Bible. "Doesn't your own life matter to you?"

Wade finally registered my mood and sobered a little. "Come on," he said softly, looking up at me. "Who cares about my school record? I know for a fact *you* don't."

I watched him wait for a response, but I didn't know what to say, and so I said nothing. The anger I felt wasn't satisfying the way that it had been when I was angry with Mr. Sorrentino. It felt terrible not to be anything but madly in love with Wade.

He got to his feet and put his arm around me. "What's going on?" he asked, concerned but not at all intimidated by the moment. "Are you really mad at me?"

After a long moment of not looking at him, I said, "I don't know."

"Is it because of the Chad thing at lunchtime?" he asked.

"Maybe. It felt weird to see you do something like that."

Again the small, mystified smile. "How come?"

We were walking along the side of the building, away from the front door traffic. His arm was still around my shoulder in a warm, protective manner. I could smell his hair and his skin, and more than anything else, I wanted to put my head on his shoulder and let him adore me. But the moment wasn't right. I had started this, and I had to take it home.

"It's like you were somebody else," I said, a little hesitantly. "It didn't really seem like something you'd do."

"Really? Why wouldn't I do that?" he asked.

I looked at him, annoyed. "Because, Wade, you're a good person."

This seemed to amuse him more than anything else I had said so far.

"I'm serious. You don't do stupid shit like that."

"That's sweet," he said, giving me a squeeze. "Not very accurate, though."

I wrestled myself out of his arm and gave him a hard push. "Fuck you. It's the truth. I *know* you, Wade. I fucking know you—better than you know yourself, apparently."

Just then, I hated him for his patience and his good humor and his ability to go confidently headfirst into emotionally loaded situations like this one or the one with Georgina the other day without any inhibitions. I turned away and made sure my face and body language reflected my utter lack of amusement.

"A couple of years ago, I broke into a bunch of houses in our neighborhood with some friends," Wade said out of the blue.

I glanced over. I had been fully committed to freezing him out and staring off somewhere insignificant, but I was caught off guard by this unexpected glimpse into his past.

"We didn't really touch anything," he continued, noting my thinly veiled, rabid interest. "Except if there was beer in the fridge—or, like, if we knew that one of the high school girls lived there, then obviously we'd steal some of her underwear or whatever, but I think that's just common sense when you're thirteen."

I snorted out an unintentional laugh. I wasn't ready to be appeased yet, but I liked wherever the hell this story was going.

"But this one guy left his credit card lying around right next to his computer. So, we signed him up to a bunch of really weird porn sites, because again: common sense! The idea was that nobody would know anything about it until the credit card bill came in the mail or the websites sent him emails or something. We thought it would be pretty hilarious, which it was for sure. But then he gets *kicked out* by his wife when she finds out. He had kids and everything, and he was good friends with my dad, so he was, like, living on our fucking couch bawling his eyes out every night."

"That's messed up, Wade," I said, smiling.

"Ya think?"

"Yeah, but whatever. You want me to tell you how that story ends? Because I already know."

"Sure."

"Okay. You confessed to the whole thing, and the wife took him back, and you didn't tell on your friends, so all the blame went right to you, and your parents had an exorcism performed on you."

He laughed.

My bad mood was unraveling quickly. We were sitting around the back of the building at this point, and it was dark out. The air was warm and thick. It was quiet except for the sounds of a whole horde of crickets and a few voices off in the distance.

"So, am I right?" I asked.

"Pretty much."

Giving in at last, I put my head on his shoulder. "I told you. I know you, Wade."

For a moment, we were content to let the conversation go stagnant.

"Seriously, though," he said eventually, and there was some earnestness underneath the playful tone of his whole spiel. "That's just one stupid example of about five million stupid examples I could give you of me being a huge, fucking idiot. And the only reason I brought it up is because—" He was struggling a little with the moment. "Because you can't have these ideas about me, Gracie. Like, that I'm—I don't know— whatever you think that I am. Because I'm not. I'm not logical and I'm not, like, known for making really great decisions about stuff. And if you have all these expectations of me being whatever . . . I feel like you're just going to be let down. So, please don't have them, okay?"

I squeezed his hand. "Relax, pal. I didn't say you were a great maker of decisions. I said you were a *good person*. And it's true—you *are*."

He seemed to think about it without answering. I could tell he truly didn't believe some part of that.

"Jesus. You're such a moron if you can't see that," I said, rolling my eyes at his silence. "You're like the best person I know, Wade." It came out almost accusingly. "You have this annoying moral compass inside of you that always makes me seem like a total callous bitch in comparison. So, now I gotta try to be a better person just because of you. And it's not fair, because you never even have to *try*. It's just the way you are. You're naturally the best person I know. So, fuck you. You can at least own up to it."

Wade scratched his cheek self-consciously. I rarely saw him uncomfortable like this. He wasn't looking at me.

"You really know how to take a compliment, huh?" I said, bumping my knee against his leg.

He looked over with a small smile, still edgy in his embarrassment. "Sorry," he said. "And yeah, thanks. That's nice of you to say—all those things. It's really nice of you."

I sighed. "No, it's not. It's just the truth."

He squeezed my hand back.

"Anyway, that's what I was trying to say," I said, pushing the point home more cautiously. "What you did to Chad—the way you just kicked him in the stomach like that—it just broke with everything I know that you are. That's all. It freaked me out a bit."

"Sorry," he said. "I didn't mean to freak you out. If it makes you feel any better, I didn't really hurt him."

"You kicked him."

"That wasn't a real kick, trust me."

"It doesn't matter. You scared the shit out of that guy."

I searched his face for any type of reluctant agreement, but there was none. He returned my stare as though waiting for a punch line. He was no longer uncomfortable, but it seemed that we truly didn't understand each other for the first time ever.

Eventually, Wade nodded and said, "Yeah. You're right," without meaning it. And then with far more conviction, he added, "But that guy's such an asshole! I mean, come on! You saw Georgie yesterday—she was crushed."

"Why do you care that much?" I asked.

It was a stupid question, but it really had to be asked.

He looked up, not understanding. "Should I not give a shit?"

"Yeah, but I mean, why do you care that *much*? Enough to fuck yourself over so easily for other people's sake? You didn't owe Georgie anything. You didn't owe anything to Michael Holt either. You do this crazy heroic shit and you use yourself like an afterthought. Like nothing."

He was biting the nail of his middle finger, listening to me, still not getting it.

"Why do you use yourself like that?" I asked again.

"I'm not using myself," he said, brushing off my question with a small laugh. "I wouldn't do it if I didn't want to."

"Whatever. The point is you didn't need to go that far for Georgie. Not like that."

He threw up his hands in surrender. "Okay, listen, I'm not saying what I did was a great idea. I'm just saying Chad was right there in front of me with his food, laughing his fucking head off with his jackoff friends and his ponytail and his face all over the drama posters, and he was never going to have to deal with what he did to Georgie. Nobody was going to make him think about it. Doesn't that stuff bug the fuck out of you? That people can just get away with stuff?"

I remembered how Georgina had almost started crying in relief when she realized that someone had taken a stand for her. The shock in her eyes. The total disbelief. And then how it had trickled back into her—the first traces of self-esteem. The confidence to be allowed to be there in the dining room like anyone else. He had a point.

"Yeah, I guess," I said, kind of defeated in my argument. I no longer knew where the morals lay. Chad was a piece of shit. Maybe Wade was right. In any case, I didn't want to think about it anymore. I just wanted to make out with Wade.

"Anyway, you're probably right about everything," Wade said as though reading my mind. He was done with this argument too. He slid down onto his knees before me and begged, "Can you just please, please, *please* not be mad at me anymore now? *Pleeeeeeese?*"

I pretended that this was a hard decision to make. "Maybe," I said. "Buy me some candy and we'll revisit the idea."

He pulled me onto my feet excitedly, and we made our way back to the dormitory.

The truth of the matter is, I was so unconditionally defenseless when it came to this boy and the way he talked, and the way he looked at me, and the way everything seemed to fall apart around him all the time in this perfect explosion of chaos—he could have done anything. I didn't have the upper hand in this at all. I decided I would gladly jump over to his side of the reasoning if it meant I could lay untroubled in his arms and eat M&M's and watch TV in the common room that night. I decided I would never be on the other side of a rift again with Wade. It wasn't worth it.

When it was time for bed, he walked me to the entrance of the girls' side of the building.

"Oh shit, I almost forgot to tell you!" I said, turning to him. "Georgie said we could use the room if we wanted to have sex."

His face stopped. All thoughts just seemed to drop midway off into nothingness, and his mouth fell open a little.

"What do you think? Is that weird?" I asked.

"No," he said. "I'd be up for that. If *you* are."

I nodded back. "Yeah. I'm up for sexual intercourse."

He laughed. "Okay, cool."

"Yeah."

For a moment, we stood there like idiots. Happy in a raging kind of way that we could do absolutely nothing about.

"So, do we just do it?" I asked. "Or do we need to plan this out?"

Wade shook his head, his face flushed with elation. "I think we just do it," he said. "Or unless—do you *want* to plan it out?"

"No, I don't want to plan it out," I said.

"All right, cool."

"When do you get out tomorrow?" I asked.

"Same time."

"I'll meet you here, then?"

He nodded again, looking a little in awe of the sudden unexpected turn his life had taken. I loved seeing him clumsy in the face of lust. His charm wobbling a little, tripping up the ease and fluidity of his mannerisms. It was another way of basking in my own power. I was doing this to him. It was nuts. I leaned in and gave him a kiss before drawing back and making my way up the stairs.

QUICK NOTE ON THE HISTORY OF OUR HORNINESS:

Ever since Goodwill, Wade and I had not been shy about acknowledging our lust for one another. Before Goodwill, we perhaps had some confused ideas about how true love ought to be pure like the driven snow and that to add anything too carnal to its natural, sacred state might contaminate the only real truth we had ever known. Something like that. In hindsight, it might have just been me that felt this way. I just assumed Wade felt the same way, since he played so perfectly off my vibes.

But then one day we had gone to Goodwill because I needed a dress for the Model UN field trip, and the only dress that seemed like it would work had an impossible zipper that I couldn't reach by myself. And all of a sudden, Wade and I found ourselves alone in a dressing room cubicle at Goodwill with an unzipped dress that I was clutching to myself and Wade's hand grazing the skin on my back as he tried to get the zipper to cooperate.

And it hit us: this was the most privacy we had ever had, and I was half-undressed and the moment was overwhelming.

The dressing room cubicle was small, and it smelled of aggressive laundry detergent, cleaning products, and a myriad of musty closets and people's personal smells. There was country music playing way too loudly over the speakers. Not exactly romance-inducing vibes, but the romance was suddenly there, full blown, all the same.

I felt one of Wade's fingers stray from the zipper and slowly, tentatively touch my back. So I dropped the dress off my shoulders. I turned around to face him with the dress hanging around my waist and just my bra between him and my nudity. We just stood there, not sure of where to take this, in desperate need of some kind of choreography. The longer we did nothing, the more we needed something to happen.

So I undid the bra, and the innocence ration dropped way out the bottom. Wade's eyes widened with an unsteady intake of breath. He almost went cross-eyed trying to focus properly. I had never seen him so paralyzed, and I could feel the glory of my magnetism. But unlike the times I'd fooled around with Derek, I could also feel my own fragility. Acutely. To the point where it almost hurt. In a way that I didn't fully understand, I knew that I needed everything from this person in front of me. Everything there was to be had. There was nothing that could be left over. I wondered if this was true passion. I wondered whether I now had the religious look in my eyes. *Probably*, I thought.

Once we started kissing, Wade's hands were on me like a grubby kid grabbing all the cookies he could get while the coast was clear.

"Hey!" someone called, knocking on our cubicle door loudly. "There's only one changing room, you know."

We hadn't gotten there that time, but ever since the cubicle incident at Goodwill, we knew that we were most definitely ready to get there. Most definitely. And with that knowledge came a blissful, full-throttle approach to horniness in whatever appropriate or inappropriate way possible. In any kind of semi-privacy, we went for it. Down by the back stairs, in the music room, the blind spot of the tennis court, the laundry room. But we had always fallen short of actual intercourse every time because of the semi-privacy element. Someone always managed to walk into a room, start a tennis match, turn on the lights, barge in with a laundry bag, and so on.

Therefore, Georgina's offer was far more precious than I had led her to believe with my nonchalant acceptance.

I should also mention that we both knew we were not virgins, and that seemed to take some of the pressure off. He had lost his virginity to some girl at his last school. All I could get out of him was that her name was Kim and she had been in the most advanced calculus class they had at the school. She had not been his girlfriend, but apparently she had pointed to him in the parking lot one day, and he walked over and she had asked if he wanted to come to her place after school to do homework. I disliked her right away. She sounded way too cool—with her confidence to point at boys and make them have sex with her. It made me a little sick to my stomach to think that he had touched this girl the way that he had touched me.

"Did she wear glasses?" had been my only question.

"Yeah."

Wade knew even less about whom I had lost my virginity to. I told him it was a guy called Kelvin (it was the only name I could think of on the spot) from my hometown—he worked at the Dairy Queen, and he also wore glasses. Wade didn't seem to want to know much about him. Good, because it was really terrible having to make up this Kelvin guy while Wade looked on with all that gullibility, asking, "Like, Kevin but with an *L*?"

"Yeah."

"Huh," he said thoughtfully. "Kim and Kelvin. That's kind of weird, right? Like they should be in a folk band together."

Once Kim and Kelvin were established, we left them alone. We didn't love that they existed, but we didn't mind them much either, because what mattered had nothing to do with the distant past.

So anyway, due to all of the above, we were very much ready to start the chapter of our relationship that involved sex. As much as we joked about it, downplaying the crazy-ass urges we felt, we were in fact breathless and giddy now that it was all going to happen. We parted ways stupidly happy. The kind of happy where you know you are an idiot.

I DIDN'T SLEEP MUCH, AND ALL THE NEXT MORNING,
I thought about "the moment." I would clean my sheets at
lunchtime. I would not eat dinner. I didn't know why this
made sense, but it just seemed wrong to make love with a full
stomach; plus, I was nervous. I would have to figure out what
to wear. It was unfortunate that I had no great underwear or
bras, but I supposed that if we turned the lights out, it wouldn't
matter very much. I definitely intended to be fully naked this
time. I wondered about whether I should wash my hair before
and entertained the idea of borrowing Beth's shampoo, which
had that mind-blowing fake tropical fruit smell—something
that wasn't too overwhelming, but also reminded the smeller
that one was a bottomless barrel of feminine mysteries.

I didn't see Wade at breakfast or even at lunch because the
International Space Station kids had a different feeding schedule, and that was fine. Somehow it all added to the buildup.
By the late-afternoon break, I had it all worked out. As soon
as the last bell rang, I would ask Beth about the shampoo, put

the sheets in the dryer, shower and wash my hair, smoke a cigarette, brush my teeth, get the dry sheets and make the bed, and then figure out what music to put on.

"Gracie!"

I turned and found Georgina running up to me in the girls' bathroom. I was washing my hands. It was the late-afternoon break, and I was wondering what my kids with Wade would look like. Not that I was planning on getting pregnant any-time soon, but it seemed more evident than ever that we would end up getting married, and of course we'd have kids once we were married. I was guessing around four kids. Wade was so beautiful, especially now that his hair was growing out all haphazardly—I hoped that my own genetics wouldn't ruin our children.

"*Grace!*"

"What?" I asked with little interest.

She grabbed my arm and pulled me over to the far end of the bathroom underneath the window. My hands were still wet.

"Do you mind?" I said, trying to push past her to dry my hands, but she stepped in front of me, blocking my path to the sinks. Her face was flushed with excitement, and her eyes were impossibly huge.

"Did you have sex with Derek?" she whispered.

Instant nausea shot through me, and my entire body went limp with terror. "What are you talking about?" I asked, man-aging to sound offended.

She leaned in closer and repeated herself, pronouncing her words slower and stressing each syllable. "*Did—you—have—sex—with—Der—ek?*"

I stared at her, paralyzed. All I could think of was that ev-erything was over.

"Oh my god!" Georgina gasped. "You did. You had sex with Derek! Oh my god!"

"No!" I said, finding my voice, I don't know where. "Why would you even say that?"

"*I'm* not the one saying it. I heard it from Carole Coleman, and I don't know where she heard it, but it doesn't even matter, because there's a rumor going around. I can't believe you didn't tell me! We're roommates, and I'm like the last person on the planet to find out! Do you have any idea how humiliating it is to have Carole Coleman fill me in on this? It's like I'm the biggest moron ever for not even knowing!"

I had to lean against the wall for support. Georgina was still whispering aggressively into my face, but I had stopped hearing her. I thought maybe I'd just die right there and everything would be fine. But instead, I had the feeling of being turned inside out, with my organs dripping off me and my soul loose and exposed.

"Does Wade know?" I heard her say.

She registered the fear in my face.

"Oh my god . . ."

She held her hand up to her mouth. Eyes wide.

"What are you going to do?" she asked. "What about tonight?" She looked wildly around the bathroom as though we were in mortal danger.

"It's just a rumor," I said, my hands visibly shaking.

"Are you sure?" she asked. "Because you look super freaked out."

"It's a fucking rumor, okay?"

She backed off. "Okay. God!"

I found myself sprinting down the hallway, through the crowds. I didn't know what exactly I was going to do, but I ran.

I wondered whether I was trying to find Wade, but I quickly

realized that this was most likely the worst idea possible, because the sooner I found him, the sooner it would all be over.
I'd have to look at him if I found him. I couldn't know for sure
if the rumors had made it all the way to ISS, but if they hadn't
already, they would soon enough. The wave of nausea came
again.

I started hiccupping and my eyes began to feel tight, and I
knew that I was about to start crying. I had to get the hell out.
Although I wasn't sure what I had to get out of. My skin? My
life? School? Probably all of it. I could never see Wade again. It
would be better to live without him than to have to look at him,
knowing that he knew. For a short moment, I entertained the
fantasy of running out of the front gates and down the road,
and hopefully being picked up by a serial killer. Only I knew it
wouldn't happen like that. I wouldn't get picked up by a serial
killer. I'd just walk until I had to pee, and then there wouldn't
be a bathroom. It would be like one of Georgina's bathroom
dreams.

So where was I running to? I wanted to stop and think
things over, but there was far too much adrenaline shooting
through my body to stop running, let alone think properly.

"No running in the hallway!" some voice called as though
on cue.

I began to run faster.

"I said, *no running!*" the voice called more faintly, farther
removed.

It occurred to me that I could find Beth. Beth was maybe
the only person on the face of the earth who might have a
plan. This sparked a small, mangled glimmer of hope. I had
no idea where she might be that time of the day, but I knew I
couldn't stop running until I had tracked her down. I had to
find Beth. I had to find Beth. I had to find Beth. My thoughts
and my body aligned under this one obsessive mantra. I had

to find Beth. I raced through the entire length of the school without finding her.

Once outside, I made my way to the tennis courts, and that's where I finally came to a stop. Covered in sweat and out of breath, I curled my fingers into the chain-link fence and felt another massive shift within me.

It was Derek. He was sitting at the far end of the tennis court, surrounded by a couple of senior kids. It wasn't his usual crowd. These people were his new "shaved-head Derek" crowd. Definitely more sophisticated than Neal and Kevin.

I forgot about Beth.

My whole body was on fire. I was no longer running. I was walking in slow, measured, steady steps across the tennis court. I couldn't have moved faster if I had wanted to, because the sudden rage burning though my body made it impossible to move with any fluidity or speed. Every step I took was like stepping through a force field of raw electricity.

Derek looked over at me, startled at my sudden appearance in front of him. I was out of breath, and I could feel strands of my hair sticking to the side of my face.

"Oh, hey, fuckface!" I said in an unsteady, weird tone of voice that creeped me out a little.

There was some laughter and clapping. I had forgotten about the audience.

"Oh my god," the girl said in a melodic, soft voice. "Who is that, Der?"

I recognized her now as one of the older girls. Dawn Henderson. Way too mature honestly for me to even register as someone in my sphere of existence.

Derek didn't bother answering her. Instead, he kept his eyes on me. "What's your deal?" he asked.

"Your breath smells like shit," I told him.

Some small particles of hurt spilled into his face. It took

me a little by surprise. I didn't care, though. It only made me
hungry for more.

"You came to tell me my breath stinks?" he said.

"I came to tell you congratulations—you're a bigger piece-
of-shit cunt than I could have ever imagined possible!"

A stunned silence had fallen over the small group around us.

"Hey, no," said Dawn, breaking the silence with the calm
confidence of a levelheaded parent. "That's not cool. That's an
incredibly offensive word."

I looked over at her distractedly. "Who the hell's talking to
you?"

Derek stepped in. "Hey, you're being a real brat right now,"
he said, trying to move me off to the side.

I shoved him away. "Don't fucking touch me!"

"What is your problem?"

I kicked him in the shin.

"*Hey!*" he said, jumping to the side. "Watch it! Seriously,
what's your fucking deal right now?"

"You're a crumb," I said, and there was a sudden immense
need to grind him into the dirt in whatever way I could. He
had ruined my life. All the emotions floundering through my
body narrowed into this one channel of rage. "You're a fucking
crumb to me! That's the relevance you have to my life—and
it doesn't even matter what you do—you'll always be a crumb
to everyone in your life. No one is ever going to take you seriously. You know why? Because you're stupid and generic and
oddly proportioned with your weird little fuck-faced head."
I gulped in a ragged breath of air before finishing my rant.
"You're nothing, Derek! And you can shove your stupid trumpet up your ass, by the way, because if you think it's somehow
making you cool or unexpected, you're wrong! You know who
is cooler than you? *Mrs. Gillespie.* And also that smooth jazz

saxophone guy that's always on the easy listening channel! Both of them are, like, five billion times cooler than you! Oh, and you're a vindictive, fuck-faced dick too."

I was breathing hard. Dawn was making a face of outraged disbelief and said something under her breath to the effect of me being seriously unglued.

For a moment, there was nothing, and then Derek grabbed my arm and pulled me to the other end of the tennis court. We were both out of breath when he let go. I caught my balance and took a few steps backward until I felt the reassuring support of the chain-link fence behind me. Leaning into it, I stared back at Derek, who looked to be crying. Not full-on howling, but his eyes were red and wet.

There was a silence. Deep and wide and utterly weird. "You want to talk?" he said flatly. "Go ahead. Talk."

I glanced over his shoulder quickly. The tennis court was empty now except for Dawn and the two guys looking over from where they stood on the other side, confused out of their minds. Thrilled, probably. It was this kind of stuff that generally kept the blood flowing at school. Drama.

"You broke my heart, Grace," Derek said in an unsteady voice, thick with emotion. "I mean, don't you *get that*?"

The conversation had totally gone down the wrong tunnel. "*What*?"

He shook his head. "What's wrong with you?"

"*Jesus,*" I said. "I had *sex* with you—I thought that was what you wanted."

"No, you didn't have sex with me. That's not what that was." A bitter laugh spewed from his lips. "You played with me. You fucked me in the head. Look at me. You think I want to be this pathetic? You think this is how I wanted to spend my senior year?"

It was actually disgusting how alike we were when it came down to it. Derek and I dealt with heartbreak in almost exactly the same way. It was like we were the Rembrandts of emotions. Maybe that's why I had no patience for him. He reminded me of myself back in the Mr. Sorrentino days.

My laugh came out as twisted as his had been. "How is this an actual conversation we're having?" I cried up at the sky. "What the fuck is even *happening*? There's no way this is real!"

"Yeah, this is real," Derek said darkly. "I hope it was worth it for you."

"Oh my *god*!" I could have killed him. "You kissed *me*, Derek! *You kissed me!* I didn't make the first move! You gave me hand-job instructions, for Christ's sake!"

"You knew exactly how I felt," he said, the tremble back in his voice. "You played with me."

"Oh, the way that you played with all those girls who are still crying their eyes out in the bathroom over you every day?"

"Every girl I've been with had fun. I make sure they have a good time, and I was always honest about what I was looking for with them. What you're doing to me is totally different. I thought there was something real happening between us during spring break. You acted like you were into me—for real—like you were having fun, and it wasn't just about sex. We laughed and made fun of stuff—that's not how you have sex if you're just trying to get the job done, all right? That's *real*. And then, out of nowhere, you're totally cold. You make me promise to pretend nothing ever happened so that you can go rub yourself up against that little fuckrag who punched me in the face. And I even go along with it. You don't think that's messed up?"

I could feel the rage being dumped back into my bloodstream. I thought for a second I would just walk away. I pushed myself off the fence and took a few steps past him, but then I turned, because it was impossible not to scratch that itch.

"I've hated your guts right from the beginning," I said. "I think I was pretty clear about that, so don't make it sound like I *seduced* you. Take some fucking responsibility."

"Oh, so you hated me but then had no problem giving it up? What does that make you? Did you ever think about that?"

We were at that point where we were going to say whatever was necessary to cause damage. "I wanted to lose my virginity. It had nothing to do with you. You were just there. Had I known what a fucking little bitch you were going to be about it, I would have waited for a real man who can handle the free sex!"

For a moment, it was as though we stood in a vacuum. Derek and I stared at each other without breathing. What I had said didn't even sound like me. Who was I to talk about needing a "real man"? The whole thing was surreal beyond repair.

"You're the worst person I ever met," he said. His voice was quiet again.

"Well, boo-fucking-hoo. Why don't you go cry about it some more?" I almost walked away again, but turned one more time and pointed at him. "You know what? *You're* the worst person *I've* ever met! You told the whole school that I lost my virginity to you after all the useless promising you did not to ever tell."

He looked confused. "What are you talking about?"

"Oh, come on! The whole school knows. My own roommate found out from some random person."

"I didn't tell anyone," he said.

"Derek, you and I are the only people who know we had sex. And I know it wasn't me who talked about it. Why are you denying it?"

"I didn't tell anyone!"

"Whatever," I said in frustrated resignation. "You're unbelievable. I hope you die."

I was done with Derek. I never wanted to talk to him again. It was the most useless endeavor I had ever undertaken. I turned away from him with finality and then stopped dead in my tracks. The bell was ringing for the second time, and the tennis court had been abandoned, except for Wade, who stood a few feet away from me. His arms limp by his side, his face utterly blank.

I froze. Terror was trickling through every part of my body. The ice-cold, acid feel of it was sliding into me slow and meticulous. There was nothing I could do anymore. I wasn't even breathing. I just stood there, waiting for the world to come crashing down on me.

Wade walked past me. He didn't waste any words or long, questioning looks. He dismissed my presence almost immediately.

He won that fight. It helped that Derek's friends weren't around to hold him down and that Derek had been taken somewhat by surprise, standing there, already half-eaten-up by emotions; but most of it was Wade. I was no longer shocked at seeing him able to drive a fist into someone's body or slam his foot into a rib cage, but there was an uncanny energy in the way he tackled Derek—something he pulled out of some black hole of the universe. Wade was a relatively tall kid for his age, but he wasn't buff. Derek was much bigger, having safely reached the other side of puberty. At the very least, it should have been a drawn-out affair of punches and equal amounts of damage done. But it wasn't. Derek lay on the ground within seconds, with his nose bleeding. I tried to make Wade stop, but it was as if I didn't exist. Nothing about what I yelled out to him even caused a blip on his radar. I grabbed his shoulders and tried to pry him off, but it was no use.

And then the rage and the accompanying supernatural strength left his body without warning, and he stopped. His whole body went lifeless, and he didn't respond to me or Derek or the PE teacher and his tennis students who had just entered the courts. He was done with having any kind of energy left inside of him.

I KNEW ALL ALONG THAT WE WOULDN'T SURVIVE IT.
The world that Wade and I had inhabited was too ideal for that kind of contamination. It was too bright and perfect—it didn't have the immune system necessary to handle Derek. It didn't matter that we were painfully in love with each other, it didn't matter that I hated Derek. None of the logistics mattered, because in the end, it didn't change that fact that Derek and I had done what we did. It. Sex. There was nothing to be done about it. It was over. We both knew this so instinctively that neither of us tried much in the way of saving what we had. There wasn't even that much to say on the matter. It was a pretty straightforward affair that took place in the library a few days later. It was all done within minutes—a frustratingly well-oiled few minutes. It should have been more of a spectacle, but I suppose neither Wade nor I had the stomach for it. And to make matters worse, the whole room was illuminated

by the cheerful late-morning sun bouncing off every surface, taunting us.

He was pushing a library cart loaded with books down one of the narrow paths between two shelves when I stepped into his line of vision. He started when he saw me. An involuntary twitch in his shoulders, and then a lethargic calm settled back over him.

For a while, neither of us spoke. I leaned against the bookshelf a few feet away from him while he went back to work, pulling books out from the cart and searching for the right place to shelve them. He was in deep shit for getting into another physical altercation only a day after the incident with Chad Werling in the dining hall, but "deep shit" is always relative, and our school didn't throw people out easily, so in the end, the shit wasn't as deep as it could have been, I suppose.

"Hi, Gracie," Wade said eventually without interrupting his work. His fingers trailed over the books in the cart, searching for the next one.

After I still hadn't said anything and the silence became suffocating, Wade stepped back from the cart and sat down on the floor, his back against one of the shelves, and stared at the carpet. It was evident that he would be the one to carry the conversation, and he took a moment to gather his thoughts. He held a book in his lap while he was thinking and began tapping his finger against it in a steady rhythm. I noticed the fingernail, bitten down painfully low, and the flesh raw around the nail.

"It's your life," Wade said, without looking up. "You honestly have the right to do whatever you want with it, and I'd be a creep if I felt like I had any say in it. If you needed to screw Derek, then, you know, that's exactly what you should have done."

I flinched at the word *screw* even though his tone of voice was oddly devoid of any severity.

"Sorry," he said, glancing up for the briefest of moments. *"Make love to."*

This was worse.

"No," I said, holding back the tears best as I could. "We didn't *make love.*"

"Sleep with, have sex," he said. "Whatever. Doesn't even matter. I'm just saying it's your life, and you have every right to go out there and do what you want."

I said nothing. Wade continued to look at the floor. The mood between us was so incredibly heavy it felt like the air was made of out of lead and we were trying to breathe it in and out of our lungs.

"It just happened," I said after a while of breathing in lead. "The whole thing wasn't planned—we didn't, like, even try to do any of it. We just . . . I just . . ."

I didn't know what I was saying or how to continue saying it. Words just crawled slowly and tediously from my mouth until they didn't anymore, and none of them were worth anything anyway. They didn't explain anything. They weren't an apology. They didn't bring relief.

"It's okay," Wade said. "Seriously. Don't explain it to me. It's none of my business." He said it with a thick kind of non-emotion, and his eyes were heavy when he looked up at me at last. "I mean it. You don't belong to me. If I have a problem with anything you do, then that's exactly what it is—my problem. Not yours." He looked down at his fucked-up finger that he was tapping on the book. "But . . . I just can't hang out anymore. I like you too much. I won't be able to take it."

My stomach was free-falling in terror, despite the fact that I had known all along where the conversation would go. I suppose here would have been the point to jump to life and grab at anything that might save us. The universe hinged on the next few seconds and what I did with them. But I did nothing with the moment. I was paralyzed. If it had been Mr. Sorrentino or Derek or anyone else in the world standing opposite me, I would have had things to say, but it was Wade standing there. The moment was too impossibly huge. There was nothing I could do.

"You can understand that, right?" he said, his eyes flicking up at me one more time.

I nodded.

"And I won't be weird about it, I promise," he said.

I knew that if I blinked, all the water that had built up in my eyes would create an avalanche. "You can be weird about if you want," I said quietly.

There was a weak smile, and then he drove both his hands over his face with a shudder that went through his entire body. He stayed like this for a second, with his face in his hands.

"Excuse me, what is going on back here? Are you supposed to be here?"

I turned with a start and found the librarian glaring over at me from the end of the shelf.

"I was trying to find a book," I said.

She didn't buy it. "Would you mind getting back to where you are supposed to be, please? You two can canoodle on your own time."

Wade scrambled to his feet and picked up the next book, and that's how we parted. No goodbyes. No parting glances. Nothing at all like any breakup I had ever seen in a movie or read about in a book. The librarian remained standing there, supervising my exit with her hands on her hips. I looked back in case there was an opportunity to say something, but there wasn't. Wade was already bent over the books, and I was walking away.

That was the end.

I TURNED SIXTEEN IN MY BEDROOM THE NEXT DAY.
I lay down on my bed and stayed there for a long, confusing amount of time that might have consisted of an entire day and night. It was the weekend, so I could go as deep as I needed into despair, but it wasn't what I had expected. After the terror had calmed down, there was nothing left. It was the strangest thing. I remembered how much I had cried when Mr. Sorrentino and I broke up. I hadn't been able to stop—I had been a useless, shuddering, slobbering ball of emotional dynamite. Anything would trigger everything. Any word, any object, any sound would lead straight to Mr. Sorrentino, and radioactive pain would leak from all my pores.

But now I just lay there, staring at the ceiling. Not moving for hours. Beyond thoughts. Beyond any real emotions. No struggles or fear. What's the worst that can happen when the worst that can happen is already real? There's a debilitating kind of peace that comes with that kind of an aftermath.

I had no interest in being happy anymore. I'd never asked for that crusade anyway. Constanze, Beth, Mrs. Gillespie, Eloise Smith, my parents, my half sisters living with my dad in Beverly Hills—it was all fine by me. For a bizarre moment, I had no problems. I fell asleep a few times. Georgina was gone that weekend, and that was all I could ask for. The loneliness of that room was the best thing that could have happened to me.

At some point on Sunday, Beth materialized in front of my bed. She stared at me for a long time. "When's the last time you moved?" she asked eventually.

I didn't know. It was strange seeing her there.

"Hey, I asked you a question!"

She nudged me with her foot, and when I didn't react, she drove it into my side a little harder. It was good to feel my nerves responding. For a short moment, that whole side of my body was alive. I realized with minor interest how dead I was in comparison to that small area that Beth's shoe had just contacted.

"What was the question?" My voice came out uneven and scraping.

"When was the last time you moved?"

I thought about it. How should I know? I didn't keep a log. I wanted to say that I thought maybe I moved my hand a day ago, but I couldn't get my thoughts to fully align, and stringing words together required too much energy. I didn't want to have to talk or crawl out of whatever I was in.

"You need to have some emotions," Beth said.

I was still lying on the bed, on top of the covers with all my clothes on from two days ago. I hadn't eaten or had anything to drink in a long while—probably since I had seen Wade in the library on Friday afternoon. After that, I had walked into my room and fallen onto my bed. I hadn't moved much since.

Beth dropped a pack of cigarettes on my bed and held up a

small box of something in her hand. "I was going to use this myself, but we're going to use it on you instead. Get up."

It was a box of hair dye. There was a picture of a woman on the box staring at me like she was about to give me a blow job. Her hair was platinum blond, flowing around her face in shiny waves.

"I said get up," Beth repeated.

I got up. She made me drink a bottle of Gatorade. Then she lit a cigarette, moved me over to the window, and stood by while I smoked it to the end. We didn't talk. I just stood by the window smoking, and she watched. I had no thoughts. I was staring out at the courtyard without really seeing anything.

After that, she took me to the bathroom and bleached my hair. An hour or so later, I sat on my bed, a towel on my shoulders and my wet alien hair dripping down over my back. I hadn't bothered looking in the mirror, so who knew what I looked like. Beth had been mechanical and driven—reading the instructions in the packet, applying the toxic slime into my roots and all the way down to the ends of my hair. Then she sat there with me, waiting for the chemicals to do their thing, reading *Ham on Rye* with her gloves still on while I just sat, staring at the faucet because it was right there in my line of vision, the easiest thing to see. She had made me hold my head under the shower as she washed out the dye, and then she had toweled off my wet hair and made me eat a protein bar.

Now she sat by my window smoking, and I sat on my bed.

"Wade and I broke up," I said.

"Yup. I know," she said.

Finally, I started crying.

THE MAIN IDEA WAS TO STAY ALIVE. TO CRANK ANY
and all levers within reach in a thoughtless frenzy of madness.
To do everything. I went to drama rehearsals. I joined the god-
damned volleyball team. I went to parties in people's rooms.
In a perfectly fucked-up kind of way, I was more social than I
had ever been before in my life.

Parties were not allowed in the dorm rooms, but people
had them anyway, and when I got word of one, I usually went,
inspired by the raging terror of loneliness. I'd sit by myself
mostly and drink whatever there was to drink. Sometimes
it was just juice, but other times someone had managed to
smuggle in some form of alcohol or another. I got high a couple of times, but generally all that did for me was the opposite
of what it was supposed to do. I felt sick and paranoid, and
being that I had a pretty bountiful supply of sickness and para-
noia as it was, I tried to stick to alcohol when I could. I kind
of enjoyed the effects of booze—not the taste, just the buzz
when it came on. It was a little more predictable. It allowed

me to have intense conversations about candy bar logos and music and politics, of which I knew just about nothing. People were far less obnoxious when you were drunk, and I was sometimes nice to people and oddly accessible. It was weird. I wondered if that had been the secret to socializing all along—inebriation. Sometimes, things were almost okay from an inebriated standpoint. Lying somewhere, listening to stupid conversations float over my head, forgetting things that mattered. But other times it backfired, and the alcohol magnified the sadness into something so monstrous that I cried all night without sleeping at all.

Beth checked in on me regularly during this period. It was nice of her even if tact wasn't quite her forte. But then again, it wasn't mine either. She meant well, and she never took any offense to my highly volatile, often snotty attitude, full of covered-up hurt and lack of patience.

"What's up?"

It was one of those times where she appeared suddenly out of nowhere in my room. I looked up. She was leaning against the doorway with her arms crossed.

"The ceiling," I said.

It was in the evening. Georgina was taking a shower or something.

"I was worried when I heard that you joined the volleyball team," Beth said, ambling in and throwing herself down on the bed next to me.

"Yeah. I hate it. They keep talking about being a team player."

She grimaced.

"But it's good," I said. "Doing things that make you feel horrible is a great way not to feel the pain of being alive, you know?"

"Oh, *geez*."

"I'm serious," I said. "It helps. Like, if there was a class where we learned how to drive nails through our hands, I'd definitely take it."

"Yeah, I bet you would, you melodramatic little nutjob."

I closed my laptop and made a point of not making eye contact with Beth for a moment.

"Have you talked to Wade—like, recently or something?" I asked her in a tone that was meant to sound offhand but didn't at all sound casual.

"I said hello to him the other day," she said.

I turned and studied her face greedily. "You talked to him?"

"It wasn't much of a conversation. I just said, 'Hey, Wade Scholfield.'"

"What did he say?"

"He said, 'Hey, Beth Whelan, your training bra is show-ing.'"

I let out a short laugh. It didn't sound like the kind of thing Wade would say, but somehow it also did. Like a grade-school insult that sounded adorable in high school.

"He hangs out with those little NSB shitheads," Beth said.

NSB = Nonsexual Boner. Calvin's band.

"Yeah. They're okay, but yeah."

Beth seemed disinterested in Wade's new social circle. Her eyes went around the room as though trying to assess my mental stability by means of my surroundings.

"So, did he seem like he was—*normal*?" I asked gingerly.

"That's not the adjective I would use in regard to little Scholfield."

"Well, I mean, do you think he's unhappy?"

I wanted him to be unhappy. I was in love with him, but not that kind of selfless love where all you need is for the other person to be happy. I wished I were that kind of person, but I knew I was the scumbag kind—the kind that felt a glimmer

of comfort in the potential misery my absence might be caus-
ing in Wade's life. I *needed* him to be miserable. I hoped he
was crying himself to sleep at night, thinking about me. I
hoped he might do something embarrassing on my account—
something like run through the halls and slam his fists into
all the lockers—or at the very least shave his head like Derek
had done. But he didn't. All he did was stay out of my way diligently, and when I did see him, he seemed to be uneventfully
well adjusted. He didn't even sit alone at mealtimes, looking
defenseless and spaced out; he sat with the Nonsexual Boner
guys or sometimes some of the chess club nerds, or even with
Michael Holt—Pizzaface guy. He talked to people. He did
stuff. I'd even seen him laugh.

Beth shook her head in irritation. "Ask him yourself. You
guys are psychotic, do you know that? Not talking to each other
after all that glory hallelujah crap. One of you should have
shown up drunk in the other one's room by now, crying and
puking all over the place and begging for forgiveness. There's
something wrong with both of you."

Beth didn't understand the clarity of the situation.

"I ruined it."

"People ruin shit all the time," she said, unimpressed.
"That's basically what the human race is there for. You think
people go through life excelling at everything and making a
long string of excellent choices and decisions?"

"This is different."

She made a derisive sound at the back of her throat.

"He would have to give me some kind of sign," I said. "I
can't just talk to him."

"That's sickening that you're actually going to wait for a sign."

"I can't talk to him. There's no way."

"Why the fuck not?"

"Because, Beth, I don't exist to him anymore! I literally do not exist! He doesn't even look at me. He looks *through* me. It's like I'm just air. Like I'm nothing. How can I talk to him if I'm not even *there*?"

She got up and rolled her eyes again—more elaborately this time. "Oh, *please*. You're probably the *only* thing that exists in his life right now."

"Doesn't look like it. He's hanging out with, like, everyone and their grandmas except me."

"Yeah, well, you have to keep in mind that you smashed his fragile little heart into a million pieces, and now he's got to put on this big show of how he's okay so that he can at least *pretend* he still has some self-esteem left."

"Thanks for laying it all out for me," I said, throwing my composition book against the wall.

Beth didn't care. She would get irritated at you for wearing weird socks, but when you had an attitude, she failed to get properly riled up by it.

"He's just trying to survive," she said. She was standing by the closet, lazily examining the few random garments I had hanging in there. "You can't really expect him to be doing anything logical right now. That's why that would be your job at this juncture. You'd have to step up. Be the non-moron in the scenario."

"Ha! That's funny," I said bitterly.

"What the hell, G," she said, holding up the bra that had one of the bra straps safety-pinned on.

"Yeah, it tore off, okay?" I said

"How old is this thing?"

"I don't know."

She put the bra down on the dresser disapprovingly. "Your daddy needs to give you bra money. I'm sorry."

"I'm never going to have sex ever again, so it doesn't even matter."

"Just because you're never going to have sex again doesn't make it okay for you to be walking around with hobo underwear."

"Beth, I don't care about me or what the fuck I'm wearing! I don't have the energy to give even, like, a nanoparticle of shit! Why are you making me talk about my bra? What does that matter? *Wade doesn't like me anymore!*"

I was close to losing it right there. I could feel the tightness in my eyes again, and I really didn't want to fall apart in front of someone else. Least of all Beth, again. I was holding on to my attitude for dear life.

"Wade does like you," she said calmly, uninterested in my tantrum. "You like him and he likes you, and both of you are determined to ignore that completely. The only actual problem I can see here is that you're a couple of half-baked morons."

I was biting the inside of my lip desperately. "I ruined it," I said. "There's nothing left to save."

Beth was leaning against the dresser, smoking and studying me. "It's like watching a bad movie. With terrible writing—where people do stuff that makes you wish you had a barf bag."

"Yeah. I'm sorry the plotline to my life doesn't float your boat."

She laughed a little. "Hey, don't take it out on me, G," she said more gently. "I'm not the one who decided it was a good idea to go on a weeklong adventure of sexual awakening with my boyfriend's archnemesis. I'm just trying to help here. I really am."

"I appreciate you checking in on me and bleaching my hair into a shit color and all that, but don't ever be a shrink, okay?"

She laughed again—the same light little laugh, unaffected by life and all its grime. "Sorry," she said, putting her arm around me. "You know I do care in my own special way."

I smiled weakly.

"All right, I gotta go," she said, getting up. "And you're

right, we should bleach your hair one more time. I know you don't care about your looks and personal hygiene anymore, but it honestly can't hurt to look a little less gross."

My hair still had that washed-out orange color. I had gotten used to it. It really was amazing how little my own appearance mattered to me at that point. All those wishes and daydreams I had had about becoming beautiful, alluring, and desirable were gone. I never wanted to make another boy horny as long as I lived. In fact, the worse I looked, the better I somehow felt.

"No, it's fine. Let's just leave it."

"No," said Beth.

"All right, whatever." I would have agreed to pretty much any hair decision.

Wade and I continued to keep out of each other's way with religious discipline. We couldn't avoid each other fully, however, being that we had half our classes together. Not to mention break times and lunchtime and dinnertime and hallways and after-school activities. It was inevitable that occasionally our eyes would meet and we'd forget to look away fast enough. The craziest thing about that was he didn't smile at me when it happened. There was nothing at all in his face except an infinite blankness when our eyes met. This was such a colossal mindfuck that I cannot begin to find a way to describe it. I told myself over and over that it was because he liked me too much. Wade was in love with me, and that's why we couldn't be together. It was too great of a love. It had been too perfect. I was even beginning to think that maybe—*maybe*—I could live with that kind of beautiful nightmare. It was, after all, the kind of tragedy that would make a good book—something dark and beautifully psychotic, written in the nineteenth century by a French writer. I figured maybe I could live with that.

And then I saw Wade talking to a girl, and everything inside of me free-fell.

It was Anju. They were sitting on the bleachers together, and she was painting his nails with blue nail polish. Beautiful Anju with the long eyelashes and the cute barrettes in her hair and her skirt rolled up so that it violated the school regulations on acceptable skirt lengths.

She was leaning over his hand, which was resting on her bare thigh, and carefully running the tiny brush over his nails. She glanced up at him and said something witty and dirty, judging by the slight smile and the way she held her head to the side. He laughed. It was a real laugh too—the one where his whole face lit up in surprise. Anju scolded him for messing up the nail polish, and he made apologies through his laughter. She leaned back over his hand with a giggle.

At that moment, I didn't know how I would survive.

It felt like I was dropping through the earth. I just fell. Thousands of miles. Hurtling into a vacuum.

I had to sit down where I stood on the football field for a moment. Like an idiot, I couldn't move. I just sat there and thought about it. It hit me hard. Anju was the right shape and size. She was pretty and petite and compact. She walked with her hips swinging rhythmically—not like a lumberjack, the way that I walked. She wasn't a popular girl; she was a *cool* girl. She was exactly the kind of girl that you would imagine with Wade.

A fucking puzzle piece that didn't have to be forced in like me. Plus, she was nice. They fit.

I TOOK IT OUT ON GEORGINA WHEN I GOT BACK TO my room. I was trembling and no doubt crazy-eyed, but being a lunatic was all I could do to keep it together. Georgina looked up as I entered and was about to ask what was wrong, but I was already yelling at her about her towel encroaching on my side of the room. She yelled back, indignant, and we argued for about an hour over the invisible line down the middle of the room. I lost three inches in the process and then told her to take down her Luke Bryan poster from the door since the door was technically half on my side (Luke Bryan being a country singer she had a crush on; and nothing against Luke Bryan—modern country just wasn't anywhere near the vicinity of my cup of tea). She ripped it off dramatically and then reattached it so that it stuck only to her side of the door and then taped the other part onto the wall across the door hinge.

"There!" she announced. "Our door looks like crap now. I hope you're happy!"

"Yeah, I'm super ecstatic about that gross guy on our door."

Once the lights were out, I couldn't stop crying. I tried my absolute best to be quiet about it, but there is a certain type of crying where dignity simply isn't an option. So I pressed my face hard into my pillow and tried to smother the sounds that way, but Georgina must have heard me all the same because after a while she said, "I'll throw away the poster, okay?"

There was so much quiet compassion in her voice that I started to cry harder. She let me cry for a while without saying anything. After about ten minutes, I pulled the pillow off my face and took a ragged breath.

"I'm not upset about Luke Bryan," I said through the dark.

"Yeah," she said. "I know."

Short silence. I had never been this openly mangled in front of her. I had always held on for dear life to my cool, shit-head façade in front of Georgina because it was all I ever really had. And now I didn't even have that anymore.

"It fucking hurts so bad, Georgie," I said to the ceiling that was presumably above me in the dark. "It hurts so incredibly bad. How do I make it stop?"

"I don't know," she said, "but it's probably okay for you to feel that way. You and Wade were in love for real."

Fresh tears were crawling down my face. "I'm still in love with him."

"Well, you guys just broke up. It probably takes a while."

Her words held little solace.

"A *while*? This is never going to end, Georgie! It's never going to get out of me."

More uncomfortable silence.

"I don't know," Georgina ventured after a while. "I really think you'll be okay eventually."

I reached for the roll of toilet paper I had on my bedside table and blew my nose. It had become almost impossible to breathe with all the goo in my sinuses. I threw the used tissue onto the floor and settled back into bed. "I wish I'd never met him," I said.

"Don't you think you'd have met someone else, though?" Georgina asked. "Someone else who would have broken your heart?"

"No. No one else can hurt me. Not like Wade."

She mumbled something about me not being able to know that for sure, and I ignored her.

"The worst thing in the world," I said, "is to meet the person that you're meant to be with. That's the big secret. Because how can you not fuck it up? It's impossible. *Something* is going to go wrong—that's just the way the world is built."

Georgina was out of her depths. She rustled around uncomfortably in her blankets and tried to say a few more soothing words about time making things better and how the situation probably only seemed bad right now, and how everything would feel different soon. She had no clue what she was talking about, though, that's the thing. All she had was her experience with Chad Werling, and that was light-years away from what had just happened to me. Still, I appreciated the effort she made, and although we never discussed my emotional implosion again after that night, it had brought us closer. I felt the bond crystallize between us the next morning when she did indeed throw out the Luke Bryan poster.

A couple of days later, I stood in front of Mrs. Gillespie's English class, slowly unfolding a piece of paper that I had folded down into a desperate, little, sweaty, one-inch rectangle. We were supposed to have written a poem about "the gift of nature" for homework, and it was my turn to read my poem out loud to the class. The unfolding process seemed to take a lifetime. I could hear chairs creaking as people shifted their positions in boredom.

"My, you're very diligent about folding up your homework assignments, aren't you?" Mrs. Gillespie said with a thin smile.

"Yeah. I guess," I said.

For a second, I paused, groping for a better comeback. I loved coming up with things to say to teachers that I would never have had the guts to actually say, but just then I didn't even have the energy to fantasize. I came up with nothing and continued unfolding the paper. When the paper was finally spread open, I took a breath. I closed my eyes for a second and then opened them again and began to read the poem out loud.

I fed upon your giving nature
Raping you of your sole possession, emotions
Ripping and screaming as you try to escape
Using what willpower remains, you surgically remove me
from your life
Left with only the empty cavity of your body, I crawl within
you to shelter myself from the rain
Love is suicide
Love is suicide
Love is suicide
Love is suicide

I was looking at Wade for the last four lines (which, incidentally, I ripped off a Smashing Pumpkins song). Openly—no efforts to veil my message. The guy next to him was suppressing a laugh, and there were some other noises of amusement that rippled through the room. Wade didn't look at me. There was nothing there. No interest, no recognition, no sign that he had even heard what I had said. Nothing. His eyes were inaccessible. Before I had even gotten to the last line, he had already turned away from the front of the room.

"Grace, I fail to see how that poem is about the gift of nature," Mrs. Gillespie said when I was done.

I looked from Wade to her, displaced for a moment. And then back at Wade, who was now turned all the way around and talking to Calvin, who was sitting behind him. I felt my sadness turn so hot that it became sticky and raw and unbearable, like I had to get the hell out of my own body.

"Earth to Miss Welles," Mrs. Gillespie was saying. "Hello?"

I swung my attention back over to her, dazed and unable to fully focus on her.

"All right, please see me after class," she said, motioning for me to sit down again.

I crumpled up the paper and threw it at Wade.

"Grace, I said sit down!"

I walked out.

I thought I would die. Surely, there was a fuse of some sort that would blow when things culminated in this kind of radio-active nightmare—like in a computer game when you get the Game Over notification. But there was no fuse. There was no anesthesia. I just continued to stay alive. I stayed alive through Mrs. Gillespie's lecture in Mr. Wahlberg's office about taking homework assignments seriously and how she wasn't in the mood for having her "chain yanked." And then I just continued staying alive after that. Through all the other lessons of the day. Through break times. Through dinner. Through the night. Through dreams about doors that were too small to get through and Mr. Sorrentino telling me that he found an alien in his poop.

I don't know why I even walked into the dining room the next morning. I wasn't planning on eating breakfast—food had become just another way to feel nauseous. As soon as I opened the doors, the smells of morning grease assaulted me with full force, and I almost pushed back out of the room, but then I noticed Wade. He was sitting at the back of the room with Calvin at the table that had always been ours. Usually, I didn't put myself through the agony of being a spectator like this, but I couldn't help it. I stood frozen, watching him be normal, with my brain melting out of my head due to the sheer lack of logic. And then I was walking toward them. There was no particular thought process involved, just my feet doing what the rest of me had been too scared shitless to do. Both Calvin and Wade looked up when my presence became apparent. I stopped in front of their table and did nothing. Nobody did anything.

After a long moment of silence, Calvin cleared his throat. "I'm the third wheel here, right?" And then, without waiting for a response: "Yeah, I can feel it. Yeah." He got up and grabbed his drink. "I'll let you kids enjoy this heartwarming sexual tension in privacy," he said, patting Wade on the back with a grin.

Suddenly, there was nothing between Wade and me except a couple of feet of nitrogen and oxygen. We were supposed to have been unbreakable. The "real thing." What a joke. We hadn't lasted long enough to compete with some of the shallowest couples in school. We were dilapidated and dead, while all around us our vapid counterparts were still holding hands.

"What's wrong with you?" was all I could think of saying to Wade.

He leaned back with no answer.

"*What the hell is wrong with you?*" I repeated, more rabid.

He looked up lazily. "Oh. I thought that was a rhetorical question. You really want me to answer that? It's a long list."

I had to take a moment to concentrate on not falling apart. It wasn't possible that he was talking to me like that—in that tone of voice, with that bored flick of his eyes. It wasn't possible. This was *Wade*. When he looked at me, everything in his face was supposed to come alive—he was supposed to dissolve helplessly in front of me. *This* was not possible.

"You said you weren't going to be weird about this," I said, "and you're being fucking weird."

"Am I?"

"Yeah, Wade. You are. You're being weird—like, on a gold-medal level."

He made a gesture of *Well, what're you gonna do?*

"That's it?" I cried, unraveling further. "*That's your response?*"

"I don't know what you want from me right now," he said, his eyes finally fixing on me, steady. "Why are you even talking to me?"

I had thought all I needed was for him to see me again, because naturally if Wade didn't see me, how could I possibly be real? I was certain that was all I needed to feel better—to have him see me. But I couldn't have been more wrong. I had his full-blown attention now, and it felt like being punched in the stomach. No hostility. Just a terribly generic unfamiliarity, as though I were some crazy person on the street, yelling at him for not accepting Jesus into his heart. It was the shittiest thing anyone had ever done to me—looking at me like that.

"You're sick!" I said, knocking his drink over.

Some heads turned at the table next to us.

The juice ran the length of the table before splattering to the ground.

Wade did nothing. He was calm, watching me make a spectacle of myself with zero reaction. Not even in his eyes.

I grabbed his bowl of soggy cereal and threw it at his chest. The bowl clattered to the floor, and I turned and walked away, not waiting for a reaction this time. Instead, I made straight for Mr. Grant, who was on dining hall duty again that day. He was standing in the middle of the room, his arms crossed and his head moving very slowly from one side, across the chaos to the other side of the room like an oscillating fan.

"Mr. Grant?"

"Yes?" he said, his focus unbroken.

"Wade Scholfield brought his skateboard into the dining room. Just thought you should know."

A zealous snap of the head. "What?"

I pointed it out, my finger going straight to where Wade was wiping cereal and milk off his lap. He looked over at the mention of his name.

"It's under the table," I told Mr. Grant, keeping my eyes locked on Wade's.

Bringing a skateboard into the dining room wasn't allowed, and naturally, Wade broke that rule on a regular basis because that's exactly the kind of combination of stupid and lazy that he was. He'd hide the skateboard under the table to have it at hand right as he left, without having to go all the way to his room to get it after he was done eating. He was pretty good at sneaking it in and out of the dining hall, usually by means of a jacket or a backpack or combo of things, but to me it had always seemed like a particularly shortsighted risk. They loved confiscating things at our school, and that skateboard was maybe the only possession Wade really cared about. God, it felt good to ruin that for him.

After I talked to Mr. Grant, I turned and went over to where Derek was eating. "I'm sitting down!" I warned him.

He was by himself (this was a new, shaved-head Derek phenomenon). I didn't wait for a response and just threw myself into the chair next to him. Derek stared at me blankly, mouth full of food, immobilized for the moment.

I looked past him and watched Mr. Grant pull the skateboard

out from under the table triumphantly. It seemed to make his day, judging by the healthy glow that suddenly emanated from his usually grayish face. He held the skateboard up to Wade and launched into the inevitable victory speech with much relish and sputtering enthusiasm.

"I thought you hated my guts," Derek was saying to me. I had almost forgotten that he was right there, next to me.

I shrugged.

"What's that supposed to mean?" Derek asked.

"Do you have a date for the prom?" I asked instead of answering him.

"I'm not going."

"I'll go with you," I said.

"What the fuck is that supposed to mean?"

"It means I'll go with you to the prom."

I focused back on Mr. Grant across the room for a second—he had started yelling. I must have missed something. He pointed at the door. Wade got up.

"What?" Derek was saying.

I turned back to Derek. "Jesus Christ! To prom. I'll go with you to prom, goddamn it."

"*Why?*"

"Why *not?*"

"I don't know—maybe because last time we talked you said I was a waste of oxygen and you hoped I'd die. Oh, and you said that easy-listening saxophone guy and Mrs. Gillespie are cooler than I am."

I threw him an impatient look. "I was pissed off. They're *not* cooler than you. It's, like, scientifically impossible to be *less* cool than those people, so don't have a heart attack about it."

Derek hesitated at the brink of something. He became all fidgety with his fork and eventually dropped it on his plate. "I told the girl who plays the tuba in the orchestra that we had sex, okay?" he said. "That's the person I told. *One* person. And she swore she wouldn't tell."

I rolled my eyes. "Good to know. Kind of irrelevant right now, though."

"So, what—you don't hate my guts anymore?" he asked. "From one minute to the next?"

"Who the hell knows? You're making this complicated. It's a simple question, Derek."

"All right," he said. "It's fucked up that you're even asking me—but I'll go to the prom with you, since I clearly have no self-esteem left."

"Don't make this super dramatic, please."

"You're using me."

"Who cares? Let's both of us just not make this into a *thing*."

He made an expression like nothing mattered anymore at this point anyway and said, "Sure."

We were sitting pretty close to the exit, and Wade was going to have to pass right by us to get to the dining room doors. I watched him as he was heading toward us with Mr. Grant behind him, holding the skateboard. His eyes were on the ground mostly as he made his way through the room, and I thought maybe he wouldn't even see us. But then, as they approached our table, Wade's eyes swung up without warning. He registered Derek sitting next to me, and for a moment, I thought he might start another fight. But he didn't, and that was far worse. His eyes moved from Derek to me, and then, with the same dead calm in his face, he flipped me off. I returned the gesture with both my hands.

I spent the rest of the day walking around school feeling some kind of relief at the finality of it all. The adrenaline smashing through my brain made everything feel loud and violent. It seemed to scratch some itch, even if it did draw blood in the process. It felt painful in a good kind of way to think, *Fuck Wade*. It felt liberating. For a moment, I thought I had grown some balls in the process of this nightmare, but who was I kidding? I cried myself to sleep again that night. Quietly this time, under my blanket like a professional.

32

"HEY, DO YOU EVEN REALIZE HOW UNCOOL YOU'RE being?"

I looked up from my book and found Anju directly in my line of sight. I was in the laundry room, sitting on the dryer and waiting for my clothes to finish. I stared at her dully for a second before the significance of who she was truly crawled into the crevices of my head and began to burn like acid. Anju stood waiting for my reaction, hands on her hips, wearing a '40s-looking, flower day dress with her Vans, and her french braid pigtails. I was wearing the gym shorts and a large T-shirt my dad had left behind at our place one time that said *Rick's Crab Shack* on it. I felt like I had already lost this battle.

"You're being so unfair to Wade," she said, shifting her weight uneasily from one foot to the other in my silence.

"What do *you* care?" I asked.

Her eyes flashed with righteous indignation. "I care because I'm his *friend*. Maybe friendships don't mean anything to you, but I take it seriously when someone trusts me enough to be my friend."

"Congratulations. You sound like a real superb human being."

She blinked at me wildly as she struggled for new ammunition. It didn't suit her very well—being confrontational. She sputtered more than she talked, huffing air in and out, clearly out of her element by a few thousand miles. All the easy grace she had as a nice person became impaired in this attempt to be tough.

"You know, he's not getting his skateboard back," she said, adjusting her stance again and crossing her arms over her chest. "And if he wants it back at the end of term, he needs to get his parents to sign this thing, and we both know he's not going to deal with asking them. So his skateboard is basically gone forever."

"So?"

Her eyebrows drew together in flustered rage. She looked around the room as though one of the washers or dryers might supply her with her next line, but there was nothing except the rhythmic tumbling sounds of wet clothes banging against metal.

"You know what?" Anju said, turning back to me with renewed spunk. "You don't deserve him. He's a really good person, and all you've done is take advantage of him. I hate when girls are like you. I thought Eloise was bad, but at least she's transparent and you can smell her a mile off; it's girls like *you* that make me sick—pretending to be one thing and then basically being a whore the entire time. You're worse than Eloise. And as if that isn't enough, you have the nerve to be upset afterward and act all vindictive on top of it, like that's even your right—you're disgusting!"

I jumped off the dryer so suddenly that she flinched back. "I have an idea," I said. "Why don't you get the hell out of my face and make all your wet dreams with my boyfriend come true?"

She gasped. "I never . . . That was never even something that I ever—"

"No, of course not," I said, cutting her off. "Not in your wildest dreams, right?"

"I told you I care about Wade as a person, and I stand up for people I care about. That might be a new concept to you."

I tossed her a smile that must have looked rabid and generally unhinged, because she took another step back, looking worried.

"Seriously, go screw him already," I told her. "Let him blow your bite-size little mind. See if I care."

She stood there for a second, and her eyes were so large and wild and perfectly beautiful that, once again, it made sense why Wade would trade me in for her. Even when she was being a nervous, fumbling pissant, she looked pretty.

"You're a horrible human being," she said.

"Oh, thanks for the info. I had no idea."

Making her exit, she threw one more look of frazzled contempt my way. "Just stay away from Wade."

"Sure. And all joking aside, suck my dick."

The truth of the matter is that what she had said to me hurt pretty badly. She talked about him as though they were on the same side of something, looking at me from across a chasm— them together and me alone. And I was the piece of trash in the scenario. I was the horrible human being. I was. I actually knew that I was. I hated myself as I watched Anju hurry out of the laundry room. She would run to Wade no doubt and tell him what I had said, and we'd be even further apart. Not that it mattered anymore at that point.

I had begun to sit with Derek more regularly during

mealtimes. Initially, it was out of revenge, but after a while it just became the norm—the new way not to be alone in the dining room. And then, it wasn't just the dining room anymore. We hung out after school a few times, or I'd watch his orchestra rehearsals, or we would go get junk food in town. He had stopped hanging out with Neal and Kevin and generally began to act less like a turd—kind of on a journey to find himself by way of shaved head. He stopped eating meat too. And the absolute weirdest thing about Derek was that he was all right.

We became friends. Nobody understood our relationship, and honestly, neither did I. Nothing about who we were or what we looked like connected in any kind of way whatsoever; and yet, so what? It was actually all right hanging out with Derek once it stopped being a performance for Wade's benefit. With time, everyone else got over it too and accepted it as one of those mysterious ways in which the Lord works. Gracie Welles and Derek McCormick—doing it on a regular basis.

Except we weren't doing it on a regular basis. Not even remotely, because my capacity to be horny had died with Wade cutting me off. It was strange how the whole concept of sex seemed suddenly null. I had never been into Derek to begin with, but now it was a positive no go. Nothing about him turned me on no matter how convenient it would have been. A couple of times, I tried being turned on by him. I made a point of watching him change his shirt in his car when we were going to get pizza in town and he didn't want to go with the school-logo T-shirt. He struggled out of his T-shirt and then searched around the back seat for the new shirt he wanted to wear. He was buff and had an almost-six-pack and everything. I was staring, waiting for something to happen, but all that happened was that I began to feel sad about Wade. Wade didn't look like that with his shirt off. My down-in-the-dumps mood ruined the whole evening and the pizza, which sucked, because it was *pizza*—and besides, I had been looking forward to getting out of school for a minute. I ended up telling Derek for the millionth time that I was not into him in "that way." He looked pissed off and said, yeah, he got the message loud and clear, and was there some law against him respecting me as an interesting human being, beyond just a pair of tits? Jesus.

"I happen to enjoy the company," he said. "Does that work for you?"

I screwed up my lips for a second and played with the cheese dangling off my slice of pizza.

"I *guess.*"

We ate in silence.

"I like the company, okay?" he reiterated.

"Okay *fine,*" I told him. "I like the company too."

"So we're good?"

"Yeah. As long as you're not secretly jerking off to me."

"Deal. If you promise not to jerk off to me either." A very Dereky smile blasted across his face. It was an expression that belonged to the old Derek with the sun-bleached hair. I never thought I'd miss that version of him, but now I thought maybe I did miss it a bit. It was good to see he still had it in him to not have a stick up his ass all the time. The shaved-head version, although far less demented, could be a handful sometimes in its own way.

My status rocketed into a different stratosphere. It was strange as hell, being so far up the social ladder at school with no warning whatsoever. Everyone has opinions and conclusions and speculations about you. I had never aspired to being

visible in school, let alone public property at the level of the ruling class. It was clear that I didn't belong there, despite having
Derek as arm candy. I didn't have the style or the hair or the
bank account—and I certainly didn't have the social graces.
I had cheated the system—everyone knew it. I had probably
sold out.

I WENT TO THE PROM IN A THRIFT STORE DRESS
with the D'arcy hairdo from the Smashing Pumpkins' "Disarm"
video—tight braids on either side of my head looped around
into two handles. Beth had dyed my hair again and finally got
it to a somewhat platinum stage. I stood back to marvel at my
reflection in Georgina's big mirror. I cocked my head to one
side, thinking that maybe—*maybe*—I wasn't even ugly. This
startled me a little. Ever since I was thirteen, it had been a
no-brainer: I wasn't attractive. Fat face, bad skin, pasty, double chin. And once that decision had been cast in stone, there
seemed to be no reason to ever reevaluate anything. What good
would it do? It felt like it would have been a waste of time—
wanting, craving, wishing I were something that I wasn't. I
had seen myself in mirrors plenty of times since then, but I
guess I'd never really *looked*. I had more or less come to terms
with my face. But now with the crazy white-blond hair color,
I really looked hard at myself in the mirror. I turned my face

in various directions, hesitant about jumping to any positive conclusions that I might have to disassemble later. But, yeah, I didn't have the double chin anymore. My face had cleared up too. My neck somehow seemed less rammed into my shoulders.

I reached for the mascara. It was old, and the little brush I pulled out of the tube was sticky and thick with black goo. I drove it over my eyelashes several times, creating a heavy, stiff and clotted canopy. Then I put on some eyeliner—I had a vague notion that maybe I was supposed to have done that before the mascara, but it was too late, so whatever. Closing one eye, I tried to draw an exact line across where my lashes connected with my eyelid. I accidentally smeared some of the mascara goo onto the side of my eye with my finger. I did my best to wipe it off with a Q-tip. Most of it came off. Good enough. I did the same with the other eye and then, lastly, I put on lipstick.

I reexamined myself. A burned-out kind of smile crawled across my face. The make-up was sloppy, but I wasn't hideous anymore, I thought. Not that it mattered. It felt like only a mildly interesting side note to my life.

My dress was basically just a slip. It was baby blue and fell down to my calves with lace at the bottom and around the top, and the strap of the new black bra I had bought slipping down my arm, which added extra points to the overall effect. (D'arcy's thick bra strap was showing throughout the entire "Disarm" video). Oh yeah, I finally bought a new bra. I didn't *want* to spend my birthday money on a bra, but it was kind of a necessity considering the hobo state of my other bras. Beth had been right about that.

But the strangest thing of all was that there was a point that night where I actually had fun. I was a little drunk. Just a little. Just enough to feel that wave of fuck-everyone euphoria, and I threw my empty plastic cup at the wall and walked onto the dance floor as the beat to "Teach Me How to Dougie" started up. For a short moment, I detached from my life, and I was just a kid at a prom dusting the cobwebs off my grade-school hip-hop moves. I closed my eyes and pretended there was nothing in the past—only a now, and who knows, maybe even a future. When I opened my eyes again, I realized that I didn't hate all the kids I went to school with for the first time ever. Granted, these kids were all older than I was and not really in my sphere of existence anyway, but still. I smiled and they smiled and everyone was united in the moment, trying to out-Dougie each other. There was sweat crawling down faces and a sense of no regret, no fear, no constipation about life. Beth was there. You couldn't miss her. Her hair was up in a simple ponytail, and she wore a black 1950s prom dress that had small silver stars embroidered onto the many layers of tulle. It flew up around her thighs when she jumped, revealing the bright white of her skin.

"Rumor has it you peed while Derek popped your cherry," she said later as we stood outside to smoke.

Constanze had started that rumor in an attempt to cling to her dignity after Derek had dumped her. The rumor didn't ever fully catch on, though. I personally didn't care about having fictitiously peed during the loss of my virginity—it was the least of my problems.

"Yeah," I said, pushing my bangs off my forehead where they had started to clump together. My dress felt wet and a little cold against my back.

"You've come a long way," Beth said. "I bet nobody even knew your name at the beginning of the school year—and now look at you."

I nodded. "I know. I allegedly peed on Derek, cheated on my boyfriend, stole another girl's boyfriend, and I'm flunking Algebra II. I wasted no time, I guess."

She patted me on the back. "I'm proud of you."

"Thanks," I said, oddly not feeling like utter shit for once.

"Your dress is pretty see-through—is that part of your new persona? I can practically see your underwear, and I can definitely see your bra."

"Well, the visibility of my underwear is accidental," I said. "Not the bra part."

"Is it a nightgown?"

"I figured it was a slip."

"Either way, I bet you some lady had a lot of frenzied sex in that."

I laughed. "Why *frenzied*?"

"Just the vibe I get. Dirty motel room, Bible salesman . . ."

"Okay, well, there's always the chance that the lady took it off before she had sex with the Bible salesman."

"Doubtful. They would have been too horny. Plus, they probably didn't have a lot of time, since she had to get back to the pot roast she was making for her husband for dinner."

I laughed again. "Oh, right, that's true."

Beth looked ridiculously beautiful, and above all, unwholesome in the glitteriest way possible. Nobody else could look that pretty and sinister in a 1950s prom dress.

"I want to be you someday," I said. "I think that's all I really want."

Smoke spilled out of her mouth. "That's stupid," she said unceremoniously. "Why would you want to be me?"

"Is that a real question?" She stared at me. I couldn't believe she was actually expecting an answer.

"I mean, you're *you*. You're Beth Whelan."

"So?"

"So you're *perfect*! You're on this other level that nobody can even dream of reaching."

"You're talking about high school," she said. "Reaching any kind of level in high school is a joke."

"No, but—" It was a little frustrating that she was being so obtuse about this. "Do you really not get that life as you know it—like, how it happens to *you*—is not how it happens to other people? Normal people don't exist like you do. This has nothing to do with just high school."

She was looking out at the courtyard, her interest in this subject matter about to eclipse fully. "I'm not a normal person?"

"Are you kidding? No fucking way. That's what you don't get. The way you live and experience things—that's not what it's like for the rest of us. You get to dictate your life and only have perfect moments all the time. That's not normal. Do you know how hard it is for me to have *one* perfect moment?"

Finally a small, annoyed smile. "I'm two years older than you, Gracie," she said. "I've had a lot of time to figure things out. When you're eighteen, you'll be bored of perfect moments. I promise."

Bored of perfect moments. Not likely.

"Well, guess what? You're wrong," I said. "I'm never going to figure *anything* out. When I'm eighty, I'll still be the same person. I'll still be in love with Wade, and he'll live somewhere across the country with Anju and their kids, and I'll be like my mom—a crazy person, obsessed with him. I'll probably have one of his old T-shirts and smell it every night, and every morning I'll tell myself that he's still in love with me."

I had been serious about this scenario, but Beth's laughter shot through the darkness of what I considered a very real possibility and annihilated it.

"Maybe you'll be married to Derek," she suggested.

"Maybe. And Derek will do everything right, and I'll treat him like shit."

She smiled.

"I want to be incapable of being in love," I said with a sigh. "I'll do the sex and stuff, but I just don't ever want to care about anybody ever again. The way I feel about Wade—it's just too much. It's not fair to have to feel that kind of thing."

Beth said nothing. I couldn't read her face.

"It's like I have a nuclear power plant of emotions burning me out all the time," I went on. "And I have to pretend that that's not happening and like I give a shit about stuff. Do you know how much energy it takes to act like you're all right, just so that other people can relax and not have to deal with the true you—the one that's rotten and dead inside?"

It came out with a little more melodrama than I had aimed for, but fuck it, it felt truthful. I wouldn't have known how else to put it. I thought Beth would laugh again, but she didn't.

"You fell in love with a boy," she said, almost gently, which was weird if you know Beth. "Don't dump on that. It's a big deal."

I took a drag of my cigarette, watching her face for clues to what the fuck was going on.

"You get to be in love. That's massive," she said.

I coughed out the last remnants of smoke from my lungs. "Excuse me—*what*?"

"It's massive," she answered casually as though changing her verdict on the subject of *love* completely and utterly, 180 degrees, was no big deal at all. "Love is one of the big feelings to be had in life—if not the biggest."

My head really cracked open on that one. "Wait, but being in love is—you said it was the worst thing that can happen to anybody!"

She gave me a shrug with her right shoulder. "Well, what the hell would I know? It's not like I've ever even been in love myself."

The whole universe trembled at that moment. Beth Whelan sounded uncertain, and she had never sounded uncertain about anything ever before. Ever.

"It's true. I know nothing about being in love," she said. No playfulness in her voice. None of the fearless security her words usually held. There was something crazy *real* in her voice and her face and the way she held her cigarette. Something human.

"I've read books where people fall in love," she was saying. "Seen it in movies, and obviously seen morons all around me in real life fall in love, but I don't personally know what it is. I don't have a clue what it feels like."

"But you . . . you said . . . it was . . ."

I couldn't even put it into words.

"Yeah, I know my stance on the subject matter," she said.

For a moment, it seemed like that would be the end of that discussion. Beth had no qualms about stopping and starting conversations in whatever disjointed way corresponded with her whims. When she was done talking about something, she usually just got up and left. But instead of leaving, she grabbed hold of the tip of her ponytail, tugged lightly on it, and continued talking.

"I've been acting on my own advice since about eighth grade, when my friends started to send nude pictures to boys and change their hair and clothes and way of talking and walking just to play into the fantasy of whatever guy decided to notice them. Then they'd puke their guts out after breakups, and cry and explain for hours why some pimply-faced dickweed was the only one on the planet for them. It seemed miserable. I wasn't interested in being superglued to another person. The couple of guys I hooked up with were handpicked for their major turnoff qualities. I had to be sure there was no chance of getting stuck. That's how I manage to have all those 'perfect' moments, if you want to know the truth," she said, like a magician revealing his tricks. "By being a coward."

I didn't know how to respond. Not even remotely.

She took a drag on her cigarette, and after all the smoke had drifted from her mouth, she said, "The way that Scholfield talked to you and looked at you—I never had that. Guys look at me—sure—but not like that."

For a moment, neither of us spoke.

"You never even *liked* someone?" I asked at long last.

"Yeah, of course I did. I'm not a *robot*." She threw a glance at me as though her being a robot was somehow an outrageous proposition. Then she continued, tugging at her ponytail again. "This guy Greg. He was a grade above me when I first got here, and lame-ass name aside, he was really cool. I mean, really cool." Her eyes detached from the moment here. "Not in the way you're thinking. Cooler than that. Not in the way guys are cool in movies or billboards or whatever. In fact, he was probably the most un-Greg-like person there is. It was like he came from another planet."

I stared at her, transfixed. Beth getting gooey over some mythical un-Greg-like Greg guy from another planet—it was incomputable.

"It was the first time that I could feel everything inside me go rogue," she said. "You know, like everything important to me was threatening to be irrelevant. Falling in love with him was just one of those unavoidable things you knew was going to happen, and when it did, it would be big."

"So, what the hell happened?"

"Nothing. I made out with his best friend at a party in front of him. I told you—only the boys I wasn't into were allowed close to me." She smiled and shrugged again like that was really all there was to be said on the matter. "I had too much common sense. Or no guts. Same thing. I guess."

The smile began to make her look a little sad. Maybe not sad, exactly—but as if she were lost in a corridor that led to some part of her life that sure as hell wasn't now.

"Okay," I said, "but you evaded the drama and the pain and the puking and the total loss of dignity. You got to have the perfect moments."

She shrugged. "I don't know. Maybe *you* had the perfect moments?"

I stopped to consider this wild, total flip side version of things for a second.

"But it *sucks* now," I said, coming to no conclusion. "It sucks to feel this way."

"So, you're an emotional wasteland. So what? At least you had the guts to go for that ride. With you, it's like, you see a shitshow about to happen, and you jump right in. That's an envious state of existence, G. I've never been able to do that."

It was surreal, watching everything around me turn into something else. It felt like realities of a different dimension pressing through into the dimension I had been living in, turning my misery into perfect moments and Beth into human shape with feelings swimming in her eyes at the mention of some past boy. Everything seemed to wobble around me as the two dimensions collided.

I shook my head, fighting it. "But it's not like I *planned* to be all courageous and dive into life headfirst. I don't choose to do anything. Stuff just *happens* to me. I—"

Beth cut me off. "Listen, you're not as big a loser as you think you are." She flicked her cigarette, letting the ashes rain down on the ground between us. "I know it makes things easier sometimes to think that, but you might as well face the facts: you're cooler than most people I know. You shot Derek in the face with a slingshot, and you called Mrs. Gillespie a 'sadistic doughnut,' whatever that even means, and you're totally fine with urinating-on-a-guy rumors going around about you.

You're not as passive as you think you are. And that other stuff you worry about—that's only a matter of time. You'll figure out how to put on eye makeup properly and have a hairstyle. Those are the little things."

I was honestly out of things to say. She had sucked all my go-to dialogue options right out of the air. There was nothing I could come up with. So for a second, I just smiled at the ground like an idiot, full of unexpected warm feelings that had nothing to do with being in love with a boy for once. I had forgotten that there even were other types of emotions to feel—that anything someone who wasn't Wade said to me could even matter. It was nice to feel the world becoming a bit more real again.

Meanwhile, Beth had begun to redo her ponytail, pulling the peach hair back onto the top of her head. I watched her twist the hairband around it and then retie the black ribbon into a new bow to finish it off.

"You know, there are probably more guys out there with bad names who are really cool," I said. "I bet you'll run into, like, a *Brad* or whatever, who's from a planet even more light-years away than Greg's planet. And then, you know, you can jump right into the shitshow, just like I did."

"Maybe I will," she said with a small smile.

"And you'd better text me super embarrassing stuff about your soul mate's exact eyelid shape."

"You bet."

Beth put out her cigarette against the wall of the building and dropped it to the ground. "All right, I'm going back in," she said, giving me a wink. "Later, masturbator."

She didn't wait for a response, and I watched her walk away, the many layers of black tulle swinging back and forth with the movements of her walk. The moment had been dropped like a hot potato, in true Queen of the Underground style. Next year would be weird without her, that's one thing I knew for sure.

Those things she said about me—I couldn't even register them fully. They made me feel worthwhile in a way that was independent of an outside force. As though there was the possibility—the small chance that even without a boy's adoration, I might be a person. Totally on my own. There was the idea that I could exist. If I really wanted to, I could exist—just by the sheer force of myself.

WHEN MY MOTHER ANNOUNCED THAT SHE WAS
coming to Parents' Weekend with my dad, and that we would
all drive home together afterward "in a rental car!" I almost
choked on my own breath.

"*Why?*"

"Isn't it great?" my mother squealed into my ear via the
phone. "Your dad happens to have a gap in his schedule right
on those days. Aren't you excited?"

It was going to be perverse. My parents were coming to
school. It would be the most official thing that had ever
happened in my life, and somehow the biggest lie at the
same time. People would look at us and actually think we were
normal.

"Uh, yeah. I'm super excited," I told my mom.

Her voice bubbled over on the other end. "Oh, you have no
idea! I'm packing already, and guess what shoes I'm bringing?
Remember the ones your dad bought me when he visited?"

"Yeah."

"I'm going to wear those. The green ones with the straps. Oh god, I need to sit down for a second and breathe. Hold on! Whooo!"

Every year before the school ended for the summer, they had a thing called Parents' Weekend, which was basically exactly what it sounds like. A boring and painful two days of parents getting tours of the school, having lunch with their kids in the dining hall, meeting all the teachers, examining progress charts with the guidance counselors, and so on. Students put on art shows, and there were science projects displayed and obnoxious dance performances and speeches to sit through. It was always that last little hurdle to push through to arrive at the seemingly eternal freedom of summer.

My parents had not made it to Parents' Weekend my freshman year because naturally my dad wasn't able to take time off from work and fly across the country just to see what pictures I had drawn in art class, and there was no way in hell my mother would have been able to do something like that on her own—the bus ride, arranging to stay at a motel, talking to the teachers. She could hardly talk to a cashier at Walmart about returning an item without all her confidence dropping out the bottom. She would never have been able to talk to one of my teachers. Teachers terrified her. So therefore I had been one of the few lucky kids spared the ordeal of having their parents ferret through their secret lives at school. Until now.

I didn't know how I felt about it. It was too surreal that they were coming for me to even worry much about my grades or progress charts being examined. Even as they got out of the rental car in the school parking lot, I couldn't quite believe it was real. It creeped me out a tad. They were both here. At school.

They saw me and waved. I waved back.

My dad's belly hung out over his pants. He had put on some

weight since I'd last seen him, which was the previous summer. He wore a light gray, expensive-looking, casual suit, but with a Simpsons T-shirt tucked into his pants. My mom stood with him, smiling her ass off, stunning in her cheap flower dress and the green platform shoes that she had described over the phone. Her dark long hair fell over her shoulders and down her back, and her skin looked healthy and glowing. She seemed so alive.

"Gracie!"

She squealed and held out her arms, bouncing up and down impatiently. I walked over slowly, and when I was close enough, she pulled me into her arms. Her hair fell over me as she kissed me, and I held on to her. All the anguish of the school year seemed to loosen in her arms. I had to pull myself together a little to not fully dissolve in the warmth and perfume and unconditional-ness of my mother.

"How are you doing, kiddo?" my dad asked. "What happened to your hair?" He put his arm around me and squeezed.

"The technical term is *blond*, Dad," I said. "You might have heard of it in California? I believe some ladies favor the color over there."

"All right, wisenheimer," he said, giving my shoulder another squeeze with a chuckle. "Just don't tell me you dyed your hair to impress a boy."

"Okay, I won't."

I was trying to be a dick to him, but it was hard. Already I found myself returning his smile. I couldn't help it. I was glad he was there, dressed as stupidly as he was, looking at me like that—confirming by his mere presence that I was connected to him inextricably whether anyone wanted it or not.

"I can't believe you guys came," I said stiffly, trying to figure out how to even *be* in this scenario.

"Isn't it exciting?" my mom said, hugging me again.

"I *guess.*"

"Oh, here's a little something for you," my dad said, handing over a plastic bag with the Apple logo on it. This confused me for a second, but my heartbeat had already picked up speed.

I pulled out the headphones I had asked him for during our spring break phone conversation, but the bag was still weighted, and then I stuck my hand in again and pulled out a new phone. A new *fucking phone.* A brand-new, not-made-in-the-medieval-ages phone—in the box from the Apple Store. I held the two boxes in my hands clumsily, turning them over and trying to get a grip on myself while not dropping anything.

"Your mom said your phone was a little outdated, and you had some trouble with the storage—getting your music on there," he said, enjoying my reaction. "I figured you could do with an update."

"Shit!" I was weirdly out of breath with excitement. "Thanks."

I was definitely going to stop being mean to him. Definitely. The fact that I was being bought off relatively cheaply did register in my mind for a fraction of a second, but—damn it—it felt so incredibly good to be bought off! He had given me stuff before, of course—jewelry for my birthdays or Christmas, clothes, and so on, but I had no idea that I could get this much out of him in one go—I mean, randomly in a *non-holiday* scenario. That had never even occurred to me before as a technical possibility in the realm of technically possible things. It was nuts. I looked up at his broad, smiling face—unshaven, with small, blue eyes stuck in a pink face, large eyebrows, slight double chin, and it sank in how much money he actually had. I mean, I knew he was rich, but richness had never been more than an abstract concept to me. It was so silly that this was the moment that brought the concept home to me, but it did. This was the realest his money had ever been to me. It meant Georgina's reign of terror would finally be over.

"Oh, your hair color!" my mom was meanwhile saying, stroking a pale strand of straw-like substance hanging over my shoulder. "You look so grown up. I hardly recognized you, bug."

"I know, it's intense," I said. "It'll grow out again."

"You're beautiful, Gracie, you know that?" My mother beamed at me from where she stood, safely nestled into my dad's arm and looking truly carefree. "God, I can't believe I *made* you," she mused, touching the strand of bleached hair again.

"We *both* did," my dad said.

"We sure did."

Yeah, they sure did. It made me a little uncomfortable that we were all standing there thinking about them "making" me.

"Well, show us around!" my dad said, waving his hand toward the building.

The best part of day one of Parents' Weekend was Mr. Sorrentino. He had shaken my parents' hands with genuine enthusiasm. After all the shit I had put him through, here he was—still on my side, my biggest cheerleader, talking about my natural talents as a biologist and my undeniable aptitude for learning and whatnot. He said I had the kind of challenging mind that would never take "the easy route to the finish line." I had poured ginger ale over his desk and broken all his pencils, and he didn't even seem to remember. God, I almost fell in love with him all over again.

Naturally, the polar opposite of Mr. Sorrentino was Mrs. Gillespie. She had her ass balanced precariously on a corner of her desk as she read off a long list of reasons why I was a lousy addition to her classroom: the lessons I had missed, the time she had intercepted a note in which I'd referred to her as "Hitleresque," the two pop quizzes I'd flunked, the grades dropping out the bottom, the weak book report on *Cry the Beloved Country,* and then she also made a point about my personal appearance, which she described as most likely "indicative of a more serious problem."

She let that hang there for a moment, giving my parents a look that invited them to suspect a really bad drug habit. My parents stared back at her blankly.

"Now, I don't doubt that she can deliver the work," Mrs. Gillespie continued, due to the shattering silence, "it's a matter of whether she chooses to apply herself or not. And to be frank, it's an attitude problem we're dealing with more than anything else. Grace shows a distressing disregard for—or rather a *miscalculation* of—her efforts in an acceptable social framework."

My parents continued to not have a clue of what to say. I noticed my mom pumping my dad's hand in a nervous rhythm.

"What I'm asking for is your help at home," Mrs. Gillespie continued into the silence, "because this is the kind of problem that can only be tackled from both ends. Without your cooperation at home, there's not much I can do here."

"Absolutely," my dad said, finally catching on to the role he was supposed to play and running with it. "We run a tight ship at home, and this is clearly not acceptable. We really appreciate your candor, and you can be sure that Grace has not heard the last of this."

I looked at him. It was surreal, hearing my dad talk to my teacher about what kind of a ship we ran at home. Threatening disciplinary actions. It was as though we were all in a play with costumes and props and everything, pretending in perfect three dimensions.

"That lady is a piece of work," my dad said as we walked out of the English room.

"Yes, she seems mean," my mom agreed. "I'm sorry you have to deal with that kind of negativity, bug."

"So much negativity, right?" I said happily.

It would have been nice to have them as actual parents, I thought. *The three of us as a team could have really torn Mrs. Gillespie a new asshole.*

After assembly was over, everyone mingled in the auditorium. Teachers, parents, and students talked in little clusters. There were drinks and cookies. With the worst of the weekend over, most of the kids finally started to relax. And the giggling and boisterous laughter that was the normal soundtrack to the school's halls began finally to flare up again as they came back to life. I, too, felt hopeful. Derek came over, still holding his trumpet under his arm from the performance he had just given with the orchestra. He was red in the face and looked nervous, shoved into a light brown suit that was clearly suffocating his entire being. He looked hulking in a pathetically sweet sort of way, especially with his head shaved and resembling the shape of an uneven potato more than ever. The suit really brought that out.

"Hi, Gracie," he said in a fidgety manner.

"Who's *this* guy?" my dad said, holding a napkin with three cookies balanced on it.

"Some stupid jerk I know," I said.

My dad chuckled, and Derek backed off a step with a flustered little pretense at enjoying the joke.

I pulled Derek forward and said, "I'm kidding. This is Derek. He's the guy that played the trumpet solo just now. He shaved his head this semester because of this midlife crisis he was going through."

My parents shook hands with Derek.

"Is this the guy you're running with?" my dad asked.

"*Running with?* I'm not sure I understand your 1930s lingo, Dad."

"You're avoiding the question."

"Sir, we're just friends," said Derek. "Your daughter is a real force to be reckoned with. I have a lot of respect for her."

That cracked me up. Derek acting like an altar boy and looking the way he did—clearly being strangled by his tie and sweating into the armpits of his suit. I really enjoyed it.

"Whatever. We practically hate each other," I said merrily, putting my arm around Derek's shoulder as best as I could with him being as large as he was.

Derek smiled through an alarmed expression.

"Well, you're right, buddy," my dad said to him. "She sure is a force to be reckoned with."

I loved that I was able to call him *Dad* that loudly in front of other people and everyone went along with it. I loved that Derek was scared of him. And when Derek's mom came up to steal her son away, she was all smiles and handshakes and polite chitchat. I had met his mother once before when Derek had taken me to his house to pick up some clean laundry. She had given me a look like I was a used piece of toilet paper stuck to her son's shoe. Her expression had blatantly been all about how to detach me from him—no qualms about making her intentions known. And now she was telling me how nice it was to see me again with a huge, chummy smile, as though I had been at her house many times before and she had fond memories of bringing Derek and me Tater Tots while we did our homework.

It was my father who inspired this kind of respect in people. Despite the Simpsons T-shirt, he had the kind of presence that commanded the entire room. Everyone who got close to him or ended up talking to him seemed to let him lead the way. There was a subtle reverence in the way that people responded to him. Even Honey Sinclair's dad, who owned a dog biscuit factory and was a pretty big-shot kind of guy, was in awe of him.

I felt suddenly proud of my parents in a preschool show-and-tell kind of way. At that moment, I had no doubt that my dad was the coolest. And my mother too: young and beautiful, looking nothing like any of the other moms. No pleated shorts. No sensible shoes. No bobs or chunky highlights. She was nothing like them. The other parents threw glances at her, debating on who/what she was, standing next to my dad like that. Second wife? Older daughter? Younger sister?

She had been nineteen when she'd met my dad, and she hadn't grown up much since then—never adopted practicality or realism or responsibility. There was an unfinished careless-ness about the way she dressed that seemed full of breathless-ness and excitement and movement—the dress, flung on last minute, and the hair loose and long. The childlike upturned nose and bright eyes. When she was happy like this, she looked so untouchable.

The next day, I packed up my stuff, which only took a few minutes. Everything fit neatly into the duffel bag that I had brought at the beginning of the year—clothes, composition books, toiletries, shoes. Georgina was packing too, although it was going to take her a lot longer. She was sitting on the floor with three large, half-filled suitcases sprawled out around her and piles of folded clothes, knickknacks, toiletry bags, and all the rest of it grouped and sorted into piles and little towers.

"Well, I'm off," I said, standing by the door with my bag.

She looked up from where she sat, pushing some stuffed animals into a backpack. The *Mamma Mia!* movie soundtrack was playing softly in the background. "You're packed already?" she asked.

I held up my bag.

"So this is it, huh?"

"Yup."

Her eyes suddenly flew open wide with panic. "Oh my god, we didn't sign each other's yearbooks!" she shrieked, scrambling to her feet.

"I didn't get one."

Rummaging through a drawer, she asked, "*Why not?*"

"Because the less I have to remember about this year, the better."

Georgina pulled out her yearbook from her top drawer and whirled around. "That's stupid. You're throwing away memories! You're going to regret this when you're older."

"I highly doubt it."

She climbed over the suitcases and handed me the yearbook. "Sign it."

I put my bag down and sighed. Georgina handed me a pen, and I propped the book against the wall to write.

Dear Georgie,

It's been really, really fucking really real.

Your music has raped my eardrums mercilessly over this unforgettable sophomore year. Your Luke Bryan poster has been burned into my subconscious (it's only a matter of time before I have weird sex with him in my dreams on a regular basis—so, thanks). Oh, and your crap—let's not forget how your crap encroached onto my side of the room about 89 percent of the time.

I'll miss you. Life will be but an empty shell in your absence . . .

Gracie Mae Welles

I handed it to her, and she flipped it open right away and read it. A smile spread over her face.

"I'll miss you too," she said, looking up.

For a split second, the bond between us was painfully thick.

"Okay, well, I'll see you," I said, picking up my bag again and giving her a small wave.

"See you," she said.

There was a good chance that we would not be roommates again next year, and we both felt it and knew what it meant. It meant this was a real ending. We'd drift away into other groups and other geological sections of the school. I certainly was not going to join the volleyball team again next year. There'd be nothing for us to argue about. So this was it. We both felt it, and that's why neither of us said more than we did.

I made my way downstairs. I knew I still had to find Beth, but I figured I'd put my stuff in the car first. When I made it down the main hallway, I stopped suddenly. Down by the doors to the office stood Wade. There was a woman standing next to him talking loudly to Mrs. Martinez. This was Wade's mother. She was petite but loud and bubbly with a no-nonsense kind of handbag slung over her shoulder and low-heeled shoes. She looked like a woman who liked to dress for comfort and then made up for it a little by wearing loud earrings—in this case, two colorful, wooden parrots dangled from each of her earlobes.

His father stood on the other side of Wade with a hand on his shoulder. He looked *patient,* for lack of a better word. Like the kind of guy who was content to have his wife run the show. He listened to the two women laugh and smiled as he shook his head occasionally, indicating that he thought his wife was a real riot. In comical contrast to Mrs. Scholfield, he was ridiculously tall—taller than was normal for a tall man. His shoulders were large, and he stood hunched over a little as though trying to detract from his largeness.

There was something so ordinary about the three of them that it was almost too hard to watch. So very much the opposite of my own family. I remembered Wade calling his parents "shitty people," and it pissed me off, because clearly he had no idea what *shitty* actually meant. Somehow this seemed to be another break between us.

Thankfully, the scene wrapped up pretty fast. Wade's dad patted him on the back, and then they shook hands with Mrs. Martinez and walked away. I didn't know exactly how I felt about Wade at that point. I knew that I was maddeningly and inextricably in love with him, but I didn't know if I still wanted him to be miserable. I didn't know if I wanted to hurt him or wish him well. I thought about it as I watched him walk away with his parents down the hallway, disappearing into the light of the main entrance.

Nope, I thought. *I don't want him to be happy.* I was too much in love with him.

I REAPPEARED IN THE PARKING LOT WHERE MY
parents were waiting for me and threw my bag into the car
with a moody, "Let's go." I'd have to call Beth to say goodbye. I
just wanted to get the hell away from school at that point.

Fifteen minutes later, I stood in a gas station shop, filling a
huge Styrofoam cup with coffee for my dad, who was outside
fueling up. I was thinking I should have said goodbye to Beth
in person. I really should have. What if I never saw her again?
I thought about all the stuff she had said to me at prom, and
how she'd dyed my hair and supplied me with cigarettes and
gave me shitloads of questionable advice. What if that was all
of her that I would ever have?

I was staring pretty intently at a napkin dispenser, feeling
nostalgic and sad about Beth, when I was suddenly jarred back
to my surroundings by a loud voice coming from just outside
the glass doors. It sounded explosive like an argument. Some
person's voice swelling up into eruptive crescendos. It wasn't
just that the voice was particularly loud but rather that it was

loaded with so much live ammunition that I could feel it in my bones even as a bystander. I turned from where I stood by the coffee area just as the door burst open.

This kid walked in wearing a yellow T-shirt that said *Happy* across the front in blue letters in this horror-film, "dripping" font. I knew that T-shirt. I knew what it felt like to touch. It was old and well used. I knew where it had a rip along the seam at the right shoulder. I even knew what it smelled like because that was Wade's T-shirt, and that was Wade wearing it—right there—so real, it was perverse.

I shrank back behind a rack of chips in a fumbling attempt to be invisible but the precaution was pointless. Wade was looking nowhere other than the floor with a tunnel vision kind of focus. And then suddenly his father was there too, a small distance behind him. He jogged a few steps to catch up with his son.

"Hey! You think we're done here?" he said, giving Wade a shove.

Wade stumbled a little before catching his step again.

"Did it sound like we were done out there?" Mr. Scholfield asked, dropping his voice to a rational volume, which somehow made the festering rage more evident. "Did that sound like a resolved issue to you?"

Wade rolled his eyes without comment. His dad grabbed him by the arm and yanked him down the candy aisle, toward the back of the store, still perfectly in my line of vision from where I was crouching.

"How about you lose the attitude?" he said, and then before Wade had the chance to lose the attitude, his dad hit him in the face hard. I mean, hard. Hard enough to make the kind of sound that comes from real impact—not the half-assed slap that happens when kids become obnoxious brats and parents lose their self-control and then feel terrible and apologize for weeks after. This was different. Wade only barely managed stop himself from hurtling into the rack of protein bars behind him.

I flinched, startled half to death and completely unable to compute what was happening. I had seen Mr. Scholfield less than an hour ago at school, and he was an oversize, shy man who patiently stood back and let his tiny wife run the show. The moment was totally irreconcilable.

I felt sick. Paralyzed and hot and terrified. Outside, I could see Wade's mom leaning against the passenger side of their car, tugging at one of her parrot earrings. She was looking off somewhere beyond the top of the building, almost in a trance-like fashion, dreaming with her eyes open. I looked around the room and there was only the clerk behind the counter, watching a football game on a small television. He had looked up momentarily when they'd come in but then lost interest when they'd disappeared down the back of the store. I couldn't see my own parents. I felt utterly alone. I turned my attention back to the candy aisle, my heart thumping so loudly that I was certain my whole body was vibrating with each pound.

"I warned you, Wade. We've been over this before. Many, many times. You don't get to play this game with me. Maybe your mother will put up with you acting like an entitled little shit, but if you believe for one second that . . ."

The worst part was Wade's own reaction to being hit in the face, which was pretty much no reaction at all. With his cheek burning red and his father's monologue flying in his face, he looked oddly unfazed. He didn't seem thrilled about it or any-thing, but there wasn't any shock—no dazed disbelief of the moment. No fear either. He was staring at a rack with candy bars to the left of his father's elbow, and when he did glance up at his father for a second, it was the same way he had looked at me in the dining room when I had confronted him—as if he didn't have a clue who this guy was. A stranger. No connection. It had given me the creeps back then—the way he could turn off his emotions like that, but now it was terrifying.

"—the consequences, you'd better believe me, Wade. You want to make it a problem, we can make that happen. Is that what you want? You want a problem?"

There was a beat of nothing, and then he clamped his hand around the back of Wade's neck and pushed him forward—all the way to the back where there was a doorway with an exit sign above it. They disappeared into the hallway, and for the moment an unwieldy calm settled over the store. I could hear the football game that the clerk behind the counter was watching and his occasional grunts and protestations at the game's developments. Wade's mother was still outside, still leaning against her car, still tugging mechanically at her parrot earring. I didn't understand where the hell my parents had disappeared to. It was like the circumstances were there just for me—a tailor-made gift from the universe.

I pushed the Styrofoam cup I had started filling up for my dad back under the coffee dispenser and pulled the lever down. I was so inflamed with adrenaline that it was hard to have any straight thoughts at all. It seemed to take forever for the cup to fill up. When it was close enough to being full, I pulled the cup out and ran down the candy aisle, burning myself a couple of times as the coffee sloshed onto my hand. I turned into the doorway at the back of the room and found myself in a short hallway. There was a grimy green door that said *Restrooms* on it, and opposite it was a door that said *Staff Only*. Other than that, there was only the exit door at the back. I went for the exit and pushed it open with the side of my body, clutching the cup of coffee in both hands in an attempt to keep it steady. I burned my hands again, stumbling into the bright sunlight and blinking madly to find my bearings. They were right there, maybe just a few yards down the side of the back of the building, next to a dumpster.

There was blood leaking out of Wade's nose by this time, and he was trying to wipe it off with his arm. His father put one hand on his shoulder and pressed him into the wall.

"When you're ready to step up to the plate and problem solve instead of being a little manipulative shit, you let me know. It's your call, Wade, you know that. I'm not the one running the show here—you are. It's always you."

Finally, there was a small crack in Wade's dead expression. Nothing much. Just a reaction as though to a terrible joke.

"Fuck you, Dad," he said, sounding annoyed, and I can't explain how spooky that sounded under the circumstances.

This time, Wade's head hit the wall behind him from the impact of the blow.

"*Hey!*"

That was my own voice. I almost didn't recognize it. It was loud and sounded pretty solid and snotty, which was interesting, because I had never been this terrified in my life.

Mr. Scholfield wheeled around, looking spooked. I didn't give him a chance to come to terms with me standing there. I just threw the entire contents of the huge Styrofoam cup at him. There was a large black splatter of liquid and a surprised sound, like a gasp that morphed into a yowl, for lack of a better word. Mr. Scholfield staggered backward with a curse, wiping at his face. I grabbed Wade's right arm with both my hands and pulled. I remember the dazed look in his eyes, murky with disorientation. It was like watching him come out of a dream. I remember tugging hard a few times before he budged. Then we were running. I had to pull with all my strength to keep Wade moving. He was like a ton of bricks.

We made it around to the front of the building. My parents still weren't anywhere to be seen. Only Wade's mother was there. She stood up straight and looked at us, puzzled as we ran past her. Her hair wafted in the wind as she held her hand up to shield her eyes from the sun.

"Wade?" she called, finally quitting with the parrot earring. "Wade! Where are you going? Where's your dad? Wade?"

We ignored her. Wade seemed to be waking up from the daze. I could feel his fingers become less limp in my hand, and he began to move faster, catching up with me.

"*Mike?*" We could hear his mother call behind us.

There wasn't anywhere great to run to, so we just ran down the side of the freeway for what seemed like hours, but realistically was probably only about ten minutes or so. Probably less. Then I stopped because I felt like I was going to vomit. I bent over, putting my hands on my knees and did nothing but try to breathe. Then I did vomit. My lunch came splattering out onto the grass in front of me in a lumpy yellow avalanche that didn't seem to end. My stomach was pumping frantically to get it all out, traumatizing my taste buds. I puked again. This time on my shoes. And again. Acid burning up my throat. And again. Eventually, it was just my stomach convulsing, desperately trying to catapult its emptiness out of me. Nothing else came. And then, at last, my stomach relaxed and my breathing evened out somewhat.

"Are you all right?" I heard Wade's voice close behind me, and I realized that he had been holding the hair out of my face this whole time. One hand on my shoulder, and the other holding my hair. It was almost too much. Too unreal.

I turned to him, drenched in sweat, smelling like vomit, and with tears streaming down my face from the effort of the puking.

"*What the fuck, Wade! Fuck!*"

"Hey, it's okay."

"*What just happened back there?*"

"It's okay. I got into a dumb argument with my dad. It's okay, I promise."

"Wade, that wasn't . . . He . . . I mean, it was—"

"Yeah, I know," Wade said, jumping in at my unsuccessful scramble for words. "My dad is a dick. Didn't we talk about this before?"

"*Fuck no!* No, we did not. You said you didn't get along with your parents—you said they sucked. Like, maybe they take your phone away when your grades drop. You didn't say . . . You didn't mention that your dad is a full-blown psychopath!"

"Okay, okay, calm down for a second!"

He took a step back and wiped his face on his T-shirt. The word *Happy* was smeared with blood when he dropped it back over his stomach. Suddenly, it looked like he might lose his balance. His face was covered in sweat. There were the beginnings of a bruise on the side of his right eye, and a cut on his cheek and lower lip. Blood smeared all across his face from his nose in an attempt to wipe it off.

"Goddamn it! Are you okay?"

"Just dizzy. That fucking wall . . ." he said, feeling the back of his head.

He took a few steps farther into the grassy area away from the freeway and lay down on his back, closing his eyes to the sun.

"Are you sure you're okay?"

"Yeah. Come on, sit down."

I sat down next to him and let my heart rate normalize. I didn't let myself stare at Wade sprawled out next to me. I only glanced over at him once briefly. He was wearing the plastic, little kid's necklace that his cousin had given him. His hair was getting long. It was the wrong time to be lustful, but my heart fell all over itself in a stupid way now that he was here, next to me, in real life. I glued my focus back on the cars flying by and my shoes, covered partially in vomit.

"I'm trying hard to wrap my head around the fact that you're here right now," he said after a while, and his voice was scratchy and warm and easy like it was back when he was nice to me. It gave me chills. "How is it even possible that you're here?"

"My parents were getting gas."

"Oh, right," he said, slapping his forehead with the palm of his hand. "Gas station—that makes sense."

He dropped his arm over his eyes to keep the sun off his face, and I noticed he was still wearing the blue polish that Anju had painted on his nails. It was badly chipping, but there was enough there to throw more emotions into the mix.

"Are you really okay?" I asked.

"Yeah." And then he opened his eyes to squint at me. "It's so weird you're here. Sorry, it's kind of freaking me out a little."

I looked over at him. "You know what's freaking *me* out a little?" I asked, and I could hear the turmoil in my voice—the fear and the underlying ocean of heartbreak and the shock of the present.

He sighed.

I hadn't meant to sound so acidic, it's just how the words came out.

Wade pulled himself up into a sitting position and pushed his hair out of his eyes.

"What *happened*, Wade?"

"Nothing. Just a bunch of bullshit. We got into this dumb argument in the car, and my dad flipped out and pulled into the gas station, and, I mean, you were there for the rest of it, right?"

"Yeah."

"Right. So that's what happened. Welcome to the shitshow that is Scholfield Inc."

I said nothing for a second. We just sat there.

Then he rubbed his left eye with a small laugh. "I can't believe you threw hot coffee in my fucking dad's face!"

I was still too dazed to be sidetracked by any stray particles of hilarity. "Your dad did that to you because of a 'dumb argument'?"

Wade finally gave in to conversation. "Yup," he said, artlessly. "Remember how he's a dick and all?"

I shook my head. "*I'm* a dick," I said. "*Derek* is a dick. You can be a first-rate dick too, by the way—but your dad . . . Wade, that's different."

He pulled out a handful of grass from the ground with a shrug. "Well, feel free to call it whatever you want."

We both fell silent for a second.

"Has he been like that your whole life?" I asked cautiously, not really wanting to ask or know. "Or was this, like, a one-off thing today, like, he just flew off the handle?"

"Are you serious?"

I felt stupid, but I didn't care. I waited for him to talk.

"Not a one-off thing, Gracie. Nope."

"When you were little too?"

He looked at me like I was being slow on purpose. "Come on, you think he just woke up today and decided, maybe he'll try slamming my head into the wall for a change of pace?"

"No, but—"

"He's an asshole, Gracie. We already went over that. I don't know what else you want me to say. He's an asshole. And what you just saw isn't even remotely as bad as it can get. But I mean, it's not like he's that way all the time either—just, you know . . ." He gave a small shrug.

"How could you not tell me?" I asked, dazed.

"Sorry. I didn't know you'd be interested in a bunch of mind-numbing sob stories about my childhood."

I sat back and said nothing because my stomach was lurching a little again. The significance of what he was admitting to began to sink in heavily. Everything began to snowball and crystallize and branch out into hundreds of new implications. Scenes spilled into my head—his whole life as I knew it and as I didn't know it. All the oddball things about him were threatening to make sense all at once in a colossal avalanche of an explosive sense-making debacle. I couldn't even look at him for a second. Everything became massively weighty and connected, and sad as hell. Debilitating.

Wade flicked my arm to get my attention.

"All right, come on," he said, after a moment. "I do my part too. Like my dad said, I can be a real obnoxious piece of shit when I want to. He's not wrong about that."

"No way, Wade," I said coldly, shaking my head. "It's fucked up."

He shrugged again.

"What about your mom?" I asked.

"What about her?"

"Like, did she know what was happening just now when she was standing by the car playing with her fucking earring? She knew, right? She was just standing there, and she knew."

"Well, what do you want her to do about it? Take down my dad?" he said. A defensive impatience was creeping into his voice.

"She's your fucking mom! I don't know. Why didn't she leave him the first time he ever hurt you? Wouldn't that be the normal thing to do? Why didn't she get a divorce?"

Wade rolled his eyes. "How the hell should I know? You think my parents came with some kind of helpful manual that explains why they blow so much? Why is your dad keeping you a secret in Florida, pretending you don't exist most of the time? And why does your mom put up with that bullshit?"

"Oh my god! That's not the same thing at all. My parents might be batshit crazy, but they *love* me. They would never hurt me! God, I feel like you don't understand the first thing about what is actually *normal*. Those people are supposed to be on your side—always—no matter what. Doesn't matter if you have an attitude problem or whatever. I mean, do you even get how massively fucked up it is that your parents treat you the way that they do? Do you have any actual idea?"

He snorted. "Some idea, yeah."

That kind of snapped me out of it—the dumb simplicity of that answer.

I squeezed my eyes closed tightly. "Ugh . . . just shut me up, please."

We were sitting cross-legged opposite each other at this point, and he put his hands on my knees. Feeling his warm, sweaty fingers directly on my skin was almost too much to handle, but I pretended it wasn't. It was hard being so turned on and also simultaneously terrified and pissed off.

"Hey, listen," he said gently with his eyes on me, unwavering and committed to burning holes into my skull. "I'm okay, Gracie. Really. I knew what I was getting into today. I could have avoided it. Believe me, I know all the tricks of how to shut the fuck up—I just don't want to sometimes. You have no idea how obnoxious he was being at school with the Parents' Weekend thing—the way he was laughing at all the teachers' jokes and looking concerned about stuff and nodding and patting my back nonstop. I wanted to rip his fucking hand off and shove it up his asshole every time he patted my back like that. Anyway, whatever. I was wound pretty tight by the end of that ordeal, and he was eventually going to blow up on me about something dumb anyway, so I just got it out of the way on my terms. And I know, I know—maybe that's the stupid thing to do—but the thing is, you *have* to start shit up sometimes. You honest to god do. It gives you a way to be in control of stuff, and you need to be in control of your life once in a while or you'll go insane. But anyway, you get it. And the point is, I don't even care anymore. You think my dad means anything to me at this point? He doesn't. He hasn't meant anything to me in a long time. So whatever he does can't really hurt me anymore—not in the way that actually matters."

He waited for me to say something, and when I didn't respond, he shook me lightly by the shoulders. "Come on, Gracie. Don't worry about it, okay? Please?"

I sucked in five seconds' worth of breath and then let it out long and forcefully. "Fuuuuuuck, Wade."

"I know," he said. "But it's just blood and vomit. Who cares? Let's talk about something else."

We glanced at each other hesitantly. There was no way to solve anything that had happened between us, and yet somehow we had gotten to being here, sitting by the side of a road, with our knees almost touching. I couldn't tell if Wade's plan was to pretend like nothing had ever happened—no Derek, no Anju—and if that really was his plan, I was confused about whether I should join the fantasy or ruin it.

"I'm sorry about the skateboard," I said. "I guess you're not getting it back."

"It's okay."

"It's not okay. It was an incredibly shitty thing to do."

"Doesn't matter. I wasn't making anything easy."

We were both hesitant about pressing our fingers further into the meat of the matter, but the matter was right there— raw and ready to be prodded.

"Well, I lost my virginity to Derek," I heard myself say,

"so . . . I guess it would have been weird if you handled things really superbly."

"We don't have to talk about that."

"Okay."

His expression had clouded over at the mention of Derek's name. It was subtle, and he was trying not to show it, but it was there.

"I'm not *with* him, you know."

"Gracie . . ." he said in a warning tone, shaking his head.

I paid no attention to his signal to abort. "I'm not into Derek—like, at *all*. You have to know that. I'm just friends with him. And he's actually not a bad person. He can definitely be a douchebag, but that's when he's putting on his act. When he's just being himself, he's actually all right."

Wade got up, full of nerves in his body language. "Why are you *telling me this*?"

"Because I know you have the wrong idea, and it's killing me that you do! I'm not *with* Derek! Even when we had sex—I wasn't into him. It was just sex. That's all."

Wade drove his hands over his face again, into his hair, and then he grabbed fistfuls of it and pulled hard. For a moment, I thought he would tear his scalp off, but he only made a frustrated sound and then dropped his hands in defeat. "Shit, Gracie! You don't have to tell me any of that stuff! It's none of my business."

"It *is* your business!" I yelled at him, scrambling to my feet too now. "Sorry to break it to you, but you and I are each other's business whether we want to be or not. You know why? Because *you* started talking to me. That wasn't my idea. You made it happen. You started talking to me. You started this."

"Okay, fine, I just don't want to talk about Derek."

"I messed up, Wade. I know I did—pretty badly—but that doesn't mean you're allowed to pretend I never even existed."

I was definitely losing it at this point. My voice going high up and weird and then cracking. "You just can't do that to someone," I went on. "You can't be *that* nice—you can't be that fucking nice to me, and change my whole entire life, and then just drop me and walk away without even once looking back. You can't throw someone away like that, Wade. Not after the things you said to me. You can't do that. You just can't."

"You dropped me too," he said quietly.

"I didn't *want* to, though! That was your call, and I had to follow your lead because I didn't have any rights in the scenario. Don't you get that? You're the one who had to be okay enough to tell me to come back. And you never did. You looked at me like I was the biggest scumbag piece of trash in the world. You looked at me like I wasn't there. You looked *through* me. You literally evaporated me. I didn't exist anymore! How was I supposed to approach you?"

He was fidgety as hell when I looked at him for a reply. "Shit," he said.

We both stopped talking for a moment.

"I'm sorry," he said. "I'm a fucking asshole."

"Unfortunately, you're not. I wish you were. It would have made things easier."

"I'm sorry," he repeated helplessly.

All I could think to say was, "I can't believe you're looking at me like I actually exist. It's so surreal."

There were streaks of tears suddenly down my cheeks. The relief was physically overwhelming. Wade put his arms around me, pulling me into his chest, and I started crying even harder.

"That poem I read in Mrs. Gillespie's class was for you, dipshit," I said, sobbing into his T-shirt.

"Yeah, I'm aware of that."

I held on as hard as I could, and he did too. We could feel how much we liked each other. It didn't matter at that moment whether it was love or something beyond that—something more vast and abstract and impenetrable. There was a lot of lunacy in that grasp too. All the darkness that had had the chance to bloom to life between us—it was intertwined now with the good feelings and made everything more acute.

We began to kiss. It was a life-saving sort of make-out session because it went beyond hormones. It went beyond lust too. There were tears and BO and blood and definitely a lot of sweat, and most likely some of my snot involved in that kiss. It was a side-of-the-freeway, everything-gone-to-shit kiss. The good, the bad, and the ugly and the beautiful. We came up for air, acting like we'd never done this before—sort of stunned and incapacitated by the glory of it. I let out a small laugh, and Wade smiled and looked at the ground, scratching his ear.

"Oh, man, sorry about the barf flavor," I said.

He looked too happy to reply. His smile broke out wider across his face, and he pulled me over to him, our faces collided, and we made out some more. It was less dark this time. More carefree, deeper, less to lose, more delirious.

I asked the inevitable question when we came up for air the second time and the mood was less frenzied and a little realer.

"Now what?"

He shrugged. "There's my mom," he said, looking off in the direction we had come from.

In the distance, we could see Wade's mother at the side of the freeway slowly making her way toward us, one hand on her purse, the other shielding her eyes from the sun. She gave a short wave when she saw us looking over. It was shitty to be reminded again that there was no such thing as a bubble. Life was always going to be attached to the perfect things.

"LET'S GET OUT OF HERE," I SAID, GRABBING HIS
arm tightly. "We could hitchhike out of here right now before
your mom reaches us. I bet we can get a car to stop!"

He shot this idea down with a small laugh.

"Or come with me for the summer!" I suggested. "You can
stay with us—with me and my mom. You'll like my mom.
She'll let us do whatever we want."

He didn't say anything. His mother was getting closer.

"Come on, Wade. Come with us!"

He still didn't say anything.

"Wade."

"I can't come with you."

"Why not?"

"I have to work this summer. I'm trying to save up some
money. And anyway, I wouldn't want to make anything worse.
I mean, between us. I just don't want to be mean or do something dumb again."

"Who says you have to be mean or dumb?"

"Nobody, but it's not like I always have a say in the matter."

I tugged at his arm. "Whatever. You won't be mean and I won't be mean, and neither of us will be dumb ever again, so it'll be perfect!"

"Gracie, I can't just come home with you. It's not that easy."

"Oh my god, it's *so* fucking easy! You get in the car with me and my parents and we drive off. That's all there is to it!"

He took a moment to respond, and when he did, he was very matter-of-fact about it, as though it was just the way things were.

"I like you too much for anything to be easy," he said, "and I'm tired of feeling like there's so much to lose all the time."

I realized then that it wasn't going to happen, and my little-kid enthusiasm chocked off. I let go of his arm. "That's a really poetic way of being a huge wimp," I said. "No offense."

"Yeah, none taken." He put his arm around me. "Just give me this summer. I promise I won't be a wimp next time I see you. I just really have to find my footing again first. Okay? That's all I'm saying. Everything is upside down right now."

I didn't exactly know what that meant, but I made a small sound of agreement. Wade gave me a squeeze and then there was his mother, making her final approach.

Wade quickly wiped his face on his T-shirt one last time.

Mrs. Scholfield stopped a few feet away from us and smiled cautiously. "Wade? What's going on, baby?"

Her voice was so warm and bottomless and inviting. It caught me off guard. I had been certain she would have had a dead, lifeless chunk of coal for a heart.

"Nothing," he said, and then he motioned to me. "This is Gracie. We go to school together."

She looked at me kindly and held out her hand. "So nice to meet you, Gracie."

I shook her hand as limply as I could. I didn't return the smile, however. That would have been too much.

"Well, I'm sorry to break up your chat, but we need to get going, baby," she said, looking back over at Wade. "You ready?"

"Yeah."

We began making our way back to the gas station. I let Wade and his mother take the lead and fell behind a few steps. It was interesting seeing him interact with her. He was feeding her with her own fantasy in nearly the same way that I fed my mother her fantasy. I watched as she put her hand on Wade's back in a comforting manner and rubbed as they walked. She leaned in close to him and said something into his ear, and he shook his head with a gesture of unconcern. They exchanged a few words like this, and then she gave him a kiss on the cheek and put her arm around him. And with that, they had brushed it under the rug. It had taken them less than two minutes to wrap up the grimy loose ends. In a way, it was fascinating—being an audience member to delusion rather than an active participant. When you're in it, you can really see the logic in all the chimerical calculations (how many times had I maneuvered my mother through her fantasy world just to keep the noise down?), but from the outside, the view was different. From the outside, it was pretty fucked up.

Mrs. Scholfield glanced over her shoulder at me with a smile. "You keeping up back there, honey?"

I nodded.

"Good. It's so nice to get to meet one of Wade's new friends."

I remained silent, and we walked back to the gas station, where my own parents were standing by the rental car, confused. As we walked up to them, I saw the back of Mr. Scholfield's head. He was sitting in the driver's seat of their car. He didn't turn around, just stared straight ahead, unmoving. I began to feel apprehensive, if justified, about having burned his face with coffee.

"Gracie!" my mom called, waving. She ran up to us and threw her arms around me. "We were looking for you!" she said, out of breath, forgetting for the moment to cling to my dad, who followed close behind her. "Where did you go?"

"Where did *you* guys go?" I turned the question around at her.

Her eyes widened at the sight of Wade's face and the blood on his T-shirt. "Did something happen?" she asked, alarmed.

I looked at Wade and his mother, inviting them to spin the explanation however they wanted to.

"Nothing happened," Wade said, taking the lead without much hesitation. "I got into a stupid fight earlier at school. It's not a big deal. Anyway, I'm friends with Gracie—we're in the same grade. Sorry, we were just talking and forgot that everyone was probably looking for us."

"Oh," my mom said, still feeling uneasy about the state of him, and probably also simply by the fact that he was a boy that I evidently knew pretty well. I could tell she had been more into the idea of Derek possibly becoming the father of my children rather than this one.

My dad was there too now.

"This is Wade," I said, introducing my parents to him with a nod.

"And I'm Wade's mom," Mrs. Scholfield said, extending her arm. "Hi. Sheila. Hi. So nice to meet you."

A lot of hand shaking took place and exchanging of names and civil smiles. Then some tedious small talk that was almost completely unbearable. My mom said nothing much. She hung on to my dad's arm while he did the brunt of the work as he always did. They talked about school, plans for the summer, and asked Wade and me a few questions about how we knew each other and blah, blah, blah. Obligatory jokes were made and exchanged with equally obligatory chuckles. Mrs. Scholfield was really smooth at small talk, as was my dad, and before we knew it, the conversation had turned to golfing. *Golfing!* They were just coasting right along on that topic as though the world were somehow a fantastic place to be.

I glared at them and decided that this is what was wrong with people. This right here. All of us standing around and talking about everything and anything that meant nothing, just so we wouldn't have to feel bad about something that was already making us feel bad anyway.

"*Great*," I said, realizing that I was about to hemorrhage. I hated the truth just as much as any of them did, and I hated them all for making me do the dirty work. "Wade's dad just beat the shit out of him, in case anyone's interested in reality," I said, staring at the ground intently, because it was hard enough just saying it. "Just now, in the store over there. Hence the blood and stuff. And then I threw hot coffee in his dad's face."

Deafening silence. The stage was still mine, it seemed, so I continued. "And whatever—my dad is married to this lady in California and has three daughters there, and they have no idea that me or my mom exist. Or maybe they do and they're just ignoring it like we are. Also, I lost my virginity to that guy Derek you met the other day, Dad—without even liking him—just to do it. And, Wade, I love you." I actually took my eyes off the ground and looked up at Wade. I was on a weird non sequitur roll. I turned to Wade fully, and my voice sped up and became urgent. Like, maybe this was the only time I would ever be able to say this. "And I think nothing else even matters, and who cares what happens—you should at least know that much. It's not a bullshit feeling, like the way I was obsessed with Mr. Sorrentino. It's real. Do what you want with it, but you can't pretend it's not real. It's the realest thing there is. Okay?"

Wade nodded, looking stunned. "Okay," he said.

Then there was another dead silence.

I was definitely ready for someone else to talk now.

My mother's eyes had grown huge. Her face turned bright red, tears forming in her eyes, and every muscle in her body was tense. It was only a matter of seconds now before she would lose it. My dad put his arm around her and was apologizing to Mrs. Scholfield, and Mrs. Scholfield was apologizing to him, and they were firing explanations at each other that had nothing to do with reality. Wade looked caught in between five or six emotional opposites.

"Oh gosh, this must look terrible!" Mrs. Scholfield was saying. Her voice was trembling and all the while she continued smiling. It was so desolate. And turning to Wade, she said, "You're fine, aren't you, baby? We're all fine."

Then there was a loud sob that sputtered violently into our midst. It was my mother. All her pain came spurting out like a geyser. I knew this was coming, but everyone else nearly had a heart attack. She began wailing. My dad tried to help her, but she slipped through his arms like a wet fish. She landed on the ground, refusing to let my dad help her up.

"Oh my Lord!" Mrs. Scholfield gasped.

"Pamela, come on, bunny—come on, let's get off the ground."

She wouldn't budge. She continued sobbing and mainly saying unintelligible things about it "not being true." My dad was trying to get her to stand up, lifting her by the arms, and calling her *bunny*, but she slid out of his grasp every time and dug her head back into her knees. Finally, he stepped back with a curse and turned away. He had far less experience with her completely losing it than I had.

"Goddamn it, Grace!" he yelled. "What were you thinking? You know your mother's state of mind—what the hell's wrong with you?"

"Yeah, I know all about her state of mind. I'm surprised *you* would know anything about her, though."

"That is *not* fair, Grace!" he said angrily. "I care very much about you and your mother, and you know that!"

I rolled my eyes. "Yeah, thanks for the scraps you throw us when no one is looking."

He stepped back, uncertain. Regarding me like I was an alien from a distant galactic cluster. "What is happening with you right now?" he demanded. "You're not like this."

"Oh, really? What am I like?"

He was stumped for the moment, so I went on.

"Why didn't you just leave us like a normal guy who accidentally impregnates a woman?" I asked. "You're already married. You don't need us. Why do you keep on coming back? It's psychotic."

"Enough of the melodrama, Grace. You're far too young to understand what I've got on my plate. We are not having this conversation right now."

"Right. You think once I hit twenty-one or something I'll get the grown-up brain and the fact that I'm a secret side project will suddenly make perfect sense? Is that when we have this conversation?"

"You're not a side project—goddamn it, Grace, how are you coming up with this stuff? Where is this coming from?"

"I can't even call you without making up a fake firm name, Dad. Bet the other girls don't need to do that when they call you."

For a second, he was out of words. We had never argued. Certainly never about anything this heavy. We had gracefully and diligently always ignored all the details.

"I do care," he said. "I care very much about you and your mother. That's the important thing, Gracie. You need to know that."

I thought maybe he meant it. He looked drained enough to mean it. His chest was heaving up and down, and his T-shirt was clinging to his protruding stomach in a struggling kind of way. Beads of sweat were stippled across his upper lip and forehead, which he was continually wiping. I began to feel bad for him. I didn't want him to look this pathetic.

"Okay," I said. "Fine. It's not like it makes a difference anyway."

It was probably around here that we noticed my mother had stopped wailing. We looked over and found Wade helping her up off the ground. Mrs. Scholfield was there too, holding her purse with a tissue ready, saying soothing things and holding on to my mom's left elbow as they got her to her feet. She was still crying a little. Just silent tears now crawling down her face. Once she was on her feet, she took the tissue that Mrs. Scholfield held at the ready for her and wiped her eyes. Mrs. Scholfield helped her straighten her dress a little and dust off the dirt from the ground. Suddenly, my mom's eyes fell on Wade and she hiccupped. After a beat, she threw her arms around him and drew him into a feverish embrace. It reminded me a little of an amoeba enveloping an unsuspecting particle of nutrition. She held on to him tightly, her head resting on his shoulders, a few last tears gliding from between her dark eyelashes.

"I'm so sorry," my mom said after a long while. She was no longer crying, but she was holding on to him very tightly. "Look at you. Your face . . ."

Wade was trying to assure her that he was okay, and she just shook her head.

"You're not okay," she was saying softly, her voice returning to the melodic quality it had when she was talking to small animals. "Maybe you don't know it, but you're not okay."

Mrs. Scholfield left them alone at this point, no doubt feeling out of place in the scene. She walked over to where we were standing and attempted a smile. It stretched across her face painfully in little miserable spastic jolts.

"She seems to be doing a little better," she told us, giving her left earring another absentminded tug.

My dad nodded and thanked her for helping out, and then there was a general lull of sticky silence. Everyone had more or less been robbed completely of their dignity at this point, and it seemed hard, making an effort of any kind at all.

My mother had meanwhile released Wade from her weird grip. Her hands were on his cheeks now, and she was staring into his eyes with that cosmic look she always got when she explained things like the "pull of the universe" to me. It was hard to make out exactly what she was saying because her words bordered on a whisper half the time, but it was something about his aura and how he needed to protect its innocence. Wade nodded a few times, letting her get it out of her system, and then he began to get some words in edgewise, and soon after that, she responded with a small laugh. The manic fervor in her eyes began to subside, and there were the beginnings of a normal dialogue. The nutcase quality began to drain out of her. She began to relax. None of us dared interfere.

"He's so good with people," Mrs. Scholfield said to my dad as we stood watching them. "I remember when he was only about three years old, how he'd talk to all the bums on the street. It scared me half to death. He was always off talking to strangers."

My dad nodded. "He seems like a good kid."

"He is. He has a heart of gold," she said with a smile. She held it for a moment before it got heavy around the edges. "He truly does. I just wish I understood him better. Sometimes I don't seem to understand anything about him at all."

She was fighting hard to keep that smile on her face. Even as she dabbed the corner of her eye, trying to disguise the threat of tears as something having gotten into her eye, the smile was there. It wavered, but she wasn't going to let it die. Not on her watch.

"Gosh. I wish I were a better person," she said with a little laugh.

"Sheila, we need to get going."

I had forgotten all about the fact that Wade's father was still part the ecosystem of things. I think we all had. There was a startled group reaction as he materialized suddenly next to his wife with a huge coffee stain down the front of his shirt, and his face slightly spattered with red discolorations. My heart plummeted through my body, and I took an instinctive step behind my dad.

"Oh, Mike. There you are!" Mrs. Scholfield announced with a nervous cheeriness.

His response was terse and mechanical in tone. "We need to get a move on. Traffic is going to be a bitch as it is."

"Hon, give us a minute," his wife said, putting her hand on his arm. "Just a minute."

He ignored her. "Wade, we're leaving," he called out. "*Now.*"

Wade glanced over. "Okay, hold on a second."

"I said *now!*"

He made a move toward Wade, and my dad grabbed him by his shirt and held him back. "Easy, chief!"

Mr. Scholfield acknowledged our presence for the first time. His glare moved from me to my dad. "What did you call me?"

"It's okay," my dad told him in that commanding lawyer-voice in which he talked to adults like toddlers. "I called you *chief*. You can live with that."

Mr. Scholfield took a step back and examined my dad with the same kind of cold violence that he had displayed earlier inside the store. "Do we have a problem I don't know about?"

"Take it easy. I'm just asking you to calm down, that's all."

The air was suddenly thick with electrical current.

"You're asking *me* to calm down? Oh, that's rich. *That's* very rich!"

My dad held up his hands in a gesture of wanting no trouble. "That's all I'm asking."

"You have some nerve sticking your nose into our business, you know that?"

Wade began walking over. "It's okay, Dad, let's go."

"No, you stay there, kid," my dad told him, holding out his hand like a traffic cop.

Uncertain, Wade stopped.

Mr. Scholfield's voice became unsteady with rage. "I said we're leaving, Wade. *Now.*"

Wade had made another step and then stopped again when my dad told him to stay. It was as though he were a remote-controlled object that moved and stopped when anyone pressed the right button.

"*Now, Wade.*"

This time, my mother stopped him. She had come up behind him and, putting her arm across his chest, pulled him backward. I honestly couldn't believe this was happening, but it only got better.

My dad invaded Mr. Scholfield's personal space.

"Hey, look," he said, "you need to stop picking on your own kid. That's a real candy-ass kind of thing to do. I'm sure you can agree with me. Now, how about you take a moment and calm down like I asked you to?"

A small *holy shit*–type noise escaped Mrs. Scholfield's lips. She clapped a hand to her mouth.

"How about you go fuck yourself?" Mr. Scholfield said, any restraint in his voice now fully obliterated.

My dad threw the first punch. It was hard to clearly determine who won in the end. Both or neither. Although it was probably my dad who was a little more on the losing end; he was older than Wade's father, as well as shorter and not to mention fatter. Still, he fought with frenzied passion. It was one of the more bizarre things that I had ever witnessed, and it was probably this moment that solidified my fondness for my dad permanently. There was tripping and falling, choke holds, elbows, rolling around on the ground, arms flailing, grunts, and curses. The kind of fight that no one in their right mind would choreograph for a movie.

Three random men broke it up eventually, and from there, the scene just kind of fizzled out faster than it had begun. Our dads didn't say anything further to each other. No one called the cops, but one of the guys got out his phone, and I suppose there was the general idea that he was going to call 911, which contributed to the urgency of getting the hell out of there. There were no parting words. I remember looking over at Wade as my dad pushed me into the car. His mother was pulling him into their car, and our eyes met for a second in the jumble of motion. I pulled down my window and leaned out, but it was too late. We were already getting onto the freeway, and the wind blew my hair into my face. By the time I pushed the hair out of my eyes, the gas station was lost behind us.

The car ride home was weird. We sat shell-shocked in silence, looking our very worst and feeling like we had all just had a group enema. But it could have been worse. We could have all stayed polite back at the gas station, smiling and small-talking our way out of that shithole of a moment. We could have stayed civil. We could have been sitting in the car now, clean and unexposed and safe and not able to breathe.

My dad turned up the radio loud when we got on the freeway, clearly in no mood to have a conversation just then. That was okay, except that it was some kind of easy-listening, smooth-jazz saxophone stuff. I stared out at the passing strip malls and electrical poles and billboards advertising sleazy lawyers and theme park rides. I knew we'd talk about everything in detail, including the loss of my virginity and all that, but for the moment, we were all locked in a semi-comforting state of shock.

"Can we change the music?" I asked, disrupting the sanctity of the state of shock. The elevator music was too hard-core for me. You honestly can't feel sad and meaningful with that kind of soundtrack.

My dad obliged my request, hitting the Seek button on the radio in a half-zombie state.

That Lynyrd Skynyrd song "Free Bird" erupted through the car's interior. Right around the "And this bird you cannot change" part.

It was pretty corny, but my mom began swaying to the words almost immediately. She rolled down the window and a gust of wind erupted throughout the car's interior. After a while, even my dad's zombie state began to crack and he started drumming out the rhythm on the steering wheel. Half-assed and absentmindedly at first, but then, slowly, the song scooped him up. The drumming became more intense, and he began to have a constipated look on his face, which I realized was his "enjoying music" face. I suppressed a laugh and slid down in the back seat and closed my eyes.

Personally, I wasn't feeling great. The barfing and the crying and the kissing and the violence and the fear and the adrenaline and the truth and the sun—it had hollowed me out.

I was pretty heartbroken too. I could still taste Wade's mouth. I could smell him on my skin, and my T-shirt had some of his blood on it. I started crying quietly. I didn't know exactly why, because part of it felt good—like mountains crumbling to pieces into the sea. It had really shaken me up, being a witness to that afternoon, and for a small moment I wished we had never stopped to fuel up the car so that I could have gone home just feeling righteously heartbroken in that easy, tunnel-vision way that required only my own self-pity.

The "Free Bird" guitar solo kicked in hard, and although I definitely did *not* want to be emotionally affected by some Southern rock song from the '70s, it was somehow impossible not to feel annoyingly free as a bird just then. Not with the wind flying through the car, and the music turned up that loud, and the speed of the wheels and the freeway under my back, and everyone's dirty laundry having been aired out so violently, including my own.

We left that gas station behind, and for the next week, we were back to being the trio from Parents' Weekend—that chemical compound that was somehow invincible as a whole. We were normal again—maybe more normal than we had ever been before, because although we made no more mention of the things we had yelled at each other at the gas station, there was still that general cleanliness that comes after shit hitting the fan. Like the pristine weather after a storm, when the air smells fresh and the humidity momentarily drops away. We might not have changed our operating basis much, but at least for those few minutes, we had actually looked at that bizarre thing that was our lives truthfully, and it rearranged things on a molecular level. We were all good to move on. Or so I thought.

The night before my dad left to go back to the airport, he showed up with a packet of tampons at my door.

"I heard you telling your mom you were out of these earlier," he said, awkwardly holding out the packet to me. "Figured I'd get you some while I was at the store."

"Wow, that's kind of intense, Dad," I said, taking the tampons.

"Well, I just felt why not save you the trip. I was already there. Not sure if that's the right brand, or if the brand even makes a difference. I'm sure it's all the same thing. The lady at the store said these were good."

"Yeah, these are an excellent choice. Thanks."

I put my hand on the door to close it again. This was his cue to go, but instead of leaving, he began to massage the door-frame with his right hand and cleared his throat a bunch.

"Gracie, you're not a side project."

If the tampons hadn't caught me off guard, then this certainly did. It was the last thing I had expected him to say. My mouth fell open a little.

"I just wanted to reiterate that before I left," he added. "You are *not* a side project, okay?"

After a moment of being stupefied by the fact that he would delve back into this hairy subject matter of his own free will, I said, "Dad, I was pissed off when I said that stuff. Not even at you, really—more at Wade's psycho parents."

He nodded. "I know you were upset, but the fact that those

words even came out of you—the fact that they were right there, on your mind, ready to go—that says a lot."

He took a deep breath, and I could tell there was a whole lot more he wanted to say—his eyes were jam-packed with emotions slushing around in them—but there seemed to be no clear way for him to start. He nodded to himself a few more times, cleared his throat again, and then eventually said, "Well, you know I love you, right?"

"Yeah," I said. "I've always suspected it, but now I've got the proof." I held up the pack of tampons.

He laughed, a little too loudly and eagerly in his relief, but that was maybe the best part.

And for the record, I hadn't been joking. You can fake paternal love by buying expensive phones and clothes and school tuition, but you can't fake it by buying a packet of tampons. That shit is real.

THINGS WERE DIFFERENT FOR MY JUNIOR YEAR AT school. Beth and Derek were gone. Mr. Sorrentino was married. I had a different roommate. I was a year older. The obvious stuff.

Wade never came back.

Of course, that was the most palpable thing of all—the real reason why nothing really felt the same. The reason for that one color pixel that had changed, pulling the entire universe out of shape. The reason Mrs. Gillespie's frizz didn't look the same, or the paint peeling off the ceiling in the back of the library felt more desolate, or the lighting in the dining hall seemed more blue than yellow.

I hadn't heard from him all summer, which was all right; I had expected as much because of the way he had talked about everything being "upside down." Plus, there was still the issue with him having to get a new phone, and me having erased his number from my own phone back when Anju had painted his nails. But it didn't matter anyway, because all that had to happen was for summer to end. He had asked me to give him the summer, and I could do that—easily enough with the promises that lay on the other side of it: us back in the same geographical location. And this time, his world would be right side up, and there would be no Derek.

But when a week of school had rolled by and he still wasn't there, I went to the office. I stood in front of Mrs. Martinez as she told me that Wade's parents hadn't signed him up this year, and I felt like my whole body had stopped existing. Then I looked around the room and realized that the building was evaporating. I crawled into bed, not bothering with a note from the nurse. I wasn't catatonic this time, and there was no Beth to dye my hair. I got through it myself. My new roommate did bother asking if I was all right that evening, and when I said, "Yeah," she returned to her homework, satisfied that she had performed her duties. She was far less obtrusive than Georgina. I had to get used to it.

It was one thing to be broken up with Wade—that rift, deep as it might have been, was only as wide as a classroom. No matter how hard he ignored me, he had been there—his voice when he'd talked to people that weren't me, the back of his head when he'd turned away, his name called out by teachers and friends.

It was another thing entirely to have an absolute physical absence of Wade at school. It was unnatural. Like he had been wiped out.

The terror became infected over the days that followed, growing larger and larger the more time I had to sink into all the details of what this meant. The permanence of it scared the shit out of me. Wade had been eradicated from my life. Just removed, and nobody had bothered to ask me about it.

I began to wonder why he wasn't back. He was supposed to

be back. He told me he was coming back after the summer, so why was he not here? I figured the only realistic explanation was that he was dead. The terror expanded further with the help of my rampant imagination. I began to feel sick about the fact that we had left him at the gas station, being packed up into the car by his parents. I was certain I had caused this to happen. I didn't know what "this" was, but I knew it was terrible. There were too many logical scenarios, the foremost being that his dad had obviously killed him and had thrown his body out into a ditch before they'd even made it home that day.

I went to the office and asked for his mother's contact info, but they refused to give it to me because of their privacy policy. I tried to hunt him down online—I knew he wasn't on social media, but maybe there was some kind of evidence that he existed—school records, who knows? All I found were some skateboarding videos on Calvin's Instagram that he was on. And one picture with Anju on her Instagram that made me sick to my stomach. I found Calvin and got him to give me Wade's number, called it, and got a lady with a slight Spanish accent who had never heard of him. I tried googling his mother, even his father, but all I found was a guy that may or may not be his dad who worked at a dental marketing company—and anyway, even if it was the right Mike Scholfield, I wasn't actually going to contact the psychopath.

I went back to the office and tried to explain to Mrs. Martinez that Wade might be dead and that I really needed to reach him.

"Don't be silly," she said. "His mother called in and cancelled his registration two weeks before the start of school. She sounded perfectly fine. He's just switching schools."

"Why?"

"She didn't give me the details."

"But doesn't she need to give you a reason?"

"Of course she doesn't."

"Okay, but what school is he at now?"

Mrs. Martinez stopped her work and gave me a no-nonsense glare over her glasses. "Grace, do you have a pass to be in here right now?"

I didn't.

She sighed. "I suggest you get your butt back to class ASAP before I decide to do my job and write you up."

It took about a week before I decided that Wade might possibly not be dead, simply because I figured it would have been in the news if a body were found. There was nothing in the news, and with the fear of his death subsiding, I was able to feel the pain of his absence properly. He was gone. Alive but gone. This was possibly worse. I swear, I was so sick of being heartbroken at this point that I could hardly stand myself. But there was just no other way to feel about Wade.

By October, the pain had become duller. A constant dull hum. By November, it was a small, sometimes undetectable vibration in my bones. By early December, there were whole strings of days where I forgot to think about him, and when I did think about him, the sadness was more poetic than directly physical. I missed him.

My life was quiet. With Beth and Derek gone, I was back to having no friends and spending my free time reading and writing novels with abstract and complicated meanings. It wasn't that bad. The previous year had been so exhausting. Maybe the loneliness was good. I remained close with Mr. Sorrentino. We really did have a connection after all, just not a pedophile type of connection. Sometimes I'd visit him at lunchtime to talk. Didn't matter much what we talked about. He mainly tried to make it be about productive things like education and plans for the future and biochemistry as a possible career move for me, but he was good about cooperating when I veered off the subject.

I'd run into Georgie sometimes and we'd exchange a few words, but it wasn't the same. She didn't tell me about her toilet dreams anymore. We were just polite strangers now with our own separate lives tugging at us. I was happy for her, though, when she started dating Byron Rosario. He was head of the chess club.

I gave up smoking after dissecting a fetal pig and taking out the tiny lungs that looked like fragile paper airbags. Mr. Sorrentino made a whole point about telling us how similar pig anatomy was to human anatomy.

I did end up being less of a pubescent mess. What Beth had said was kind of true—you start to figure things out. I had dyed my hair light gray over the summer. I grew out my bangs, clipping them to the side. More fat started to disappear from my face. I began to wear lipstick sometimes and got really good at doing the lip liner. I had better bras and underwear. It just happened—I don't even remember going bra shopping. I had a shampoo and a conditioner that smelled like artificial fruit.

Anju Sahani was back at school. Naturally, she was. The one person I could have really done without showed up like clockwork on the first day back at school with her boobs more developed and her hair cut short and slightly flipped out at the ends in this '60s way that was totally at odds with everyone else's hairstyle—and also annoyingly amazing. I tried my best to ignore her completely. She still made me sick to my stomach. Every time I saw her, I remembered her sitting with Wade in class or outside by the tennis court, her head on his shoulder, or painting his goddamn nails or writing cute things on his T-shirt with a Sharpie. I wondered whether she had his address or phone number, and it nearly killed me to think that maybe she did, and that this whole time they were texting or talking on the phone, planning their lives together. I didn't know if I could bear Wade and Anju getting married someday. I didn't think I could. If they had kids, I'd probably have to kill myself. My imagination was having a hard enough time dealing with Wade's disappearance; it didn't need Anju on top of it. So I denied her existence. When she entered a room, I left it. When I saw her coming down a hallway, I retraced my steps and went the other way. When we were stuck in the same class together, I pretended her side of the room didn't exist.

This worked out well enough until we were teamed up together in our cooking class to make a chocolate hazelnut cake. When Mrs. Friebe called out our names, I nearly fell off my chair. Anju was walking toward me with her bowl and recipe clutched under her arm—flesh and blood and bottomless eyes and 1960s hair. She was as real as she had ever been. I could feel the battle build up inside me. All the hatred. All the sickness. When she reached my table, she put down her bowl and glanced hesitantly at me. Then she sighed.

"I don't want to be your enemy," she announced.

I ignored her.

"Seriously," she said. "I've thought about it a lot, and I've decided I'm not going to dislike you."

I flattened the recipe out on the table, continuing to ignore her.

"And just so you know, you can't make me change my mind about it," she went on stubbornly. "We don't have to be friends or anything, or hang out or even talk, but I'm not going to hate you. I thought you should know."

I raised my hand. "Mrs. Friebe, can I have a new partner?"

Mrs. Friebe glanced over her shoulder from across the room. "Everyone is teamed up already. What's wrong with your partner?"

I wavered for a moment. "Uh . . . she smells like my boyfriend's dick," I said.

To set the record straight: I was not cool enough to say things like that to a teacher in front of a whole classroom—not by a *long* shot—but it was either that or bake a chocolate hazelnut cake with Anju. The latter being unthinkable. There was no way in hell I was measuring out sugar and whipping eggs with my archnemesis. No way. Mrs. Friebe sent me to the office, and I was so thankful I nearly fell over myself trying to get the hell out of there.

But that wasn't the end of it. I was cleaning the downstairs girls' bathroom later that day, because of the unsavory language in class and all that, and then:

"Hey . . ."

Anju's voice came from right behind me. My heart sank.

I couldn't believe she had the nerve. I honestly could not believe it.

I turned to her and dropped my sponge on the floor.

"I just want to talk for a minute," she said with determination threading through her slightly wobbly voice. "Just for a minute."

I realized this was going to happen one way or another. I was powerless to stop it.

"Don't you think we should at least talk about what happened before the holidays?" she pressed on. "We said some awful things to each other."

"Oh my god," I gasped. "What is wrong with you? *No.* No, I don't think we should ever talk about *anything.* I think you should get on a spaceship and go live in another solar system—that's honestly what I think would be a pretty fantastic idea. I don't like you, okay? I'd feel happier if you didn't exist in this dimension or time zone or even this particular armpit of this state—but if you just weren't right in my fucking face, that would be a decent start too."

Anju screwed up her mouth but didn't budge. She continued to stand there, her feet planted firmly on the ground in a battle stance of peace and love.

"You don't have to like me. That's fine," she said. "I'm just uncomfortable with what happened between us. I want to clear it up."

I picked the sponge off the floor and started with the next sink. *Maybe if I ignore her, she will just disappear,* I thought. You can't have a conversation by yourself. The words will fizzle out.

"I hate when girls do this to each other." Anju' s voice came floating from behind me. "I've always hated it. And I realized I was acting right into that system. I said some awful things. You're not a whore, okay? Please disregard everything I said to you. I don't want to be the kind of girl who says things like that."

"Well, that's too bad," I said, not doing a great job at ignoring her, "because you *are* the kind of girl who says things like that, and I *am* a whore. I had sex with Derek, remember?"

"You're not a whore," she insisted firmly. "Did Derek pay you? Was there a monetary exchange?"

I squeezed my eyes shut tightly. "Stop it. Seriously, stop!"

"Well, it's *true.* You're not a whore."

I poured a perverse amount of Comet into the sink and continued scrubbing. "Fine! Even if I'm not—still makes you the kind of girl that calls other girls whores," I pointed out.

"I wouldn't be here right now if I were that kind of girl. That's my whole point. We don't have to be what everyone expects us to be."

I stopped and turned to face her. "Why are you making me

a part of this? If you're having some kind of religious break-through, that's *your* business. Why the hell would you pull me into it? Don't you think that's kind of fucked up?"

For the first time, she seemed at a loss for words. In hind-sight, I can't blame her. My accusation didn't make much sense. There are no fast rules about sharing or not sharing your religious breakthroughs as far as I know.

"I don't mind being what everyone expects of me," I told her.

Her eyes went to the ground for a second. I thought we were finally done, but again I was wrong.

"Wade made you sound so cool when he talked about you," she said, shifting gears.

A small part of my heart exploded at the mention of Wade's name. It still unsettled me to be reminded of him. Every time someone mentioned him, it was like a small, private earth-quake. Everything rocked a little around me.

"And he had more insight into things than anyone I've ever met," Anju added as a dreamy afterthought. She liked him a lot. I could tell by the way she was trying to sound matter-of-fact in her observation.

"Wade could be way off his fucking rocker when he wanted to," I said callously, turning back to the sinks.

"Yeah, but he was different," Anju mused. "And all the ways that he was the same as other kids, you know—the things that made him like the rest of us—I feel like they were just an act he put on."

"Oh, geez. Save it for your diary."

I hated her talking like this. He was *my* subject matter. I was the only one allowed to make philosophical judgments about Wade. It was probably worse because there was some truth in what she said. It hurt that she knew Wade that well.

"He wasn't into me," Anju said quickly. "I mean, not romantically. He was nice to me because he's a nice person and he could talk to me when he was at his worst—you know, about you—stuff he couldn't talk to Cal about. But that's all. He wasn't into me." She stopped and looked at me cautiously, and it seemed as though this was what she had been trying to talk about the entire time. "I don't know if you understand how heartbroken he actually was."

I rolled my eyes.

"No, listen, he was really destroyed over you," she said. Her voice took on a more intimate tone. "I know he was good about hiding it—you probably don't even have a clue, but he was *so* lost. It kind of freaked me out, actually. Like, that day when you started hanging out with Derek at lunch, I found him behind that equipment shed way in the back by the back entrance, and he was just sitting there crying. His whole body was shaking. It scared me pretty bad because I've never seen anything hurt him before ever—and then I was holding him and he was falling apart like a little kid, and—I mean, you'd think that would be romantic—me holding him and him clinging onto me, but it really wasn't. It was hard-core. It was scary and sad."

I didn't have the ability to say anything. I moved over to the next sink with my cleaning supplies, and Anju continued talking.

"That's why I said what I said to you in the laundry room. I'd just seen him lose it like that, and I had to make him feel better. I was pissed off. You did this to him—you broke him into all these little pieces—and it didn't even matter, because he was still in love with you. And he would never like me the way he liked you—even though I would have done everything right. It seemed wrong. But then I realized that he had done the same to you. You were doing it to each other, and it was pretty obvious to me then that I didn't fit in anywhere with what you guys had going on. I wasn't even close to playing a part in it, and honestly, I didn't want to."

She took a little, trembling breath. I could feel her wait, probably wondering if I would react. I didn't.

"Anyway, I just wanted you to know that," she said. "I wasn't ever a threat to you. The way that Wade was in love with you was bulletproof. And I'd really hate for you to think it wasn't what it actually was just because I was there with my stupid crush."

She waited a moment longer.

"That's all," she said.

"Great," I replied. I was staring into the sink in front of me, scrubbing so hard that my wrist was hurting from the way I was pressing my hand into the sponge. "*Now* can you fuck off?"

Finally, she sounded resigned. "Sure."

She left.

It was irritating the way she had said all the things I'd really needed to hear. It wasn't fair. She couldn't be that person. She couldn't be the kind of person who realizes her mistakes and takes responsibility for them by performing touching monologues out of the fucking blue. That wasn't fair. I hated her too much to let her be a good person. God, the thought that I might have to think of her in less black-and-white terms made me queasy, and I finished the rest of the sinks with unhinged belligerence. It was all I had left—her being a piece of shit. She should have had the good sense to see that.

Still. There was no point in lying to myself. What Anju had said made me feel safe in a way that I hadn't felt before. I lay in bed that night, running her words through my head over and over. I had sometimes struggled to remember how real things had been between Wade and me. The more time happened, the more I thought maybe I was insane because, after all, where was the proof? I had nothing to show for it. There was nothing there except the way I remembered it, and what if I remembered it wrong? What Anju had said gave me back the whole thing. She made it the truth. It might have ended, but it had been real, and beautiful, and honest—as honest as the natural laws of existence—those things that you can't dispute: gravity, mass, light, skin, atoms, neutrons, motion, cytoplasm, blood, wind. Not even someone as cool as Anju Sahani had the power to come between that reality.

It had been nice of her to tell me that. She could have kept it to herself, but she didn't. Fuck her.

About a week or so later, I happened to be around when someone accidentally bumped into her outside the history room and all her notebooks fell to the floor. I don't know what possessed me, but one of the notebooks landed right by my feet, and I picked it up for her. The entire back of it was covered with tiny, weird, block-letter writing. The kind that serial killers have in movies when they write all over the walls of their bedrooms. I stared at it for a second because the words looked familiar. Yup. They were.

FREAK OUT AND GIVE IN. DOESN'T MATTER WHAT YOU BE-LIEVE IN. STAY COOL AND BE SOMEBODY'S FOOL THIS YEAR. 'CAUSE THEY KNOW WHO IS RIGHTEOUS. WHAT IS BOLD. SO I'M TOLD . . .

And on and on and on. They were all lyrics to Smashing Pumpkins songs.

"Yikes," I said, handing the notebook back to her.

She took the notebook and piled it underneath her history book before slinking away like a sad, bullied child on a playground. I let out a breath of air and felt mean. This is exactly why it sucked that she had said all those things to me in the girls' bathroom. Everything I did and said now in regard to her made me into an asshole. Not to mention it sucked ass that she liked my band.

We had computer science together as our last period that day. And when we somehow ended up next to each other in the congestion of kids trying to get into the classroom, I asked her, "So, what's your favorite SP album?"

She blinked uneasily at me, uncertain of what was happening. I felt just as uncomfortable as she did, to be honest. The whole thing was weird—me, instigating a conversation with Anju. What the fuck?

"Um . . . I don't know," she said slowly, looking around as though waiting for a booby trap. "I like all of them."

"That's not a real answer. You have to say something specific, like a song, an album—whatever."

Anju turned to face me more fully, and the trepidation in her face began to intermingle with curiosity. "Wait, do you know the Smashing Pumpkins? I mean, pretty well or something?"

I shrugged. "No. I just don't like vague generalities when people talk about music. If you can't back something up with a specific reason, you're full of shit in my opinion. It's like those people who buy used-looking AC/DC or Iron Maiden T-shirts at Urban Outfitters or whatever for like forty bucks. I don't care if you're going to listen to that kind of stuff, but I'll definitely have a problem if you're wearing the T-shirt and you *don't* actually listen to that stuff."

She nodded, still looking a little spooked, but also with a growing expression of interest in her eyes. "Okay, yeah," she said. "There's this part on the first album—*Gish*—that song 'Bury Me'—about a minute into the song where there's a break, like the song is going to end, and then the guitar comes in again—"

"'I love my sister so,'" I said, quoting the lyrics.

Her eyes went wide, and she had a physical reaction like someone had just popped a balloon in her face. "What?! No way! How do you know what I'm talking about?"

"It's a cool part," I said, still sounding like a dick about it, though.

She laughed excitedly, saying, "No way!" a couple more times. Then she shook her head and laughed again. "*Fuck me. Of course.* All my friends make fun of me for being obsessed with that band, and then you come along—the biggest asshole in school—and you get it. I mean, of course that's what would happen!"

I smiled a little and tried to hide it by looking at the floor over my right shoulder. "Yup," I said after a moment. "This sucks."

"Shit. So much," she said.

It was probably the first thing we ever agreed on. I mean, besides Wade.

"Did you listen to their last album?" Anju asked.

I bit my lip, terrified. There is nothing worse than sharing a favorite band with your nemesis. I was either going to like her a lot more now or like the Smashing Pumpkins a lot less. It was one or the other.

"Ladies!" This was Mr. Lee, holding open the door to his classroom. "Are you planning on joining us? You have two seconds before I call roll."

The hallway had grown empty. We followed Mr. Lee into the classroom, and I sat down next to Anju, because fuck it, I knew that I was never going to like the Smashing Pumpkins any less.

AND THEN I GOT THE LETTER.

It was the beginning of December by this time. Florida at its best. The heat had gone down, and the air was fresh and sweet again. Everything always seemed so much more hopeful when the weather stopped being a dick. You could walk outside without clothes sticking to your skin or the sun feeling like acid on your face. It was like the universe letting you out of a choke hold. It was easy to feel hopeful that time of year despite all the Christmas decorations.

I had gone to the office expecting to pick up a package from my mother, but instead, I was handed a normal-size envelope, thick and battered up—too much paper stuffed inside of it. There was no return address, only my name on the front of the envelope with the school's address, and on the top left-hand corner of the envelope it said *Wade S*. I stood paralyzed for a moment. I don't know how long I was frozen like this, but I snapped out of it when my lungs began to burn from lack of oxygen.

"Holy moly!" Miss Klein said with a little laugh as she passed by. "Everything all right there?"

It felt like three tons of adrenaline had suddenly been dumped into my bloodstream. I began to feel dizzy, like I might pass out. My body seemed to be under the impression I was in the middle of running a marathon and responded accordingly—sweat pouring off me, breathing uncontrollably. I had to prop myself up against the wall.

Miss Klein circled back around, looking more genuinely concerned. "Is something wrong?"

I managed to shake my head. I told her I was fine and ripped the envelope open as soon as I was outside. I had taken the first exit door there was. It led to the back parking lot, and the fresh air gave me some of my sanity back. I slid down the wall next to the back entrance until I was sitting on the ground. My hands were unsteady, and the papers trembled. I had to lay them out flat on my lap. It killed me to see Wade's handwriting again—the large, messy scrawls and the tendency to capitalize words for emphasis.

Hi, Gracie.

Yeah, I'm alive. I know you probably thought I was dead at some point. I know how that brain of yours works. Just kidding. I have no idea how it works. Anyway, I'm sorry. I should have called you a long time ago. What the hell is wrong with me? I'm sorry.

Remember I told you I like you too much for anything to be easy? That's the best that I can explain it. I like you waaaaay too much—just use that as a reference point for all my bullshit. Including this letter.

Anyway, I'll start with the easy part:

I'm living with my aunt's family. My mom's older sister. She lives in Missouri, so that's where I am, in case you were wondering. Springfield. I have three cousins. They're all girls, and the oldest one is at college. The other ones are the girls who gave me the tattoos during spring break— remember? Anyway, I'm staying in their older sister's room while she's at college. She said it was okay. It's only temporary anyway. But it's cool, except I'm really stressing out about keeping all her plants alive. Why does she have THAT many plants in her room?? Also, on the ceiling, right above the bed, it says RYAN GOSLING—spelled out in those glow-in-the-dark stars. You know my deal with insomnia. I stare at the ceiling a lot in the middle of the night—so that guy's like a big part of my life right now.

Anyway, my aunt and uncle are nice. Sometimes I think they're TOO nice. I haven't really gotten the hang of their rhythm or whatever you want to call it. They really LOVE to talk about stuff and get to the "bottom" of everything all the time even when there IS no bottom. But anyway, they're nice, so there's no point in blaming them. It's kind of stupid to think of how comfortable I actually was with the way my parents ran the show. It sucked, but I knew my way around that shit better.

Oh yeah, my parents are getting a divorce, btw. Weird. It's like a dumb punch line to a fucked-up joke that started before I was even born. Not that I'm against it or anything.

And you were probably right about my mom and that she should have left my dad a long time ago and all that. I mean, no question—you were right for sure. I just don't like to think about it. No fun to admit that things could have been NOT screwed up, you know? Like that was an actual <u>option</u>. You get into the what-ifs, and I don't wanna know about my what-if life. No point. Anyway, sorry if I was a jerkoff when we briefly talked about this last time.

Hey, MOVING ON!!!!!!

I still haven't even said what I should ACTUALLY be saying. I don't know how good I will be at saying it, but I'll just write it in whatever dumb way it comes out of me and you'll just have to deal with it.

Okay:

I've never felt like I belonged anywhere specific. Or more like: every place I ever was felt like the wrong place to be. Like no place was mine. I was in other people's places where their bullshit rules were the ones that worked. All I could ever do was play along or blow those places up. Those were my choices, more or less. Mostly it didn't matter which one I chose anyway. I for sure didn't give a fuck about myself, so there were no real consequences that I cared about ever. That's a lot of really twisted freedom to have by the way.

With you around it wasn't like that. I had more than those two choices maybe for the first time ever in my life. It felt like things were right—not just to be hanging out with you—I mean my life actually seemed right because of you, and that is fucking CRAAAZYYYY. Trust me. I didn't have that sick freedom anymore, and maybe I didn't know how to deal with that and I fucked up a bunch and I'm sorry.

But the point is: nothing about being with you felt the way that everything else always felt. Maybe that's what I was trying to say. In a way, you made my whole life worthwhile. Sorry to be corny about it. There's no cool way of saying that exact thing. I tried.

Anyway. Not sure what else to say. I'm in love with you, okay? Just in case that wasn't clear. That was supposed to be the main point of this whole letter. And I can't explain how much it blows being away from you—it does—but I'm stuck here while my parents are getting a divorce, and I don't know where I'll be stuck after that. One day, I'll probably get to make an actual decision about something, Can you imagine?

So yeah, I don't know what happens after this letter. I have no clue. Let's just pretend that anything could happen, okay?

I miss you.

Anyway, enough bullshit.

Yours truly,
Wade

I put the letter down on the ground. For a moment, I had no thoughts at all. I leaned back against the wall and watched a couple of freshman kids run by screaming with water guns. Then I picked up the pages and the envelope and began to search for a return address or his number. There was none. I got up and stuffed the letter into my pocket. I wanted to be with Wade. He had promised it by the side of the freeway. He was a liar. No phone number, no email address, no return address. Nothing. Fuck his romantic puritanism. I wanted real things. I wanted Wade to tell me that we'd wait for each other, and I could visit him or he could visit me for the next holidays, and we would text all night long and talk on the phone and write each other until we were done with school. I wanted plans and goals and deadlines and calendar days to cross off. He was shutting us down, and he knew exactly what he was doing.

All those months of getting over him were for the birds. I was back where I had started with my heart in shreds, bleeding, hurting, rotting. When I got to my room, I threw the letter under my mattress, wishing he had never written me at all. Then I ripped the lamp off my bedside table and threw it across the room. The lampshade ripped, and the light bulb shattered. Good. I slammed the door on my way out. I didn't know where I was going but probably to dinner. It was right around dinnertime.

I stopped the first guy that crossed my path. A skinny, tall kid. I vaguely knew him from art class. He was the one who had made a pretty cool Darth Vader helmet out of papier-mâché.

"Hey, you wanna go to the Christmas dance with me?" I asked him.

The guy looked startled. He stopped and made a weird face. Then he scratched a patch of bad skin on his cheek and said, "Yeah. Definitely."

It wasn't until the day before the Christmas holidays that

I pulled the letter out from under my mattress again. I had been doing some research in the library earlier that day and came across the yearbook from the previous year lying on one of the tables. I stared at it for a while before flipping it open to our page: "Sophomores—Overlooked, but Not Forgotten." There was Wade's picture toward the bottom between Laura Salvaterra and Tim Streeter. His smile was almost not there at all, but his eyes were full of that ten thousand wattage that powered him. I felt this inexplicably massive relief, seeing his face again—I mean, it was pretty unbearable at the same time, but still—relief, like it was good to be reminded that he existed. Somewhere.

The letter was badly crumpled when I pulled it out from under my mattress that night, and the second page was almost ripped fully in half. I taped it back together and laid the pages out on the bed. My roommate was with her study group. The room was mine. I picked up the first page and started reading it again. It felt like an entirely different letter. I had gone through it so fast the first time that I had shortchanged myself. Most of it had gone over my head. I had been too hungry to get it in me, and I had devoured it—torn the words apart and only half-registered anything about it. The only thing that had mattered was my anger.

This time, I read with no hopes, no fears.

I started crying right off the bat, because everything about that letter was too much exactly like him. And goddamn it, it was so insanely beautiful. I ended up reading it about twenty times, and each time the entire world changed. Eventually, though, I wasn't crying anymore. I had emptied myself out, erupted into flames, melted all over the place, and finally I was all right. I didn't necessarily *want* to be all right—the moment was too perfectly melancholy—but I couldn't help it. I was all right. I realized there was no point in being mad at Wade, because fuck it—I liked him too much. Way too much. The real thing I felt for him was not this generic, synthesized, auto-pilot production of hormones-going-apeshit love. It was much calmer than that. It was constant and actual. Unkillable. The kind you don't ever need to worry about.

Maybe all that mattered was that Wade was going to be okay. Maybe it wasn't only about what I needed from him. I sat back on my bed and examined the ceiling. It kind of blew my mind that I had gotten to that non-scumbag way of loving someone. I had been pretty certain that I was incapable of being that kind of person.

There was a soft-water stain in the corner of the ceiling. I was staring at it intently without seeing it. I figured maybe I loved Wade for real.

My bedroom door crashed open, and I dropped the page of the letter I was holding.

"Miss Welles, rumor has it you were present earlier today at the assembly where a select group of teachers from the English Department, wearing backward baseball caps, took it upon themselves to perform a rap about education being fun."

Anju was standing in the doorway, aiming her phone at me, filming.

"Would you care to comment on this unfortunate incident?" she asked, walking up to me, phone still in my face.

"Can you maybe *not* take an extreme close-up of my fat, sweat-glazed face right now?"

Anju ignored my request. "How did the performance affect your sanity? Is there a chance that you will be able to move past this traumatizing experience and hope to live a normal, productive life again one day?"

I glanced at the letter one more time. *Anyway, enough bullshit. Yours truly, Wade* and folded the pages carefully back into the envelope.

"Well," I said, slipping the letter into the drawer of my bed-side table and turning to Anju, "I think it's too early to tell. This is not the kind of thing one just moves past, but maybe with the help of a lobotomy I can dare to hope again."

Anju laughed, and I grabbed the phone out of her hands. "Gimme that," I said and aimed it at her. "Live from Midhurst School, our investigative reporter Ms. Sahani is going under-cover to report on the very serious matter of teachers letting loose and what exactly this means for those unsuspecting vic-tims tragically blindsided by such 'entertainment.'"

We spent the rest of the evening interviewing people about the teachers' talent show at assembly. After that, we stayed up pretty late, hanging out in Chandra and Angela's room. Some-how, I ended up being a girl who hung out in that room with the other girls, listening to music and talking and draping our limbs over furniture. I remembered the days when I used to walk past those rooms, looking in, condemning everyone, be-cause it was all I had. Before Derek, before Beth, before Wade. Back when there was only Mr. Sorrentino and Stephen King.

It seemed a lifetime ago that I was fifteen years old.

Song List

Chapter 1: "Bullet with Butterfly Wings" by the Smashing Pumpkins

Chapter 2: "You'll Never Change" by Bettye LaVette

Chapter 3: "Teenage Wastebasket" by Beck

Chapter 4: "Sabotage" by the Beastie Boys

Chapter 5: "Hey" by the Pixies

Chapter 6: "Stumbleine" by the Smashing Pumpkins

Chapter 7: "Cheerleader" by St. Vincent

Chapter 8: "Where I'm From" by Digable Planets

Chapter 9: "Geek USA" by the Smashing Pumpkins

Chapter 10: "Return of the Rat" by the Wipers

Chapter 11: "See See Rider" by the Animals

Chapter 12: "We Can Get Down" by A Tribe Called Quest

Chapter 13: "Bury Me" by the Smashing Pumpkins

Chapter 14: "Lounge Act" by Nirvana

Chapter 15: "Freedom" by Rage Against the Machine

Chapter 16: "Sex Beat" by the Gun Club

Chapter 17: "Better Off Dead" by La Peste

Chapter 18: "Soma" by the Smashing Pumpkins

Chapter 19: "Mama Said" by the Shirelles

Chapter 20: "What?" by A Tribe Called Quest

Chapter 21: "Would You Be My Love" by Ty Segall

Chapter 22: "Low" by Cracker

Chapter 23: "Passin' Me By" by the Pharcyde

Chapter 24: "Cherub Rock" by the Smashing Pumpkins

Chapter 25: "Dancing the Manta Ray" by the Pixies

Chapter 26: "Add It Up" by Violent Femmes

Chapter 27: "Marquis in Spades" by the Smashing Pumpkins

Chapter 28: "Between the Bars" by Elliott Smith

Chapter 29: "Getchoo" by Weezer

Chapter 30: "Pennies" by the Smashing Pumpkins

Chapter 31: "Hell No" by the Falling Idols

Chapter 32: "She's Got You" by Patsy Cline

Chapter 33: "Sex" by the Urinals

Chapter 34: "So What'Cha Want" by the Beastie Boys

Chapter 35: "Today" by the Smashing Pumpkins

Chapter 36: "Locust" by Black Lips

Chapter 37: "The Truth" by Handsome Boy Modeling School ft. Róisín Murphy and J—Live

Chapter 38: "Disarm" by the Smashing Pumpkins

Acknowledgments

FIRSTLY, THANK YOU TO MY PARENTS, GOTTFRIED and Renate Helnwein, for being the complete opposite of all the parents in this story—and for the freedom, inspiration, and the opportunity to grow up with art as the focal point of everything in our lives.

Thank you so much to the people who made this book with me, but most of all, my agent, Elizabeth Bewley, whose enthusiasm was the true beginning to this story becoming an actual book, and my editor, Sara Goodman, for guiding this adventure so perfectly. Thank you both for your incredible support and guidance.

Thank you to everyone at Wednesday Books.

Thank you, Olga Grlic and Ana Hard, for the cover.

And thank you, Berni Barta, for your faith in this story so early on.

Thank you also to the following people:

Christopher Watson, for his brainstorming capabilities and for everything else.

Vivian Gray, official advisor on all matters of everything since before either of us hit puberty.

Michelle Green and Gina Ribisi, for thoughtfully replying to my many texts over the course of a few years about things like "what's another way of saying 'dickwad'?"

Francesca Serra, for being the first person to read this story, chapter by chapter, as I was writing it. Thank you for the many amazing, illuminating, and in-depth emails, back when no one else knew these characters.

Alex Prager and Jodi Leesley, for also surviving the insane early version and for the much-appreciated encouragements.

Olugbemisola Rhuday-Perkovich, for the notes and invaluable feedback.

Brandi Milne, Sirene Evans, Eve Darling, and Jamie Marvin—thank you for being guinea pigs at various revised stages.

Tiffany Steffens, for introducing me to her brilliant oeuvre of teenage poetry and letting me use a few lines in this book.

Amadeus Helnwein, for the many literary discussions in the kitchen in Ireland.

Paul D'Elia, for the legendary punk music playlists.

And special thanks to the Smashing Pumpkins, A Tribe Called Quest, and the Beastie Boys—the Holy Trinity of the soundtrack to this story.